Lightwarriors

Brian L. Jackson

ISBN: 9781982984359

DEDICATION

To my wife Melanie, my partner in crime.

ACKNOWLEDGMENTS

I would like to thank my friend and former law partner, Judge Joseph M. Gardner for his feedback and suggestions; and my mother and sister for their encouragement and advice.

I would also like to express special thanks to Miss Sasha Figarella of Chrissha's Art for her breathtaking cover illustration. You have truly brought my characters to life.

To my loving wife and children; I appreciate your support, encouragement and patience. I am blessed to have you in my life to share this moment.

Lastly, I wish to express my deep and heartfelt appreciation to my father, Dr. Barry L. Jackson, this has been a long and sometimes arduous journey and I would not have gotten this far without you.

Lacrimosa dies illa

Qua resurget ex favilla

Judicadus homo reus.

Huic ergo parce, Deus,

Pie Jesu Domine,

Dona es requiem.

//

Oh how tearful that day

On which the guilty shall rise

From the embers to be judged.

Spare them then, Oh God.

Merciful Lord Jesus,

Grant them rest.

"Lacrimosa" from Requiem
Wolfgang Amadeus Mozart.

The only hope or else despair

Lies in the choice of pyre or pyre

To be redeemed from fire by fire.

TS Eliot

Prologue

Great events often happen with little notice or care, on days so ordinary as to be forgotten by men. I have seen many great things over the course of my long life. Events of great joy and great sadness have unfolded before my eyes and I have watched and waited.

I have lived by many names though my true character remains hidden. I am not a good man but I am not without sympathy. It is with great sadness that I relate to you the tragedy that began to unfold on an unremarkable day, in an unremarkable town, affecting seemingly unremarkable people. This day passed without any concern by men and women despite being of import nearly as great as that fateful night when a carpenter's boy came into the world and changed t1he history of man. For on this day a child came into the world who would once again change the fate of man. Cursed with power that she neither requested nor desired, her fate is sealed before she draws her first breath...

I

A warm breeze stirred blades of grass, carrying upon it newly mown grass, barbecue, hints of gasoline, and new spring blossoms. Dusk had turned to darkness. and a father and son walked together in a field behind their house among the chirrups of the crickets. A father in more than one sense, this man had adopted the boy when he was only six and the two had lived as s family ever since.

On this night, they would sleep outside and stargaze as the temperature had finally warmed enough to permit camping. The boy, aged twelve, carried a telescope under his left arm and walked with purpose. He felt excitement in his chest, for this would be a special night. On this night it would be just him and his Dad.

After walking for a short time father and son stopped to set up camp. The boy set his telescope down on the long, deep green grass, then turned his face to the sky and smiled as a thousand twinkling stars greeted his eyes. In the distance an owl hooted, and a coyote answered with a low cry.

Though his eyes remained transfixed by the gorgeous night sky, the boy was aware that his father had begun to set up their tent.

The boy had just begun learning astronomy from his adoptive father and identified many of the visible starts and constellations with ease. One in particular held his attention as it shone brighter than the others and hung directly overhead as if to signal some event of great import.

Nevertheless, this was an ordinary night and could have happened anywhere in America, though father and son were far from ordinary.

Having never seen this particular star, the boy turned to his father to ask its name. Before he could speak his father released the tent pole he had been muddling with, allowing it to clang off the ground and eased himself upright. As he did the color drained from his face, leaving behind bleached bone flesh.

In that moment the boy sensed fear from his father and became frightened himself though he had no knowledge of what had so frightened his dad. He knew only that he felt…*something*, a sensation of cold desolation and warm comfort at the same time. His flesh crawling, the boy began to tremble as the first beads of oily sweat rose on his back and chest.

The boy watched his father's eyes travel from his watch and back to the sky. Fear radiated from Dad in icy waves.

A stiff breeze tugged at the boy's jacket. It no longer carried the sweet scents of spring but rather the cool, musty scent of night long since fallen. An invisible force soundlessly pulsated in the air.

Purple lightning forked across the still cloudless sky followed a moment later by an angry growl of thunder. The boy stared at this unexpected development with wide-eyed fascination and fear.

What's happening? How can there be lightning if there are no clouds?

As the boy watched in frightened amazement a second bolt of purple lightning cascaded from the sky and shattered upon the earth in a brilliant white explosion. Thick ozone choked the air with invisible hands. This time there was no low rumble but rather a deafening roar that the boy would have only imagined possible from a nuclear blast. He turned once again to his father and with trembling lips asked the only question on his mind.

"Wha…what's happening?"

His father did not reply at first but only stood there, still as a statue, eyes fixed upward upon the sky. Then in an instant, he turned and met the boy's frightened glance with an overly jovial smile.

"Oh, it's nothing." He forced a laugh. "I've just never seen a lightning storm on a night this clear before."

II

At that exact moment in a hospital far across the country, orderlies wheeled a young woman on a gurney down a corridor. She was about to give birth to her first child. Contractions pulled at her body yet no cries escaped her lips. Her mind, though preoccupied by pain, exhaustion and *yes* something reminiscent of excitement, noted the sights and smells of the hospital. She detected chlorine, alcohol and that overpowering, medical smell that always seems to permeate hospitals and clinics. Her ears caught the sharp clack of hard soled shoes on tile and the rattle of a loose wheel.

Despite her condition, the woman instinctively scanned around noting the two orderlies and one nurse who accompanied her gurney.

"Hold on." The nurse insisted in what she no doubt intended to be a comforting tone. "We're almost there."

A moment later the gurney turned and the woman found herself in the delivery room. For a moment her eyes fixed on a large poster featuring a cutaway of a woman's uterus.

The nurse had taken her hand and began to squeeze. The woman fought back an urge to break the nurse's neck. Yet she felt more than an edge of anticipation now. She would soon be a mother despite so many doctors telling her such a thing would be impossible.

"Push!" The nurse urged. The woman could have easily turned this nurse in her green hospital scrubs into a corpse but that would serve no purpose.

At the woman's side stood her husband, his expression stoic. Though his eyes fixed intently on hers, he remained silent and betrayed not a hint of emotion. For a moment, the woman became aware of the soft, smoky scent of his cologne and his out of place black Armani suit, and red silk shirt and tie.

The woman pushed untroubled by the complaints of her fatigued muscles. The doctor, who had crouched between her legs, suddenly popped his head up.

"I can see the head. One more push and she's out." The nurse must have intended her tone to be comforting or encouraging or something. In truth, it sounded inane. Without a response or sound, the woman bore down with all her strength.

A moment later the doctor reappeared, this time holding a small bundle in his arms. He turned to face her and though a surgical mask covered his mouth the woman detected an unmistakable a smile on his face.

"Congratulations! It's a girl!"

He turned and handed the child to a nurse who proceeded to clean the blood and birth fluids from her body. When she had finished she carried the small bundle over to the woman and placed it in her arms.

"She is beautiful." Her husband's voice was calm and level but she could not help noticing a hint of what had to be…*Joy? Can he still feel joy?*

The moment she saw her daughter's face the woman fell in love. The baby girl in her arms looked up at her with placid eyes that pierced to the soul. Her beauty exceeded anything the woman could have imaged prior to that very moment. The child had fair porcelain and rose skin, a small tuft of downy fine blond hair on her head and perfect, sky blue eyes more beautiful than the woman had ever seen before. The child did not cry but rather lay in her mother's arms looking up with wide, gentle eyes. The child's soft scent replaced the hospital smells pervading the air.

She felt the afterbirth coming but paid little mind. Pain had never troubled her and she had focused her attention on this tiny girl that should not have been.

Intense joy flooded through her though the woman didn't so much *feel* it as she was logically *aware* of it. She managed a thin smile. "Hello little girl. I am your mother." The woman's voice came out hushed, little more than a whisper. She turned to her husband who she saw wore the hint of a smile.

"She is beautiful. Do you want to hold her?"

Without a word he nodded and then took the child from her arms.

"That's is your father." The woman whispered to her daughter.

As the new mother and father marveled over their baby daughter, the doctor pulled his watch from his wrist with a cry of pain. It struck the tiled floor with a *-clink-* before coming to rest at the foot of the steel counter along the right hand wall.

An unexplained, large and very angry blister had cropped up on the back of his wrist.

A second degree burn. Huh?

The watch body itself had become hot enough to burn it's leather band. A small tendril of smoke curled from the joint between leather and gold as a faint smell of burning flesh filled the doctor's nostrils.

Rather than being frightened the doctor felt both intrigued and irritated at once. He crossed the room to find that the watch's second hand had frozen. The minute and hour hands had come to rest at exactly eleven fifty-seven. A wrinkle of annoyance crossed his face. He had just had the damned thing fixed. Now he would probably end up replacing it as the heat would have almost certainly fried the watch's electronics.

Still feeling aggravated, the doctor scribbled out the birth certificate, setting the time of birth at eleven fifty-seven, exactly three minutes before midnight.

Close-a-fucking-nuff. Goddamned watch.

As he filled in the day's date, thunder exploded above bringing the floor to life beneath his feet. A moment later the air became electric with power and then ignited with intense heat. For a brief instant brilliant light flooded the delivery room, followed by a fountain of sparks and flame and then choking smoke-filled darkness. The stench of ozone and burned rubber lay heavy on the air. Several dozen screams rang out from neighboring delivery rooms and the hallway together with a number of loud crashes and bangs followed by deathly silence.

Chapter 1
The Chase

I

The clock radio buzzed at six thirty awakening Jack MacLeod from a deep sleep. His eyes flicked open and he silently reached for the alarm then sat up smoothly. It was Friday, July twenty-third and he was scheduled to travel to Eastern Europe, Romania, on one of his "missions" That was what his handlers always called Jack's assignments, "missions", giving them an almost military sound, as if he were being dispatched to bomb an airfield or capture a hill. In fact, Jack's "missions" had as little in common with regular military objectives as a Mafioso has in common with a soldier and Jack was no soldier, not anymore. His official title was FBI Special Agent. Unofficially Jack was known as an Asset and he worked as a hitter, a highly prized and very expensive assassin. Jack's primary employer was the United States Government though he occasionally took contracts from certain well connected and well-funded private clients.

Jack slid to the edge of the bed and slowly stood up, his fine-tuned senses rapidly coming into sharp focus. Unconsciously he swept the room for threats and found none. Everything looked as it had been when he drifted off to sleep the night before, save for the absence of his wife and the low light of early morning. For a moment he listened to the sound of silence and stretched out with his "other" sense, that sense that had grown from more than just years of experience with "missions" that could only be described as suicidal. Jack crossed the room with soundless footfalls. This too came by instinct and from more than his years of experience.

As he walked his back crackled irritably. Not for the first time, Jack realized that his body was aging prematurely. He was only forty-five but already he felt the beginnings of old age creeping up on him. His joints were stiffer than they had once been, and it took him longer to come around in the morning. There was no emotion attached to these thoughts, only cold logic.

His wife Dana was more fortunate. She had remained in more or less the same physical shape she had been in when they married fifteen years ago. But then she was also ten years younger than him.

It's not just the age difference. I have used my body beyond its capabilities for far too long. This is the price to be paid.

Jack strode into the bathroom to take his shower. He stopped in front of the mirror and looked himself over critically. He didn't look bad for a middle-aged man. He had a muscular though not ripped frame and his skin remained taut with few scars or blemishes. Only a couple of small wrinkles on his forehead and around his eyes and a scattering of gray flecks in his black hair and the red stubble on his face betrayed his true age. He stared at himself coldly for a while, then took off his boxer shorts and stepped into the shower. When he emerged twenty minutes later his stiffness had passed, and his body felt energized and ready for action. Before leaving the bedroom, Jack picked out a black sports jacket from the closet and slung it over one arm. Minutes later he walked into the kitchen.

A different man might have described his kitchen as a good room. The lighting here was always bright and warm. He might have called this room his favorite if he had a favorite. Jack had many memories that originated in this room that could have been described as happy. The kitchen walls and cabinets were white with black trim as were the Formica countertops. A single long Formica bar separated the cooking area from the rest of the kitchen. Three bar stools stood along this. Behind them stood the kitchen table. Several large windows bathed the room in golden sunlight.

The rich scent of freshly brewed coffee wafted on the warm air.

Jack's six-year-old daughter Charlene, Charlie since she had been a baby, sat at the table slurping up Cheerios. She looked up and smiled when he came in.

"Good morning Daddy." She chirruped.

Jack smiled back. "Good morning Charlie. How did you sleep?"

"Good." She replied with a child's cheer.

For the first time that morning he felt a touch of emotion. His daughter was one of the few people who could elicit such a reaction from him. For most of the rest of the world, he felt mere indifference. Still, he smiled more for her benefit than out of any true sense of happiness. He loved her, would have died for her if necessary.

"That's good." He answered in his best "Daddy" voice. "Don't take too long eating your breakfast. We have a lot to do today."

"Ok, Daddy." She looked up from her Cheerios.

He looked down on her feeling something like faint fatherly pride. The sensation was uncommon enough to be nearly alien. Charlie was one of his few pleasures in life.

When we're done running errands, I have a surprise for you."

Jack spoke in his best "Daddy" voice; to him, it sounded alien.

She renewed her smile. "Really?"

He smiled back. "Yes really."

"Oh goody," Charlie replied joyously before returning to her Cheerios.

Behind her, Dana offered a slight smile as she poured milk into a bowl of cereal. Dana was his other pleasure and she too could stir emotion in him that he felt for precious few others.

As Jack came to the table, Dana turned, and their eyes met as she gave him a perfunctory hug before she sat down. Jack poured himself a bowl of cereal and sat down at the table across from Charlie. She had by this time finished her cereal and was munching on a piece of toast. Jack watched her for a moment feeling something like contentment.

If there is such a thing as the American Dream, then this must be it.

Jack smiled inwardly as he ate forgetting for a few moments who and what he was. He and Dana both functioned as Agents. Officially the FBI employed Jack as a Special Agent in its Counter Terrorism branch. This assignment gave him cover to travel the world without raising suspicions. Dana, on the other hand, had been with the Department of State as a translator since leaving the service. Unofficially both Jack and Dana worked under a handler whom they knew only as Vic.

Both Jack and Dana completed "missions" at the behest of Vic and were well paid for doing so. Still, that money, though significant was not free for spending, lest they attract the wrong sort of attention. While both Jack and Dana earned respectable federal salaries neither earned so great a salary as to allow for lavish spending. As a result, both had worked hard to get where they were. It took them two years to save enough money to put down on the house they lived in and they still had to scrimp some months to make the mortgage payments, but things were working out. Together Jack and Dana earned enough legal money to fund a comfortable middle-class life and Jack took faint pride in the knowledge that he had done right by his family.

II

When breakfast was finished Jack went upstairs to brush his teeth. Ten minutes after that he and Charlie were in his nineteen ninety Pontiac Sunbird on their way to interstate 80. His neighbor Rob Striker waived as they passed.

Rob was the closest person to a friend in Jack's life. Jack felt intense loyalty since their days in the service. Rob had been the only one of his friends to stand by him following the procedure. Better not to think about that now though. Better to push the thought away before the guilt could come and distract him.

He had the whole day planned out perfectly. They would go to the travel agency to pick up their airline tickets and hotel reservations, then to Bank of America to withdraw three thousand dollars in cash. Jack had already wired approximately twenty thousand dollars to himself from his extra-legal funds. Then he would take Charlie to her pediatrician for Yellow Fever, Hepatitis A and B and Meningitis vaccinations. After she had finished they would get lunch at whatever restaurant Charlie chose. Then they would head to Sugar Lake for an afternoon of swimming. He used to take Dana to Sugar Lake on dates. This would be Charlie's first time to the water park. Jack knew she would love it. Charlie enjoyed swimming more than anything. He put on a subtle smile as he thought of her splashing around in the town pool. She had only learned a year ago and she was already a strong swimmer.

Charlie's voice broke his train of thought. "Daddy how long before we get done running errands?"

Jack turned to her. "About three hours hon."

As he looked at his daughter Jack felt a certain awareness of the precarious nature of their existence. There was no guilt in that awareness, rather cold knowledge of the danger they faced if certain facts ever came to light.

III

Jack's ambition as a young man was to be career military, specifically special forces. He had entered the Army through the ROTC program at the University of Oklahoma. Following basic training, he applied to and was promptly rejected by the Rangers program. It was then that he met his future wife Dana. It was also around this time that they participated in a secret program that would change their lives forever. The program director, Major Hoess, promised him "the assignment of his choice" if he agreed to participate. He further assured Jack that the program would easily give him the qualifications for any assignment he wanted. Hoess promised him there were no serious risks. The procedure he and Dana would undergo had been vigorously tested and none of the many participants who had gone before them suffered any serious adverse effects.

For his part, Jack didn't care. He saw only the career opportunities ahead of him, where this program would take him, the skills he would gain, the adventures he would have. He saw all of this and gleefully signed up. That was when he could still feel glee.

The military scientists presented the procedure as harmless. They explained that he and Dana would first be given a mild analgesic painkiller followed by a series of cortisone shots. In truth, the "painkiller" was a frighteningly powerful hallucinogenic stimulant that brought on bizarre psychic phenomena in those exposed to it. Jack remembered feeling as if he had taken a massive hit of methamphetamine. His heart raced so hard that he felt it would explode and his body temperature shot up so high he thought his skin would catch fire.

The drug did other things to him as well. He remembered feeling terrible fear. He also remembered learning things, things he shouldn't know. All at once he knew everything about the technician that had injected him. That the young man had served for three years in the Army, that he was not an Army regular. That the technician had killed seven people, four men and three women. None of them in combat. He also remembered being able to *push* things, not with his hands but with his mind. He had tried pushing a metal instrument tray near his cot and had watched its contents go skittering across the floor.

While the most powerful psychic manifestations faded with the drug's other effects each of the subjects retained a variety of psionic talents including telekinesis, ESP and enhanced natural senses. These abilities were limited, and overuse would bring on a variety of neurological symptoms including headaches, dizziness and nausea.

The "cortisone" shots were actually some sort of synthetic anabolic steroids that magnified their physical prowess, augmenting their physical strength and agility.

There were other things as well, things only remembered in flashes and fragments of memory. He remembered being taken to a featureless room where he was wired up to some kind of machine. The machine did something to him. He didn't know what couldn't remember. It *hurt*.

The procedure exacted a heavy price. Both Dana and Jack were stripped of many of the characteristics that make a person human. Neither felt emotions as they once had. Joy, humor, love, fear, anger, guilt all had been blunted and muzzled within their minds, replaced with cold, calculating logic and a strong predatory instinct. Both became capable of committing terrible acts without feeling a bit of remorse. Both became perfect killers.

For some inexplicable reason, Jack and Dana had feelings for one another despite feeling nothing but cold indifference towards the rest of the world. They fell in love and married. At some point, without actual discussion, the two decided to have a child. It was then that they discovered the cruelest side effect of the procedure. Jack and Dana both had suffered near sterility as a result of their participation and were told that they could never have children. Charlie was a miracle.

After years of failed attempts, Dana unexpectedly became pregnant. Charlie was the result. Her birth had been quick and easy, no complications, no problems. Everything seemed to be going perfectly but it was too good to be true. It was evident very soon after her birth that Charlie was not normal. Two days after she came home from the hospital Jack and Dana put away the crib forever after discovering that when they put Charlie to bed her pillow would *smolder.* That night it had gotten hot enough to blister her cheek. Jack found a tube of burn ointment, but she still cried most of the night. That first year had been dangerous and required constant vigilance. There were fires in the trashcans; sometimes it would be the drapes. One time they were awakened by their daughter's screams and found that she had set her own *clothes* on fire and burned them almost completely off. It was fortunate indeed that they had found Charlie when they did, or she might have died. As it was she suffered severe second-degree burns all over her body.

It wasn't until she got older that Charlie began to gain a tentative hold on her power. But as she grew older the power grew stronger making Charlie's control tenuous at best. Last week she had inadvertently started a fire in the garage after slamming her fingers in the car door.

The power was called *pyrokinesis*; Jack had researched it as thoroughly as he could. Information on this so-called wild talent was almost non-existent. Jack was only able to learn that it was a very rare and dangerous psychic ability that was usually involuntary and activated by strong emotions. Most of those who possessed this power were discovered only after they had burned themselves to death. The handful of cases involving living subjects generally centered around young girls approximately Charlie's age. It was theorized that the talent was somehow connected to certain poorly understood and otherwise unused portions of the brain, but no one knew for sure.

There were other things as well. When Charlie went in for aptitude testing before entering kindergarten she scored off the charts. The child psychologist who had administered the tests said that her IQ was higher than any current test could measure. He then added that Charlie was more alert and acutely aware of her environment than any child he had tested before. The young man recommended right then that she be enrolled in a special school for gifted and talented children. Jack and Dana both rejected this suggestion. Neither of them wanted to separate Charlie from normal children. Jack also thought it unwise to draw too much attention to his daughter and suspected that Dana had reached the same conclusion though they never discussed the issue.

It was for this reason that he had, from her earliest years, told Charlie again and again that she should never, never use her power. That her power was a bad thing. This was for her protection only. In truth, Jack was proud of his daughter. As young as she was Charlie was powerful and possessed remarkable intelligence. Her instincts were sharper than his. Charlie's pyrokinesis was a rare gift that was as much a part of her as her direct blue eyes, and double-jointed thumbs. Logically Jack knew Charlie was going to need help controlling her power. Nevertheless, he was resolute in his decision to keep his daughter's power a secret. He did not fear for her, he was incapable of feeling fear, rather he understood with perfect clarity the consequences of revealing her power to an outsider. His daughter would be institutionalized. She would grow up being studied like a rare specimen in a petri dish. The military would certainly become involved and they would no doubt sweep her up and make her disappear. They would pick her apart, experiment on her, scoop out her soul and finally weaponize her. Jack wanted Charlie to have a normal life and thus ensured that her power was kept secret.

Though he recognized the danger his decisions had wrought Jack felt no guilt, could feel no guilt. Jack reflected on his decisions with cold logic. He had participated in the program because he was promised the opportunity to join the Rangers program, the opportunity to advance his career. He was also paid a significant amount for his cooperation, but the money was unimportant to him. It was an ambition that made him agree. Dana's motivation, on the other hand, had been money. She had faced eviction from her home and participated in the program to pay off back rent

For their part, the military kept their end of the bargain, after a fashion. Jack and Dana were each paid ten thousand dollars for their participation and Jack did go to Army Ranger school. Then he received an honorable discharge for medical reasons, he was given his position with the Bureau, and he met his handler, Vic. He became an Asset. Yes, he had gotten everything he wanted, and his daughter's future was irrevocably changed.

The year Charlie was born Jack was assigned to the FBI field office in Taylor, Illinois on the pretense of investigating a white supremacist group suspected of domestic terrorism right next to his old buddy Rob Striker. He had his suspicions about the real reason for the assignment, but it didn't matter. They were safe as long as they kept Charlie's talents a secret.

IV

As they continued down the highway Jack felt some pleasure. Today he would show his daughter a good time and tomorrow he would take his family to Romania with him. Everything was coming together perfectly.

After completing his errands Jack took Charlie out to Friendlies for lunch. Then they got back on Interstate 80 for another twenty minutes before getting off at exit 190. As soon as she learned where they were going Charlie's eyes lit up with excitement. Her excitement grew as they stood in line for admission and then went to the locker rooms to put on their bathing suits.

They stayed at Sugar Lake until closing time, swimming and riding the water slides again and again. The day was perfect, like a mission flawlessly executed. Jack only regretted not convincing Dana to join them. He had asked her the night before and she had declined saying that she wasn't feeling very well. She had been suffering from migraines the last couple of days.

After leaving the park Jack and Charlie got dinner at a small diner near the park. It was then that everything changed. Jack had taken the first bite of his hamburger when his stomach lurched and his flesh chilled. It was a feeling he knew well. Sharp, stabbing pain exploded from his bottom jaw as if someone had drilled into his teeth without Novocain. Charlie was watching him. All pleasure had drained from her face, replaced by frightened bewilderment. In her eyes, Jack saw that Charlie felt it as well.

"Finish your food Charlie so we can get on the road."

She sat motionless for a moment. Then she picked up her hamburger and took several quick bites before setting it down and scooting towards the open end of the booth.

"I'm done, Daddy."

He nodded. "Ok let's go take care of the bill."

Without a word, she followed him to the cash register. Jack left two fives on the table, twenty percent exactly. Enough to keep the waitress from remembering a middle-aged cheapskate and his blond haired, blue eyed little girl but not enough to be remarkable. As he drove down the highway Jack's mind analyzed the premonition he had experienced with rapid efficiency.

Something has happened? Is Dana hurt? Did someone hurt Dana?

He took his iPhone from his pocket and dialed her cell. The call rang through to voicemail unanswered.

Should I be concerned? She said she was not feeling well. She could be sleeping, might not have heard the phone ring. Or maybe it was on silent?

There was no answer, but he already knew. Something terrible had happened. Jack glanced at his watch. It was seven thirty in the evening. They were passing through rural country on an otherwise deserted highway stretch.

No risk of encountering a local cop, very unlikely I will see any sheriff's deputies or state troopers out here either. I can go a little faster and I need to get home fast. Something has happened.

Jack leaned on the gas a little harder. He had already been speeding, now he had brought the car up to eighty. Still, he was not satisfied with his progress.

This car cannot go much faster.

"Daddy what's going on?"

He did not reply. He was deeply focused on his objective, his mind clicked away with a computer's cold logic.

"Daddy, I think Mommy's in trouble."

He did not reply.

"Daddy? Daddy I think Mommy's hurt."

He knew. Something was wrong. He couldn't tell what for sure, but he knew something was very wrong.

"Daddy please…"

Charlie was terrified, but he couldn't help her. His only focus was on getting home.

The drive seemed to take forever. Somehow an hour turned into three days. By the time he had reached Blakeville Road Jack had begun to feel agitated. He was not frightened (he believed himself incapable of fear) rather he felt a powerful need to do *something*. Charlie sat beside him shuddering in fear, but he paid no attention.

Jack parked his car along the curb in front of the house, shut off the lights and engine and got out. Charlie started to unbuckle her seat belt to follow.

"No, you stay in the car and wait for me. Your mother and I will be back out in a few minutes."

Jack's voice came out calm and gentle, like that of a normal father rather than of an Agent who had sired a child. As he got out of the car and stood up he drew a suppressed jet-black Colt Commander 1911 from inside his belt. This was his favorite weapon, a signature of his if he could be said to have one.

By the time he reached his house, Jack felt coiled, ready to strike, his agitation having turned into hard determination. He did not know what he would encounter (though he had his suspicions) but whatever lay ahead he would be ready. He found the door cracked open. Jack opened it wider without making a sound, his focus sharpening further.

"Dana! Dana are you okay?!"

There was no answer. Jack stepped through the doorway, his eyes swept the entryway looking for threats. The house was dark, the air hot and stale.

"Dana!"

There was still no answer. Everything was deadly still. Jack moved through the house with great care, sweeping each room for threats, searching, listening, finding nothing. Something, an ember of heat, long forgotten, glowed within his chest.

She had better be ok... "Dana!!"

Still nothing. Jack's only answer was a soft rustle of leaves outside. He went into the kitchen. There was a half-eaten sandwich on the counter, an overturned glass of Pepsi lay beside it, still dripping onto the floor.

The ember flared and became a glowing coal. He recognized this feeling it was...*anger?*

"Dana!!"

He studied the room with care. Everything seemed to be in place. Other than the half-eaten sandwich and the spilled Pepsi everything looked as it should. Still, he knew better. His intuitions told him that something terrible had happened. There was a pool of liquid on the floor by the cellar stairs. Jack approached it with care and bent down.

Blood.

There wasn't much of it, but Jack immediately decided that this was not a good sign. The coal in his chest glowed brighter. Jack descended the basement steps two at a time.

"Dana!"

"Dana!!"

There was still no answer.

He was standing in the family room now. It was pitch black as with the rest of the house. The air down here was much cooler than it was upstairs. No, it wasn't cool it was cold and very still, like a tomb. Jack reached out with his right hand and flipped the light switch with care. The overhead incandescent lights flicked on to reveal a cluster fucked murder scene. There was a huge pool of blood in the center of the carpet. A single nickel .45 ACP shell casing lay at its center. A nickel plate Colt Commander 1911, belonging to Jack, lay on the floor nearby. In one precise movement, he took it up and slipped it in his jacket pocket.

Somebody died in here. I know someone else who is going to die soon,

Jack scanned his surroundings. The room was in shambles. The couch and two chairs had been overturned along with one of the bookcases. The other lay in pieces on the floor. Books were scattered everywhere.

There had been a struggle. Someone was shot. Jack reasoned that it had to have been Dana though he had not yet found her body.

I will kill the one who touched her…

Flames licked around the hot coal in his chest. Jack felt his heart rate increase slightly.

All at once Jack turned and sprinted up the stairs. He had searched the ground floor and found nothing, so he ran up to the second floor. Dana was in their bedroom lying on the bed in a small pool of blood. There was a fist-sized chunk missing from her forehead. She had been executed.

The coal erupted into flame. Hot blood coursed through his body. She was dead. Dead and gone forever. It was still hard for him to grasp. She had been alive that morning. She had hugged him, planted a delicate kiss on his cheek, offered a slight smile.

"I am sorry I was not here Dana, but not as sorry as the person who killed you will be when I find them."

Jack knelt beside the bed and ran his fingers through Dana's blood matted hair. Her skin was pale with tinges of blue and her face was bruised and cut. Jack's eyes trailed down her face to her mouth. Blood trickled out of both corners. Her lips were slightly parted revealing more blood. Jack brushed the hair from her face and closed her eyes with a gentle touch before carefully pulled her mouth open to find that four of her incisors had been torn from their sockets.

Butchers! She put up a fight and they tortured her.

His mind fixed on what he had already known. There were a number of possible scenarios that could have led to his wife's death. He had made enemies over the years, any one of them could have found him and done…*this.* It could have been a random break-in for all he knew but he knew better. His instincts told him all he needed to know.

The people he had been doing "missions" for, his handler. They had come for him, or more likely his daughter. If they wanted him, they would have taken him. The same for his wife. No this was connected to the program. They must have been watching for some time observing unnoticed from a distance. They had probably assigned him to the Taylor field office so that they could keep a close eye on his family. His purchase of three airline tickets to Romania had most likely convinced them that he was about to take his family and run.

So, they came and killed Dana while Charlie and I were gone. Probably pulled out her teeth to get her to tell them where to find us.

A soft implacable voice spoke up in his mind.

Charlie.

Cold understanding flooded him. *Oh, fuck Charlie!!* In all his anger over Dana's death, he had forgotten about her. *Shit, Charlie's still sitting out there in the car!*

Jack shot up. In the same instant, several men in black suits appeared with weapons drawn.

"Hold it right there Mr. MacLeod."

Jack's heart began to race, the flaming coal exploded with fury. Still, he remained calm on the outside. Black, cold rage flooded his body.

"You killed Dana."

As he spoke Jack thrust out at them with his mind. A great invisible hand leveled the five men. In the same instant two flaming spikes slammed into his skull. Jack swayed on his feet for a moment before catching his balance. The men were already getting up by this time. Jack drew the nickel plate 1911 from his pocket and in the same smooth movement shot one man in the forehead and a second through his left eye socket. He turned on a third man and was about to fire when he remembered…

Charlie!

Instead, Jack bolted through the survivors who attempted to block his path jamming their guns with his mind as he passed. This set off a fresh wave of stabbing pain severe enough to cause him to teeter at the edge of the stairs. Jack's anger mixed with another, cold sensation he recognized as being close to fear. If he could fear.

What if Charlie's gone? What do I do?

He would kill them, make them suffer if they touched his daughter. It seemed to take forever for him to reach the car. To his relief, Charlie was still sitting where he had left her looking pale-faced and frightened.

"Daddy where's Mommy?"

He couldn't deal with this right now. He had to get them out of there before the men inside caught up with him.

"Buckle your seatbelt, Charlie."

She did as he asked then immediately grabbed him when he got in the car.

Once inside Jack threw the car into gear and gunned the gas. As he sped away Jack knew this would be the last time he would ever see his house on Blakeville Road.

There was a car following him, a silver Crown Victoria. Fresh anger erupted within him. The logical part of him understood that he had to get his daughter to safety. There would be time for retaliation later but for now, she was the priority.

Have to get Charlie to safety so they cannot harm her.

Except that wasn't what they wanted. They wanted Charlie and him alive. Or rather they wanted Charlie alive. He was expendable. They would capture them both if they could, but they would kill him if necessary.

As he thought this Jack pulled the car around a sharp turn at high speed, tires screaming in protest.

At this point, Jack was so infuriated that he was calm. His thoughts became very clear, clearer he thought then they had been in a long time. It was strange despite the odd things that had happened since the experiment, even despite Charlie's abnormalities, he had firmly believed that he could hide his family, his *daughter* in plain sight. Something akin to regret came over him.

No one is untouchable. You of anyone should know that no one is untouchable. And that there is no such thing as a secret. They always get out in the end. Oh, but the people who did this...

Jack leaned harder on the gas bringing the car up to seventy. They were on Harrison Boulevard now. Jack weaved his way through traffic desperate to lose the silver Ford. The car matched his every move without fail.

The people who did this will die. Every one of them!

They were nearing the highway now and Jack's headache was getting worse. His vision doubled, then trebled. Tears welled up in his eyes though he was not crying. His stomach churned with nausea. It was becoming very difficult just to keep the car going straight. He would not be able to drive much longer. The interstate entrance was straight ahead on the right. Jack floored the accelerator bringing the car up to ninety. The silver Ford followed suit. At the last second, he yanked the wheel to the right nearly sending the car into a spin. It was fortunate that it was late. The Harrison Boulevard exit was busy during the day and early evening hours. At any other time, he would have surely collided with another driver doing this maneuver. The silver Ford tried to follow but was not so fortunate in that it slammed into the guardrail and flipped over. They were safe for now.

Jack turned to Charlie. "Look at the road signs and tell me what the next exit is."

"Okay Daddy." She was still visibly frightened and confused.

The next exit was Fallstaff. Jack found a Days Inn a mile off the interstate. He had Charlie sit in the car while he checked them in. Jack paid cash. It was fortunate that he had made a withdrawal from the bank for his Romania trip that morning. He knew from experience that using his credit card would be like putting up a banner saying, 'This way to the fugitive Agent and his daughter.' As soon as they were in the room Jack collapsed on the bed, telling Charlie to wake him at seven the next morning before drifting off into darkness.

V

When Charlie shook him awake six hours later Jack's headache was raging and shudders wracked his body. Charlie explained that she had turned on the air conditioner when the room got hot but couldn't figure out how to turn it off. Jack smiled and ruffled her hair.

"It's okay Charlie." He didn't feel much like smiling but he forced one for Charlie's sake.

Jack struggled to his feet and plopped back down as two gigantic bolts of pain ripped through his skull.

Charlie looked at him with concern. "Daddy are you okay?" Her voice sounded faint as if heard from very far away.

"I will be fine." He put a hand to his head. "I just need to eat." He paused for a moment waiting for the pain in his head to lessen. "This is the plan Charlie.

We're going to get back on the highway and drive for an hour or so. Then we will stop and eat. Then we'll get back on the highway and drive for the rest of the day. Okay?"

She looked at him with a question in her eyes. "Daddy, when are we going to get Mommy?"

Jack sighed. "Charlie sit down." He patted the bed beside him. She walked over and sat down next to him, a puzzled expression on her face. "Your mother's…some men came to our house…they…" He ran out of words. As cold and emotionless as he had become he still could not bear to see his daughter hurt.

Charlie's mouth widened into an O and she covered it with her hand. "Oh no, Daddy say it's no."

He tried again. "Charlie…"

"Say it's no!"

"Charlie I'm sorry."

"Say she's all right! Say she's all right! Say she's all right!" She was shaking her head. Her hair whipped from side to side in a flash of gold. "No! No! No! No! No!"

All at once the room became explosively hot. Thick oily sweat beaded up on Jack's skin. Charlie's forehead shone with moisture. Jack understood the danger at once. "Charlie! The bathtub, quick!"

She screamed, then turned towards the bathroom. There was a bright white flash and a sharp crack followed by a clatter of porcelain. Thick choking smoke filled the room and there was a strong odor of scorched towels and singed plastic.

"I'm sorry Daddy I didn't mean to!" Charlie's voice was pleading. All at once she burst into tears.

Jack took her into his arms. "It's ok Charlie. I know you didn't mean it."

"I want Mommy." Charlie wept.

Jack clutched her to his chest. "I know. It's going to be all right Charlie." He did not recognize the voice that came from him. It sounded fatherly. Inside he felt only murderous rage, for the death of his wife and for the pain they had inflicted upon his daughter.

He cradled her as blank rage washed through him. "I promise you somehow everything will be all right again."

Chapter 2
Fate

I

It was early morning and there was a light dusting of snow on the ground. The weather was cold and slightly breezy, but a brilliant sun shone down from the clear blue sky making for a gorgeous day for a walk.

Both David and Catherine were in their early twenties and still looked more like teenagers than adults. David was twenty-three years old and tall and slender. He stood at six feet two inches and had close-cut dark brown hair, light skin, and mysterious wolf gray eyes. Catherine, his wife of two years, was five feet nine inches tall with long red-gold hair and coral green eyes. She was slender with all the right proportions. Both David and Catherine wore casual dress. Catherine dressed in blue jeans and a button-down blouse covered by a blue denim jacket. David also dressed in blue jeans, together with a white t-shirt, an open green button-down long sleeved-shirt and a leather bomber jacket.

It was a typical Monday morning in the city. The sidewalks were bustling with people. Business executives in black or blue suits toting attaché cases, teenagers in trendy clothes, blue-collar workers in uniforms or street clothes, and children in school attire all jostled for space on the concrete walkways. Among them and ignored by design were the ubiquitous denizens of the street, the lost, forgotten souls who haunt every city street in America. Homeless people lay in doorways or alleys or pushed pilfered shopping carts filled with their meager possessions while street dealers and hookers peddled their illicit wares among crowds of indifferent pedestrians. The streets too were busy, crowded with cars transporting commuters to work or children to school, transit buses filled with the city's less wealthy residents, trucks loaded down with a cornucopia of goods and the typical scattering of VIPs in limousines.

David watched this all with a wry smile feeling grateful that he was no longer a part of the obligatory morning rush. It was only two years ago that he was reading manuscripts for the Lafayette Agency in the Village for twenty-five thousand dollars a year and braving the crowds and commuter traffic. Then his boss found a copy of a book manuscript he had written and showed it to the senior literary agent and president of the agency, Rikki Lafayette. And so, in the span of a night, he had a writing career. Instead of bucking crowds in the subway or traffic if he took his car David was riding in limousines and instead of working from nine to five reading half-assed submissions he was being wined and dined by senior editors from major publishing houses. It was strange how fast things changed for him. Lafayette got him a publishing contract with Raven-Pratt and a one-hundred-thousand-dollar advance on his book, titled *Shadows*. Two months after the deal was made David and Catherine moved out of their cracker box studio apartment in Harlem and into a roomy two-bedroom townhouse on the Upper East Side. He had had to use his entire advance as a down payment and still needed to take out a one and half-million-dollar loan to cover the asking price, but it was worth every penny. The apartment in Harlem was little more than a standard sized hotel room and it was located in a dangerous neighborhood with poor schools. Both David and Catherine wanted to become parents but neither wanted to raise children in such a bad neighborhood. Their new townhouse was located in a nice neighborhood with good schools. It was a perfect home for children.

II

They had entered Central Park now. The grass was brown with some tinges of sickly yellow and was covered in white powder. The trees and shrubs were bare skeletons. As they walked David and Catherine talked of unimportant things. An hour later they stepped off the path with the intention of fooling around. There was a small break in a stand of trees to their left. Behind it was a narrow disused dirt path. David and Catherine followed the path to where it abruptly ended in a round clearing. Upon entering the clearing, David spotted a small child cowering under the largest of the surrounding bushes. He nearly took the little girl for a ghost. She was slender to the point of emaciation and dirty. Her face was pale, her hair was tangled and matted, and she was dressed in rags. A long scrape skidded up her right arm. It looked infected. What looked like the remains of a pair of canvas high tops barely covered her feet. She had once been a beautiful child. Now her long mousy brown hair was clotted with dirt and her wide-set blue eyes were red and swollen with dark circles beneath them. She was young, no older than nine, yet her eyes were those of an old woman rather than a child. David approached her with gentle care.

"Are you alright sweetheart?"

The little girl cringed and tried to pull herself further under the bush. It was a pathetic sight. David's heart filled with deep compassion.

"Oh, sweetheart you don't have to be afraid. I won't hurt you, I promise."

Catherine moved in beside him offering the girl a friendly smile. "We want to help you, honey."

The little girl tensed and started to pull herself into a fetal position but then stopped and looked up at David with sudden realization in her eyes.

"You have it too." Her voice was soft and filled with sorrow.

David looked at her with curiosity. "What do you mean honey? What's wrong?"

The girl appeared oblivious. "You have it too." Her voice had become very tired.

David was confused. The girl seemed to be delirious. What she said made no sense. *What do I have too?* "Honey, what's wrong? Where are your mommy and daddy?"

The little girl staggered to her feet. "You have it too." Her voice a mere whisper this time. She took several clumsy steps and then pitched forward. David had to move fast to catch her. The girl's skin was burning up. Blood stained the back of her ragged shirt.

David spun around to Catherine. "Call 911! Hurry!"

She nodded, pulled out her cell phone, and fired off the number. David gathered the girl up cradling her in his arms. Her body felt loose and boneless like a dead thing.

Catherine hung up her cell phone in frustration. "Busy! Damned city! Come on."

All at once David became terrified. The main path was strangely deserted. David called for help but there was no answer. He wasn't surprised. The essence of

New York was to mind your own business and let other people mind theirs. In general, people made a point of not seeing things; you lived longer that way. David hugged the girl to his chest and sprinted along the path continuing to shout for help. There was still no answer. David's fear was mounting. It was too quiet. David felt no human presence anywhere. It was as if the entire park was deserted.

He had reached the edge of the park now. There was still no one in sight and he had no feeling that there was anyone nearby. David hurried across the street and ran another three blocks along a side street before reaching his front door. Catherine fumbled for her key before opening the door.

She pulled her phone out again and dialed. "I'm calling Judy. Hopefully, she can help."

"Help me get her into bed," David replied quickly.

In the back of his mind David knew he should be taking the little girl to the emergency room but in that moment, it occurred to him that to do so would endanger not only the little girl but also Catherine and himself. Anyway, he knew he could trust Judy.

Judy Taylor was David and Catherine's doctor. She was also one of both his and Catherine's closest friends. They had known her since moving to the city three years ago.

As he carried the little girl upstairs David was overcome by a sudden and powerful sense of danger he was unable to ignore. Though he knew not why David felt certain that he and Catherine and the girl were all in imminent peril. He did not like to trust his psychic senses, David had spent eight years trying to forget them and the other things he could do, but he could not ignore what he felt now.

II

An hour later David sat at the kitchen table with Catherine feeling both confused and more than a little frightened. Judy was still in the guest room with the little girl.

David couldn't help but be amazed at how fast things had changed. Only an hour ago this had been an ordinary day. Then they stumbled across the girl and the day went from ordinary to downright bizarre. The girl had said something about him 'having it too' but she had been delirious. How could she have known about the powers he had rejected so many years ago?

She's only a little girl. She couldn't be more than nine. It's not possible.

A voice spoke up inside him. *But what if she wasn't delirious? What if she's not just another little girl? She could be like you...different.*

It was a disturbing thought, but it was possible, and it would explain his growing sense of danger. As he thought about it now he was certain that she had the power. His unconscious mind had known it all along. Now that he was aware of it David could feel the girl's power. The air felt alive with energy as it did before a thunderstorm. He looked up at Catherine and their eyes met across the table. Something silent passed between them.

She feels it too.

Catherine too was gifted *or cursed* with the power. It was in part why they had fallen in love. They had both been outcasts, in a way they still were. Now it seemed that fate had brought them a child who was also an outsider. But her problems ran much deeper than being an outcast. The girl was in some kind of trouble. David didn't know what for sure. He knew only what he felt, and he felt very strongly that this child was in serious danger.

As he thought that Judy appeared through the kitchen door. Judy Taylor was a slender woman of thirty-five. She had average looks but her impeccable dress and personal care more than made up for any deficiencies in her natural beauty. Judy entered looking deadly serious and strode across the kitchen. David and Catherine both pushed away from the table.

"You don't need to get up." Judy's voice was low and somber. "She's in pretty bad shape but she'll be all right. She's running a slight fever; her chest is infected, and she has food poisoning. She also has an infected cut on her arm and her back is all scraped up and infected. She says she cut herself when she crawled under a barbed wire fence to get away from a 'dog that got mad at me' which is a strange thing for a little girl to be doing. Do you know anything about that?

"No," David answered truthfully. "I don't even know her name."

"She says her name is Danielle and I don't believe that any more than I believe that I can buy the Brooklyn Bridge for ten dollars from the guy on the corner. She also says she doesn't remember much about the past week and that I do believe. She's in pretty rough shape and she's been traumatized. She should really be hospitalized overnight for observation."

"Yeah…I would rather not do that." What Judy was suggesting made sense, but he felt more strongly than ever that to follow her advice would be a deadly mistake.

"Okay." Judy's tone suggested that she was more than a little suspicious. "But all the same I'm going to have to report this to the police."

David looked up at her warily. "I thought you only had to report shootings and stabbings?"

She inclined her head. "Yeah that's the law…but then there's the letter of the law and the spirit of it." She paused "Look you've got a sick and injured little girl whose parents are missing. She's obviously been traumatized and she's trying to hide something."

She was right of course. The whole situation was strange, and he felt that there was more going on than was readily apparent. But he couldn't let her call the police. "Judy we've been friends for three years now. You know me, and you know I wouldn't ask you to do this unless I thought it was important."

Judy's expression grew troubled. "She's in trouble, isn't she?"

"I'm not sure but something doesn't feel right. I don't want to get the police involved until I know more about what's going on."

"All right," Judy replied. "But what do you plan to do? You can't keep her a secret forever. Sooner or later somebody's going to start asking questions like where she came from and why she's not in school. And if you try to register her for school then they're going to want to know her medical history, they'll want to see her ID card and if they pull up her records then they'll see she's not yours and that you haven't legally adopted her. Even if you keep her inside there's still the mailman, the paperboy, people from the water and electric companies, hell the neighbors could show up. You going to keep her locked up in the basement? That's a fine life for a kid."

David frowned. "I haven't thought about that yet."

"Yeah well, you'd better start thinking about it." Judy retorted. "Because she's a little girl not a house cat."

David nodded. "I know but I don't know what to do right now."

"All right. I'll keep my mouth shut for whatever it's worth but don't forget she's a little girl and you can't keep her shut away forever." Judy handed him a small brown paper bag. "I'm leaving you some Amoxicillin for her fever and a tube of antibiotic ointment to clear up her infected cuts. Keep her in bed for the rest of the week and don't give her anything but broth and juice for the next forty-eight hours. Then you can give her rice or chicken soup if she feels up to it. Take her temperature every two hours and make sure she drinks lots of clear liquids. I'll be back to see her again on Wednesday." Judy started to leave and then stopped at the door. "There's something damned strange about that little girl."

David nodded. He felt something too though he did not understand what it was.

III

After Judy left Catherine got up, telling David that she wanted to give the little girl a bath. She was gone for a long time and when she returned she looked tired and deeply concerned.

"How is she?"

"She's sleeping." Catherine crossed the room and sat down across from him. "She was so quiet. The whole time she barely said a word. She didn't even ask me to leave while she bathed. Judy's right something happened to her."

He nodded. "Something's really wrong. I feel like we're in danger…All of us."

David and Catherine sat at the kitchen table for the rest of that day. They talked some but for the most part, they sat in silence each lost in thought. Every hour one of them would get up to go check on the little girl. She still wasn't talking much, and she wouldn't give her real name. David and Catherine both called her 'Danielle' lacking knowledge of her real name. 'Danielle' was deeply depressed and in shock. When David went upstairs to give her, her medicine he found her lying on her back staring straight up at the ceiling, face devoid of any emotion and his heart filled with deep concern.

After dinner, David and Catherine moved to the living room. They turned on the television but neither paid it much mind. At some point, David glanced up at Catherine.

Her eyelids drooped and there were dark circles above the tops of her high cheekbones.

"Go to bed you look tired."

She met his gaze with weariness. "I'm alright." Her voice didn't sound so all right. It was heavy with fatigue from too much worry.

"It's okay hon you can go to bed I'll sit up with Danielle."

"No." She yawned. "That's not fair to you. If you're going to stay up with her then I will too."

David smiled. "Thanks, but I think you need sleep more than I do." The truth was he felt about as tired as Catherine looked but he thought he could stand a sleepless night better than she could.

Catherine yawned again. "Okay but in a little while."

David nodded. "Alright."

Catherine's expression became troubled. "What do you think we should do about Danielle?"

David shook his head. "I don't know. I wish I knew where her parents are. They must be worried sick."

"They're dead...my Mommy and Daddy are dead."

David and Catherine both spun around to see 'Danielle' standing at the bottom of the stairs looking all the more pallid now that she was clean. Her waist length hair which David had at first taken for mousy brown was actually perfect golden blond and her skin which had been pale before was now ghost white. She stood tall for her age and floated in one of Catherine's old nightgowns. 'Danielle' approached them with careful deliberate strides. Her wide-set deep blue eyes glistened with tears.

"Please help me...I'm lost...I don't have anywhere to go...they want to kill me...they k... killed my Mommy and tried to take me away….and then they caught us and they tried to kill me and they…they…k…killed Daddy…" She dissolved into incoherent sobs.

David bent down and held his arms out to her. "Oh, come here, Danielle."

She ran to him. David clasped her to his chest his heart filled with compassion as sharp and cutting as a razor that threatened to tear him apart from the inside. He wanted to tell her it would be all right, that everything would be all right, but he could not lie to her and in truth, he did not know.

I'm so sorry Danielle. Whatever happened, you didn't deserve this.

David could not read the little girl's mind, but he felt her anguish and fear and that made his own feelings of sadness for her that much more profound. David wanted to help her, but he knew whatever he did for her he could never give her father and mother back. As he held the girl David felt himself beginning to cry. He did nothing to stop this though he had not cried in years, not since he was thirteen and his first girlfriend had dumped him for Jimmy Cristopherson, his worst enemy in junior high.

She's just a little girl and she's lost both of her parents. Even if she's not in danger nothing can bring them back.

IV

David squeezed her against his chest his tears wetting 'Danielle's' hair. He knew the pain she was suffering. His own childhood had been traumatic, filled with great emotional pain and fear. His mother rejected him only days after his birth when she realized that he was not normal. From that time on only his father cared for him. It was because of his father that he was not put up for adoption. Looking back David believed that his mother had loved him at first but was unable to deal with the reality of what her son was. So, she became distant, spending as little time with him as possible. It was his father who was always telling him he was loved, his father who made meals for him and comforted him when he had nightmares and read to him and sang him to sleep at night. David's father was always there when he needed him. Still, David missed having a mother and there was nothing his father could do to remedy the situation. When David was five his father was shot and killed. It happened on the way to the playground. A man with a gun suddenly appeared from behind a tree and without saying a word shot him in the head killing him instantly. On that day everything changed. David's mother became cruel and abusive. She began to drink heavily and abuse heroin. She blamed David for his father's death and she made this painfully clear when berating or beating him. As time went by the situation got worse. David had to endure increasingly severe physical and emotional abuse. Some days his mother would lock him in his room with no food or water. Other times she would beat him with leather belts, or wooden coat hangers; whatever happened to be handy at the time. Once she locked him out of the house overnight and another time she forced him to eat garbage. Still, the worst was the emotional abuse. David's mother told him she hated him, that he was a curse, a worthless child, a rotten brat, a freak, and a monster. It was his fault that his father had died, and she wished she'd had an abortion because then he would still be alive. This continued for a year before David was finally taken from his mother after she was arrested for prostitution. Not long after that, she died of a heroin overdose.

Now as he stood holding 'Danielle', David remembered his early childhood in more detail than he had in a long time. Fragmented memories both good and bad flashed through his mind as tears streamed down his cheeks in rivers. It took David a long time to regain control of himself and when he finally did he felt very tired.

V

Sometime later, and without a word, 'Danielle' pulled out of his grasp and sat down in the big armchair by the stairs. She lifted her eyes to meet his with slow, care. Her expression was unreadable, and her face was very pale.

"Please help me. I'm so scared." Her voice was strained, and David feared she would burst into tears all over again. She did not but her expression suggested that she thought he would say no.

David approached her slowly. "I'll help you, Danielle. I promise."

Behind him, Catherine added. "We'll take good care of you sweetheart. You can trust us." Her tear-stained voice suggested that she too had been crying.

David knew little about Catherine's childhood other than that her father had also died when she was very young and that she had endured horrible abuse at the hands of her mother and stepfather. Catherine refused to elaborate but David suspected that the abuse was, at least in part, sexual. This suspicion was confirmed the first time he and Catherine made love and he discovered that she was not intact. David tried to talk to her about this later, but she refused to discuss it and then burst into tears. David never again brought up the subject and Catherine never talked about it.

'Danielle' was studying him with care. "What's your name?"

"My name is David McAuliffe." He extended his hand.

'Danielle' looked at it with suspicion for a few seconds before cautiously extending her own hand to shake it. "Hi. I'm Charlie…Charlie MacLeod."

David shook her hand gently. "It's very nice to meet you, Charlie. Is that short for Charlene?"

She gave a tentative nod.

He offered her a warm smile. "That's a very pretty name." David half turned and glanced at Catherine. She approached with care. "This is my wife Catherine."

Catherine smiled kindly. "Hi, Charlie."

Charlie offered her a shy smile in return. "Hi." Then she turned back to David. She looked tired. Her face was very pale and there were dark circles under her eyes.

David renewed his gentle smile. "Come here Charlie I'll take you back to bed."

"Okay." She slid out of the chair and allowed him to pick her up and carry her back upstairs.

As he carried Charlie up the stairs David tried to put her mind at ease. "You're safe now Charlie. We'll take good care of you."

She smiled, eyelids heavy with sleep. "Thank you, Mr. McAuliffe."

"It's okay to use our first names Charlie," David replied in a soothing tone. "Catherine and I want you to treat us like friends."

"Ok." She replied in a soft tone.

VI

David stayed with Charlie until he was sure she was asleep. Then he tiptoed out of her room leaving the door a crack open so that he would hear her if she awakened in the night. As he walked down the hallway towards the bedroom he shared with Catherine, David found himself again wondering who this Charlie MacLeod was and what had happened to her. He had not wanted to press her, she was too upset and frightened, but he had many questions.

Who are 'they'?

And why did' they' kill her mother and father?

And of course, the most vexing question of all: *Why would anyone want to kill a little girl?*

As he asked himself that he remembered Judy's last words before leaving.

There's something damned strange about that little girl.

David nodded without thinking.

Yeah, there is.

He did not understand what it was about her, but he felt some strange…*force? Energy?* He didn't know what for sure but there was this sense of power whenever he was near her. The air around her felt alive with energy like before a lightning storm. The feeling made him uneasy. Not for the first time, David found himself wondering if Charlie was gifted with similar talents to those which cursed Catherine and him. If so then he pitied her for her life would only get more difficult as she got older. At some point, she would face the difficult decision of what to do about her power, whether to embrace or reject it. David hoped that she didn't have the power but he suspected that she did. Her words echoed in his head.

You have it too.

Yes, I have it too. David thought sadly. *We are all cursed.*

VII

In the guest bedroom, Charlie had awakened once more and lay listening to cars go by on the street outside her window. Any one of them could be coming for her and then it would be all over. But she did not feel that any of them were. She was afraid but for now, at least she was safe. David and Catherine McAuliffe seemed confused and surprised, but she sensed that they wanted to help her. She wasn't sure what they were going to do but she didn't need to think about that now. Better to drift, listen to the swish of cars outside the window, relax. The weight of the rainbow afghan on her chest was comforting, soothing her troubled mind. She lay like that for most of the night drifting somewhere between sleep and wakefulness.

Fragmented images drifted through her mind. She remembered cowering under the bush in the park praying as hard as she could that she wouldn't be seen. She remembered first seeing David and being paralyzed with fear. Later Charlie remembered Dr. Taylor. She was very kind and gentle, but Charlie didn't trust her. She asked too many questions and that made Charlie nervous.

Never mind that now just rest.

Charlie's mind drifted back further. She remembered little of the two weeks between the day her father died and when David and Catherine found her in Central Park. All that remained of this time were fragmented images, flashes of memory separated by long blackouts. Dr. Taylor said that it was called amnesia and that it was probably caused by shock. That had upset Charlie because the only thing she knew about amnesia was that people who have it forget their names and families. She didn't want to forget her father and mother. Memories were all she had left of them. If she lost her memories of her parents, then they would truly be gone, and she would be completely alone.

Never mind.

She still remembered her mother and father as if they had died just yesterday. It was only the last two weeks that were lost. Or rather they were badly fragmented with large parts missing. Charlie remembered walking away from the Fallow Point compound and she remembered hitching a ride with a bunch of ravers in a Volkswagen minibus. They smoked and took pills almost constantly and called her shorty. When they asked her where she was going she answered "North" earning a raucous cheer. The next thing she remembered was scraping her back open crawling under a barbed wire fence to escape an angry guard dog that tried to eat her. Her last clear memory was of the young man she had spoken to at Fox News. Everything else was a total blank until she met David and Catherine. It frightened her a little to know that she had lost almost all of the last two weeks of her life, but it didn't matter now. Whatever happened was over and was probably not anything she wanted to remember anyway. As she thought that a brief image of her eating out of a garbage can behind a restaurant flashed in her mind. Charlie cringed

Oh, that's nasty. I'd never do that.

She was at least certain of that much. There was no way she could ever eat out of a garbage can even if she was starving to death. But the image persisted, and it was too clear to be a figment of her imagination.

Oh, stop it. What does it matter anyway? I'm safe now and I'll never have to do that again so what does it matter?

With that, Charlie pushed the image aside.

For a while, she laid still in bed listening to the night sounds outside, not thinking but drifting. Eventually, sleep came upon her.

VIII

Over the next few days, Charlie's health steadily improved. On Wednesday Dr. Taylor returned and pronounced her improved. Then she returned on Friday and pronounced her much improved. Charlie had a slight relapse Friday night spiking a fever of a hundred and three but by Saturday afternoon the fever was down, and she was able to walk around the house albeit unsteadily. She was still very weak and suffered from sporadic attacks of vomiting and diarrhea, but these were becoming less frequent and severe.

Early Sunday morning Catherine went to the grocery store alone leaving David to care for Charlie. She was still asleep when David finished his breakfast, so he sat down in his office to write. After a while, Charlie came in and sat down beside him. She watched him in silence for a time before meeting his gaze with nervous eyes.

"Don't you want to know what happened?"

David offered her a gentle smile. "I figure you'll tell us when you're ready." He did want to know but he didn't want to press her.

Charlie seemed to sense this. She gave a slow nod. "I'll tell you."

She began with slow reluctance, speaking with careful detail and was still talking when Catherine returned two hours later. She came in without a word and sat down to listen as Charlie droned on and on in her young and yet somehow old voice. When she was finally finished David and Catherine both understood how high the stakes were and how much danger they were all in.

David had many questions, but he kept them to himself. Charlie wasn't crying but she looked exhausted. David took her into his arms and carried her upstairs to bed. He stayed with her until he was sure she was asleep. Then he crept out of the room and went downstairs. He found Catherine sitting at the kitchen table looking very concerned. She had poured herself a cup of tea and was sipping it with deliberate slowness. She didn't look up when he came in.

David crossed the kitchen and sat down without a word. He still didn't know what he thought about Charlie's story. It seemed incredible and yet he felt certain that it was true. And if she had told the truth then they were all in very serious danger.

As if hearing his thoughts Catherine broke her silence. "What do you want to do?"

David sighed. "I don't know. I'm still having trouble believing all of this."

Catherine looked up at him. "You think she's lying?"

David shook her head. "No. That's just it. I know she's not lying. I can feel it. Can't you?"

"Yes." Her face was taut with fear. "I'm scared, David."

He nodded. "Me too." He was still having trouble taking it all in. He had sensed that Charlie was in some kind of trouble, but he hadn't thought it was this serious. He had assumed she had run away from abusive parents or a children's home. This was beyond anything he would have guessed possible. "I mean let's be honest about it. As much as we may care about Charlie, she could get us both killed."

Catherine's expression of fear deepened, and her face paled a half shade.

"Maybe we should call the police. They could protect Charlie better than we can and we should tell someone what's going on."

Sudden anger flashed within David's heart. "Do you know who these people are Catherine?" His voice had taken on a subtle edge. "This is the NSA we are talking about, the fucking National Security Agency. If we report this to anyone then they'll squash any investigation and come and kill Charlie and probably us too. The only hope we have is if we can keep her a secret."

Catherine picked up her cup of tea and took a sip. "Then let's go to the *Times* or CNN or Fox. They're sure to put Charlie on if they see what she can do, and the NSA couldn't hurt her if enough people know about her.

"No, they couldn't." David paused thinking the idea over in his head. It wasn't a bad idea except for one glaring problem. "But if the NSA finds out then they'll squash it before anything gets out and then they'll know where she is…where we all are. They've probably already thought of all this. I could take Charlie to CNN or Fox and there could be a dozen guys in the lobby with guns. We could get Charlie killed that way." He gave a tired sigh. "That may not even be the worst that could happen. God forgive me for saying this but I'm afraid of what might happen if she gets the drop on *them*. You heard what she said happened at that Fallow Point compound. If her power gets out of control like that again…there are over a *million* people in this city. I don't want to be responsible for something like that."

"But what else can we do?" Catherine asked. "We can't keep her a secret forever. She has to get out to exercise sometime and she needs friends. I don't think that little girl has had any friends her age since she was six. I wouldn't be fair to keep her locked up in here all the time and anyway it'll never work. Sooner or later somebody will come by and see her here."

"I know Catherine," David replied in a fatigued tone. "But I don't know what else we can do. If we screw with these people they'll kill us and Charlie and maybe our families too."

A brief image of his adopted father flashed in his mind. David hadn't spoken to him for over a year now.

"I guess you're right David." Catherine conceded. "I'm just really scared. I don't want to see Charlie hurt and I don't want us to get hurt either." She slid to the edge of her seat and stood up with slow deliberation. "How did we ever get ourselves into this mess? Jesus, we only helped a lost little girl."

IX

Outside the kitchen door, Charlie stood shivering with fear. She was not so much frightened for herself as she was for David and Catherine. What had she brought upon their house? Charlie's cheeks flushed with shame. Here she had been so concerned for herself that she hadn't even thought about what kind of danger she was placing David and Catherine in.

She could get us both killed.

No...please...

Like she did her mother...

Please don't say that...

Like she did her father...

Please, I didn't mean to...it wasn't my fault...I...they came and killed Mommy and Daddy.

To get to me.

She was crying now, softly and hopelessly. Tears spilled down her cheeks to her chin where they dripped down onto the collar of her nightgown.

It's all my fault. If it wasn't for me Mommy and Daddy would still be alive. They would be happy instead of dead. A sob escaped her throat. *And now David and Catherine are gonna get killed too. All because of me.*

To her surprise, the kitchen door opened, and David appeared. His expression was tight with fear and he looked angry. Charlie backed away guiltily still sobbing. David took a step towards her. Charlie looked up with pleading eyes.

"Please, I'm sorry I didn't mean to...I didn't think...I'm so sorry."

David took her into his arms. "It's okay sweetheart. You didn't do anything wrong. Everything's fine."

"No, it's not. The NSA men are coming. You said they are. You said that I... could...get...you...." She forced the word out. "...killed." Then she burst into fresh tears.

David drew her tight against his chest hurting her a little. "Charlie you haven't done anything wrong. It's not your fault that your parents died."

Charlie looked away. She didn't believe him. The NSA killed Mommy and Daddy to get to her and now they were going to kill David and Catherine too.

David gently turned her face towards his. "Listen to me, Charlie. Whatever happens, what's going on now, it's not your fault. I'm sorry I said that you could get us killed. It wasn't right. You didn't do anything to put Catherine or me in danger."

Charlie tried to turn away again. *It's all my fault. Daddy and Mommy died because of me and now I'm going to get David and Catherine killed too.*

David would not let her. He gave her a gentle shake. "Listen to me Charlie this is *not* your fault. Those NSA men are bad people. They're the ones who are doing this not you. You haven't done anything wrong."

Charlie looked at him in disbelief. "Really?"

"Yes." He gave her a gentle smile. "You can't help being who you are, and you certainly didn't do anything to deserve being chased and threatened."

"Okay." Her voice dropped to a whisper. "But David…I'm scared."

Me too. David thought. "It's okay sweetheart. Everything's going to be ok." *I hope.*

Chapter 3
The 'Suicide' of Judy Taylor

I

A week after David and Catherine found Charlie Judy pronounced her physically well though she had much psychological healing ahead of her. She still felt weak and tired much of the time and her appetite remained poor. Food was tasteless and nauseating. Some days simply getting out of bed took all of her energy. She would often sit alone in her room staring into space, lacking the energy or will to do anything more, barely able to keep from bursting into tears. It didn't matter. Nothing was fun anymore. Everything she used to enjoy had become meaningless and often unpleasant as it brought back painful memories. David and Catherine did their best to comfort her and make her feel loved and she had grown close to them. She had only known David and Catherine for two weeks, but they had become her family. She felt as if she had known them for years. She thought perhaps this was because of the power. It connected her to David and Catherine in a way, made them brothers and sisters afflicted with the same curse. This curse that made the three of them other and brought them together in a way that transcended time. They felt like family and…they were the only family she had left.

Still, it wasn't enough. They weren't her parents. One-night David and Catherine went out and bought *The Little Mermaid*. It was Charlie's favorite movie, but she couldn't enjoy it, it reminded her too much of her parents. She sat through half of the movie and then asked to go to bed. Charlie missed her parents terribly. The pain was unbearable. Most of the time she tried not to think about them at all. Sometimes she couldn't help it. She would see something or hear something that reminded her of Mommy and Daddy and burst into tears.

Fear hung over her like a dark storm cloud. Charlie was plagued by flashbacks and horrible nightmares. In these, she was plunged back into the terrifying prison of the NSA's Fallow Point Compound or running scared from men intent on spilling her blood. She would awaken from these with shuddering suddenness, her body coated in sweat. She was not so much pulled from sleep as ejected like a fighter pilot from his cockpit. Often, she would be screaming and unaware of it frightening David and Catherine into her room.

On Monday morning she had a bad one.

She was in the park with David and he was pushing her on the swings. At first, it was great fun. Charlie laughed and squealed with pleasure begging him to push her higher and higher. At the height of one swing, something caught her eye. She recognized it at once in that strange way that one always recognizes things in a dream. It was Robin Striker the man who had pretended to be her friend and then killed her father. He was standing on the edge of the playground, his back to the sun, his figure little more than a shadow in the bright sunlight. As she watched him Robin drew a long rifle from within his long coat and stalked towards her with deliberate slowness. Charlie was terrified. She wanted to cry out to David, to scream a warning but she could not find her voice. Rapid panic set in. Charlie's breathing became swift and shallow and her heart began to pound so hard that she thought it would burst from her chest.

Oh, please no…Please not again.

David had stopped pushing her and the swing was still. Charlie sat frozen in place, wanting desperately to jump up and run away yet unable to.

Robin stopped six feet away. His silver eyes were cold. He raised his rifle and took aim. A cruel smile played across his thin lips.

Then she was awake, sitting bolt upright in bed, muscles wracked with fierce shudders, her body soaked in sweat. She wasn't screaming but she was badly frightened. Robin was dead, she had killed him herself, yet she was still terrified. The image of him standing over her lingered for a moment longer before it faded leaving only fear behind. The power raced within her mind, turning the bedroom air explosively hot. Charlie bit it back fiercely, sending twin spires of searing pain ripping through her skull.

STOP IT! STOP IT NOW!

The power continued to spiral upward, sharpening the pain in her head to a terrible, screaming crescendo. She wanted desperately to let go for she knew that the moment she did pain would immediately turn to pleasure. Yet dared not. The images of the inferno at Fallow Point remained fresh in her mind. She did not want to hurt David and Catherine. They had tried to help her.

STOP IT!

For a moment the power continued to accelerate, then something within disengaged, spun free for a moment and the power went silent.

Charlie remained frozen in place for several minutes before rational thought returned.

Robin's dead. He can't hurt me anymore.

The thought brought little comfort. Charlie knew that Robin was dead. She had watched him burn to death in her flames, but the dream's grip permeated her emotions. Charlie's eyes drifted around the bedroom. It was still dark out. Dim, artificial light filtered into the room through the large windows in the right wall. In the daylight, the room had a warm, cheery air that she found comforting. Now it felt cold and haunting in the dim twilight of the night. The antique furnishings made her feel as though she were in a haunted house. Charlie shuddered hard. Something wasn't right. She could feel it. This fear, it wasn't only from her nightmare. There was something more. Charlie turned and picked up the Big Ben from the bedside table.

One o'clock.

It was so late that it was early. The room was silent save for the muffled sounds from the city streets below. Nothing was out of the ordinary and yet she was afraid. Something was very wrong. Her instincts were screaming. Charlie's heart began to race. She slid to the edge of the bed and crossed the room in total silence without bothering to turn on the light. She had to tell David and Catherine.

II

The sound of the telephone awakened David from a deep sleep. At first, he took it for part of a dream and ignored it. After the fourth ring, David realized he was not dreaming and fumbled for his iPhone.

"Hello?" Before the caller even had a chance to reply a sudden and powerful sense of foreboding struck David.

"Hello David, it's Rob." Rob Perkin was Judy's boyfriend. David didn't know him as well as he knew Judy but they were friendly. "Something's happened…"

He didn't have to finish. David already knew that something horrible had occurred and was terrified. Still, he wanted to hear it. "What happened?"

Rob was silent for a moment. "Judy's dead." He paused. "I don't know what happened. The police said it was suicide. They found her on the floor in her office with a bunch of pills all over the place. They said she overdosed on barbiturates." He broke off. "I don't understand. She was happy. We were going to get married next year. I can't believe she would kill herself."

The phone slipped out of David's hand. Thick, oily sweat coated his skin. "Jesus…" His voice was little more than a frightened whisper.

"Who was that?" Catherine's voice was thick with sleep.

David did not reply. He could still hear the faint whisper of Rob's voice on the phone, but it no longer held any meaning or interest to him. His mind was focused on only one thought. *Charlie!*

"What?" Catherine asked still more asleep than awake. "What's going on?"

"Judy's dead," David replied in a dull tone.

"What!" Catherine was wide-awake now. "What happened? Who did it?"

"They said she committed suicide, took an overdose of sleeping pills or something." David was shaking with terror now. "Jesus…" *Charlie!* His mind repeated. David jumped out of bed. "We have to go. Now!" His calm and controlled tone surprised him.

Catherine gave him a strange look. "Where? What do you…" She broke off. "Oh God, you don't think…"

David nodded. "She saw Charlie three weeks ago and now she suddenly kills herself. Do you really think that it just happened?"

Catherine's eyes widened but then she shook her head. David could feel the force of her denial and fear. "You think it was the NSA?"

David said nothing.

"Why would they kill Judy? She didn't know anything about Charlie's power."
As she spoke David could sense that Catherine already knew the answer but
refused to acknowledge the truth.

"Catherine the NSA does signals intelligence and surveillance. All it would take
would be an intercepted phone call or a few minutes of video. Charlie used to
live in Manhattan with her father, they had to have been looking for her here."

Catherine did not reply. David sensed her internal struggle as she did not want to
believe what was happening. Finally, she resigned herself to the reality of the
situation. "What do you want to do?"

David opened the dresser and took out a pair of jeans. "Get dressed. We have to
go."

As he spoke David heard the bedroom door open. He turned to see Charlie
silhouetted in the light from the hallway. "You know too." She spoke with the
resignation and sadness of one who has experienced prolonged suffering from
which there is no escape. "We have to run. I'm so sorry."

David and Catherine both went to her. In his heart, David felt deep compassion
for this young girl who had suffered so much in her short life. "It's going to be
ok Charlie. Somehow it will all come right." As he spoke David was struck by
the sudden realization that nothing would be alright for a long time. Instinctively
David drew Catherine and Charlie to his chest and hugged them with desperate
strength.

Catherine met his gaze with a question in her eyes. David said nothing. He had
no plan, no idea of how to handle the situation. He only knew that they were in
danger.

III

Ten minutes later David watched Catherine dress in silence. He knew that this
was a turning point. Once the three of them left the house there would be no
going back. They would become fugitives. Their lives as they knew them now
would be over. Part of him balked at the thought. He had spent half his life in a
desperate struggle to be normal. He would be throwing all of that away if he
tried to run with Charlie.

But it was already gone. Any hope he had for a normal life had died when he and Catherine found Charlie in Central Park.

Catherine finished putting on her sneakers and the two of them went to get Charlie before heading down the stairs and out the front door. Ten minutes later they entered the building's underground parking garage.

David had no idea of what to do but he knew they couldn't use his car to flee. The NSA would know they were running the moment he started the car. Having no other options David used the power to steal a car from the garage. He felt bad about doing this, but he needed a way to get to safety without tipping off the NSA too soon. It didn't make it ok, but it at least was a good reason. It was surprisingly easy. All he had to do was reach out with his mind and the car kicked over by itself.

Not long after the three of them were headed north towards the George Washington Bridge on their way out of Manhattan for the last time. From the bridge, David would take Interstate 80 across northern New Jersey and into Pennsylvania on their way west. David had no specific plans, but it had occurred to him that they could catch a container ship out of the Chicago port, across the Great Lakes to the Atlantic and then to Europe.

Black despair welled up in David's heart. They would have to show ID to get out of the City and the moment they did the NSA would know they were trying to run. The situation was hopeless.

IV

An hour and a half later they had driven through Manhattan and the Bronx and were approaching the checkpoint before the George Washington bridge. Ahead the road split into six cattle chutes. At the end of these was a structure that resembled one of the old tollbooths, except that this structure was made of concrete and was sealed at the opposite end by a row of twenty-foot electrified steel gates. Two heavily armed state troopers guarded each gate. David carefully applied the brake stopping beneath the overpass. His heart was racing, and he had to struggle not to tremble. Both state troopers lowered their M4 carbines and ambled up to the car flanking it on either side. *This is it. In a couple of minutes, the NSA will know we're trying to run.* David could feel Charlie and Catherine's fear radiating out at him.

The trooper on David's side knocked on his window. David rolled it down.

"Yes, officer?" Somehow, he managed to keep the fear out of his voice.

"May I see your identification sir?"

David turned off the car and gave the cop his ID card. The man reached in with one leather-gloved hand and took the small plastic card while keeping his rifle leveled with the other. He gave it a cursory glance. "I'll need to see your passengers' ID as well."

Catherine handed her ID card over as she mumbled something about Charlie having lost her ID at a rest stop. Her fear was palpable. The state trooper motioned with his rifle. "Please step out of the vehicle." David, Charlie, and Catherine got out without a word. A cool breeze stirred the otherwise quiet air. A slight shiver took David. He was thankful that it was cold enough out to warrant wearing a heavy jacket. Otherwise, the two state troopers would have seen his shirt plastered to his chest and back.

He glanced at his wife and adopted daughter. Both looked deeply frightened. Catherine's excuse was paper thin and would likely get them caught.

The first state trooper motioned with his rifle. "This way please sir." David followed him into the booth on his left. Inside were a card reader, a thumbprint analyzer, and a retinal scanner. David stared at them with fear in his heart. In another minute he would be arrested and dragged off to be taken by the NSA. They would verify his ID; a red flag would come up and the three of them would be arrested. David studied the state trooper. He was of average height and build but he had a 10mm Glock pistol in addition to his rifle and he looked like he could handle himself in a fight. Belatedly, David found himself wishing he had listened to his father and developed his powers.

David went through the entire ID verification process expecting at any time to be dragged away in cuffs. To his surprise, he passed without a problem.

David was incredulous. *What the hell?*

Instead of feeling relieved he was more frightened and suspicious. The NSA had to have put a flag on his file. But the state trooper was letting him go. Why? It didn't make sense. David walked back to the car feeling confused and frightened.

As he drove away from the New York City checkpoint David again wondered what it was he and Catherine had gotten themselves into.

Their progress was agonizingly slow. With each passing minute, David's fear and tension increased as he expected to encounter a roadblock at any moment. After an hour had passed he was gripping the wheel with white knuckles and trembling.

V

It was close to dawn. The sky had gone from jet black to deep purple. David had stopped at the top of the exit ramp for Ashford Pennsylvania waiting for the light to change to green. There were no signs or billboards indicating a nearby hotel, but he and Catherine were exhausted and could drive no further.

"Do you see any place where we can rest?"

Both Catherine and David had left their cell phone at home and they dared not use GPS for fear of being tracked.

Catherine yawned and glanced at an old road atlas for a moment before shaking her head. "Ashford's to the right but I don't see any hotels."

David felt his chest fill with desperate exhaustion. They would have to sleep in the car then because he couldn't go much further safely.

Without thinking and without concern for the still red-light David turned right. Trees floated by on both sides in a blurry dream. David's head swam with exhaustion. Someone was talking but he could not make out the words.

"David!" It was Catherine and her voice was upset though he could not understand why. "Be careful you almost ran off the road."

David shook his head clear and suddenly realized he was driving on the shoulder. Without slowing down David cut the wheel to the left, hauling the car back into the driving lane. Though a small gesture, getting the car back onto the road took tremendous effort. David had little energy left in him and had to fight to keep his eyes open.

After traveling an unknown distance David carefully applied the brakes and turned left onto a heavily wooded, narrow dirt road.

David could feel Catherine's gaze. "David where are we going?"

"I don't know." He replied as he gave the engine a little gas. The car lurched forward and began to bump and thud along the dirt road. "I think we're going to be sleeping in the car tonight and this road looks fairly private."

In truth, David was unsure of why he had chosen this particular road when any road would have suited his purpose.

The road wound its way through the woods for several miles before terminating in a steel cattle gate. David stopped in front of the gate and got out.

Catherine called after him. "David? What are you doing?"

Upon reaching the gate David found it latched but not locked. David unlatched the gate and pulled it open. It seemed to take a tremendous effort. David's legs felt like lead. A few moments later he was back in the car and they were on their way again. After another mile of bumps and thuds, the road abruptly ended in front of a derelict log cabin.

David stopped the car and turned to Catherine. "Wait here with Charlie. I'm going to have a look around."

David intended to find out if the log cabin was indeed empty and if so he would break in. He was not proud of this, but he saw no other options. They needed shelter, someplace quiet and at least somewhat safe where they could rest for a few hours before getting back on the road.

David found the cabin was indeed abandoned. The front windows, while not boarded up, were festooned in cobwebs and dirt. David found electric and gas meters that had long since been shut off. He tried the front door and found it dead bolted.

David let out a tired sigh. He could open it with ease, but he hated to use the power. After a moment's pause, David reached into the power, feeling it flow in an invisible river. Then he thrust it out at the lock. A warm, pleasurable sensation washed through him as the bolt thudded clear and the door fell open.

David returned to the car to find both Catherine and Charlie fast asleep. For what he hoped would be the last time that evening, David shook Catherine awake and then gathered Charlie up into his arms before heading into the log cabin.

VI

As David, Catherine and Charlie settled into the abandoned log cabin in Ashford Pennsylvania, a chestnut-haired woman sat behind a wide red oak desk drinking an espresso and reviewing a report on Charlie Macleod and the McAuliffe's flight from Manhattan to Ashford Pennsylvania.

Two agents were assigned to dispatch Dr. Judy Taylor, the physician who had treated the girl. The chestnut-haired woman had sent another two dozen NSA operatives together with an Asset to find and kill the girl and the McAuliffes. Fortunately for the McAuliffe's and the girl the operatives arrived late only to find an empty house.

The chestnut-haired woman gave an involuntary shudder. Though her position within the NSA gave her cart blanch to dispatch Assets as needed, she nevertheless hated to do so.

The blank-faced, soulless assassins deeply disturbed her and, though she would not have admitted it to anyone, they absolutely terrified her.

The chestnut-haired women skimmed further down the report. They had intercepted a call between one Judy Taylor and a David McAuliffe discussing the recovery of a mysterious little girl that David and his wife, Catherine had found in Central Park a week ago and had placed both Taylor and the McAuliffes under surveillance. Then at 2000 hours last night the girl used her power confirming that she was indeed Charlie MacLeod, the same little girl who had burned her way out of the Fallow Point compound a little over a month ago.

Jane Rickman, Captain Rickman, to those who worked under her, commanded the NSA's Office of Covert Action. Although she had no direct involvement with the program that gave birth to the Assets who would later be placed under her command, Captain Rickman had become as familiar with the program and its aftermath as any of the men and women who had overseen it.

Project Black Wolf began in the 1970s as an offshoot of the MKUltra experiments. The original goal at that time had been to test bio-modifying drugs as a means of inducing physiological and neurological enhancement in human test subjects. Unofficially the intent had been to artificially breed, so-called Enlighteneds, or men and women gifted with inborn psionic abilities such as telekinesis, electrokinesis, ESP, and other related abilities; together with an instinctive knowledge of weapons and combat. These Enlighteneds were considered the ultimate super soldiers. The ability to artificially breed them would have been invaluable to the arms race against the Soviet Union.

Sadly, the program was a failure in that regard. While the test subjects did indeed develop some psionic talents and became proficient with weapons and in many forms of combat their abilities were inferior to those of a true Enlightened. Nevertheless, the program director, a Dr. Alexander Richter soon found a new use for the surviving test subjects. While the limitations on their abilities made the surviving test subjects unsuitable for use as soldiers they could be employed in the far more specialized field of assassination.

After several generations of additional experimentation and tinkering with the process, Dr. Richter managed to engineer a highly intelligent, emotionless, amoral and frighteningly effective breed of assassins which he codenamed Assets.

These Assets were used by the US government and occasionally by wealthy private parties, to perform the most difficult, dangerous and above all the most sensitive assassinations. They were managed through an organization officially known as Intelligence Support Activity. Officially the Activity, as it was known was under the control of the US Army and was tasked with gathering actionable intelligence in advance of missions by other US special forces units. Unofficially, the Activity engaged in numerous black bag operations, including the Asset program.

Rickman flipped through the file further. At the core of Project Black Wolf, was a drug codenamed D-13. First discovered during the MKUltra experiments D-13 was a chemical cousin of Methamphetamine. However, D-13 was a unique drug. Like Meth, D-13 was a potent stimulant. It also had potent hallucinogenic and dissociative properties, but it was not these qualities that made it of special interest to the NSA. Rather, it was the drug's ability to activate psi talents in persons exposed to it that led to it becoming part of Project Black Wolf.

D-13 performed exactly as promised, proving to be a powerful psychic stimulant. Unfortunately, when the subjects were at the height of their power they would also be tripping out of their minds and in the grip of violent paranoia. After coming down from D-13's immediate effects the subject would retain moderate psychic abilities including telekinesis and limited ESP, but the use of those abilities would harm the subject's health. Moreover, the damage was cumulative and would shorten the subject's life to a significant degree.

Overuse of the subject's psi abilities would result in severe headaches; impaired judgment and reasoning; severe nausea; episodes of extreme violence; and eventually cerebral hemorrhage, stroke, and death.

Another interesting side effect of D-13 was its ability to remove both the subject's emotions and any sense of empathy or morality. This combination of traits made it clear that the test subjects were not Enlighteneds and would make poor soldiers in any case. Those same qualities contributed to making the subjects ideal assassins.

In addition to being injected with D-13, the subjects of Project Black Wolf were also injected with synthetic anabolic steroids and subjected to neurological reprogramming.

The end result was a perfect assassin. Assets were proficient with any weapon imaginable. Without a conscience or sense of empathy, Assets would kill without hesitation. Without emotions, Assets would experience no fear, regardless of the danger confronting them. Equipped with ESP and telekinesis they would be almost unstoppable. Yet their powers would be limited and their lifespans short, thereby ensuring that they would remain under the thumb of the federal government.

Although Project Black Wolf failed as a means to breed Enlightened it was a total success as a means to produce assassins.

Successful that is, until Jack MacLeod and Dana Blackwood, entered the program fifteen years ago. There was nothing remarkable about either MacLeod or Blackwood at first. Both were ambitious low-level Army officers looking to advance their careers. They had been offered the usual inducements to enter the program and both joined without any hesitation. Both underwent the procedure without any unusual occurrences.

A year after submitting to the program MacLeod and Blackwood fell in love and married. An unusual occurrence to say the least. Five years later Dana MacLeod became pregnant and gave birth to a baby girl, something that should have been impossible.

Assets were generally rendered sterile from the Black Wolf process. The handful who remained capable of siring offspring would have children with horrific birth defects. Yet the MacLeod girl was born without any of the usual birth defects. In fact, she was born without any apparent defects. She was of unprecedented high intelligence and possessed powerful psi abilities, including an exceptionally rare and dangerous ability called pyrokinesis.

It was this ability that attracted the NSA's attention although at first, they had had no idea of the full extent of the girl's power. As they would later learn the girl was far more powerful and dangerous than anyone could have predicted. *She* was an Enlightened, though her parents were not. But she was more than a garden variety Enlightened, even among Enlighteneds, power such as hers was rare.

Captain Rickman had met a dozen or so Enlighteneds in her time with the NSA and none of them had demonstrated power on the scale of the girl's and these were all older teenagers and young adults. Furthermore, none of them were capable of pyrokinesis.

The girl was indeed powerful, she was also extremely dangerous. Attempts to capture and control her had ended with much death and destruction. It was for this reason and this reason only that Rickman had elected to use an Asset to attempt to kill the girl.

Rickman sipped her espresso as she continued reading through the girl's file. Charlene MacLeod was far too dangerous to be left alive. She was indeed powerful, and she could not be controlled. Furthermore, she was not afraid to use her powers. These characteristics made her death a necessity.

As she completed that last thought Rickman picked up a photograph of the girl from the desk. The picture had been taken a few months before they had captured the MacLeod girl and her father. It depicted an eight-year- old girl with waist length perfect blond hair and deep blue eyes. In the picture, the girl was winding up to throw a snowball. She wore a broad smile of pure bliss as her long hair streamed out behind her in a golden comet tail, set aflame by the dying afternoon light. Her father stood a few steps behind her looking on with pride. The girl in the photo appeared normal, innocent and harmless as children are. Nothing about the girl's outward appearance suggested that she represented a more dire threat than even the most fanatical terrorists or that she possessed a power greater than the largest of nuclear warheads. This would make what Rickman had to do that much more difficult. Difficult but necessary.

Rickman put down the photograph and reached for the burner phone on her desk. She dialed a number and listened while the line rang.

VII

As she slept in the abandoned cabin in Ashford Charlie had a terrible nightmare. In it, she was walking with David and Catherine in the woods. It was late summer. The weather was warm but not hot. The sky was a perfect, cloudless span of blue. A soft breeze tugged at her hair and clothes. Gentle sunlight bathed the forest in perfect gold.

Charlie smiled. *It's so beautiful. It's like heaven.* She heard her own words as if she spoken them aloud though her voice remained silent.

David touched her shoulder. *I'm glad you're having a good time. Come on, we're almost there.*

This is the best place for picnics. Charlie turned and saw for the first time a large picnic basket in Catherine's right hand.

They were approaching a clearing. Golden panes of sunlight kissed its soft grass and gentle trees. Charlie ran ahead calling to David and Catherine to hurry. As she neared the clearing the sunlight grew warmer and brighter. Charlie's smile widened as her heart filled with indescribable joy. As she entered the clearing the sky began to darken. Big black storm clouds began massing on the horizon. Thunder rumbled in the distance. Charlie stopped short, frozen in place by sudden fear. Within a few seconds, the sky went from blue to haunting green and then pitch black. Purple lightning forked above followed a moment later by an angry peal of thunder. Charlie cried out in fear and whirled around to see that David and Catherine were gone. A panicked sound, half moan half sob, escaped her throat.

Charlie tried to call to David and Catherine; heeding the advice of the remaining logical part of her mind that insisted that they couldn't be too far away but found that her voice had deserted her. Panic began building in her chest. A second bolt of lightning slashed through the air, illuminating the entire world in brilliant purple for a second. This time there was no peal of thunder but rather a furious roar that nearly took her off her feet. Charlie screamed in terror. She spun around intending to run but froze instead. Standing before her, outlined by the flashes of lightning was the dark figure of a man. It was hard to make out any details of the man's appearance, but she was certain that it was indeed a man. He was very tall, much too tall to be a woman, slender and powerfully muscled. His arms were thicker than her thighs. The man's dress was dark, and nondescript save for

the long black cape that swirled around him as it was caught by the gathering
winds. As she watched in terror the figure plodded towards her with deliberate
slowness. She screamed again; a shrill animal sound filled with panic and fear.
Charlie tried to run but found herself frozen in place. Tears spilled down her
cheeks.

Stay away. She tried to speak the words but found her tongue rooted to the floor
of her mouth.

The man continued towards her. Charlie's heart began to race and she began to
tremble. Thick, oily sweat beaded up on her skin.

Please stay away.

She was terrified, one step away from total panic. The man did not stop. As he
neared her Charlie could hear his breathing; slow, raspy, artificial; and the snap
and flutter of his swirling cape. When he was within a foot of her the man
paused for an instant. At the exact same moment, lightning exploded above
illuminating the clearing in brilliant purple-white. In that instant of twilight,
Charlie saw the man's full features. Heavy black plate armor covered his entire
body. His hands were covered by thick, black leather gloves, and his feet were
encased in black, armored knee-high boots. A long black sword with a leather-
wrapped handle hung from his left hip. Above the shoulders, the man's head was
encased in a black armored helmet. Beneath the helmet, the man had no face.
There was only a skeletal steel mask; even his eyes were invisible. A moment
later he was hidden by darkness. The man's gloved hand closed on her wrist. His
strength was incredible, yet he did not hurt her. Charlie screamed again and tried
to pull away to no avail. She tried to lash out with the power but found that it too
had abandoned her. Panic swept over her in an instant. She shrieked and
struggled in vain to free herself from the man's iron grip. He held her fast. His
grip was like steel, though not crushing it was impossible to escape. The man
drew her towards him even as she struggled to get away. He then turned her
around and pulled her back against him with one hand, while he closed his cape
over her with the other. Charlie uttered one final, terrified shriek. Then the
darkness broke and she found herself sitting up in bed, sweat pouring from her
body and shuddering with terror. Someone was screaming. It took Charlie a full
minute to realize that it was her and another three to stop.

David and Catherine had come into her room and were trying to comfort her.
Charlie remained deaf to their words as her mind was awash in terror. They
were in grave danger and from something far worse than the NSA. She could not

feel what it was, only that it was something horrible.

Chapter 4
A Threat in the Shadows

I

A tall slender man in a tailored black business suit sat alone in the corner booth of a dingy diner sipping a slug of mud. A burner phone lay on the table in front of him. He had just ended a call with command. The man was intrigued. He had never encountered anyone like this little girl.

A pyrokinetic is she? Dangerous? Rickman's warning about the girl might have frightened another man but the tall man found it all fascinating.

Anyway, he was incapable of fear. Like the girl's father, he had been stripped of that hindrance.

The tall man's lips curled into a slight smile. This would be an interesting mission. A child, and a powerful and dangerous child at that. He enjoyed a challenge and this girl would make a difficult mark. The fact that her adoptive parents possessed similar powers was a bonus.

Rickman had warned that David McAuliffe possessed an electro kinetic talent and his wife Catherine was a telekinetic. He was to target the girl without alerting either parent or the girl herself. Failure would mean certain death.

The tall man took a final sip of black swill, stood up and dropped a few bills on the table before walking out the back door of the diner. No one saw him leave.

The tall man took a second burner phone from inside his suit jacket, dialed a number and spoke two sentences to the male voice that answered. "It's time. Location as previously confirmed." He then disconnected the line and discarded the phone in a dumpster behind the Starlight Diner.

II

A short time later he was behind the wheel of a battered gray primer Ford Econoline panel van on his way to the cabin where Charlene MacLeod and the

McAuliffes had stopped to rest.

The tall man was armed only with a suppressed nickel plate Colt Government 1911 in a left-handed shoulder holster, a black canister in his left hip pocket, and a nylon garrote in his right inside breast pocket. Nothing more.

He had been ordered to spray the girl in the face with the contents of the black cannister but that would be no challenge. For the same reason, he had decided against using the Colt. The tall man desired a real challenge and so he decided upon the garrote.
Ten minutes later the tall man had pulled onto the dirt road leading up to the log cabin. He parked the car far enough away to avoid arousing suspicion and approached the cabin on foot. He found the small building dark and quiet. The sky had gone to a deep red and purple hue. He would need to be quick to avoid detection.

As he neared the cabin the tall man mentally reviewed the description Rickman had given him of the interior layout. The cabin was a loft design with a great room and single bedroom on the ground floor and a loft with a second bed above the great room. The tall man speculated that the girl would most likely be sleeping in the loft while the McAuliffes would be in the ground floor bedroom.

As he approached the cabin, the tall man noted that the windows had been shuttered behind caramel wood slats before silently trying the front door. The knob slipped through his fingers.

Locked.

He slipped a hand inside his suit jacket and withdrew a set of lock picks from his right breast pocket. The lock opened without effort and within five minutes he was inside.

A single sputtering kerosene railroad lamp provided the cabin's only illumination, leaving the majority of the great room cloaked in shadow.

The tall man scanned his surroundings. The great room's furnishings were of old and tattered leather. The floor consisted of scuffed hardwood planks. A bearskin rug, frosted gray from dust lay before a cold, fieldstone fireplace. To his left, a shadowy hallway led away to the cabin's ground floor bedroom and sole bathroom. Ahead of him and a little to his left a narrow, wooden plank, stairway led up into the cabin's loft.

The heads of numerous slain animals festooned the walls. In the flickering shadows of the railroad lamp's dim lone flame, they had become grotesque gargoyles. Without a sound, the tall man crossed the great room and skulked up the stairs into the loft.

The railroad lamp's meager illumination did not reach up here leaving the room bathed in shadows broken by slivers of crimson sunlight from a single narrow window in the loft's back wall.

As he had expected he found the girl curled up on her left side in the loft's lone, double bed. Her long blond hair splayed across the yellow and brown stained pillow beneath her head.

The tall man slipped his right hand inside his jacket, found the nylon garrote inside and withdrew it. The girl mumbled something in her sleep and turned onto her back. Her blond hair fell away, exposing her pale, slender neck.

Without pausing the tall man grabbed the girl by her nightie, hauled her into a sitting position and wrapped the nylon garrote around her throat, drawing it tight enough to stifle any sounds.

As the girl struggled he slowly tightened the ligature. The tall man enjoyed the sensation of strangling the girl. The garrote felt almost alive in his hands as if it were conducting the girl's life force. He enjoyed the sensation of her fighting for beneath his grasp, the terror in her pale face and deep blue eyes. Still more he enjoyed the knowledge that he could draw the nylon cord tighter and cut into her carotid arteries or crush the vertebrae in her neck thus ending the matter instantly. The all man had no desire to bring a quick end to the struggle. This would have made for a messy and unprofessional kill. It was his intent to leave the girl dead with no blood and no damage to her body and so he was careful not to draw his garrote any tighter than necessary to cut off the girl's air.

III

Charlie was dragged from sleep by sudden, painful breathlessness. She fought a desperate struggle to feed air to her starving lungs but could draw no breath. Something hard and tight dug deep into her throat. She opened her eyes onto a hazy image of the loft, dimly lit from the guttering lamp and the early morning sky. Charlie fought desperately against the hard thing that had cut off her breath. Instinctively she reached for the power. To her immense terror, Charlie found it far away and hard to reach. Worse she could not control it. Before she could stop it, the power flowed out of her and splattered against the wastebasket by the wall painting it in fuzzy orange. Charlie bit the power back before it could do any further damage. The sudden realization came to her that she could not use the power to defend herself. She had lost control of it and in any case, she could not burn her attacker without harming herself as well. She was helpless.

All at once David appeared out of the growing gray blur of the loft. Charlie met his eyes. She could feel his power flowing through the air and knew what had to be done.

IV

David stood facing Charlie in her bedroom, having been yanked from sleep by the certain knowledge that something was terribly wrong. Catherine too had awakened but he had ignored her and raced to Charlie's loft bedroom. Upon reaching the top of the stairs he found Charlie sitting up in bed wide-eyed with terror. A tall, slender man of indeterminate age stood behind her. The man had wrapped a silver ligature around Charlie's neck and was brutally strangling her. Upon seeing David, he pulled the cord still tighter and addressed David in a calm, professional tone.

"Do not come any closer or I will open her carotid arteries."

David stood frozen, too frightened to think with any clarity. He had to do something. The tall man was choking Charlie to death. David felt the power stir.

In the same moment, Charlie locked eyes with him. Her voice came to him as clear as if she had spoken aloud.

It's okay David. I'll be alright. Use the power. It's okay.

Her eyes seemed to confirm what the voice in his mind had suggested. David reached into the power, at the same moment extending his hands. Jagged sheets of blue-white lightning leapt from his fingertips and lanced into the tall man and Charlie both. David was careful to keep the electrical current of his attack low while maintaining a high voltage. Enough to disable but not kill. Both Charlie and the tall man tensed for a moment as tens of thousands of volts ripped through their bodies. There was a sharp pop followed by a spray of white mist. The tall man let out a grunt and released Charlie who fell forward gasping. Both lay on the bed trembling. David ran to Charlie and took her into his arms. When she was safely out of the firing line David struck out again with his power. A blazing net of white lightning raced through the air and danced over the floor, bed, and walls before tearing into the tall man's body. This time he didn't tense but instead jerked hard enough to launch himself onto the hardwood floor. He remained in this state frozen as thick tendrils of electricity arced into his body. The air filled with the scent of burning human flesh as dense smoke poured from the tall man's body. Then, in another instant, David withdrew his power and it was over. The tall man lay sprawled out on the floor, obviously dead. Deep black charred burns covered his face and exposed skin. His clothes smoked and smoldered. But David had already forgotten him, having turned his attention to Charlie. She was weeping and still gasping for breath.

David examined her to ensure she wasn't seriously injured. There was an angry, deep red mark across her throat where the nylon cord had been. David also found a second, bright red mark on the left side of Charlie's abdomen that had already begun to blister. Neither mark seemed dangerous and Charlie appeared otherwise unharmed. David took her into his arms and tried to soothe her. After a few moments, her crying died out and she looked up at him with frightened eyes.

"They're coming David. We have to get away." As she spoke, he felt it too.

"Yes, I think you're right." He turned to Catherine. "We need to get out of here. I think we are out of time."

She nodded without a word and descended the steps two at a time. David took Charlie's hand and helped her to the edge of the bed. As soon as she put her weight down, Charlie's right leg buckled and she collapsed to the floor.

"Careful." David forced a laugh. "Don't want to fall and bust your ass. There's already a crack in it."

"Are you ok Charlie?" Catherine asked with more than a hint of concern.

Charlie let out a short, high pitched giggle. "I think so. I just twisted my ankle." She continued to smile but her eyes were wide and her breathing quickened. "We should get going."

"Yeah, I think you're right." David agreed. In his mind he saw a dozens of men in black business suits pouring out of late model cars outside the front door. It would not be long before it was too late to run.

Chapter 5
Fugitives

I

As David pulled the car onto the old tar and pitch road, Charlie's flesh suddenly turned to ice and her heart began to pound. They were about to walk into a trap. Somebody was waiting only yards away. Charlie screamed,

"David, Catherine look out!"

and then dropped onto her side.

She never heard the gunshot, only the crack of glass as the bullet passed through the windshield. The car swerved to the right and then to the left. For a moment she was terrified that David and Catherine had not heard her in time. Then David called to her.

"Stay down! I'm going to try to get us out of here."

Catherine's voice followed. "Christ, what the fuck was that?"

There was a second gunshot followed by the sound of a bullet tearing through metal. Charlie's terror carried her almost beyond all rational thought.

Oh, please no! Please, not David and Catherine too! An image of her father's death flashed through her mind. She heard another gunshot and then his gasp of pain.

NOOOOO!!! The shriek echoed sickeningly in her mind.

"It's okay Charlie. Everything's going to be all right. Just keep your head down." David's voice was frightened.

Charlie felt the car accelerate. A moment later David drew in a sharp breath and the car stopped hard nearly throwing her into the back of Catherine's seat. Charlie eased herself into a sitting position and looked around. Two cars had parked across the road ten yards ahead. Dozens of men in black stood in front of them with rifles leveled. They were NSA and they were going to kill David and Catherine unless she stopped them.

No! Not again! It can't happen again! She began to tremble, both with fear and rage. *I won't let it!!* The power sprang up within her, sparked by her anger.

"Stay down!" David's voice, sharp with terror, broke through to her. Charlie ignored him. She eased open her door and got out.

"No Charlie don't!" David sounded close to panic. "Don't get out!"

Catherine cried after her. "Charlie for God's sake!"

The NSA men shifted their aim in her direction.

David screamed. "Charlie look out!!"

The NSA men's eyes were wide. Charlie could feel their fear. Her anger was growing.

You bastards killed my Mommy and Daddy! And now you want to kill David and Catherine! I won't let you!

The power was racing within her now, eager to suddenly leap out and destroy. Charlie held onto it only a moment, just long enough to focus her mind. Then she lashed out with the power shoving all of it out of herself in one huge pumping bolt of force. Both cars exploded in a brilliant white fireball. The shock wave caused her to stumble. Several of the NSA men were instantly devoured by fire. The concussion threw the rest of them clear of the flames. Shards of metal and glass sprayed in all directions. One of the NSA men was neatly decapitated by a whirling piece of steel as it flew through the air. Another lost his right arm to a long shard of metal shot through the air like a harpoon. Yet another NSA man was impaled through the stomach and chest by two long pieces of steel. Two others lay motionless on the ground with no visible injuries.

Something whizzed by her head. Something else painted thin fire across her wrist. The power was screaming within her mind, wanting to jump out again. Charlie turned and sent the power out in the direction of the NSA man who had fired on her. A thick trench of fire swept across the ground in his direction. He screamed and turned to run but it was already too late. In an instant, he was swallowed by flames and collapsed to the ground shrieking in agony. Charlie spun away from him as more gunshots zipped by her small body. Two NSA men stood firing rifles at her. Charlie shoved the power out at them. Fire swept across the ground in a wave enveloping the two NSA men before they had time to react. Their screams echoed in the trees.

David screamed at her. "Jesus Charlie stop!!" Charlie could feel the force of his fear.

The power was raging now. She had to stop it. The NSA men were gone, either killed or fled. Heat baked out at her from numerous directions, the blazing cars, the scattering of burning human remains and numerous flaming trees. The air was thick with smoke and the heavy, sick stench of burned human flesh and raw gasoline. Charlie fought the power back fiercely.

STOP IT!!

STOP IT!

GO AWAY!!

Sharp, burning pain closed around her in a net. The power was still racing in her mind, fighting to get out. Charlie clamped down tighter with her will.

NO!

NO! YOU'RE NOT GETTING OUT!!

"Charlie you have to stop it!!" David's cry was little more than a whisper through the growing pain.

The power was raging within her. She was in agony; invisible flames had swallowed her body, burning her to the core. She had to fight not to scream

STOP IT!

STOP!! PLEASE STOP!!

The power was still blazing, dancing on the edge of her ability to control it. The pain was unbearable, the pleasure of using the power irresistible. She wanted so much to let go. Charlie spun around looking for somewhere, anywhere to expend the force building in her mind. She saw nothing, nothing except trees and the cars.

STOP IT NOW!!

The power continued to rage. Suddenly something inside her mind disengaged, spun free for a moment and then dissipated. The power was silent. Charlie breathed a huge sigh of relief. A wave of dizziness swept through her. She swayed on her feet for a moment before catching her balance.

David's expression became concerned. "Charlie, are you ok?"

Charlie turned to face him. "I'm ok." She spoke in a soft and very calm voice and did not yet realize that she was crying. Charlie staggered toward David. He bent down and took her into his arms.

As David carried her back to the car Charlie's anger dissolved into fear and horror. She buried her face in his shoulder and began sobbing. David stroked her hair and spoke to her in a soft voice. Charlie did not hear what he said. Her mind was lost in memory. She took only passing notice when he placed her back in the car and belted her in. As the car bounced along the remaining distance of the tar and pitch road Charlie saw her father's face and remembered.

II

The day it began was like any other day. She awakened early and went into the bathroom before dressing and hurrying downstairs for breakfast.

Not long after she sat down at the kitchen table Daddy came in looking handsome in his black suit. She offered him a blissful smile and he returned a tentative smile of his own. Today he would take her to run errands. They would have the whole day together.

Charlie scarfed her breakfast and then scampered off to brush her teeth. As young, as she was Charlie was meticulous about caring for her personal hygiene. After she finished Charlie hurried back down the stairs to wait for Daddy.

He arrived a short time later and then she was kissing Mommy goodbye. A quick peck and then she hurried outside. She would have done more if she had known that this was the last time she would see her mother alive.

Robin Striker, Daddy's friend, and their neighbor for as far back as she could remember waived as they passed by. Robin was always nice to her. He lived in a neat old farmhouse and would let her come over and play whenever she wanted. She supposed he was lonely. He lived alone and didn't have any friends other than her father. There was something odd about him she couldn't place but that didn't bother her.

The day promised to be glorious. The sun was shining, and the air was warm without being hot. The last errand they were going to run would be a trip to the doctor's office for some shots which she was not looking forward to, but it would only be for a short time and afterward, Daddy had promised her a surprise.

After the doctor, Daddy took her out to lunch and let her pick the restaurant. Then he took her to Sugar Lake. Charlie had never been to a water park before and was very excited when he told her where they were going. She couldn't remember ever having more fun in a single day except maybe on Christmas. It was a wonderful time and Daddy let her stay until dark.

After they left the park Daddy took her out to dinner and it was during this time that everything changed. She remembered the exact moment. Cold fear born from nowhere welled up within her. Her stomach churned with nausea removing all appeal from the hamburger in front of her. Daddy too felt it and immediately became tense and quiet. Within minutes the two had finished dinner and were on their way home. They were already too late. Charlie knew this from the start but would not believe it. Even after Daddy emerged from the house alone, confirming her worst fears, she would not believe her mother was gone. It wasn't until she heard it from her father's lips that reality sank in.

Daddy got sick that first night and had to stop at a Days Inn to rest. Charlie awoke him early the following morning and it was then that he confirmed her worst fears. His words cut her deeply, awakening the power. Without meaning to Charlie nearly set the little motel room on fire and completely destroyed the bathroom. He had assured her that it was not her fault, but she felt intense, burning guilt for what she had done and sobbed hysterically partly out of shame but mostly for the loss of Mommy. In that moment it had seemed too terrible to be true and yet she had known from the night before that Mommy was gone, Daddy's sorrow-filled words had only served to drive the point home.

When she finally calmed down Daddy gathered her up and took her to the car. They drove all day that first day getting off the highway only twice, once to get gas and once to avoid the checkpoint at the state line. When they finally stopped it was late at night and they were halfway across Ohio. They were both exhausted and slept all day the following day. When they left the hotel, it was dark outside. Daddy drove most of the night that second night. Finally, when the sky had turned from black to deep purple, Daddy pulled into a ramshackle motel in a little town somewhere in Pennsylvania. As they were leaving the next morning Charlie asked her father where they were going.

"Pittsburgh. We'll find someplace to stay and try to start over again."

"Okay," Charlie replied with little enthusiasm.

They arrived in Pittsburgh that afternoon and checked into a Best Western on the edge of the city. That night, after dinner, Daddy sat her on his lap to talk. He told her that the men who had taken her and killed Mommy were still looking for them, so they had to be very careful. They couldn't tell anyone their real names; she was Brittany Thomas now and he was Paul Thomas. (Daddy explained that he would get them identification with these names.) She couldn't go outside without Daddy or somebody he said was okay. He was going to pick her up from school and she was not to go with anyone other than him. She wasn't allowed to answer the door or talk on the phone and she wasn't allowed to look up at the sky. Though she was only six Charlie vaguely understood the necessity of the new rules, except for not being allowed to look up at the sky. Daddy tried to explain to her about the spy satellites watching from space, but she was too young to understand.

Now his instructions had become clear. The NSA men could look down from space using their spy satellites and if you looked up at the sky they would see your face and recognize you.

At the time Charlie had asked who these men were and what they wanted. Daddy's eyes narrowed, and Charlie sensed what she thought was anger tinged with guilt. "Those men are from the government. A bad part of the government. I think they're after you because of what you can do. Because you can start fires."

Guilt flooded through her and she burst into tears. "They killed Mommy because of me?!"

Daddy clutched her to his chest. "It's not your fault Charlie. You can't help being who you are. You haven't done anything wrong."

Charlie was not comforted. "It's all my fault. Mommy died because I'm bad."

Daddy gave her a sudden, rough shake. "Charlie look at me."

She looked away face flushed with shame.

"Look at me." He repeated in a sharp tone.

She looked up at him.

"You are not bad." He gave her another shake. "I love you and you haven't done anything wrong. This is not your fault."

Charlie did eventually regain her composure after that, but she still blamed herself for her mother's death.

III

They stayed at the Best Western for a week before Daddy found them a nice apartment only a few blocks away. Not long after that he sold the car and got a job working as a locksmith. Summer turned to fall. Charlie went to school. Winter came and then Christmas and New Year's. Everything seemed to be going back to normal.

Then in February, it all fell apart. It began with a terrible nightmare which Charlie no longer remembered. She awakened bolt upright in bed, tears streaming from her cheeks and the power raging. Charlie went into the bathroom and pushed the power into the toilet. The water inside the bowl immediately erupted into a furious boil, filling the little bathroom with thick steam. A moment later a sharp -crack- broke the night's silence as the porcelain toilet split down the center from the heat.

Fresh tears spilled from her eyes as guilt twisted her heart.

I'm sorry... I didn't mean to.

Charlie went to find her father, knowing that he would be understanding and yet fearing that he would get angry.

Daddy never raised his voice with her or even betrayed a hint of anger. Rather he took her back to bed, telling her that she had done nothing wrong and then went into the bathroom to clean up her mess.

IV

Later that same night Charlie's father shook her out of a deep sleep. She awoke to find herself looking up into his intense eyes.

"Get dressed Charlie, we have to go."

Charlie did not ask why. She felt it too. *They* were back. Cold fear pulsed in her blood as she pulled her nightgown over her head and threw on the clothes she had worn that day. After she had dressed Charlie started to go to the closet to get her backpack. Her father stopped her.

"We don't have time to pack, we have to go now." His voice was low and tightly controlled. Charlie heard a slight edge of steel. She complied without a word following her father down the stairs and outside.

"Where are we going, Daddy?"

He shook his head. "I don't know Charlie, just away someplace."

He took her hand and they turned right on Hanover Street. Charlie glanced back over her shoulder. It would be the last time she saw their little brick apartment building.

"Come on Charlie." Daddy's voice was calm and but filled with anger.

She looked up at him. His face was hard and showed cold, focused anger. The street looked empty, but she felt it, she felt *them*. Charlie picked up her pace to a sort of walk-run. She began to tremble.

"Daddy I'm scared. What if they catch us?"

"They won't." He replied in a firm voice. "Just keep moving."

Charlie obeyed mutely. A big black car appeared from a side street and turned in their direction. It was *them*. Charlie felt her heart drop into her shoe. "Daddy they're coming!"

Without warning, he bent down, grabbed her by the waist and hoisted her up. Then he broke into a full out run. Charlie looked back over his shoulder. The black car was close behind them. It wasn't going very fast but then it didn't have to. She could see the driver now. He was middle-aged and beginning to bald. His face was blank. Charlie felt the power stir within her.

Oh no! Please not now!

Her trembling intensified. The black car was only a few feet behind them. She could have set it on fire if she wanted to.

No please! Daddy said it's bad!

She turned and looked over her shoulder. They were nearing the bus stop and to her immense relief, there was a bus waiting there. Daddy balanced her on one arm and waived to the driver.

"Hold up!"

The bus driver gave no sign of recognition, but Charlie sensed that he understood. Her relief immediately turned to terror. The men were getting out of their car. Charlie turned around to see four of them rushing forward. Another car appeared out of nowhere and four more men piled out. She screamed.

"Daddy hurry!! They're right behind us!!"

He did not turn around. Instead, he clasped her to his chest with both arms, bent forward and sprinted for the bus. As they approached Charlie heard the hiss of the door opening. Or maybe it was the breaks being released before the bus drove off.

Oh no please don't leave!!

They barely made it. As the bus pulled away from the curb Charlie and her father sat side-by-side. His arm was around her and she clung to his chest. Charlie felt both relieved and deeply frightened. From her father she sensed cool, calculating anger. *No not just anger but cold fury.*

It had been very close.

V

Half an hour later they were sitting in a grungy diner across from the train station waiting for their train. Daddy had bought tickets to New York, telling her that they would be safe there. Charlie knew he was only telling part of the truth but said nothing.

A gray-haired waitress came to take their orders. "What can I get ya' hon?"

"Just a coffee please." Daddy glanced at her. "Do you want anything Charlie?"

She looked up at the woman with a nervous smile. "Can I have a Pepsi please?"

"Coke okay hon?"

"I guess so." She didn't like Coke, but it didn't matter.

The woman smiled back, "Sure thing cutie." then turned and left.

Charlie watched her until she disappeared through the kitchen door. Then she let her eyes wander around the diner. She had never seen any place like this. There was an old pair of skis on one wall and beneath them was an old pair of snowshoes. A tennis racket hung from the wall above their booth and there was a big Chinese fan hanging over the coffee machine and the toaster oven.

A motley collection of people sat in the diner's dozen or so booths and at the front counter. There was an old man and an old lady in the booth in front of theirs and a young woman drinking coffee at the front counter. A man in a dogcatcher's uniform sat beside her and beside him was a young man in a navy officer's uniform. He was a SEAL; Charlie recognized the insignia. Daddy had taught her all about military uniforms one rainy afternoon. It was a long time ago, but she remembered it like it was yesterday.

As she watched, the man in the SEAL uniform turned and flashed her a slight smile. Charlie returned a nervous smile. Something wasn't right. She felt that this man was one of *them,* one of the people from the government who wanted to take her away. A cold shiver wormed its way up her spine. There were others too. She thought maybe two or three, but it was hard to be sure. She was too frightened. The power stirred within her. Charlie held it down as best she could.

I won't do it. I won't.

She was terrified. She knew any moment now the three people at the counter would turn around with guns drawn. As she watched the two men and the woman at the counter stood up and walked towards them. Charlie drew in a sharp breath and had to fight to suppress a scream. None of them were visibly armed but she knew they all had guns. Daddy looked up suspiciously but remained still. Charlie too felt paralyzed.

The man in the SEAL uniform spoke first. "Hello Jack. Hello Charlie." His voice was soft, almost gentle.

Charlie glared at him. "What do you want?" She was surprised by the steadiness of her voice.

"We need you to come with us, Charlie." He turned to Daddy and his voice dropped to an almost whisper. "I suggest you come quietly, Mr. MacLeod. You don't want to hurt all these people." As he spoke he withdrew the grip of a big gun from his pocket.

Daddy glanced at Charlie with as comforting an expression as he could muster and then stood up. "Alright." Without warning, he lunged forward thrusting his fist into the man's s throat. There was a wet sound of crunching bone and the man collapsed to the floor. It was all the opening they needed. Charlie jumped up and ran for the door. Her father's footsteps thumped close behind her. Just before she reached the door he scooped her up and carried her outside. As they crossed the street Charlie looked back over Daddy's shoulder and saw the man in the dog catcher's uniform and the young woman close behind, outlined in the harsh white glow of the Wash Tub Laundromat's sign. They were rapidly closing. Charlie screamed.

"Daddy hurry!!"

He leaned forward and stumbled into a full sprint. As he did, Charlie felt him reach into the power and thrust out at the man in the dog catcher's uniform and the young woman from the counter. Both were caught off guard and went sprawling. A sharp wave of pain radiated from Daddy.

Poor Daddy... He had used the power even though it hurt him.

As Daddy ran through the train station door he tripped and lurched forward almost dropping her. The train station was empty save for a scattering of tired looking men and women and a few children.

"You can put me down if you want."

"I don't mind carrying you, Charlie."

Charlie looked at her father and felt terrible guilt. His face was pale and sweaty. His eyes showed exhaustion and were bloodshot. "Please, Daddy put me down."

He nodded and set her down. Just then the door banged open behind them followed by the ring of footsteps on concrete. Charlie grabbed her father's hand and began to run. He was having trouble keeping up. His hand was soaked in sweat and trembling. He was getting sick again. Now she was really frightened; not just of being kidnapped but also for her father. The last time he had gotten really sick he had fallen unconscious and almost died. She had lain beside him on the bed crying soft tears, terrified he would stop breathing. She turned and glanced over her shoulder. A tall blond-haired man in a black and gold Steelers jacket and a similarly dressed dark haired woman had appeared less than twenty feet behind them. Both were from the government. Charlie pulled hard on her father's arm.

"Daddy hurry!!"

He glanced back and then lurched into a run. Charlie matched his pace to the step, wanting to be there to help him if he should stumble. They had reached a set of stairs and were hurrying up to the platform. Daddy's gait had become very unsteady. He was struggling to keep his balance.

"Daddy?"

"I'm fine Charlie just keep moving."

He didn't look fine. His face was ashen with little black and blue tinges. She sensed he was in a lot of pain. Charlie gave her father's hand a gentle squeeze. He returned a feeble squeeze of his own.

Poor Daddy.

Charlie could feel dozens of men and women bearing down on them. They were almost within arm's reach. She gave her father's arm another tug.

Oh, Daddy. I'm sorry.

He staggered up the last two steps and then stopped for a moment swaying as if drunk. Charlie's eyes darted around the platform. She didn't see the train.

Oh no!

She had been so concerned for her father that she had never thought that the train might not be there. She spun around. The tracks on both sides were empty. There was a train on the track beside the next platform, but they wouldn't be able to get to it in time. They were trapped. Charlie pulled hard on her father's arm and then turned and ran for the far end of the platform. As they neared the edge, Charlie stopped and glanced back towards the stairs.

The man and woman in their matching Steelers jackets had reached the platform and stood a little over a hundred feet away. But there were more than two of them now. Charlie counted fifteen before she stopped counting.

Oh no, please!

She bit down the urge to scream. The power came alive within her. Charlie's fear grew to almost blind terror.

Not now, please not now!

She was going to have to use the power to protect her father.

No, please.

It was the only way.

Please, Daddy said it was bad.

These people would kill her father if she didn't.

But she was more frightened of what would happen if she didn't use it. Charlie glanced up at her father. His eyes were half closed, and he looked only semi-conscious.

The government men and woman slowed their approach and began to fan out across the platform closing off all possible routes of escape. Charlie could sense their combined excitement and fear of her. They knew, at least in part, what she was capable of and as a result were cautious. And yet fear was not enough to make them go away.

Charlie steeled herself for what she had to do. The power boiled within her. She held on for a few seconds longer, waiting until it was obvious that there was no other way.

She never let go. Just as she was about to use the power the train roared into the station. The two dozen or so men and women from the government continued to approach but Charlie knew she and her father would escape. As soon as the train stopped Charlie pulled her father towards the train.

Once inside she led him to the nearest empty seat and helped him sit down. As she slid in beside him Charlie glanced out the window and saw that the men and women who had been chasing them were gone. The platform was empty. Charlie continued to stare out the window for several minutes before looking up at her father. His eyes were closed, and his breathing had slowed and deepened. He was asleep. Charlie leaned over and kissed him.

"Good night Daddy."

She reached into his pocket for the train tickets. After giving them to the conductor Charlie sat back in her seat, closed her eyes and drifted off to sleep.

VI

"Charlie?"

"Charlie wake up."

She opened her eyes, expecting to see her father and was dismayed to find herself looking into David's gentle gray eyes. For a moment she was confused. Then she remembered. Her father was dead, and she was on the run again. She must have been dreaming though she did not remember falling asleep. Charlie looked around slowly. It was mid-morning and they had stopped at an Exxon station. Golden panes of sunlight shone down, glinting off the gas pumps to her right and warming her bare legs.

David had stopped to refill the gas tank and to give everyone a chance to use the bathroom. Charlie wanted to get out and walk around but she felt too tired and weak to do so. Catherine had to help her stand up and keep her balance on the way to the bathroom. Once inside Charlie vomited and almost collapsed to the floor when her calf muscles went into spasm. When she was finished Catherine had to carry Charlie back to the car.

Charlie felt worse and worse as the day wore on. By sundown she was in extreme pain and having difficulty just lifting her arms.

VII

Less than an hour after the firestorm in Ashford an emergency meeting was convened to deal with the Charlie MacLeod situation. Among those in attendance was Vic Garling. Officially a nobody, in reality, he held more power than the director. He said little during the meeting, but his presence was ominous.

Garling did not get involved in a situation unless it was serious and when he did somebody always died. The other NSA officials watched him out of the corners of nervous eyes as they discussed the situation. As they filed out at eleven-thirty that morning, the same time David, Catherine and Charlie were crossing the Ohio state line, Vic Garling intercepted Captain Rickman.

After Charlie's cataclysmic escape from the Fallow Point Compound Garling had assigned Rickman to oversee her recapture and termination. It was her idea to use an Asset to assassinate the girl, a plan, which turned out to be a miserable failure.

"I want that girl killed." Garling's voice was low and threatening.

Rickman looked frightened. "I'll take care of it right away."

"Do that."

VIII

That was twelve hours ago. Now as Charlie lay sleeping Garling and two others, one man and one woman, met in a dimly lit conference room in the underground complex beneath the NSA's headquarters in Fort Meade, Maryland.

The woman was young looking and very beautiful. She was slim with large breasts, tapered legs, and a muscular butt. Her skin was pale, and she had intense blue eyes and long blond hair. During her career with the NSA, she had personally killed eighteen people and was involved in another fifty murders. She had also personally tortured and maimed two-dozen people and was instrumental in framing another thirty people for serious crimes ranging from trafficking in child pornography to capital murder. One of them went to the electric chair last spring. The woman went by the name Nicole McDermott. Her real identity long since erased.

The man was older but still in good shape. Unlike McDermott, he was a troll of a man. His hair was reddish-gold and thinning on top. His skin was also pale and freckled in places. He was short and heavily muscled. His deep-set eyes were brown with hazel flecks and he had a short and rounded querulous face. This man went by the name Orson Tarken. Like the other two, his true name and identity were destroyed. Tarken like McDermott and Garling was responsible for numerous murders, frame-ups, and other atrocities. However, unlike the other two, Tarken preferred to arrange for others to do the actual murders, rapes, and torture rather than doing it himself. Still, his hands carried the blood of many victims.

Garling arrived last. He entered the room and sat down at the end of the long wooden table that served as the room's only furnishing save for the high-backed leather chairs that surrounded it and a short countertop with a sink along one wall. The room itself was dimly lit from overhead incandescent bulbs hidden beneath a long layered wooden lamp.

"What is the latest on the girl?" Tarken's voice was low and harsh.

"She escaped again this morning. Rickman's ambush failed." Garling's soft words positively dripped contempt.

Tarken's lips twisted into a sardonic smile. "Stupid cunt I could have told her it wouldn't work. Not that it matters that little bitch is poisoned. Our men on the scene found a ruptured can of binary nerve agent. She won't get far."

"She might not get far," McDermott interjected. "But the McAuliffes know about her and what she can do. If we don't take them out, then they could go to the media."

Garling took out a cigarette, lit it with his silver Zippo and took a long drag. "They could but they won't."

McDermott looked down the table at him. "What makes you think they won't?"

Garling took another drag off his cigarette and blew the smoke out of his nostrils. "Because they know that if they go to the media then we'll know exactly where they are."

McDermott, unconvinced, gave him a contemptuous look. "Yeah and by then it will be too late."

Garling smiled as a cloud of cigarette smoke drifted around his head. "No. I don't think so. If they try to go to the media, we can quash the story and kill or discredit everyone involved."

"That may be," Tarken replied. "But it's still risky. Something could leak out."

McDermott nodded. "Orson's right we need to put a lid on this now. How much do we know about the McAuliffes?"

Garling stubbed out his cigarette, took out another and lit it. "Apparently both David and Catherine McAuliffe lost their fathers at a young age and were then taken away from their mothers. David McAuliffe was raised by a Catholic priest, a Father James Lenox, at a parish church in Loganton, Pennsylvania. He left Loganton at age eighteen and attended the University of Pennsylvania on scholarship.

David met Catherine Donnelly, as she was then known when he was fifteen. She was sent to a children's home operated by the Loganton Catholic church after running away from a foster home in Friarville. The two hit it off and were married when they were sophomores in college. After graduating David and Catherine McAuliffe moved to Harlem where they resided until David landed a lucrative deal for his novel *Shadows* after which they moved to the Upper East Side. The facts here also suggest a strong possibility that they are both gifted similarly to the girl."

Tarken sat up and edged forward. "Do we know this for a fact?"

"No." Garling puffed and blew more smoke out of his nostrils. "But NSA personnel found Rickman's Agent dead on the floor of the cabin where we caught up with the McAuliffes with unexplained deep electrical burns."

McDermott nodded. "Yeah, they probably have some kind of talents. Why else would the girl trust them so readily?"

Garling took another drag off his cigarette. "It doesn't matter really. Even if they have the power they can still be killed easily. They are not Lightwarriors."

"That may be," McDermott replied. "But we should still proceed with caution."

Garling flicked ashes into the crystal ashtray in front of him. "I agree." He lifted his cigarette to his lips and drew more smoke into his lungs. "That's why we should do nothing. We watch them from a distance until the girl dies of the poison. Then we move on the McAuliffes."

McDermott was silent for a moment. "I suppose that is the safest course of action. The girl has already proven more than willing to use her power in self-defense." She paused. "Do we know where they are?"

"No," Garling replied. "But it will only be a matter of time before the girl uses her power again and when she does we will have her location."

For years, they had been able to find the MacLeods through the girl's power for whenever she used it she would be igniting a bright torch in a darkened room. There would be no mistaking her location.

He stubbed out his cigarette and stood up. "If you'll excuse me I have some business to take care of."

Both McDermott and Tarken raised their eyebrows but neither said anything.

IX

Thirty minutes later Captain Rickman received a phone call from an unidentified man instructing her to meet him in room 311 of the Star Motel. The Star Motel was near the interstate in a part of Washington frequented by long-distance truckers, hitchhikers, hookers and pushers. When she saw the motel Captain Rickman became uneasy.

It was a small two-story building covered in graffiti. The parking lot was mostly empty save for a few shitty looking ghetto cruisers. The office was a ratty little cubicle about the size of an ATM booth.

Rickman parked her car under the motel's single sodium lamp and got out. As she did her unease grew to outright fear. Rickman had no idea who the man was that had called her. She had never heard his voice before. She didn't even know if he was NSA. He'd had the proper identification codes, but this could still be a setup.

There was a scattering of people in the lot, mostly hookers and their johns, but any one of them could be an assassin. She was armed, and a crack shot with a pistol, but the NSA employed the most skilled hitters in the world. As she crossed the parking lot Rickman tensed, expecting someone at any moment to draw a gun and shoot her.

A hooker glanced at her for a moment but other than that her presence went seemingly unnoticed. Rickman knew better. The motel was probably crawling with agents although they wouldn't be anyone she would recognize.

Rickman slipped a hand beneath her trench coat to where her sidearm hung in its shoulder holster. If someone were planning to kill her she wouldn't make it easy for them. Rickman found the room with no delay. Before knocking she withdrew her weapon from its holster, cocked it and slid it into her left pocket. She kept her hand there, fingers curled around the black-checked grip.

I won't make it easy.

Rickman tapped on the door with the back of her hand. A soft voice from within told her to come in. She grasped the doorknob with tentative fingers and turned it. The door opened to reveal a darkened room. There was no one visible within. Rickman cautiously entered the room. Suddenly something struck her from behind. White light exploded in her head. A gunshot rang out and then everything went black.

Once she was unconscious Garling dragged Rickman to the ratty motel bed, stripped her of all her clothing and chained her to its steel frame. He had carefully chosen and specially prepared the room. This motel was located in one of the worst neighborhoods in Washington DC and the room was located at the far end of the motel, well out of earshot of the office. Once he had obtained the room Garling had the existing bed frame removed and replaced with a heavy gauge steel frame. This was all done under cover of darkness and in neighborhoods such as this people were used to not asking questions about what they saw. Once she was restrained Garling pulled up a chair and waited for Rickman to come around. After some time had passed she stirred, and her eyes fluttered open.

Garling smiled down on her coldly. "Good to see you're awake."

"What do you want?" Rickman was terrified despite her calm tone.

Garling's smile faded to a look of pure contempt. "I warned you about the consequences for failure." His expression was superficial for inside he felt not anger but excited anticipation. More than anything he enjoyed the rush that came from having someone totally under his power.

Garling reached under his sports jacket and withdrew the slim dagger that hung beneath his left arm. The blade gleamed in the shadowy room.

Rickman's terror exploded as she began to realize what he intended.

Garling walked around to the right side of the bed, deliberately taking his time, drawing out the moment of anticipation as long as he could. He enjoyed the time before the actual act, when his victim knew what was to come and awaited their fate, almost as much as the act itself.

He paused for a few seconds at the edge of the bed watching her, enjoying the total fear in her eyes and heart. She was his and she knew it. He held the dagger steady, as if he intended to strike but remained still, feeding off her terror.

Rickman closed her eyes and looked away, expecting the dagger to fall. Instead, he unzipped his pants and climbed onto the bed straddling her hips.

Understanding dawned on her. In that moment her skin broke out in goosebumps and she began to tremble. Rickman's breathing became rapid and shallow. Her mind was lost in terror.

Garling watched her with childlike eagerness, enjoying her fear of him. The dance was everything and every step had to be followed. To strike too soon would spoil everything.

He began suddenly and with great force wanting to inflict as much pain as possible both to punish and to accentuate the moment. Rickman fought back hard trying to push him off with her hips while struggling against her restraints. At first, he laughed and intensified his attack. When she continued to struggle he struck her across the face with his knife hand drawing a thin line of blood across her cheek. As the attack reached its climax she began to scream. Garling responded with a second-strike slicing open her other cheek. Moments later he slowly straightened up, raising his dagger as he did. Rickman stared at it in wide-eyed horror reading at once his intent. Garling paused again, drawing out the moment, enjoying her fear of him as much as any physical pleasure he had ever experienced.

Rickman struggled with great desperation as terrible knowing swept through her mind. Garling renewed his smile. Then he thrust the knife into her as hard as he could and twisted it. Hot blood gushed from her body. He yanked the knife from the wound inflicting more damage and releasing more blood.

Rickman screamed. Garling laughed in response enjoying the sight of her suffering.

Then he raised the dagger and thrust it into Rickman's body. Again, he twisted it before ripping it free and spilling more of her blood and part of her small intestine onto the bed. Garling stabbed her

again, and again until her entrails and their contents leaked out onto the already filthy sheets. A revolting stench filled the air.

Rickman no longer made a sound, but he knew she was in agony. Garling caressed her cheek with the back of his gloved hand. A gesture of thanks for a pleasurable evening. Then he stabbed her in the abdomen and twisted peeling back a thick chunk of flesh. She screamed again. Garling chuckled then slashed her throat. Blood sprayed everywhere, soaking his clothes and hers. Garling watched Rickman until the last flicker of life had left her eyes.

When she was gone he stood up slowly, a cruel smile on his face. Then he casually removed his bloodstained clothing and put it into the duffel bag he brought with him. Before leaving the room, he removed Rickman's restraints and covered her with a blanket. Then he closed the door and locked it, leaving the keys on the nightstand within. As he walked back towards his car Garling whistled softly.

X

Charlie awoke feeling hot. She was dimly aware that the power was awake again. Charlie sat up slowly, slid to the edge of the bed and stood up. Her body felt as if it weighed ten tons.

The room was dark. Both David and Catherine were fast asleep. Their breathing was slow and even. Charlie clumsily stumbled across the bedroom still more asleep than awake and went into the bathroom. Once inside she shut the door, lifted the toilet seat and pushed the power into the water in the bowl. There was a low sizzle-hiss and the power was silent. The air instantly became steamy hot.

As she was lowering the toilet seat Charlie realized that she was parched and drank two glasses of water before returning to bed.

XI

David, Catherine, and Charlie awakened early the following morning and ate breakfast at a nearby diner. Then they got back on the highway. They drove for many hours before finally stopping in Gary, Indiana. The day was altogether uneventful. Even getting around the checkpoint on the state line seemed easy, almost too easy. All day Charlie felt nervous and watched. Yet nothing happened. That night she slept soundly undisturbed by fear or illness. The next day was more of the same. They drove all day without incident, crossed the border into Illinois without any trouble and drove until they reached Taylor. Taylor her old home. The place where it had all begun.

As they drove towards downtown Taylor, Charlie's heart ached. She had not been here in three years and yet it seemed like just yesterday. Everything was painfully familiar. She recognized buildings and houses, each seeming to carry with it its own fragment of memory. She remembered going to work with her father, going shopping with her mother, going downtown with both of them. Tears came to her eyes. David must have sensed her sorrow for he turned and glanced at her with sympathetic eyes.

"Is this where you lived with your parents?"

Without a word Charlie nodded. More memories of fun times spent with her father and mother drifted through her mind. She remembered trips to the park, rides on the elevated train, eating at McDonald's or Burger King.

She saw a green road sign ahead. *Harrison Boulevard exit fifteen miles.* "I used to live there." She said more to herself than to David or Catherine.

"Where?" David asked gently.

"Off that exit. We lived on Blakeville Road."

"It's very pretty Charlie." Catherine's tone was gentle and overly bright.

It was. They had had some good times there before the NSA came and destroyed it all. Charlie sat in silence for a moment her heart burning in her chest. She began to cry.

Catherine reached around her seat and took her hand. "I know sweetheart. I know it hurts."

"I'm so sorry Charlie. I'm so sorry they did this to you."

Charlie sensed, for the first time, that David was unsure of what to do. She felt sorry for him. He always tried so hard.

Charlie took his right hand with her left and gave it a gentle squeeze. He returned an even more gentle squeeze. "We can stop if you want to."

"Or we can keep going. It's up to you."

Charlie wasn't sure what she wanted to do. Part of her wanted to stop, to go home one last time but another part of her couldn't bear the pain of being reminded of all that she had lost. "Where are we going?"

David was silent for a moment. Charlie sensed that he didn't know. "Chicago. We're going to get you help and then rest and try to figure out what to do next."

Charlie still felt watched and was afraid that if they stayed in Chicago too long they would be caught by the NSA, but she kept her fears to herself. "Can we get something to eat?"

"Sure." Catherine's voice was too cheerful. Charlie sensed her thinly veiled concern.

They stopped at a Friendly's two miles up the highway. Charlie ordered a burger with French fries and ate only half of each. She also drank two Cokes and a glass of water. She was still upset and felt nauseous, but she was also very thirsty. Throughout dinner, Charlie could feel David and Catherine's concern though they did not speak of it.

XII

After dinner, they got back on route eighty and drove for another hour before stopping at the Executive Motel near the center of Chicago. It was still early so after they had checked in David took Charlie shopping for clothes. Catherine had offered to take her, but Charlie had asked to go with David instead. For some reason, she couldn't name she felt more comfortable with him. Maybe it was because she had touched his mind first, or maybe it was because he had carried her out of Central Park. She wasn't sure.

Charlie sensed that David was worried about her. He wanted her to talk about what had happened. He wanted to help her, but he didn't understand.

She had told him, both of them, a lot going back as far as that first horrible day when her mother was killed but there was also much she had not told. While she had told David and Catherine her entire story from that first horrible day to the day they had found her in Central Park she had told them little of the torrent of emotions within her. She was haunted by fear, hurt and anger that she could not speak of. She dared not talk about these feelings for fear of what might happen if she let them out, and, though she would not admit it to herself, fear of what David and Catherine would think of her. So, she was forced to face her emotions alone as she was forced to face her power alone.

Yet somehow her own feelings, the fear, and hurt and anger, seemed so much more terrible than the power, even when it was at its height. Like the power they tempted her, drawing at her heart and pushing her to do wrong.

What was worse was that she *wanted* to give in. She wanted revenge so badly. She was frightened of the NSA but more than that she was enraged at them. They had killed her father and mother and tried to kill her. They had terrorized her, and they had wounded her to the core. She had burned down their compound but that wasn't enough. Her father and mother were still dead, and the NSA was still out there, watching, waiting to swoop down and snatch away what little she had left in life. She wanted to destroy them. The desire was powerful and very tempting. She had the power; she could burn them all up.

But it's bad. Daddy said it's bad.

She didn't want to kill anyone else but part of her insisted that it was her right. They had taken her parents' lives. And that was what frightened her. That was why she could not talk about her real feelings. She could not even think about them for fear of giving in to her desire for revenge.

And what would David and Catherine think if I told them? What would they say? They'd think I'm bad. They wouldn't want me around anymore. They'd send me away.

She would be alone again.

David and Catherine were so nice; how could she ruin this by telling them? How could she throw away the only family she had left?

Maybe they won't be upset. They were so kind and understanding when I told them what happened at Fallow Point. Maybe they'll understand.

A cold voice spoke up within her. *They won't understand. They'll throw you out on your ass when they find out. David and Catherine will leave you on the side of the road alone and that's if they don't decide to turn you over to the NSA.*

She didn't want to believe the voice, what it said was bad, but she felt it was true. Something deep inside urged her to keep silent, some deep inner instinct, and she had learned to trust her instincts for they were always right.

XIII

Upon returning to their motel room Charlie went straight into the bathroom to take a shower and change clothes. After showering she sat down to watch television before going to bed. Sleep overcame her and brought with it, nightmares of the past.

Chapter 6
Sound and Fury

I

Charlie snapped awake, soaked in sweat, trembling, heart racing in her chest. She was petrified and unsure of why. She felt as if she had awakened from a terrible nightmare, but she did not remember dreaming. The room had filled with oppressive heat. The power stirred within the back of her mind. By instinct, Charlie slammed it down.

GO AWAY!

A slim dagger dug into her skull for a moment before the power quieted down and was silent.

Charlie sat up and reached for the clock.

Six thirty.

She had an hour before it was time to get up, but she was too frightened to sleep. Charlie struggled out of bed and walked out into the hallway.

She felt a veiled threat, a shadowy danger lurking just beyond her knowledge. The apartment was dark and quiet. Daddy was still asleep. For a moment she considered waking him but then decided against it.

I probably just had a nightmare and don't remember it.

Charlie walked down the hallway and went into the bathroom. She showered and dressed then went into the living room to wait for Daddy to get up.

Charlie sat down on the couch and turned on the television. Popeye came on. Zombie-like, she stared at the screen without comprehending. The television was little more than a source of light and noise.

What's going on?

The question repeated over and over again in her mind. Something was very wrong, but she was too frightened to sense what. So, she just sat and stared.

After an unknown period of time Daddy strode into the living room.

Charlie looked up at him and smiled. "Good morning Daddy."

"Good morning Charlie. Why are you awake?"

"I couldn't sleep."

Charlie wanted to tell her father what she was feeling, to warn him of the danger she sensed but she remained silent. She wasn't even sure what it was she had felt.

"Did you have a nightmare?"

"No." Charlie lied. "I just couldn't sleep." Her voice came out slightly confused.

"Ok." Daddy's voice was his usual level and calm tone, but she sensed slight concern. "How about pancakes for breakfast?'

Charlie smiled. "Yeah!"

"I will need some help."

"Ok, Daddy."

Charlie followed Daddy into the kitchen, her sense of danger forgotten. As she helped her father make and then eat breakfast Charlie felt nothing but happiness. She was able to forget if only for a little while, all of the misery that had been inflicted upon her. For that hour and a half, she was an ordinary little girl spending time with her daddy.

II

After breakfast, Charlie went into the bathroom to brush her teeth. As she was putting toothpaste on her toothbrush the sense of danger returned. It was stronger now and more urgent. Her toothbrush dropped out of her hand onto the floor narrowly missing the toilet bowl. The sound of it striking the floor was deafening. Now she understood. The men from the government had found them again.

It had been over two years since they arrived in Manhattan; long enough for Charlie and Daddy to begin to believe that they could be safe. Daddy found work as day security for a construction company while Charlie went back to school. Charlie made friends again. In the spring Charlie's seventh birthday came and Daddy took her to the Statue of Liberty. While in the summer they took day trips to the beaches of Long Island. Then fall came and to Charlie's surprise Daddy let her dress up as Ariel from The Little Mermaid and go out trick or treating. By Christmas time they had almost forgotten that they were on the run.

Winter gave way to spring and Charlie's eighth birthday came. This time Daddy allowed Charlie to invite a few friends over and threw a small party. Life had almost returned to normal. That had been six months ago, now she felt less certain.

Charlie was terrified. She wanted to run to her father and tell him what she felt but she could not. Her feet were rooted to the floor. She could only stand and stare at herself in the mirror. Her face was very pale, and she was trembling. Her heart was racing. She imagined she could hear its pounding. After a moment her fear receded enough to allow coherent thought.

She was shuddering hard and could not stop.

They're coming. They're coming for us.

As she thought that, she absently bent down and picked up her toothbrush. It was clean save for a single blond hair that had stuck in the toothpaste. After several minutes of trembling and fear she realized that it was hers. Charlie picked the hair out of the toothpaste and half-heartedly brushed her teeth. When she was finished, she returned to the kitchen to wait for Daddy. Not long after she sat down, he appeared and the two of them left the apartment and got on the subway.

III

Half an hour later Charlie was sitting in Ms. Peters' class. A social studies textbook was open in front of her. Ms. Peters' was reading from chapter two. Charlie was barely aware of what was in the chapter, something about people living in cities and towns. She wasn't sure. Her mind was preoccupied with fear.

She had not told her father of the danger she sensed and now the feeling was growing stronger. The men from the government had found them again. They were coming for Daddy and her.

Charlie tried to force herself to think rationally. She tried to devise some sort of escape plan should the government men appear through the classroom door, but she could not think of anything.

Time dragged by. As the morning passed Charlie grew more frightened and wary. Every time she heard footsteps outside the classroom she would tense and look up expecting to see the blank-faced government men in their black suits appear through the door. But each time the footsteps would pass without slowing.

At nine thirty they finished with social studies and started math. Charlie was usually very good at math but today she missed six problems. Ms. Peters gave her a disapproving look to go with the sad face she drew on the paper. Then she said that she wanted to talk to Charlie later. Charlie hoped that she would be there later. After math came spelling. They had a quiz today.

Just as Ms. Peters was handing out paper Charlie heard the faint but unmistakable sounds of footsteps in the hallway. As they grew closer she realized that it was not just one person but two. Her heart began to race.

Oh, please don't come in here. Please don't be here for me.

The footsteps grew louder and closer. They were slowing now. A moment later, as Ms. Peters was putting a piece of white lined paper in front of her there was a knock at the door.

Charlie's heart flash froze. *Please no...*

Ms. Peters crossed the room, slipped the door open, and stepped outside. From where she sat Charlie could not see who was there. Fear clouded her mind such that she felt nothing about the person outside. Ms. Peters and this unknown person spoke for a few moments in hushed voices. Then Ms. Peters turned towards Charlie.

"Sally your daddy's here to pick you up."

Charlie went weak with relief. "Okay, Ms. Peters."

She stood up on rubbery legs and crossed the classroom to where her father stood waiting for her. As soon as she saw him she knew something was wrong.

His eyes had that focused look of cold anger that always appeared when he sensed a threat to Charlie.

"Daddy...?"

"Shh. Don't say anything yet." Daddy's whispered to her in a soft, implacable tone.

Ms. Peters bent down and gave her a sympathetic look. "You be a good girl Sally." She gave Daddy s momentary glance and then turned and went back to teaching the class.

Before Charlie could say a word, Daddy took her hand and led her out of the classroom. They walked down the hallway in silence for a few minutes before Daddy made a sudden turn and led her into an empty classroom. He closed the door behind them and then bent down to her level.

"I need you to listen very carefully." His voice was low and intense. "We have to run again Charlie. The men from the government have found us."

"I know," Charlie whispered fearfully.

"They know who we are, and they've probably already given our new names to the police. Give me your ID card."

Charlie reached under her shirt, pulled the lanyard that held her ID card over her head and placed it in her father's hand. He took her ID card from its protective plastic case and snapped it in half. Then he slipped in another. This one had the same photograph of her but identified her as Karen Harrington.

Daddy held the card up to show her. "If anyone asks you your name is Karen Harrington. Mine is Luis Harrington. Say it back to me."

"My name is Karen Harrington." Charlie recited. "My Daddy's name is Luis Harrington."

He flashed a brief smile. "Good girl." Then he took her hand again. "There's a cab waiting for us outside. The driver's going to ask to see your ID before he lets us get in. I want you to give it to him and let him scan your thumbprint and retinas. Answer any questions he asks but don't talk to him and don't tell him anymore than he asks. Understand?"

Charlie nodded.

"Good." He gave her hand a gentle squeeze. "Come on. We need to get going."

Without a word, Charlie followed him through the hallway and out of PS 81 for the last time. The taxi was waiting for them outside just as Daddy had said. Charlie gave the man the ID card her father had given her and then let him scan her right thumb and eyes. When he was finished the man smiled and told her she could get in. Charlie sat down, and Daddy climbed in beside her.

"Grand Central. Quickly!"

"Okay, buddy."

The driver pulled onto the street and slammed the pedal to the floor. As they sped away Charlie glanced back and saw two men getting out of a black car that had stopped in front of her school. Charlie knew immediately that they were from the government. A moment later the two men disappeared inside the building.

They had just made it. If they had been in there a few minutes longer then the government men would have caught them. Charlie turned away from the window and hugged her father around the waist.

"What is it Charlie?" His voice was steady, inquisitive.

She did not answer.

IV

It didn't take long for them to reach Grand Central Station. Soon they were waiting in line to board the subway. Then they were on their way to Coney Island. It was lunchtime when they arrived, and they were both hungry, so they went to TGI Friday's. After lunch, they got back on the subway and headed for Staten Island. This was how they spent the rest of the day, going from subway to subway traveling all over New York.

Charlie sensed the government men close by all day but somehow, they managed to stay ahead, barely. Eventually, they ended up back in Manhattan and it was there where their luck ran out.

As Charlie and her father emerged from the subway to catch the bus a black car appeared out of nowhere and began following them. Charlie knew immediately that it was the government men. They had been found.

Daddy must have felt it too because he picked up the pace. Charlie had trouble keeping up. They had been walking fast before, now they were almost running. Her legs were much shorter than her father's and she was tired. Still, she pushed herself to move as fast as she could; they had to get away. Daddy glanced at her for a moment and then scooped her up and started running.

Charlie glanced over his shoulder and saw that the black car had slowed to match their pace. Its windows were dark making it impossible to see in but Charlie sensed at least four people in the car.

Arctic terror gripped her heart. It was getting dark. They were heading up a side street in one of the poor neighborhoods. The street was deserted save for the occasional car or person hurrying home. The government men could take them here.

Frantic, she scoured the street and sidewalk for some kind of escape. There was nothing. They were approaching an intersection with another, busier street. Daddy turned right on this street and began pushing his way along the crowded sidewalk. Charlie glanced ahead and saw that there was another intersection a short distance ahead. As she watched the light turned red.

Oh no. Please don't stay red.

They were closing upon the intersection and the black car was right behind them. Charlie's heart began to race. This was where the men would take them. All at once Daddy became very focused and tense. His anger, cold as ice, was palpable.

Please no.

The light was still red. A knot of people was building up on the sidewalk in front of the crosswalk. Charlie and her father soon became trapped within this knot. She glanced back again and saw the black car stop. Three men piled out. They were young and looked considerably fresher than she or her father felt.

Charlie screamed. "Daddy they're coming!!"

Daddy looked around quickly and then she felt him suddenly *push* out with his mind at a limousine approaching the intersection on the cross street. It skidded to a stop almost instantly. Daddy ran to it then opened the door and almost threw her inside before jumping in himself.

Charlie had never ridden in a limousine before and under other circumstances would have been awed by its plush interior. At that moment though she was too frightened to notice or care. All that she could think of was the men who had gotten out of the black car. The men who were no doubt right behind them and would in another few seconds throw open the car door and haul the two of them out.

The window that separated the driver's seat from the passenger compartment rolled down and the driver turned and gave her father an annoyed look.

"Hey, this ain't no taxi cab. Take your kid and get the hell out of my limo."

Daddy reached into his pocket and produced his Colt Commander. "Drive or I will kill you."

Charlie shuddered in fear. *What are you doing?* She couldn't believe that her father was doing this. Not Daddy. He was distant but always kind and gentle with her. How could he ever do something like this?

Daddy gave her a mild, reassuring glance before jamming his gun against the man's head.

"Okay, buddy whatever you want just cool it with that thing." The driver's expression was fearful. He pulled out quickly, just before the government men could reach the car, and sped through the now green light.

Daddy relaxed a little but kept his gun trained on the driver. "I do not wish to harm you but don't think I won't kill you if I have to." Charlie looked up at him with fear in her eyes, as fierce tremors took her. She remained thus for a long time before exhaustion overtook her.

V

Charlie awakened sometime later to find that the car had stopped, and she was alone inside. Fear cropped up within her.

"Daddy?" She sensed him nearby but could not understand why they had stopped. She scooted to the door, opened it and got out. Then suddenly she understood. Her father meant to kill the driver. He had decided this man was a threat and resolved to kill him. Horror exploded within her.

Oh, Daddy no...

Please don't...

Deep inside she knew who and what her father was. She had long since sensed the truth. But he was still her father and she loved him. He was the strongest, bravest, smartest man in the world and he was always so gentle and loving with her. He was a good father.

Please, Daddy, don't...

She looked around. The driver had parked the limousine in an empty lot between two dilapidated buildings. It was dark here save for a narrow pool of light from a single street lamp. No one was around. The air felt chilly and deadly still. She detected a faint odor of rotting garbage.

Charlie began to walk, not knowing where she was headed. She crossed the empty lot and entered a dark, narrow alley. Two silhouettes stood at the far end. She recognized her father and the driver at once.

"Get down on your knees." Her father's voice was cold and business-like.

"Please, buddy you don't have to do this." The driver's voice registered panic. She could feel his fear radiating out at her in cold waves. "Please..."

"I'm sorry but I do. I cannot have you going to the police." Daddy's cold indifference shocked her.

"Please! I won't tell a soul. I swea..."

BANG!!

She jumped and nearly shrieked with fear at the sharp report of her father's pistol. He had done it. Charlie burst into tears as the reality of her father's act sank in. He had *murdered* that man.

Oh, Daddy, how could you?

And yet she could not hate him. He was her daddy and she loved him with all her heart. He turned and for a moment she thought she sensed sorrow and guilt from him, not for the deed itself but rather for the fact that she had seen it.

"Charlie. I'm sorry you saw that. You should have stayed in the car."

She ran to him, throwing her arms around his waist and holding him as tightly as she could. "Oh, Daddy." She sobbed. "Daddy…Daddy."

He hugged her to him. "I'm sorry you saw that." He repeated dully.

She clutched her father desperately as the tears streamed down her cheeks. "Daddy please say it's not. Please say you didn't."

"I'm sorry Charlie."

She cried harder. Yes, she had known for a long time but this. This somehow made it real. Her Daddy was a killer, a professional murderer. The fact that he was indifferent to having ended this man's life made it even worse. Charlie wept for her father because she still loved him and she knew deep inside that he was lost. Charlie cried and cried in that dark, filthy alley until finally exhaustion overtook her once more and she passed again into darkness still clutching her father.

VI

When she awoke again they had reached the Lincoln Tunnel and her father had gently roused her to have her identity confirmed. Charlie was nervous throughout the procedure. The fake IDs had always worked before, but she still harbored the fear that this time they wouldn't.

And what happens if they find that man? She pushed that thought aside quickly. It hurt too much to think about that.

Daddy had explained to her when he got the fake IDs that only one of them would be active at a time and that once you used a new one the old one would become invalid and the new one would become active.

Something else troubled her as well. Daddy had gotten four fake IDs and they had already used three. If the government men found out who they were again then they wouldn't be able to hide anymore.

The new ID card worked as intended and they were soon on their way. The remainder of the ride to Philadelphia was long and uneventful. Charlie slept the entire time. When she awakened again it was dark out and the limousine had stopped. She looked at her father questioningly still more asleep than awake and not yet remembering everything that had happened.

"Where are we?"

"Philadelphia International Airport." Daddy replied.

Charlie groaned and sat up rubbing her eyes. There wasn't a clock in the limousine and she didn't have a watch, but she knew it was late.

Daddy switched off the car and turned to her. "Can you walk for a little while?"

"I think so." Her sleep had been restful, and she felt fairly fresh. "Where are we going, Daddy?"

"Croatia." He responded, his voice all business. "But first we're going to catch a flight to London."

"Where is Croatia?" She knew that Croatia was a country *somewhere* but that was about it.

"It's in Eastern Europe, near Italy. It is bordered to the north by Hungary, and Slovenia and to the east by Serbia and Bosnia. Croatia is a non-extradition country and we will be able to blend in there."

Charlie was silent for a moment. She understood that she would need to learn a new language, make new friends again. More than likely she would never return to America. That was alright, but she sensed something else that frightened her. Daddy had some deeper intent that he had buried deep in his thoughts, some darker intent for her future. "Will we be safe there?"

He met her eyes with a sober gaze. "I don't know Charlie. Croatia is far away, and I don't think the NSA will have the same resources available there, but I don't know."

Both Charlie and her father got out and hurried away from the limousine. Twenty minutes later they were standing outside of the main terminal building.

When she saw her father under the bright overhead lights Charlie became very frightened. He looked terrible. He had been fine when they were in New York. Now he looked very sick. Daddy's face was as white as a sheet and his skin was soaked in sweat. He was trembling slightly and swaying on his feet.

"Daddy are you alright?" Her voice was little more than a whisper.

"I'm fine Karen. Let's go inside." Daddy's voice was shaky and pained.

He took her hand and led her towards a large glass door. Charlie followed him without a word, still very frightened. It was easy to tell by looking at him that Daddy was in agony. It wouldn't be long before he wouldn't be able to stand up at all. She was going to have to take care of him.

Charlie helped her father pull the heavy glass door open and then held it while he stumbled inside.

The government men were nearby. She could feel them. They had to find someplace to hide until Daddy got better. He couldn't travel far the way he was now.

Charlie scanned the airport terminal. She didn't see anyone who looked like one of the government men or agents as her father sometimes called them. There was a scattering of people; mothers with tired, up too late kids; teenagers in jeans and t-shirts, or halter-tops, or white undershirts and open button-down shirts. It was the middle of October but still warm enough for summer clothing. There was a policeman standing beside the American Airlines counter and a fat lady talking on a cell phone by the door. To her right a group of skaters was hassling an old man and his wife; a tall man in a business suit was talking to a young woman in a white halter-top and behind them and a little to the left a young man in a Naval Officer's uniform was talking on a cell phone. The Navy man was sitting in one of the waiting areas before the security checkpoints.

Charlie led her father in that direction acutely aware of the worried and disapproving glances from the people they passed.

They think he's drunk.

When they reached the seats, Daddy flopped down in the nearest chair and closed his eyes. Charlie sat down beside him and gently kissed his cheek.

"Poor Daddy."

He slowly turned and opened his eyes. They were bright red and swollen. One eye looked bigger than the other. When he spoke, his words were slow and filled with pain. "I need you to do something for me, Karen." As sick as he was he remembered to use the fake name. "Those agents are still out there. It won't take them long to catch up with us." He paused. "I need your help. I spent our last twenty dollars on our subway passes. We will need money to buy our airline tickets and you are the only one who can get it."

Charlie looked at him questioningly. She knew what he had in mind but refused to believe it despite all that she had seen that horrible night. "How could I get money?"

"You know." His voice was steady.

Charlie shook her head. "No. I can't. It's bad. That's stealing. It's not right to steal." She was already frightened and upset by what her father had done to the limousine driver Now he was asking *her* to go against what she knew was right and wrong.

"I know." He replied. "But there's no other way. Those agents are still searching for us. Our only hope is if we can get far enough away that they will not be able to find us."

"Do I have to Daddy?" She was close to tears. The thought of stealing was bad enough but what was worse was that it was *Daddy* who was telling her to do it.

"Karen, it is our only option. We don't have any more money and we don't have anything left to sell. We can't stay here; those men will find us."

Charlie shook her head, struggling to hold back the tears. "It's not right. Please don't make me. It's not right to steal!"

"I know." He repeated. "But we will need money to escape. I explained this to you, or at least I tried. Remember?"

"About doing what you have to to survive?"

He nodded. "That's right."

"But Daddy. I don't want to…"

"Karen, I cannot do anymore and we need the money." His voice was heavy with pain.

Charlie looked at him and felt terrible. He was suffering terribly, she didn't need psychic senses to tell her that. She could see it on his face.

She was terrified and that made it difficult to think clearly. Daddy would soon be too sick to stand up and they had to get away, the bad men from the government were coming. Charlie looked at her father with great compassion. "Does your head really hurt?"

"Yes." His voice was afflicted with suffering.

"Ok." She replied reluctantly. "I'll try." On impulse, she leaned forward, hugged her father tightly and kissed him on his forehead. Then she stood up and walked away.

Charlie walked quickly and with purpose. She was in one of the few places where a little girl could go alone unremarked after midnight. If she had been crying, then one of the skycaps or airport police might have approached her and asked if she knew what flight her mommy and daddy were on, but she wasn't crying, and she looked like she knew where she was going.

Charlie didn't but she definitely knew what she was looking for. As she continued down the concourse Charlie studied her surroundings. She saw dozens of people; some of them were the same people who she had noted earlier, others were people who had trickled in since then. She passed a group of teenagers in jeans with leather jackets and wild hairdos. Later she passed a fat black woman with a gaggle of kids around Charlie's age. One of them was whining that he wanted a soda. Not too far away from her was another woman dressed in a peach business suit. She was sitting by one of the front windows typing away on a laptop. Beside her, a tan-skinned man in a black business suit was talking into a cell phone in a soft voice. Charlie eyed him suspiciously for several minutes, but she had no feeling that he was one of the government men. The man was talking to his girlfriend. His voice was high pitched and carried a tone of false remorse. Charlie had a strong feeling that he was trying to trick the woman on the other end.

Probably cheated on her. I'd never let a boy do that to me.

There was something suspicious about this man, but she was sure he wasn't from the government. Charlie gave him one last distrustful glance before turning away and continuing along the concourse.

Further along, she saw a bunch of vending machines. She could get some money from there, but it wouldn't be that much. Charlie passed them by and continued walking. She passed a garbage can with a plastic Wal Mart bag sticking out of it.

Charlie took the plastic bag and continued walking.

A little further along she saw what she was looking for. Ahead and to the left was a small glass cubicle with a blue ATM sign above it. Charlie's heart quickened. She looked around quickly. The man in the Navy uniform she saw earlier was standing at the bar across from the ATM cubicle drinking a beer. To the right of the machine a slender woman in a white dress was talking on a cell phone and to her right, another man was sneaking a cigarette in a little alcove that led to the men's and ladies' rooms. Nobody was paying attention to her.

Charlie drew in a slow, steadying breath and casually walked over to the ATM cubicle. At the door, she stopped again, looked around and then nervously entered. Charlie looked up at the ATM machine inside and became afraid because her father had told her again and again that she mustn't do it.

She had the power like her father, only her power was much stronger, and she never got sick from using it but sometimes, afterward, there were fires. She couldn't always control the power and that was why she wasn't supposed to use it. Sometimes it would get away from her. Like the time she had almost burned the house down. *My mommy and daddy have to wear bandages because of me. Because I was bad.* The image of the massive fire that she had started in the living room burned in her mind. *It was all my fault.* What if something like that happened now?

The other reason she wasn't supposed to use the power was because the government men might see her.

I don't know who these people are or how much they know about you but I don't want them to find out anything more than they already know. Your power is different than mine. You don't get sick from using your power, do you?

No-oo.

And you can move things and light fires. If these men see strange things happening and connect it to you…

If they saw her now she and Daddy would be caught. They had no money and nowhere to go. And this was stealing and that was bad too.

What does it matter? They stole Mommy's life. And we need the money.

Charlie approached the ATM machine slowly and placed her hand on the little door marked 'Cash'. She glanced around once more to see if anyone was being nosy. Nobody was. Charlie turned and reached into the machine with her mind. She found the cash release catch quickly and shoved at it.

Charlie smiled as she did it. No, there was no pain involved. It felt good to use the power and that was another thing that scared her. What if she got to like this dangerous thing?

All at once the cash door opened and the machine began spitting out money. Charlie hastily positioned the bag underneath the machine but not before most of the money had fluttered to the floor. She quickly bent down and scooped up large handfuls of tens and twenties from the bottom of the cubicle.

When she had picked up all of the money Charlie opened the bag and looked inside. It was stuffed almost to the bursting point with more money than she had ever seen in her life. There must have been over a million dollars there.

Charlie did not waste time staring. She snapped the shopping bag closed, stood up and casually walked out of the ATM cubicle. The power was racing in her mind, trying to get out. It was hard for her to hold it in. Charlie hurried into the ladies' room.

There were a number of women inside and only a single open stall. An older woman was headed for it. Charlie rushed past her and slammed the door in her face.

After closing the bolt Charlie turned and pushed the power into the toilet. There was a loud hiss followed by a sharp crack as the toilet split right down the center from the heat. In an instant, the room was filled with thick steam. Several frightened cries rang out followed by a number of bewildered voices asking: "What was that?" "Is everyone okay?".

Charlie hurried out of the bathroom in a frightened daze. She knew she had gotten herself in trouble again. Any one of the women in the bathroom could have been a government agent. Even if none of them were it was certain that one of them would tell an airport cop what they had seen. Sooner or later it would get back to *them*.

Charlie hurried back to her father carrying the now heavy shopping bag from the bottom so that it would not rip. Daddy was sitting in the same chair she had left him in. He had closed his eyes and he looked almost as if he were asleep, except for the pain stamped on his face. Charlie approached him fearfully. She knew she would be in trouble.

"Daddy?" As she spoke she realized for the first time that she was crying.

He looked up at her slowly the pain in his eyes immediately replaced by concern. "Charlie, what happened?"

"I got the money like you said." As she spoke she handed the heavy grocery bag to Daddy. "But when I used the power I... I couldn't stop it." She was sobbing hard now. "I…Daddy I didn't mean to."

"Didn't mean to what Karen?"

"I couldn't stop the power, so I went into the bathroom and put it in the toilet and the toilet got too hot and it cracked and everyone in the bathroom heard it." She broke down sobbing.

Daddy took her in his arms. "It's alright Karen. Nobody was hurt. You did the right thing."

"But…they…saw…me. I…let…them…see…me…do…it. Now…those…government…men will…. know…. where…we…are." She struggled to get the words out between sobs.

Daddy stroked her hair. "You've done nothing wrong. They would have found us anyway. This just means we have to move a little faster." He took her hand. "Come on. Let's go catch a plane."

Charlie glanced up at him incredulously. "You're not mad at me?"

"No." He produced a slight smile. "This is good news. You were able to hold onto it long enough to get to the bathroom. Last year you would not have been able to do that. You could have set someone on fire. You could have really hurt someone, but you didn't."

Charlie looked away guiltily as the image of the fire in the living room returned. "Not like I did to you and Mommy in the living room."

Daddy squeezed her hand and gently turned her face towards his. "You don't have to think about that anymore Karen." He lowered his voice. "I know you didn't mean to hurt us." They had reached the ticket counter now. There was no line, so Daddy walked right up to the counter.

"Hello. I would like two tickets to London please."

The young woman behind the counter smiled. "Certainly sir. I'll need to see your ID first."

Daddy took out his wallet and produced his fake ID card.

The woman took it, swiped it through a card scanner and handed it back. "Thank you. Now I'll need you to place your thumb on the panel." She glanced at a small glass panel behind her computer monitor.

"Daddy placed his thumb on the glass pane without a word

"Thank you." The woman reached below the counter and produced a retinal scanner. "Please look into the eyepiece sir."

Daddy did as she asked. A moment later there was a low beep.

The woman smiled again. "Okay, Mr. Harrington I'm going to need to verify your daughter's identification before I can issue you your tickets."

"Of course." Daddy replied nonchalantly. He bent down, took her by the shoulders and whispered in her ear. "Act normal." Then he hoisted her up to the counter.

Charlie gave the woman her fake ID card and let her scan her thumbprint and retinas.

When she was finished the woman offered Charlie a warm smile. "Thank you. You were a very good girl."

Daddy set Charlie down a short distance away and then returned to the counter. "I would like one-way first-class tickets and I would like priority boarding because of my daughter."

The woman nodded and began to type Daddy's order into the computer. "That will be three thousand forty-three dollars and six cents."

"Do you accept cash?"

"Sure."

Daddy reached into the plastic shopping bag and counted out three thousand and fifty dollars. The woman made change and then handed Daddy two small plastic packets.

"These are your tickets. The flight will be approximately ten hours with a thirty-minute stopover in Montreal."

Daddy inclined his head. "Thank you. Which gate do we depart from?"

"Gate one twenty. Have a nice flight."

Daddy took her hand again. "Come on Karen it is time to go."

"Ok Daddy."

As she spoke Charlie suddenly became frightened again. The government men were back. She could feel them someplace in the airport, someplace very close.

When they were out of earshot from the ticket counter Charlie turned to Daddy. "Daddy, I feel those government men around again."

Daddy inclined his head again. "Then we should hurry."

Charlie didn't think they would be able to get on their plane now, but she said nothing.

As Charlie approached the security gate with her father they stopped short. The gate looked normal but they both knew better. Two men in black business suits were standing at the window to the right of the security gate pretending not to watch the people passing through the gate.

A man in a Navy uniform was standing on the other side of the gate talking to a young woman in a matching black blazer and suit. They were both government agents.

Without warning, Daddy turned and ran for the door dragging her helplessly behind. Charlie struggled to keep up as her father sprinted across the concourse.

Fear pulsed in her blood. The government agents weren't following but she felt they would soon. It seemed like an eternity before they finally reached the exit. The automatic door opened in slow motion. Charlie and her father bolted through without waiting for it to open fully.

Charlie's fear was mounting.

They're going to catch us. They're going to catch us this time.

The words repeated over and over in her mind. The government agents were close behind them. It was only a matter of time before they would be caught.

Outside the curb was lined with cars. Taxis, limos, and private cars of all sizes jostled for space. A white Chevy Tahoe with black tinted windows was parked several feet down from where they came out between a taxi and a blue car. The Tahoe's passenger side window was rolled part of the way down. Without a word, Daddy pulled her in that direction.

Charlie knew, perhaps even before her father did what he had in mind.

"Daddy what are you…"

"Shh." He offered her a half smile that was meant to be reassuring. "It's ok Karen. Everything's going to be fine."

They reached the car. Daddy reached through the window and opened the front passenger side door. As he did Daddy gave her a passing glance. "Don't say anything. Let me do the talking."

"Ok, Daddy." She was very frightened.

Daddy got in the car and she slid in beside him. A tall, muscular man sat behind the wheel. Daddy drew his gun from under his coat.

"Go."

The man nodded and pulled out onto the road.

"Now, I am going to give you a destination and you are going to take my daughter and I there without a word. I have no desire to harm you, but I will kill you if I have to."

The man nodded again without a word.

Charlie watched the exchange fearfully still not believing what her father was doing. *How can he be like this?*

Daddy must have sensed her upset for he placed a hand on her back and began to gently massage her muscles. "Everything's fine Karen. Don't be afraid. We are safe now." Warmth trickled through her flesh where her father touched her, but her blood and heart remained as ice. She knew he was lying through his teeth. In truth, he was as tense as she was frightened.

Charlie looked at her father and was terrified. His face was white as a sheet and he was sweating heavily. There were tinges of blue around his mouth and his eyes were bloodshot. The hand that was stroking her back was trembling. He would not be able to travel much further. She was tired and didn't think she could go much further either. They had to find someplace to hide.

The government men are still out there.

They had to get away first. She glanced at the man behind the wheel. His face *looked* kindly, but she knew better. He was very dangerous. He was afraid but for him fear provoked action. He would take advantage of any opportunity he was given.

He's a policeman! She felt this with absolute certainty.

The policeman was already talking to Daddy in a friendly tone trying to gain his confidence. "Your little girl is very beautiful. What's her name?"

"Never mind her. Keep your eyes on the road."

The policeman smiled at her kindly. "Hi, honey. What's your name?"

Daddy jammed the gun into his ribs. "Do not talk to her."

"Ok." The policeman's voice was steady. "Listen you don't want to do this. I'm a cop. Whatever trouble you're in we can work it out."

"No, we cannot." Daddy replied flatly. "I have no wish to do this to you, but I have no choice. I have to protect my daughter."

"You're doing a great job of that. You're taking good care of your daughter but you're not helping her but putting her in danger." The policeman looked into Daddy's eyes. "Please give me the gun. Nobody will hurt your little girl. I give you my word."

"Sorry…" Daddy withdrew the gun from the policeman's ribs. "You cannot protect us from them. This is the only way."

Charlie's fear grew stronger for this was not like her father. He was usually very controlled, always taking care not to reveal information about them. Even when he was sick he had never before told anything.

"Who's after you?"

Daddy was silent.

"I promise whoever's after you won't hurt your little girl or you. They won't get near you. Just tell me what's going on."

"Never mind." Daddy answered. "Just keep driving."

"All right sir." The policeman's voice still held that friendly quality. "But I want you to know I'm on your side. Whatever situation you're in. I can help you if you let me."

Daddy stared at him with what would have been a threatening glare were it not for his tired, bloodshot eyes.

After that the policeman was silent.

VII

That night was an agony of fear and suspicion. Charlie was exhausted, but she would not allow herself to sleep. She had to stay awake because she did not believe her father was capable of handling the policeman alone. She was terrified of what might happen if she were to fall asleep. Charlie remembered little of the actual car ride all she remembered was the fear; icy and heart chilling.

I have to stay awake. Have to stay awake or we'll be caught. She repeated the words over and over to herself.

In the end, her efforts were in vain. As the sky was changing from black to purple she felt herself drifting off. She struggled against it but her body was too exhausted. Darkness swallowed her, carrying her away to a place where even fear could not touch her.

VIII

Charlie awoke suddenly soaked in sweat and sobbing miserably. Everything had seemed so real, the feelings, the images. It was as if she had stepped back in time to that night, to when her father was still alive. And now it was gone. Her father was gone, dead, and she was alone again. Charlie cried for several minutes before sitting up and sliding to the edge of the bed. She wasn't thirsty but maybe a glass of water would help her feel better. Suddenly her muscles drew tight and she collapsed to the floor. The attack was so sudden and severe that she didn't even have a chance to scream.

White-hot pain ripped through her body in waves. Her muscles drew very tight, to the point where she felt certain she would tear in half. The muscle spasms grew in intensity with each passing moment. Charlie wanted to scream but she could not. Her vocal cords were paralyzed. The pain continued to grow, burning through her like molten metal, searing her to the core.

Please...make it stop...it huuurts... She wanted to scream the words but her paralyzed throat muscles would not allow her. *Please no more!!*

Her muscles drew tighter still causing her to arch off the ground. The pain was excruciating, almost insupportable. She was going to pull apart. There was no question.

A moment later her muscles relaxed for a second. Then they drew tighter still once more plunging Charlie into excruciating pain. She imagined she knew how it must feel to be put in the electric chair. She felt as if she were being electrocuted or burned alive. Her flesh felt as if it were being seared off. She began to honestly believe she was on fire. The pain was almost beyond feeling.

Her senses grew dull, blunted beneath a growing red haze of suffering. She was one with the pain and it was all that mattered. Though she remained conscious throughout the attack her awareness of her surroundings faded until it became almost peripheral. Charlie was vaguely aware of David screaming to Catherine to get help and sometime later remembered being lifted onto a stretcher and pushed into an ambulance. Later she was strapped to a bed in a white tiled room, surrounded by white masked faces.

The air in this room was hot and close and stunk of smoke. Flames were shooting from a trashcan in one corner. The white masked faces ran around frantically as the air filled with their frightened shouts. One of them grabbed a fire extinguisher from the wall and sprayed it at the blazing trashcan. Everything after that was a red blur of searing pain.

IX

When the attack finally passed Charlie found herself lying in a hospital bed surrounded by machines.

There was a needle in the back of her hand and a tube in her nose. She was naked except for a flimsy hospital gown and the blanket that covered her. Little suction cups had been pasted to her chest; these were connected by thin wires to a machine to the left of the bed.

David and Catherine stood over her with worried expressions.

"Charlie? Can you hear me, Charlie?" David's voice was very concerned.

"David?" Her voice was little more than a whisper.

Charlie felt like crying. She was embarrassed to have them see her like this.

"Thank God." Catherine too was close to tears. Her eyes glistened in the room's low light.

David and Catherine both took her into their arms.

Charlie hugged them tightly. "It's ok. I'm fine now."

It was a poor lie. She didn't feel fine. She was exhausted. Her body felt heavy as if it were made of lead, and she was still in pain. She did not have much time left.

Charlie glanced out the window and saw that it was dark out. "I must have been asleep for hours."

"Actually, it's Sunday. You were unconscious for almost three days." David forced a smile. "But don't worry. You're going to be fine now."

Charlie felt like crying again. He was trying so hard not to upset her, but she already knew the truth. She was dying. She would probably be dead in a few days. "I know." She replied softly. Just then another question occurred to her. "Where are we?"

"You're in the hospital." David's voice was troubled.

Cold fear raced through her blood. "We have to get away! We'll get caught!"

David took her hand. "Shhh. It's okay we're all right for now."

"But…"

"Shhh." David stroked her hand. "Relax. Sleep. You'll feel better."

Charlie glanced at Catherine. She looked frightened but nodded her agreement with David. "Everything's going to be all right Charlie." Her voice held no conviction.

Charlie was not comforted but she kept her feelings to herself.

This is all my fault. The NSA is going to catch us here and kill us all.

Guilt welled up in her heart. Again, she felt like crying but she continued to hold back the tears.

Not in front of David and Catherine.

X

After a time, Charlie fell asleep. She was awakened by the doctor.

"Hi, Sue Ann. I'm Dr. Hale. Your Mommy and Daddy told me that you were feeling better. I'm glad to hear that."

Charlie offered him a slight smile. "Hi."

Dr. Hale offered her a friendly smile. "I'd like to examine you. It won't take long and then you can go back to sleep. Is that ok Sue Ann?"

She nodded shyly. Charlie didn't sense any menace in this man, but she was still distrustful.

Dr. Hale's smile widened. "Thank you, Sue Ann."

The examination only took ten minutes. Afterward Dr. Hale spoke to her briefly.

"How do you feel Sue Ann?"

"I'm tired," Charlie replied. "And my body hurts."

"Where does it hurt?" Dr. Hale asked.

"Everywhere."

He glanced down and wrote something on his clipboard. "Is it a sharp pain or a dull ache?"

"It burns," Charlie replied. "And it's sharp. Like somebody's stabbing me."

He nodded and wrote on his clipboard. "Other than the pain do you feel all right? Do you feel sick to your stomach or anything?"

Charlie shook her head. "No."

"Okay." He scribbled some final notes on his clipboard and then offered her a friendly smile. "You had yourself quite an episode there Sue Ann. You were unconscious for a long time."

"No, I wasn't," Charlie replied steadily. "I had a seizure, then I fainted."

Dr. Hale's smile disappeared momentarily. "Who told you that?"

"I remember," Charlie answered softly.

Dr. Hale's smile was gone now. "That's not possible." A moment later his smile returned. "You must have been dreaming."

Charlie knew that her memories were genuine and not dreams and she sensed that Dr. Hale knew this as well.

"Don't worry Sue Ann. You're going to be fine now. You'll be out of here in a couple of days." Dr. Hale's voice was much more confident than he was.

He left with a smile on his face. Charlie strongly felt his fear. It added to her own, bringing tears to her eyes. Charlie blinked them back fiercely.

David and Catherine were asleep on cots next to her bed. She did not want to disturb them. So, she simply laid awake shivering and fighting back the tears. Sometime shortly before dawn Charlie fell asleep. She slept for eleven hours before finally awakening.

XI

Over the next week, Charlie's condition deteriorated rapidly. By the next Thursday, she was no longer able to stand up. By Friday she had no control over her bowels or bladder.

Friday night she had her most severe attack yet and went into a coma for several hours. When she regained consciousness, Charlie was too weak to lift her head.

She cried for several hours that night before she was able to regain control of herself. It wasn't fair. She had been able to walk when she came into the hospital. Now she couldn't even lift her arms. The pain had quadrupled over the week and so had the severity of her seizures.

"I'm going to die." She sobbed miserably. "I'm going to die."

David held her tightly in his arms as he stroked her sweat soaked hair and tried to comfort her. "You're not going to die, Charlie. You're going to be fine. You'll feel better soon."

Charlie knew he was lying and that made her cry even harder. David tried so hard. He was always so kind to her. She didn't deserve such kindness.

Not long after she finally stopped crying Charlie fell asleep still cradled in David's arms.

XII

When she awoke the next morning, he was still holding her. His eyes were closed, and his breathing was even.

He must have gone to sleep holding me.

She was so touched that she nearly burst into tears. She wasn't his child. They weren't even related. He had found her hiding under a bush and taken her into his home. He had cared for her and loved her as if she were his daughter. He and Catherine both had given up everything for her. It hurt her to think of how much they had sacrificed.

Big round tears welled up in her eyes and trickled down her cheeks. She cried not for herself but for David and Catherine.

In that moment she wished she had been killed with her father. Everyone would have been happier that way.

Not long after Charlie had awakened, David stirred and opened his eyes. Charlie gulped back her tears, not wanting to upset him.

"Good morning Charlie." David's voice was still thick with sleep.

"Good morning David."

"How do you feel?"

"Tired." She replied in as upbeat a tone as she could muster.

David smiled gently. "How about some breakfast?"

"Oh no, I'll get sick." Charlie had been unable to keep solid foods down since last Tuesday.

"You should try to eat something. How are you going to get better if you don't eat?"

"But I'll just throw it up," Charlie replied miserably.

"Maybe you won't this time." Despite the confidence in his voice Charlie knew David didn't believe his own words. "Besides you don't want another shot, do you?"

She shook her head weakly. Suddenly the room had become cold. Her skin turned to gooseflesh and she began to tremble.

Since Wednesday all of her meals had been injected into the large vein in her neck. The procedure was very painful, and it took several hours. As she thought about it she suddenly became aware of the large catheter jutting out of her jugular vein. It burned and throbbed agonizingly. Fresh tears spilled down her cheeks.

"Please don't let them do that again! Please, David, it hurts!"

He stroked her cheek. "I know Charlie. I know but if you don't eat they're going to have to. You can't go without food."

As he spoke Catherine stirred in her chair and awakened. "What time is it?"

David glanced up at the clock on the wall. "Ten thirty."

She groaned. "I need some coffee." She stood up laboriously and walked up to the bed. "Hi, Charlie. How are you feeling?"

"Tired," Charlie repeated morosely.

Catherine stroked her cheek. "It'll be all right. I'll be back in a few minutes. I'm going to get some coffee. Would you like a glass of orange juice or a soda or something?"

"No that's okay." In truth, she would have loved a glass of juice, or milk or even water. Her throat was parched. However, she knew she would just throw up whatever she drank. Fresh tears spilled down her cheeks.

"You can have something if you want. Anything at all." Catherine's voice was so gentle it hurt.

"No, I can't." She had meant to add something about not being able to eat or drink without vomiting but before she could Charlie dissolved into tears. She wept bitterly, mourning the total unfairness of it all.

Mommy and Daddy are dead, David and Catherine are in trouble because of me and I'm going to die.

Suddenly her body went rigid as every muscle drew taut at once. A strangled cry escaped her throat before her voice box was paralyzed.

No please not again! Her mind screamed the words her mouth could not speak. *PLEASE!! I can't take any more pain!*

In response her muscles drew tighter, twisting and contorting against themselves. White flames swept her body. A scream was building within. She wanted so badly to scream, to beg for help.

Let me die. She thought desperately. *Please let me die. Anything to make it stop.*

There was no answer and the pain continued to grow. Every inch of her body blazed hotly. For a moment she wondered if she had not lost control of the power again and set herself on fire. But she saw no flames.

Suddenly her back jerked into painful spasm catapulting her off the bed. She landed on her side drawn into a fetal position by her own convulsed muscles. She was unable to control any part of her body. To her immense embarrassment, Charlie soiled and wet the bed. A moment later another back spasm rolled her over into her own urine and feces.

Stop...Please...Stop...Please

Charlie's mind fragmented from the pain, making clear though difficult. Even her vision and hearing were obscured.

Catherine was screaming for a doctor while David tried to hold Charlie steady. His efforts were a waste as Charlie threw him off within minutes while in the grip of another powerful muscle spasm.

The muscles in her chest were tightening as were the muscles in her throat. Breathing became increasingly difficult. Charlie choked and sputtered, struggling to get breath into her screaming lungs. Terror swept through her.

No! Please, I don't want to die! Please, I'm just a kid! I'm only nine!

There was no answer.

Her chest and throat continued to constrict. She began to wheeze. Her lungs felt as if they would burst. The pain was almost beyond feeling…*almost.*

Tears streamed down her cheeks as she fought desperately to breathe. Suddenly the pain didn't matter anymore. All that mattered was getting air into her lungs. She struggled valiantly to breathe but her strength was waning. Black spots began to fill her field of vision. Then all at once, her chest and throat muscles went slack.

Charlie drew in a deep shaky breath and let it whistle out between her teeth.

A dozen frightened faces floated above hers. Charlie recognized David, Catherine, and Dr. Hale but the others were strangers. Dr. Hale spoke first.

"Charlie? Can you hear me?" He had used her real name but that didn't matter anymore.

"Yes." Her voice was a hoarse whisper.

"Are you, all right?" David's voice was frightened.

"Do you feel any pain?" Dr. Hale's voice was steady despite the fear she sensed in him.

"Yes."

"Where?"

"Everywhere." She replied with a sob.

"Shh." David soothed. "Don't cry Charlie everything's going to be all right."

Charlie bit back her tears.

"Just relax and the pain will pass."

Charlie closed her eyes and tried to bring her emotions under control. It took several minutes but she was eventually able to calm down.

She would die soon. Since awakening that morning, deep inside, she had known that she would die today but she had not been able to consciously accept it until now.

The realization struck her like lightning from above. She was going to die today. Probably within the next few hours. Her body was too ravaged to survive another seizure. The next attack would certainly kill her. Now was the time to say her good-byes.

Charlie looked up at David and Catherine with tear stained eyes. "I'm so sorry I put you through all of this."

"It's not your fault Charlie." David's voice was husky. "You didn't do anything wrong. None of this is your fault." He hugged her tightly to his chest. "You've been an angel through all of this." He was crying though he was doing his best to hide it. Charlie felt bad for him.

"Everything's going to be all right now Charlie. You'll never be in pain again. You'll be with your father and mother in heaven." David was smiling through his tears. "It's ok to let go, Charlie. When the time comes don't fight it just let go. You don't have to go through any more suffering for us."

Catherine nodded. She was crying too hard to speak but Charlie sensed that her feelings were the same as David's.

"We love you, Charlie. We'll always love you."

Charlie hugged David as tightly as she could despite the pain it caused her. "I love you too. Thank you for taking care of me."

As she spoke those last words Charlie felt her muscles draw tight. Within seconds her body was again alight with pain. White flames swept her head to toe penetrating her to the core. Again, her chest and throat contracted this time closing her airway entirely.

David's words echoed in her mind. *Let go, Charlie. You don't have to fight anymore. Just let go.*

She couldn't though. Her heart insisted that she fight for survival. Her lungs had swollen to the bursting point. Dr. Hale was standing over her shouting.

"Breath Charlie! Damnit, Charlie, you have to breathe!"

I can't. My throat's closed, my chest is crushed.

"Charlie listen to me. You have to breathe or I'm going to have to cut your throat open and it'll hurt."

No please don't do that. Please don't do that.

Charlie redoubled her efforts to breathe but her struggle was in vain. All she succeeded in doing was aggravating the muscle spasms in her chest and throat.

Dr. Hale turned to one of the nurses. "Get me a trache tube stat."

Icy cold liquid was smeared on her neck. Dr. Hale turned and picked up a small silver knife from a nearby cart. Without pausing he bent down over her and drew the knife down the length of her larynx splitting it open almost to her collarbone. White fire exploded from the wound as blood rushed out and ran down her bare chest.

A nurse handed Dr. Hale a small plastic tube and a roll of white tape. Dr. Hale thrust the tube into the slit in her throat and taped it in place. Fresh pain ripped through her body, but no air entered her lungs.

Her senses were growing fuzzy. Her ears began to ring. Black butterflies danced in front of her eyes. Only the pain remained strong.

Her body was growing heavy and limp. Charlie was terrified. She wanted to scream but her throat was paralyzed.

Please help me. Please, I don't want to die.

There was no answer and she remained unable to breathe. Her lungs cried out for air. A moment later she felt her heart stop.

Blind terror raced through her bringing with it mind-numbing panic.

NO! PLEASE, I'M JUST A KID!

"She's coding. Give me fifty ccs of epinephrine stat." Dr. Hale's voice was faint, but his fear was palpable.

One of the nurses handed him a large syringe. Dr. Hale thrust the needle down driving it deep into her chest. Fresh pain radiated out from the place where the needle penetrated her body.

The clear liquid intensified her fear, but her heart remained still. Charlie's mind was nearly gone. She was beyond panic, beyond reasoning, only base survival instinct remained.

The power suddenly jumped out of her sending flames dancing up the privacy curtains. The air reeked of sweat, smoke and human waste; the stench was heavy and choking.

"It's no good. Get the paddles. Charge them to three hundred joules." Dr. Hale's voice was distant as if he were standing at the opposite end of a long hallway.

A male nurse moved quickly to comply. There was a high-pitched whine as a machine came to life. A moment later Dr. Hale took the paddles from him. The nurse quickly squirted a thin blue gel on both paddles and Dr. Hale rubbed them together. Then he applied both paddles to her chest.

"CLEAR!"

White fire ripped through her chest as her body arched off the bed.

A second nurse touched the side of her neck. "No pulse."

"Charging."

The machine whined to life. Dr. Hale rubbed the paddles together and reapplied them to her chest.

"CLEAR!"

Again, white fire swept her as her body jerked upward. The second nurse moved in again. Her touch was like ice on Charlie's hot skin. "Still nothing."

"Charge it to three fifty." Dr. Hale barked.

The male nurse pushed a button on the white box that was attached to the paddles. "Charging." The whine was louder and sharper this time.

Dr. Hale pressed the paddles down hard on Charlie's bare chest.

"CLEAR!"

Searing pain tore through her for the third time as her body arched off the bed yet again.

Please no more. Please don't hurt me anymore.

"Again! Five hundred!" Dr. Hale's voice had risen to an angry shout.

"Charging."

Weeeeeee

The sound was a nightmarish howl.

Dr. Hale slammed the paddles down on her chest. There was a low crack as one of her ribs broke.

"CLEAR!!"

The white fire returned. Charlie felt herself jerk upward. *Please no more. I can't take any more pain.*

"Come on Charlie stay with me!" Dr. Hale's voice was angry but tearstained. Behind him, David and Catherine looked on with tears in their eyes.

It's okay to let go Charlie.

Even now with all of this pain, she could not bring herself to give up.

"Charging." Sharp whine as the machine charged, then cold steel against her skin.

CLEAR!!

A horrifying call in a nightmare. The voice was no longer Dr. Hale's. It was the disembodied voice of some horrible monster.

White hell fire swept through her. The muscles in her body pulled tight, lifting her off the bed and cracking more bones. The pain continued even after the shock was gone.

The female nurse who was monitoring Charlie's pulse shook her head. "Her pupils are fixed and dilated. She's gone."

"Charge the damned paddles." Dr. Hale snapped. "Set them to six hundred."

The male nurse gave him a sad look. "It's over. I'm sorry."

"It's not over. We can still save her." He looked down into Charlie's eyes. "Damnit kid come on! You're too young for this shit!"

The female nurse put her hand on Dr. Hale's arm. "Let her go Jack."

He lowered his head and dropped the paddles on the bed. He made no sound, but Charlie knew he was crying. Behind him, David and Catherine stood holding each other and weeping.

The pain remained strong for several minutes longer. Then it began to gradually fade until she felt nothing. Her flesh grew cold and her muscles stiffened. Terror exploded within her for she knew what had happened.

Chapter 7
Fallen Shroud

Dead.

Gone.

She's gone Mr. McAuliffe.

I'm very sorry.

I

He walked in a daze only partially aware of his surroundings. It was still hard for him to grasp. She was dead. Nine years old and dead. It was hard to accept and made harder by the fact that it was not a natural death. How could someone bring themselves to do something so horrible? How could anyone murder a nine-year-old child? Grief pierced and twisted in his heart. Bitter anger burned in his soul.

The hospital corridor was a scene out of a nightmare, piercing bright lights, sharp pungent odor of chlorine. And the quiet. That horrible ear shattering quiet. Both eerie and maddening at once. Each of his footsteps rang like thunderclaps off the hard-tiled floor and cinder block walls. It was cooler down here than in the rest of the hospital. It wouldn't do to return bloated, half rotten bodies of loved ones.

David stared ahead bitterly. *She doesn't belong down here. She's only a little girl for God's sake.* Unshed tears burned in his eyes. David blinked them back fiercely. He would not cry anymore. He had to remain strong for Catherine's sake.

The doctor beside him walked briskly not speaking, not even making eye contact. The corridor seemed to go on forever. They passed numerous doors leading various laboratories and offices. After a while the doctor stopped in front of one and opened it with a key.

"She's in here." His voice was nonchalant, almost bored. For a moment something familiar moved within David, then it was quiet.

Behind the door David found Charlie lying naked on a bare metal table. She had not even been covered with a sheet. Even that small dignity had been denied her. Bitter anger bubbled up within his heart. The air inside the room was cool and fetid with the stench of urine and feces.

They didn't even bother to clean her up.

Despite the rancid odor David bent down and hugged Charlie to his chest.

"I'm so sorry Charlie." He whispered. "You deserved better than this."

"Sir…Mr. McAuliffe, you can't touch the body. It's not safe."

David glared at the doctor. "Get out. Leave me alone."

"I'm sorry I can't…"

"I said get out." David growled.

The doctor nodded, then turned and left. David ignored him.

"I'm so sorry." Little more than a tearful whisper this time. David stroked Charlie's forehead. "Nobody will ever hurt you again now."

She looked so small and fragile. Her flesh was cold and clammy to touch. Her skin was pale bone china. Her expression was doll like, a slight smile suggestive of peaceful slumber instead of cold death. It was a sad, pathetic sight. She was only a child.

David's heart burned. He began to tremble. Tears of rage spilled down his cheeks. The power was spiraling within him, raging with his emotions. He squeezed Charlie tighter against his chest as he fought for control. The power continued to grow, gaining strength with each passing moment. David pushed it aside angrily.

Fuck Off!

The last thing he needed to do was cause any further trouble for Catherine and himself. The power seemed to lose some of its intensity, but it remained active, spinning within his mind.

"I'm so sorry."

It was all he could say, all he could think. She had done nothing to deserve this. Nothing. David stared at her small fragile body and felt only rage and hatred for the ones who had done this.

He would have to leave soon. Charlie was to be autopsied in another five minutes. Standard procedure when someone dies under such mysterious circumstances.

He began to tremble anew. In his mind he saw her, chest flayed open in a giant Y, organs lying out on display. He felt himself flush, as his heart raced with fury. Charlie had already been dehumanized, stripped of her dignity as well as her life. She did not deserve to be made a side of beef to be butchered and manhandled.

David clutched Charlie's small body to his chest for a long time before gently releasing her and stepping back.

Hate and fury burned within him bringing with them a power like nothing he had ever felt before. It pulsed and raged. The room resonated with its force. David made no attempt to control it; he could not have stopped it if he wanted to.

Cold hate and righteous fury exploded within sending alternating waves of icy cold and burning heat rippling through the air. The power was coalescing around Charlie. Slowly, almost gently, she lifted into the air above the metal table. Unbridled energy was building in the air, humming softly, then growling and finally roaring. The room shook with its rage. Cracks appeared in the floor and ceiling. David watched them grow, his heart thundering with calm fury, the blood in his veins turned to ice water. He would not try to restrain it this time. He would allow it to run its course. The cracks blossomed into fissures as the roar grew still louder. The power intensified still further as the fissures joined to form two massive chasms. Between these floated Charlie, still undisturbed by the chaos surrounding her. Even her hair remained exactly as it had been when she laid on the table.

This was not his doing. Before him was a scene unlike any he had seen before. Above Charlie, the ceiling opened into heaven itself. Angels beyond counting looked down on her, their faces showing unmistakable sadness and pity. Among them men and women in white looked on with sorrowful eyes. A bright light shone around them. Just to look at it was to feel joy and contentment beyond description. For that moment David's hate and fury were gone. Then he looked away and a Red Sea of emotion flooded his heart.

The fissure below her opened into a vision from *Dante's Inferno.* Screams echoed from the abyss as millions upon millions of men and women were tortured and mutilated over and over. Devils and demons of all sorts lined up to stare with cruel smiles at the small child floating above them. Fire and magma intermingled with rivers of blood. Booming, malevolent laughter rang in the air mixing with the shrieks of the damned.

David felt his hate and rage grow, stoked by the dark energies flowing from the pit. It hurt to look down, but he could not turn away. The dark power drew him; eroding what little self-restraint he had left.

With a great effort David was able to tear his gaze away. In the same instant he felt the power intensify exponentially. White lightning streaked down from above as its blood red twin leapt up from the abyss. The two struck Charlie at once surging around her, through her. Brilliant white light radiated from the center. The roar of power filled the air, adding to the haunting cacophony from the abyss. A sharp gasp rang over the din followed by a child's anguished sobs. David stared with blank eyes. Sight and sound bled together, losing form and meaning. The world went gray and then rapidly faded to black.

II

David found himself lying on the floor. He slowly sat up and blinked. The room looked the same as it had when he had come in. The great chasms had closed. The bright lights and roar of power were gone. All was silent. Except for the soft cries of a child. With his heart in his mouth David stood up.

Charlie once again lay on the metal autopsy table, but she was no longer on her back. She had drawn herself into a fetal position and was weeping, moving, breathing.

ALIVE!

She's alive!

The realization struck like lightning. David ran to the table and gathered Charlie up headless of the overpowering stench of human waste. She wrapped her arms around his neck and buried her face in his chest. She was filthy dirty. A yellow pool on the steel table indicated that she had pissed herself out of fear. It made no difference. She was alive.

"Charlie!" He was unaware until that moment that he was crying. "Oh, Charlie thank God!" He drew her tight to his chest and rocked her back and forth. "I thought I'd lost you."

She looked up eyes swimming with tears. "David." He could feel the force of her fear. Whatever she had seen, whatever lay on the other side must have been terrifying.

"It's ok Charlie." He soothed. "Everything's going to be all right now." David was so grateful that Charlie was alive that he forgot to be shocked by what he had seen.

But had he really seen it? The room looked untouched. There were no cracks in the tile floor or the concrete ceiling. Even the steel autopsy table appeared undamaged. Perhaps he had been hallucinating. Perhaps Charlie had not died but rather had gone into cardiac arrest. He looked down at her and knew that wasn't true. In his heart he felt that she was fine, her body cleansed of the poison. Still he had to ask.

"How do you feel?"

"I'm scared David. I…. I'm so scared." She began to sob anew.

David clasped her to his chest. Then something horrible occurred to him. *If the NSA finds out that she's alive then they'll…* Then they would come after her again and this time they would employ more aggressive tactics. And if they didn't already know Charlie was still alive they would soon.

David fought to keep his voice calm. "Can I put you down now Charlie?"

She looked up at him with slow reluctance. "Okay."

David gently laid her down on the table. After helping her clean up David hurried out of the room to find her something to wear. He found nothing except some doctor's scrubs and surgical slippers that would be several sizes too large for her. David picked out the smallest pair he could find and carried them back to her. Charlie studied them with care before dressing. The scrubs were way too big for her. David had to pull the drawstring out of the pants and tie it around Charlie's waist to make them stay up. The shirt came down to her knees. Under other circumstances it would have been a comical site.

III

When she was dressed David gave Charlie his coat. Then he gathered her up in his arms and hurried from the morgue. As they were approaching the elevator David spotted the doctor who had brought him in. Without pausing David ducked into an office before the doctor could spot him.

"I need you to be very quiet Charlie. That man out there is the doctor who brought me down here. We can't let him know you're alive."

"Okay." Her voice was only a frightened whisper.

What are we going to do David? He heard the words as if they were spoken aloud but Charlie had said nothing.

We're going to try to get away Charlie. He heard his mind reply. *We're going to go someplace far away where they can't find us.* Fear pulsed in his blood.

who is she what is she what who The questions spun madly deep within his mind below that which made conscious and reasoned thought. There was more to this, much more than was readily apparent. More, he thought, than even Charlie knew.

special...she's very special...very special...why?

Charlie must have sensed his fear for she tensed and withdrew from him. He believed he sensed guilt and fear in her, but he could not be sure. Her mind was closed to him now.

Sorry.

She's only a little girl. She's probably more confused and frightened then you are.

Still he could not shake his fear. *Who is she? What did I see in there? Was she really dead?* The questions spun round and round.

The doctor passed by outside. His footsteps rang on the hard-tiled floor before fading to whispers. When he could no longer hear the doctor, David pulled open the office door and hurried towards the elevator.

"Come on Charlie. Let's get out of here before anyone else shows up."

"David where's Catherine?"

"She's upstairs we'll meet up with her in a little while." He hadn't thought that far ahead yet. He had not thought beyond getting out of the morgue. He would have to find a way to sneak Charlie out of the hospital and contact Catherine without attracting attention. She was still upstairs in the waiting room with one of the nurses. She had no idea what had happened though she must have felt the tremors and would certainly have sensed the buildup of power.

But what was it? Was it real or just a dream? He didn't want to use the word hallucination because that would mean he was losing his mind. If that were true, then he might not have seen anything at all. Charlie might never have died, or even been poisoned.

Or she might never have been revived. I might be holding a corpse in my arms and just be imagining that she's alive or she might not be here at all. He quickly pushed the thought aside. He couldn't afford to travel this road. The elevator door slammed shut like a vault and the car lurched upward.

He glanced down into Charlie's eyes. *How much does she remember?*

He could not worry about that now. He had to think about how to safely get her out of the hospital. He could worry about what she remembered later.

The elevator stopped on the ground floor and the doors opened onto a blank white hallway. David scanned the corridor and, seeing no one, stepped out. A sign on the opposite wall indicated that if he turned left he could find cardiology, urology, radiology, ophthalmology and infectious diseases. To the right were obstetrics, gynecology, pediatrics and the west entrance. David hurried to the right.

"David I'm scared." Charlie's voice was little more than a frightened whisper.

"I know Charlie I am too." He soothed. "Don't worry we're getting out of here."

She hugged him tightly. She was trembling. David gently massaged her back as he continued down the hallway. He was moving quickly, not quite running; it was more of a fast walk, almost a jog. He passed solid wood doors with small plastic signs and others with large glass windows. At some point the hall widened into a large atrium that served as a waiting area for the ob/gyn clinic. The air was cold here. A slow shiver wormed its way up his spine. Charlie began shivering anew. He squeezed her to his chest.

"It's okay Charlie. Nobody's going to hurt you."

She did not reply.

David hurried through the waiting area, which was now dark and desolate (during the day it would have been bustling). The air was dry like a tomb and reeked of disinfectant. A cold hand gripped his heart.

His footsteps were gunshots in the deafening silence. It seemed to take forever to cross the atrium to the opposite corridor. As he left the waiting area David felt something loosen within him. Charlie must have felt similarly for she relaxed a little and loosened her grip around his neck.

He patted her back gently. *It's going to be all right now Charlie. Nobody will ever hurt you again.*

I hope…

The corridor lights seemed to be dimming again. Shadows deepened and grew. Slowly, white light turned to orange and then crimson. His heartbeat thundered in the silent air. Charlie's echoed in tandem. He could feel the steady pulse beat through her back. A sign on one wall indicated that they had entered the hospital's pediatric wing. Children's drawings adorned walls decorated with bright colored balloons and animals of all sorts. Further along he passed another darkened waiting area. This too was deserted but it held none of the cold shadows of the atrium. This was just a room. David hurried through and came to a set of glass double doors leading into the parking garage. David passed through these quickly. The air on the other side stunk of gasoline and oil. It was very cold out here. Charlie shivered in his arms. David wrapped his coat more tightly around her shoulders.

"Hang on Charlie. We'll only be out here for a few minutes."

"Okay." Her voice was listless.

He hurried through the garage and out onto Carson Avenue. Cars raced by trailing gusts of cold air. Charlie shuddered with each rush of wind. David clutched her to his chest. A cab sat beside the curb a few feet up the sidewalk. David hurried towards it.

"57th Street and step on it."

"Okay buddy." The driver spoke with a strong midwestern accent.

Charlie looked up at him with questioning eyes. "When are we going to get Catherine?"

"Shhh." He had to struggle to keep his voice calm and level. Though he did not feel it, he knew this man could still be an NSA agent. *He can't know who we really are.* He touched her hand and whispered. "We'll call her when we get there Charlie. I promise."

She nodded. Her face was very pale, and she was trembling. In her eyes he saw cold fear and…yes doubt. She did not believe him though he knew not why.

"It's alright." He was saying, more to himself than to her for she did not appear to be listening.

IV

In truth she heard every word he said as if they were not words but her own thoughts. It was not his voice she heard though. She felt herself being pulled back, back to another time, and place where she had heard words like this once before.

Charlie sit down.

Your mother…some men came to our house…they…

Catherine's dead. She's dead and it's all my fault. Tears trickled down her cheeks as she began to shed soft tears.

"It's okay." David was saying. "Everything's going to be all right."

It was a lie. She felt it in her heart. She could sense David's fear and sadness.

Catherine's dead because of me.

What made it worse was that he feared *her.* He knew as she now knew, that she was different, special somehow beyond the power.

Or maybe it is the power. Maybe that's why.

She didn't know. She wasn't even sure what had actually happened.

V

Everything was a confusing jumble of images and sounds. Her last clear memories were of Dr. Hale shocking her with the paddles. She remembered the pain and the touch of cold metal on her bare chest. The image was strong in her mind but after that everything became hazy. She had many other vivid memories, but they made no sense to her. She remembered feeling the pain fade, slowly draining from her flesh. She remembered standing over her own body, watching as her skin turned dark blue. Sometime later a white sheet was pulled over her head and her body moved to a gurney. She followed as they took her down to the hospital basement and watched as they took off her hospital gown and laid her on the metal table.

She was terrified, knowing and not knowing what was happening. Time seemed to be at a standstill and yet it moved swiftly. The air filled with a strange sound, soft and beautiful, melodious. It was like nothing she had ever heard before. Even now she could not have described it. The sound drew her, pulling at her heart. It seemed to be calling her away, urging her to come relax and rest, to forget. She resisted it with all of her will, but it was too powerful. With great reluctance she turned from her body and went in the direction of the sound. She passed through a wall unawares. Her mind was blind to all but that which drew her. It was no longer even a sound, more of a pull, something warm and gentle tugging at her heart. Her fear was gone, replaced by an overwhelming sense of peace and contentment. Still she was confused.

Is this what it's like?

Is this all it is?

She passed through another wall and found herself standing outside. Bright light shone all around her. The tug became a yearning, an insatiable thirst. The light was calling to her and she wanted more than anything to go to it. She moved forward with gradual, trembling steps. All at once the light was gone, replaced by choking darkness and cold desolation. Fear and despair swelled within her for she knew the light had rejected her.

I'm going to hell for killing all those people.

Her fear was racing now, racing in her still cold blood, racing in her silenced heart.

I'm going to hell.

She was frightened but her heart did not rebel against her fate. It was just. She had burned all of those people to death. Now she would know how they had felt as they died. She would burn for all eternity for their suffering. She began to tremble with terror. As she watched the ground split open to reveal a vision of hell. A cold hand closed around her heart and began to pull. She did not want to go but to her dismay she found herself betrayed as she moved forward towards the abyss. This was to be her fate. She was powerless to resist.

Darkness swelled within her bringing back old feelings of fear and anger. Something else began to blossom within her as well, something she had not felt before. The name for this feeling came to her like a ray of sunlight trying to poke through a thunderhead.

Hate! The word clanged in her mind. *Hate!* For the people who had killed her father and mother and chased her and terrorized her and killed her. *Hate!* She began to tremble, not with fear but rage. Strangely enough though the power remained silent. She was puzzled. In a clearer state of mind, she might have realized that this was because she was dead and with her body the power too had died.

Her puzzlement did not last long as it was quickly swept away by the growing tide of fury. Her father was dead, her mother was dead, David and Catherine were hurt, she was dead. *Hate!*

Hate! for the people who had killed her mother. *Hate!* for the people who had killed her father. *Hate!* for the people who had terrorized her. *Hate!* for the people who had chased her. *Hate!* for the people who had imprisoned her. *Hate!* for the people who had forced her to kill. *Hate!* for the people who had taken away David and Catherine's home. *Hate!* for the people who had poisoned her. *Hate!* for the people who had hurt her. *Hate!* for the people who had killed her. *Hate!* for the people who had made all of this happen. *Hate!* for the NSA. *Hate!* for Captain Taylor. *Hate!* for Robin Striker. *Hate! Hate! Hate!*

Hate! for life. *Hate!* for people. *Hate!* for herself. *Hate!*

Memories flashed before her outlined in fiery damnation. She saw her mother and her father. She saw herself when she was little. She saw herself at age eight running down the streets of New York with her father. She saw the Philadelphia Airport and the jail cell in the Ephrata Police Station. She saw the two of them driving south west. The little cabin in the woods. Snow and ice. Fire and smoke.

Her apartment at the NSA. Robin Striker. *Hate!* With each image her grief and fury burned brighter and with them the fires of her damnation.

She moved closer to the abyss. Heat baked out at her fanning the flames of her rage. She was afraid, but her fear was almost peripheral as it was sublimated by fury.

The abyss grew closer, as if it and not she had moved. She stared into it enrapt, her mind consumed with *Hate!*. Its power drew her as her power had once. The word itself, *Hate!*, held power. It spoke to darkness, and something beyond mere anger, something that she even yet did not understand. The abyss grew closer still. She tensed as terrible maddening pain swept through her. She screamed as rivers of tears streamed from her eyes. The pain grew. It was not the pain she had suffered from the poison. This pain was like nothing she had ever felt before. With it came a black despair that swept her through and through. Emotion and pain grew and grew building to a crescendo as she moved ever closer to the abyss.

All at once something powerful took hold of her and yanked her away. She was rapidly sucked back, as though caught in a tornado. The feeling was strange. She imagined she knew now how a piece of dirt felt as it was sucked up in a vacuum cleaner. Fear pulsed within her but also relief to be saved from the fiery abyss.

What's happening? Where am I going? The only coherent thoughts in her mind as fear had so completely swept it clean of all others.

The pain was still growing but it was also changing, changing back to that which she had felt before she died. Everything bled together. For a brief moment she saw the metal table and her own dead body. Then everything turned to a white-red blur. When her vision cleared she found herself floating between heaven and hell surrounded and penetrated by white and blood red lightning. She gasped and began cry.

Fear prevented her from realizing the significance of this. She knew only terror. All else was forgotten. Perhaps not all for deep within, beyond the awareness of consciousness but not beyond memory's knowing burned *Hate!*. A blood red stain that would never fully leave her.

As she sat beside David in the cab, Charlie looked down at herself and felt that stain still burning upon her heart.

The pain and the fear grew within her as she levitated between heaven and hell.

She could feel the energy now. Its force was overwhelming, beyond even that of her own power. Its power intoxicated her.

A bright light radiated out from her body. Its intensity should have been painful, but she felt none. It brought pleasure even as she continued to suffer. She was momentarily confused before it was swept away by fear.

Her vision was gone now. Everything had become a solid white field. Instinctively Charlie pulled herself inward. She remained this way even after her vision cleared and she found herself lying on the metal table.

VI

The taxi slowed and pulled over.

"57th Street."

David took out his wallet and gave the man a handful of bills. "Here. Keep the change."

"Sure."

They got out. The street was dark and dingy. The day people were gone, replaced by hookers in suggestive clothing and cheap makeup, flamboyantly dressed pimps and vague outlines of the homeless huddling in the shadows. The buildings along the street were typical of what she had seen of most major cities; rundown stores with cramped and dirty apartments above, brick and steel outsides covered in graffiti.

The air had grown colder, and the wind had picked up. Big white snowflakes fluttered in the dim light suggesting the beginnings of a storm. David took her hand and led her down the street towards a dingy little diner set in a recess between two larger three-story brick buildings.

As she walked through the door Charlie was thrust backward to a time when she was younger and ever so much more innocent. The diner in Pittsburgh, her father, the two of them running from the government men, men of whom they had no knowledge, men who were after her for what she could do.

She saw the two men; the one who wasn't a dogcatcher, the other not a Navy SEAL and the woman in her jeans and white t-shirt. Fear, also remembered from that time, came flooding back upon her. She was no longer nine but six and she knew not who these men were. It was not until much later that she would learn that they were from the NSA. Right then she knew only that they were from the government.

The power stirred within her, awakened by this echo of remembered fear.

Stop!!

The man who was not a Navy SEAL's voice: *Hello Jack. Hello Charlie.* A frighteningly realistic echo as if just spoken rather than heard in memory.

no ..No NO **NO!** *I can't remember! I can't remember! I can't!* The words repeated again and again in her head.

Charlie. Are you okay? David's voice brought her back to the present, melting away memory as fog melts away with the sun.

"Yes." Her tone was emotionless. Fear still pulsed in her heart.

A waitress approached them. "Smokin' or non?"

"Nonsmoking please." David glanced back at her his eyes repeating the same question *Are you ok?*

The waitress took them over to a booth in the corner and laid two menus in front of them. "Can I get you's somethin' ta drink?"

David glanced at the back of his menu. "Bring me a Sam Adams lager."

Charlie looked up at the woman. "Can I have a Pepsi?"

The waitress nodded and scribbled their orders on a pad before turning and heading back to the counter.

When she was out of sight David leaned in close and whispered. "I'm going to go buy a burner phone. You wait here. If anyone asks I went to the men's room. Understand?"

"Yes."

"Good girl." David stood up and crossed the diner with a casual stride on his way to a little alcove marked exit. Charlie watched him go with trepidation.

What are we going to do now?

She knew that they couldn't stay in Chicago any longer. If the NSA didn't already know she was alive they would soon and then they would come after them full force. They had at best mere hours. The waitress returned with their drinks.

"Where's ya Daddy?"

"He went to the bathroom." Charlie replied in a nonchalant tone.

"Okay." She set the drinks down on the table. "Here ya go. Tell ya Daddy I be back in a few to take ya order."

"Ok." She looked up into the woman's dark face and smiled. "Thank you."

"Sure." The waitress turned and went back into the kitchen leaving Charlie alone.

What are we going to do?

She was very afraid. She felt that the NSA was already coming for her.

They'll kill David and Catherine to get to me. They'll kill David and Catherine just for knowing about me.

The thought filled her heart with cold terror and burning guilt. What had she brought upon them?

David returned. "We'll meet Catherine in an hour."

Charlie nodded. She was relieved to hear that Catherine was okay but also still very frightened. *What are we going to do?*

"What are you going to order?" David asked changing the subject.

Charlie picked up her menu and glanced over it. "Spaghetti and meatballs."

She didn't care. Food was the furthest thing from her mind. Charlie sipped her Pepsi. It was flat and tasted more like water than soda. Without realizing it she made a face.

David laughed. "That bad?"

Charlie giggled. "It's all flat and it tastes like water."

He smiled. "When the waitress comes back we'll get you something else."

"Okay." She became serious. "What are we going to do now?"

"We don't have to worry about that right now." David's tone was unconcerned, but Charlie saw through the illusion to the fear beneath. "Just relax, let's enjoy our meal."

"Okay."

The waitress returned. "What can I get fer ya's?"

David looked at Charlie.

She gazed up at the waitress. "Can I have spaghetti and meatballs?"

"Okay." The waitress scribbled something onto her pad and then looked down at David. "What about you's?"

"I'll just have a plate of fries."

The waitress scribbled that onto the pad as well and then turned and left.

David and Charlie sat in silence until the waitress returned with their food. Neither of them felt particularly hungry. Charlie spent more time poking at her food than eating it. David ate a handful of fries then pushed the plate aside.

Thousands of questions, answers, things to say spun within Charlie's mind but she spoke none of them. Fear and confusion sealed her lips.

Charlie gazed blankly at her plate of now cold spaghetti and carefully picked at it with her fork. She usually loved spaghetti but now it looked less appetizing than vomit. She took a sip from her soda. The flat, watery liquid rolled over her tongue and down her throat without leaving much more than a faint flavor of cola. Its cold was soothing but otherwise it brought her no pleasure.

What are we going to do now?

Where are we going to go?

She was very afraid.

VII

The waitress came and took their mostly uneaten food back to the kitchen. She didn't bother to ask them if they wanted desert instead simply bringing the check. David paid for their food then took Charlie outside and hailed another cab.

This one took them to The Rusty Nail on Tremont Avenue.

The bartender eyed them with suspicion as they entered. Catherine sat alone at a table in the corner sipping a glass of beer.

When she saw Charlie, her eyes lit up. "Charlie!" She ran to Charlie and scooped her up into her arms. "I'm so glad to see you."

Charlie hugged her tightly around the neck. "Me too."

Catherine carried her back towards the table. David followed without a word.

When the three were seated Catherine turned to David. "What now?"

Her voice was calm, but she was very frightened, and Charlie felt that it was not just because of the danger they were in.

"We have to get as far away as we can. When the NSA figures out that Charlie's not dead they're going to come after us full force."

"Where?"

"We can go to my Dad's. He'll help us." *And he'll know how to help Charlie.*

David's thoughts rang in her mind as if spoken aloud.

"David your father lives in Scotland." Catherine replied levelly.

"I know." He said. "We'll be safe there for a while. The NSA won't be able to find us as easily if we're not in the US."

"But how are we going to get out of the country?" She persisted. "We don't have clearances to leave the US and our identities must be flagged by now."

"Don't worry about that I have an idea."

VIII

David's voice sounded a lot surer than he felt. In truth he had no plan, but he knew they could not stay here.

"Come on, let's get the hell out of here before they find us."

As he spoke David gathered Charlie into his arms and headed for the door. Her mind was still closed to him, but he sensed that she was very frightened. He didn't feel much different.

If the NSA catches us now….

He didn't want to complete that thought. He forced himself to think of escape. They had a small window of time before the NSA mobilized against them. It was best not to waste it.

David hurried out of the bar with Charlie in his arms and Catherine in tow. Once outside he hailed a cab and had the driver take them to the Chicago Seaport.

As they entered the cargo section of the Chicago Seaport David's nerves screwed tight. It was quiet here, security in freight depots was generally much lighter than what could be expected at a passenger terminal, but he still expected to encounter some TSA agents checking ID at a minimum.

Fear made it hard to think clearly. Nevertheless, it had occurred to David sometime between hailing the cab and giving the driver directions that the safest, and perhaps the *only* way for them to leave the country would be by sea. The TSA screened ticket holders on passenger liners and cruise ships as closely as airline passengers and in theory the law required the same for those who would book passage on a freighter but in practice this rule was enforced sporadically. It was a risk, but David could think of no other option. He supposed they could try to sneak across the northern border and book passage on a Canadian freighter. Canadian port security was far looser than in the United States and he doubted they would be actively looking for two young adults and their tow-headed daughter. He doubted the three of them would make it that far though. Surely the US Border Patrol had been notified of their identities by now.

David paid cash for passage for two adults and a child aboard a German container ship named the *Bismarck* that was scheduled to leave for Glasgow within the hour. To all outward appearances Port security was nonexistent. David, Catherine and Charlie boarded the *Bismarck* without so much as passing through a metal detector. David was not fooled. There were eyes everywhere, watching and waiting. He sensed danger all around them. Charlie must have felt it too for though she said nothing her blue eyes were wide and glistened with frightened tears.

David's heart went out to her and again he found himself feeling immensely guilty. Not for any wrong he had personally inflicted upon her, just guilty.

I'm so sorry Charlie. I'm so sorry. It just goes on and on and there is no escape.

David took her into his arms. "It's all right now Charlie. Everything's going to be fine. We're going to go to our cabin, the ship will get underway soon and everything will be fine."

It was a lie. The oldest lie told by parents to children since the dawn of time. Told not out of malice but because there is nothing else to say. That little droplet of opiate fed to young trusting minds to quell the dark shapeless fears of childhood. Sweet poison passed on to each generation of innocents too naïve and trusting to suspect the sugar cube which they swallow is laced to distort and blind. David remembered hearing these very words when he was a child and now he was repeating the lie to Charlie so that she could go on and pass the same lie to her child continuing the cycle of deception. He hated himself for saying what he knew to be false, but he had nothing else to say.

How do I tell her that we'll probably get caught and killed before we leave the port?

"Everything will be all right now."

He heard himself speak the words, but it was not him. It was not his voice. He would not lie to Charlie like this. He loved her too much to deceive her in this way.

It made no difference. She knew the truth, probably better than he did and would not be placated by his lies. David hugged Charlie tight to his chest for a moment and then stood up and walked across the ship's deck to where a sailor stood smoking a cigarette. As he approached the man stubbed out his smoke and looked the three of them up and down for a moment.

"So, you're the stowaways huh?" His voice was curious, not menacing. "You guys don't look like the usual types we take as passengers."

David remained silent.

He shrugged. "Whatever man. I get it. Your business is your own. We don't have guest rooms aboard this ship, so you'll have to sleep in the crew quarters. Meals are served in the dining hall at 7am, noon, 7pm and midnight. There are no private bathrooms, but I think something can be worked out for your wife and little girl." The man motioned for them to follow. "Come on let's get you settled in."

IX

Fifteen minutes later David was sitting beside Charlie on a three-tiered bunk bed listening to the low rumble of the ship's engines as it trundled out of port to the open waters of Lake Michigan. The crew quarters were cramped and musty with scents David associated with working men. The entire room was the size of a large hotel room. Bunk beds lined both sides of the narrow chamber. David, Catherine and Charlie had been assigned the bunks closest to the bathroom.

Charlie had wrinkled her nose in distaste upon seeing their accommodations but said nothing. This would be a long and uncomfortable trip, but they had escaped. They were safe for now.

The trip was indeed long and uneventful. For that short week and a half, they lived almost like a normal family. It was as if they were on vacation, save for the cramped quarters, bad food and lack of privacy. Still David had not forgotten how they had gotten here nor was it lost on him how lucky they had been. They could have easily been caught at the port, or the NSA could have sent the Coast Guard after them. Neither had occurred and yet instead of feeling fortunate David felt more afraid.

Did we really get away clean? They couldn't possibly be this incompetent. They must know where we are?

X

They arrived in Glasgow on Friday. David stood on the deck with Catherine and Charlie watching as the massive ship trundled into port. It was dark out. Silver moonlight glinted on waters smooth as glass.

Nothing out of the ordinary.

Something isn't right.

They were pulling up to the dock now. Engines powered down. Two sailors were setting up a gangway. David took Charlie's hand absently and began to lead her off the ship.

Something's not right.

The feeling grew stronger with each moment. Inside something was screaming at him, nerves screwing tight, screaming.

Something's wrong.

A light sheen of sweat coated his skin.

"Owww. You're hurting me." David loosened his grip on Charlie's hand, even yet failing to realize that he had been almost crushing it.

Something isn't right.

They had reached the gangway and were making their way down to the dock

Shit!

His heart leapt within his chest. Two British Secret Service agents armed with Glock 17 pistols awaited them at the bottom of the gangway. David started to turn and run, not yet realizing the futility of the act. One of the agents intercepted him.

"Sir, I'm going to have to ask you to come with me."

"Why what's going on?" He knew what had happened, but knowledge had not yet caught up with speech.

"Sir, I need you to come with me."

David complied, having no other options, fully expecting to be handed over to NSA agents upon leaving the port.

There were none. They were escorted to a large office building near the main entrance to the port. Once inside they were placed within a small cinderblock room, unfurnished and featureless save for the metal table and three chairs in the center and the long one-way mirror running along the left-hand wall.

The British agents told them nothing of why they were being detained or for how long. They knew only that something had happened.

XI

For Charlie life as far back as she could remember was a nightmare of frightening forces she could not control, broken by brief periods of happiness, like sunshine poking through the clouds at the eye of a hurricane. She often felt like a small boat on rough, storm tossed seas, powerless and at the mercy of fate.

Even her mind seemed outside of her control. High intelligence gave her an understanding of the world superior to that of most adults. Yet for her, intelligence was a curse. For though she understood much, her understanding was purely academic. Like one might understand the workings of a nuclear bomb through reading but could not build one if offered the necessary materials. Deep inside, beyond logic and reason, where emotion and visceral knowledge lie, she understood none of that which poured forth from her powerful intellect. At this level knowledge only brought confusion and fear. For though she was very bright she was still only a young child and nothing in her short nine years of life had prepared her for the harsh realities of the often cruel and violent adult world. For her knowledge had long since become fear.

Memory too brought much fear and confusion for there was much there as well that she did not, even yet understand. And it was not conscious memory that troubled her most. Conscious memory was merely an untrained dog, which could be tamed and made to be silent. This was the dog's, larger and more dangerous cousin the wolf. Unseen, gray and sometimes black wraith skulking just beyond sight, visible every now and again by its glowing yellow eyes. Unconscious memory, waiting unseen in the shadows, waiting for the right moment to strike. When the mind was at its weakest, besieged by fear, confusion, anger or exhaustion the wolf would pounce. This was the time.

As she sat in that tiny cinderblock room, between David and Catherine, memory began to creep upon her unsought. Memory that would not be suppressed. She had seen rooms like this many times before, but one in particular came to mind now.

Charlie drifted from sleep to wakefulness. The first thing she became aware of was that she was no longer moving. Golden sunlight shone down on her face, warming her, making her eyelids glow red.

At first, she tried to turn away from the light, to sleep a little longer but she could not. Something insisted that she must awaken. It wasn't fear or danger or even knowledge, just something.

Slowly her eyes opened. Her vision was blurry, but she was immediately aware of being in an open space, or at least a space more open than the front seat of a police car. The golden sunlight continued to shine down on her but now it was broken, slit into bars by black stripes.

What's going on? Just a question. There was no fear behind it, only curiosity.

Her vision cleared slowly, and she still could not see her surroundings. Maybe they were in a hotel room. Maybe Daddy had stopped the policeman and gotten a room. She didn't sense any danger. Everything seemed okay.

Her eyes began to come into focus. As they did terror began to take shape within her. Even before she saw she knew. This was not a hotel room but a jail cell. They had been caught.

Steel bars surrounded them on three sides. The golden sunlight streamed in from a single window secured by steel bars. She was lying on a bed in one corner; Daddy was on the bunk above.

Before conscious thought began, animal instinct reacted. In an instant she was on her feet and in another she was at the bars struggling with all her might.

The power was wild within her, but she had not yet thought to use it on the bars. Fighting it came as second nature to her. To use it was counter intuitive.

The power was raging, screaming. She fought against it, with intensity equal to that with which she fought the bars.

Hands closed on her shoulders. Charlie let out a cry and turned to release the power. It was her father.

Panicked, she jerked the power back, driving steel spikes through her skull. Tears spilled down her cheeks. She was not crying but her eyes ran just the same. The pain was intense; she would not be able hold the power back for long.

She spun around and sent the power out in the direction of the toilet in the corner. There was an immediate loud sizzle as steam poured from the bowl and tank, this was followed a moment later by a sharp crack as the toilet split completely in half.

Charlie immediately burst into tears. "I didn't mean it Daddy!"

He hugged her to his chest. "I know Charlie. I know."

She hugged him back fiercely still crying hard then suddenly stopped. Footsteps rang on the concrete floor.

"Daddy somebody's coming." Her heart pulsed with fear.

He nodded and set her down behind him.

The policeman whose car they had stolen approached the bars. "Good morning. How did you sleep?"

Neither of them said anything. Charlie's heart was racing. The power became restless.

"Would you like some breakfast? I can have Mike bring something back here for you?"

Still neither of them spoke.

Charlie stared up at the man fearfully. He was not one of the government men nor was he working for them, but he was still dangerous. The power moved again.

The man offered her a gentle smile. "It's okay sweetheart. You don't have to be afraid. You're not in trouble." He turned to Daddy. "I wanted to know why you kidnapped me before I filed any charges."

Daddy said nothing.

"If you're in some kind of trouble I can help."

Daddy still remained silent.

Charlie's fear cranked up a notch. She felt that the policeman knew nothing, but she was still very afraid. He could arrest Daddy at any time and if he did then they were finished.

The policeman's expression hardened. "Look if you don't talk to me I'm going to have to place you under arrest and take your little girl away. She is yours?"

No please... The power had awakened. She began to tremble. *Please just let us go.*

"She is my daughter." Daddy answered in a low, level voice.

"Is she with you legally?"

"Yes." Daddy replied in flat tone.

"Okay. Then let's try this again. Why did you kidnap me?"

Daddy did not reply.

"I can't help you if you don't talk to me." The policeman's voice betrayed annoyance.

Charlie's heart was racing now. Her trembling had become fierce shuddering and a light sheen of sweat coated he skin. The power was racing within her. She clamped down hard on it before it could escape.

Stop it!

Stop it now!

Daddy still did not reply.

The policeman's expression softened again. "Look I know how it is. Your wife divorces you. You're going to lose your little girl. So, you snatch her and run."

"I did not kidnap her. Her mother died." Daddy replied in a cold menacing voice. "And if you accuse me of kidnapping in front of my eight-year-old daughter again I will tear out your windpipe." He spoke with great sincerity.

Charlie was frightened still more. She knew what the policeman was accusing her father of and she knew that her father was only telling part of the truth.

The power continued to race within her.

Stop please.

Stop!

"Why did you kidnap me?" The policeman demanded. "Did you want to fuck her?!" He barked. "Is that it!? Did you snatch her, so you could fuck her!? That's it isn't it? You saw her on the playground and you wanted her. So, you grabbed her so that you could fuck her! Say it! Tell me the truth!"

"She is my daughter." Daddy's voice was an icy wind, filled with absolute hate. He was enraged and yet his tone remained calm. "I did not kidnap her, and I would never hurt her. And you will not talk like that in front of her."

The policeman's anger was an act, but Daddy's was not. It pulsed and raged in the air.

The power grew still stronger. Charlie forced it down driving white-hot spikes through her skull. It was only by a great effort that she was able to suppress a cry of pain.

"If you won't talk to me then I have no choice but to place you under arrest."

The words echoed sickeningly in her mind.

We're caught.

The power continued to spin wildly, only barely under her control. *Stop. Stop it now!* Fresh pain ripped through her skull.

The policeman turned. "Hey Mike. I need a hand in here."

A moment later a slender policeman appeared.

"Open the cell for me please."

Mike took a large key ring from his belt and unlocked the cell door. When it was opened the first policeman stepped inside, grabbed Daddy and tried to handcuff him.

Charlie screamed. "You leave my daddy alone!"

"It's okay sweetheart." Mike was saying as he slowly approached her. "Everything's all right. We just want to talk to your daddy."

"No!" The power was racing madly within. It took all of her will to hold onto it.

Mike took another step towards her. "Come on sweetie. Let's go for a walk while Jake talks to your daddy."

"NO!" She stepped backward. "Leave my daddy alone!"

The power was nearly out of control. Her heart was thundering in her chest, her head throbbing in time with its pulse.

Mike took another step forward. "You don't have to be afraid honey. You can trust us. We're policemen."

Charlie returned a cold stare as she gathered herself for what she knew she had to do. She was very frightened but now she felt something else as well, something bright, hard and shining. Her heart chilled but it was no longer just with fear. Cold fury now washed through her, steadying her tremors and bringing goose bumps to her skin. The power was raging. She held onto it for a moment longer. Long enough to be sure that there was no other way.

Mike continued to approach. "It's okay to trust policemen sweetheart. We won't hurt you. We want to help."

The air inside the little cell was heating up. Still Charlie held the power, knowing that in a moment it would be too late but unable to bring herself to let go. To use the power would be to go against everything Daddy and Mommy had ever told her. She was never to let it go, she was never to use it on purpose and she was especially never to use it on people.

If you don't do it now, then you won't be able to use it later.

Still she held back. Waiting, waiting until he actually tried to grab her.

Mike was within three feet of her now. "Just relax. Nobody's going to hurt you."

If she was going to use the power, it had to be now. Charlie gathered her courage, retaining a mere tenuous grip on the power. *I'm sorry Daddy...*

"Everything is fine Charlie. The policemen just want to talk to me. That is all."

The sound of her father's voice broke the spell. Charlie slammed the power down, setting off still more stabbing, burning pain throughout her body.

"Everything will be fine." Daddy turned to Mike. "Leave her alone. She is not hurting anyone in here."

Mike ignored him and continued to approach Charlie until Jake called to him. "Leave her be Mike. She'll come out when she's ready."

"Sure." Mike turned away from her in disgust and roughly grabbed her father's arm. "Let's go."

When the two policemen had gone Charlie once again turned her power on the toilet. This time there was a momentary loud hiss, followed by a sharp crack as the toilet exploded. Water sprayed from the pipes. Charlie could feel its cold even before it splashed on her t-shirt and jeans. Mike appeared again.

"What the hell...?"

He broke off as he saw the shattered and scorched pieces of porcelain scattered across the floor. For a moment he stood and stared dumbly before regaining his composure. "What the hell happened?"

Charlie said nothing. She was close to tears. *I got us in trouble again.*

Mike approached her slowly. "Come on. Let's get you out of here."

Charlie backed away towards the gushing water pipes. Cold water soaked her to the skin. None of it was clean.

Mike sighed. "Look. You're soaking wet. Can I at least get you dried off?"

Charlie followed without speaking as Mike took her to the shower room. He left telling her to clean up and that he would be back shortly with some clothing for her. Charlie watched him leave in silence, then undressed and stepped into the shower. Mike returned a short time later with a pile of clothing and a towel. Charlie was still in the shower and remained there until he had left. When he was gone she turned off the water and quickly crossed the locker room.

Neatly laid out on the wooden bench were a pair of plain white cotton panties, a frilly pink dress, a pair of frilled white ankle socks and a pair of patent leather girls dress shoes. A white towel lay on the bench beside them. The clothes were old fashioned and not of her usual taste, but Charlie was grateful none-the-less.

She wasted no time in drying off and dressing. To her surprise the clothes fit quite well. On her way out, the door she paused to glance into the mirror above the sink nearest the door. Save for her hair, which hung dripping and limp about her shoulders, she looked exactly like a picture she had once seen of a girl from the nineteen-sixties.

Charlie smiled despite herself. Then without intending to she burst into laughter.

I look like a refugee from the twentieth century.

She looked so foolish that she couldn't even feel embarrassed, she was laughing too hard. It took her a full twenty minutes to stop laughing and she had to avoid looking in the mirror to maintain her composure for every time she saw herself she would start laughing anew.

Upon leaving the locker room Charlie was met by a young, blond haired policewoman. "Hi, my name is Miranda." She approached slowly and bent down to Charlie's level. "What's your name?"

Frantic, Charlie searched her mind for the name on her fake ID. After a few moments' pause she found it. "Karen."

"Hi Karen." Miranda offered a warm smile. "You look very pretty."

Charlie returned a blank gaze.

"Karen I'm going to need you to come with me." She held out her hand.

"Where's my Daddy?" Charlie asked plainly.

"He's with my friends Mike and Jake." She renewed her smile. "Why don't you come with me to the break room and I'll see if I can't find you an ice cream bar."

"Okay." Charlie replied with some reluctance.

This woman meant her no harm, but she wanted to take her away from Daddy. She was going to call child protective services and they would take her away. The government men would find her. She might never see her father again. She had to find some way to escape. She had to find some way to get to Daddy.

Charlie went with Miranda, mind frantic as she searched for a solution.

There has to be a way out of this. There has to be. The words repeated over and over in her mind.

Miranda managed to find her a chocolate fudge bar and sat and talked with her as she ate it. She asked many questions, all intended to garner information about Charlie and her father.

Charlie took care in answering, sticking closely to the information on her fake ID and taking care not to reveal more than was asked. As she spoke she maintained tight control over her body and tone of voice, not wanting to betray even the slightest hint that she might be lying. She spoke, casually laughing at the appropriate times, and displaying a trace of smile upon her lips. Her posture was relaxed but not withdrawn. To all the world she would have looked normal. Miranda was completely fooled. And yet Charlie still felt uneasy. She sensed no suspicion from the policewoman but still… Something wasn't right. No, she wasn't just uneasy. She was terrified. Her heart pounded in her chest as she spoke in her most plain and casual voice, as she smiled and laughed at a joke, as she ate her ice cream bar.

The ice cream was a lead weight in her stomach yet when Miranda offered her a second, she accepted, if only to avoid raising concern.

After finishing her second ice cream bar Charlie felt sick. Her stomach was doing nauseating hula hoops around her ass. Miranda offered her a Coke, but Charlie asked for water instead. The water calmed her nausea a little, but she still felt ill.

Miranda's questions had become more pointed. Charlie's nerves tightened another notch and her heart rate picked up again. A thin sheen of sweat beaded up on her skin. Miranda still suspected nothing but the feeling that something wasn't right continued to intensify.

All at once her vision changed and she found herself looking at Jake. He was sitting at a desk talking on the phone. At first, she couldn't hear what he was saying but then his voice came into her mind.

"Male, about thirty-five maybe forty. Caucasian. Dark hair, with some gray flecks, red moustache and beard neatly trimmed and also flecked with gray, green eyes about six foot even."

"Name?" The voice on the other end was female, and young. It was the voice of one of the government agents.

"His ID says he's Louis Harrington. He has a child with him. Female, eight, also Caucasian, blond hair, blue eyes, four and a half, maybe four and three quarters tall. Her name's Karen Harrington."

"Hang on." The female voice was silent for a few seconds. "Hold them there we'll send someone to pick them up."

"Why? What's going on Sally?"

"They're wanted by the feds."

"A man and a little girl. What for? He kidnap her?" Jake asked.

"Doesn't say." Sally's voice was confused.

"What do you mean?"

"I mean there's no information. Both of their names are on the wire but there's no other information on them. It just says to detain if seen."

"Oh?" Jake's voice was also confused. "How long will it take you to get someone here?"

"We're sending a car now. Should be there in an hour. In the meantime, keep them separate and keep a close eye on both of them."

As quickly as it had come the vision dissolved and she once again found herself sitting across the table from Miranda in the police station break room. Her head swam with newly gained information.

The woman on the other end of the phone, Sally, was a government agent. Her name wasn't even Sally. Everything she said was a lie or pretense to convince Jake that she was indeed whom she claimed to be. The only part that was true was that there was a car on its way. Except that wasn't true either, there were at least a dozen cars on their way, each filled with armed men and women in black suits.

Cold terror exploded within her. They would be there soon. She had only minutes. Charlie fought an urge to jump up and run away.

"Are you okay honey?" Miranda's expression was concerned.

"Yes." Charlie's response was perhaps a little too quick for she felt Miranda's concern growing and along with it the first hints of suspicion.

She was silent for a moment.

"How about another glass of water?"

"Okay."

Miranda stood up, took her glass and filled it from the sink. Then she turned and set it in front of Charlie before sitting down across from her. "There you go."

Charlie forced a smile. "Thanks."

She picked up the glass to take a sip. Her hands were trembling so hard that she came close to spilling it all over herself.

Miranda was watching her carefully though she said nothing. Her suspicion was growing.

Charlie's vision changed again. For a moment she could see the men and women in their big black cars. Then she was looking at Miranda again.

Everything had become deadly silent. All of the usual office noises were muted. Even the low hum of the refrigerator was gone leaving her with the pounding of her own heart. She heard voices. *Their* voices. The government agents were here

We're here to pick up the man and the girl.

May I see some identification? Thank you. The man is in the interrogation room with Officer Mikousky. Officer Barrett has the girl in the break room.

Johnson, Michaels go get the girl's father. The rest of you come with me.

There were fifty of them, ten inside the other forty surrounding the building. Terror exploded within her. *Oh God what do I do? What do I do? What do I do?*

She didn't know. Panic welled up inside her. Charlie bit it back as best she could. It was hard. She was confused and frightened. She had to get away and help Daddy. She knew how she could.

But it's bad. Daddy said it's bad. Daddy said to never, never...

The rest of the thought was swallowed by terror and panic. She had only, seconds to act and she didn't know what to do. Inside the power was already racing. The door opened, and two men came in. Charlie was on her feet in an instant.

The first was very tall and slender. His face was young and handsome. He had jet-black hair, light tan skin and wore a black suit with a white button-down shirt and black tie.

The second was also tall and slender though he was more than a hint shorter than the first. His face was rounded and blank looking. This man's hair was sandy brown, and his skin was paler than the first man's. He too wore a black suit with a white button-down shirt and black tie.

Neither held a gun but slight bulges under the left breast of each man's jacket indicated that they were both armed. The first man offered her a false friendly smile.

"Hi Charlie." His smiled broadened. "You don't have to run anymore now."

She returned a cold stare. "Go away."

"I'm afraid I can't. I have my orders." His tone softened. "Nobody wants to hurt you and your Daddy."

She knew before he spoke the words that the man was trying to deceive her. He took another step forward.

Charlie backed away. "You liar! You're supposed to kill everyone and take me away. You leave us alone!" The power was spinning furiously, just barely within her control.

Miranda got to her feet. "What's this about?"

The two men reached into their jackets and produced badges. "FBI. These two are wanted for questioning in connection with a murder."

"Whose murder?"

"Dana MacLeod. The girl's mother."

Miranda's expression did not change. "She's frightened. Why don't you let me talk to her?"

"No. We need both of them." He took another step forward. Miranda did not move to get in his way. "Come on sweetie. Everything will be fine. You'll see." He extended his hand.

"NO!"

She took several quick steps backward. The power was racing, screaming to be let out. She bit down on it hard.

No, I can't. Daddy said it's bad.

Blood soaked pain ripped through her head. She had to fight to suppress a scream. The man continued to approach.

"Please don't make me do this." she pleaded. The man ignored her. The power was alive within her; the pain grew with each moment.

The man took another step forward and made a grab for her wrist.

Charlie stepped back releasing the power as she did. Fire swept over the man's shoulders and hair. He screamed beating at the flames with his hands. In the same instant the second man had reached into his jacket and produced a gun. Charlie released the power again. In an instant fire engulfed the second man's head and torso. His screams joined those of the first man as they both frantically tried to extinguish themselves. Miranda stared wide-eyed. Her fear was palpable.

The room was deadly quiet. The power was out of control spraying in all directions like blood from a severed artery. Flames licked across the floor in front of her. Fire swept over the counter and engulfed the cabinets. There was a low sizzle followed by several sharp pops as the refrigerator's motor burned out. A moment later it exploded into flames.

An artificial calm came over her. She no longer felt frightened and her mind was strangely clear. Slowly she walked around the fires on her way to the door. The two men whose hair she seared had succeeded in extinguishing their flaming heads and clothing but neither made a move to stop her.

Fire followed close behind her. As she passed through the doorway it burst into flames. Flames swept up the walls and along the ceiling. A gunshot rang out and something hot whistled by her head.

One of the men was shouting: "Not the girl! Not the girl!"

He had his gun out. As she watched he turned and fired at her father who was struggling with two other agents.

Charlie turned the power on him. Fire swept up his pant legs and sleeves. He was screaming but she was only peripherally aware of it. She felt no anger towards the man though he had tried to kill her father. Inside she felt nothing but the power. Flames enveloped the man. He ran screaming towards the fire extinguisher on the wall, no longer a man but a blazing scarecrow. Through the yellow sheets of flame, she saw his face, twisted and contorted with pain. His features seemed to be *running* like hot wax. A moment later the man collapsed and was still. His body sizzled and popped like bacon on a skillet as the room filled with the acrid smell of burning flesh. Muscle and fat were rapidly consumed exposing bone that was quickly charred. Charlie watched this all impassively until the flames died down leaving only charred skeletal remains.

The rest of the room was silent; everyone was frozen in place, staring at the pile of ashes and fused bone that had once been a man.

Charlie walked away from the remains calmly. The power continued to flow from her mind. Computers and telephones exploded as she passed. Desks burst into flames. Fire swept across the ceiling and floor as if they were soaked in gasoline. The air became explosively hot and choked with smoke.

Several of the agents drew their guns as she approached. She swept them with fire. They scattered, screaming and beating at their flaming hair and clothing.

The power continued to pour forth. As she approached her father, the one-way glass of the interrogation room bubbled and began to melt. Tears of molten glass ran down onto the floor. The door exploded outward throwing her father head over heels to the ground. He was calling to her.

"Charlie that is enough!"

"Stop it!"

She couldn't.

"You have to stop!"

She looked at him. "I can't." Her voice came out calm and collected.

She turned, and the glass front foyer exploded filling the air with twinkling shrapnel. Three more agents went down in the hail of glass and blood. Charlie started towards the large gap in the wall that had once been the door. Behind her Daddy staggered to his feet.

"Charlie!"

She kept walking. All at once she became aware of the carnage surrounding her. Lying among the agents she had killed were a dozen or more dead police and office workers. They had all been shot. Their blood lay in bright red pools on the floor.

Charlie looked at them and felt nothing. Though she felt regret that they had died there was no emotion attached to the feeling, it was pure cold logic.

They didn't deserve to die.

She passed them with slow strides, eyes taking in every bit of gore. Then she was outside. For a moment everything was quiet. Then all at once men and women in black suits swarmed the parking lot.

Charlie's reaction was swift. The agent's screams rang out on the cool morning air as their clothing and hair burst into flames.

The power continued to flow unabated. Trenches of fire swept across the tar parking lot itself, as if trails of gasoline had been laid there. Sparks and flame rained down from above as the overhead street lamps burst. Then the cars began to explode.

Thinking back later she realized that they had exploded from the rear, where the gas tank is. The cars went up in a series of earth-shattering booms like a giant string of firecrackers. The concussions came close to knocked her off her feet.

The agents scattered after the first car exploded. Three were unfortunate enough to be caught in the blast from the second. The rest were peppered with safety glass. Cries of terror rang on the gasoline heavy air. A third car exploded throwing shredded metal through the air. Hot shrapnel mangled several agents; two others were thrown into another car. Two agents made a break for a large black car at the far end of the parking lot. Both men were swallowed by fire when the car exploded a few seconds later. Three other agents ran towards another black car only to be incinerated when it detonated along with a smaller blue hatch back. Shock or shrapnel from the blast struck down the remaining agents.

One man was sliced in half at the waist by half of a cherry red car hood. Another agent, sex unidentifiable, lay in a pool of blood by the curb. He or she had lost their head, both arms and one leg. A third agent lay on the grass moaning and clutching at the mangled remains of his right arm. The limb was severed save for a few strands of skin. Beside him lay another man's leg and a hand. More limbs littered the parking lot and surrounding grass. A woman's head lay at her feet. Its glassy blue eyes stared up at her accusingly.

She looked back down into them and felt nothing. The power continued to flow free bringing with it indescribable pleasure. She felt warm almost to the core.

A pistol left behind by one of the dead agents spun and danced on the parking lot as its shells exploded one by one.

Charlie stop! Out of nowhere a hand struck her across the face. She turned to see her father, his eyes were intense. *Charlie!* His voice seemed to come from very far away. The hand came again. There was no pain. The power flowed out of her towards her father.

Charlie pulled it back suddenly. *No! Stop!* Sharp pain exploded in her skull. Then it was gone. For a moment she stood and stared. Then the spell broke. Sudden horror and guilt washed through her.

"DAAAAAAAAAAAAAAAAAAAAAAAAAAAAAAADDY!!!"

The scream built and built as the full intensity of emotion sank in. Her vision blurred, and the world began to spin. Then everything fell away leaving only darkness.

XII

The door opened and a man in a black suit came in. The moment she saw him Charlie knew something terrible had happened. "Names?"

"David McAuliff."

"Catherine McAuliff."

"This is our daughter Danielle." David said flatly. His fear was palpable. "What's going on?"

"Your identification please."

David and Catherine gave him their cards. Charlie nervously explained that she had lost her card in O'Hare Airport. The man listened to her explanation without speaking. David dropped three hundred-dollar bills on the table, which the man snatched up. The man then looked over David and Catherine's ID cards without bothering to verify their accuracy.

David caught his eyes. "What's going on?"

"What purpose do you have in our country?" The man asked plainly.

"Why are you holding us? What did we do?" David's voice was calm but there was an edge to his words. Charlie could feel his fear.

"Are you here to work, for business perhaps, a military post, or are you just a tourist?"

"What's going on?" David repeated.

Instead of answering the man turned and left shutting the door behind him. He returned a moment later followed by a woman carrying a laptop computer and set it down on the table in front of them.

"...sixty thousand people died on impact. All that remains now of the city of New York is a burning pile of rubble." The reporter's voice was heavy with emotion.

Charlie realized he was crying. It was hard to tell as his face was obscured by the large yellow helmet he wore. As the camera panned backward Charlie realized that he was wearing a radiation suit.

"I...I don't know if you can see this but this is all that remains of Manhattan."

The image on the screen changed to an overhead view of fire and thick clouds of smoke. It was hard to see but beyond the thick smoke and haze visible in the bright orange glow was mile after mile of flaming rubble.

"You're looking at Lower Manhattan. This is all that is left after the blast." The last sentence was little more than a sob. "Once again for those of you who are just joining us now. A five-megaton nuclear weapon was detonated over New York City at five thirty pm local time. At least sixty thousand are confirmed dead. Hundreds of thousands have been reported missing. Authorities believe the death toll may reach into the millions." The man was crying out right now.

The image changed again. This time the smoke was much thicker and there was no fire, nor any rubble. The little bit of the ground that was visible was barren, scorched black and gray by the heat.

"You're looking at midtown, ground zero of the blast. Damage extends out from here in concentric circles as far north as Yonkers and as far south as Staten Island."

The image changed again to show the reporter in his yellow radiation suit. Behind him was a massive mushroom shaped smoke cloud.

"New York City...destroyed...at five thirty. There is no information available at this time concerning who may be responsible for this atrocity." He broke off sobbing. "I... I can't even imagine what purpose an act like this would serve other than mass murder."

The man closed the laptop. "Somebody detonated a nuclear device over New York at eight fifty-seven. We have been ordered to detain everyone coming into the country until their identity and purpose can be ascertained."

Charlie did not hear the rest of what the man said. Her vision changed for a moment and she saw a brilliant flash of light followed by fire sweeping up from the ground in a single titanic pillar.

It took several minutes for her to understand what had happened. It was difficult to comprehend. New York, her home for over a year, the place where she had lived with Daddy and then where she returned and met David and Catherine; New York huge, bright, loud, overcrowded; erased, gone forever. For a while she sat and stared too numb to react. Then all at once she burst into tears crying harder and harder.

The people…

Those poor, poor people.

Her vision changed again and again. She could see them dying. The fires, the smoke, the collapsing buildings she could see it all. The horror and sadness of it all flooded through her, overwhelming her young mind.

Oh God. Those poor people.

Her stomach lurched violently. She was going to be sick.

Those poor people.

Without even realizing it she vomited all over the floor.

She was standing up. Someone was leading her away. It was a woman. She was not Catherine. The woman spoke with a pleasant English accent. Charlie barely heard what she said. They were in a hallway now, walking slowly. The woman was still talking. Something about everything being all right, about getting her all cleaned up. Now they were in the bathroom, she was sitting on the toilet and the woman was wiping her face with a wet paper towel. Hot tears streamed down her cheeks.

All those people…dead.

It was hard to accept, hard to believe that so many people could die in such a short time. Yet she knew it was so. She had known it all along though she was not aware of it until now.

Deep down, beyond rational thought, she felt that something had begun;

something bigger than the destruction of a city and the death of millions; something dark and terrible. Cold darkness coiled about her like a python. The shadows were gathering. She became calm despite the deep terror boiling within her heart.

The woman gave her a paper cup of water and then took her back to the room where David and Catherine were.

For the first time Charlie saw their faces. They wore pale, blank expressions of pure horror.

The man was still questioning David. He answered in a dry and emotionless voice. Charlie sat down between David and Catherine without speaking a word.

The fear and horror in the room were choking. The air felt thick and cold, a strange sensation that she had never felt before.

Sometime later the man finished questioning David and left. He returned ten minutes later and laid their ID cards on the table. "You may leave now."

They neither spoke nor moved for nearly a minute. Then David picked up his ID card and put it back in his wallet. Catherine took her ID back a moment later. David got to his feet with slow deliberation. Charlie followed him with Catherine. A woman met them in the corridor.

The woman offered them a curt nod. "Have a pleasant stay."

"Thanks." David's voice was flat and emotionless.

XIII

The woman escorted them from the office building, through the front gate, and out of the port. Twenty minutes later they were standing in the shadowy bar room of a seedy Glasgow pub. The air inside was stagnant and soaked with whiskey and stale beer. There was a line of mahogany booths along one wall, the opposite wall opened into a large single pane, picture window that was part way shaded with dark cherry shutters. Mahogany pillar tables and three-legged chairs clustered around a long mahogany bar that ran the length of the back wall. The man behind the counter looked them up and down before speaking

"Ello, can I help you?"

"Yes." David replied. "I would like to rent a room."

"May I see your identification sir?"

David complied without hesitation.

"I'm going to need to see your wife and daughter's identification as well."

Catherine approached the bar first. When she was done Charlie reluctantly stepped forward with the same explanation she had offered to the Secret Service agents. In the back of her mind she feared that the man would turn them in to the police. To her surprise the man accepted her excuse without question, and made no attempt to establish her ID.

Instead he smiled at her. "You are a pretty one young miss"

Charlie blushed and returned a shy smile. Inside her heart remained cold with horror.

David paid the man with the last of their cash.

"I'm putting you in the bridal suite. Yer paid up until Monday." He handed David a single key on a big plastic keyring and pointed towards a narrow doorway to the left of the bar. "Stairs are through there. Your room is on the third floor. Have a pleasant stay."

"Thank you." David took her hand. "Come on Charlie let's go to bed." He was confused and frightened despite the natural tone of his voice.

She looked up at him with listless eyes. "Okay." Charlie might have been confused and afraid herself were she not still overcome with horror.

Charlie followed David and Catherine up the stairs in silence. The bridal suite was laid out in the shape of a rough T with the living room at its center and bedrooms on its left and right. David took her into the left-hand bedroom.

The room was small but beautiful. Despite being exhausted and miserable Charlie couldn't help being awed. On the wall opposite the door was a big, elaborately carved, four-poster bed with a lace canopy and spread. To the right was a pretty honey brown wooden dresser with a huge oval shaped mirror on top and to the left was an elaborately carved black wood wardrobe. There was a little wooden chair with a maroon cushion by the bed and a larger wing-backed chair against the wall by the door. There was even a little round table with two matching dark cherry wood chairs with red crocheted cushions.

Everything about the room felt as if it were made just for her. Someone had even turned back the blankets and left a terry cloth robe on the bed.

"Wow!" The word was a hushed whisper, spoken without thought.

David released her hand. "Why don't you get ready for bed? You can call me when you're ready to be tucked in."

She looked up at him with a weary smile. "Okay."

Charlie was slow to undress, taking time to look around the room and enjoy it. She knew that this would be the last time she would have a room this nice. In her heart she knew that this was only the beginning, that things would become much worse, not to improve for a long time, if ever.

Whatever was happening, Whatever, it was she had felt beginning at the seaport, was accelerating, building into a groundswell of horror and sadness and hurt and terror. She could feel it all in her heart and she could feel the darkness, cold as ice, building, swirling like the first wisps of smoke before a blaze. *It* was coming, Whatever *It* was.

After wrapping herself in the bathrobe and tying it shut Charlie went to the door, pushed it open a crack and called to David. He came into the room a moment later with Catherine and scooped her up into his arms.

"Come on Charlie let's get you tucked in."

She grasped him in a tight hug, heart still cold with fear.

Catherine stroked her hair. "It's okay Charlie you're safe. No one's going to hurt you anymore. Not while we're here." Charlie wanted to believe her. She wanted to believe her so badly. But she knew differently.

David gave her a gentle squeeze and then carried her over to the bed and laid her down. As he drew the blankets up to her chin he whispered to her. "Just relax. You're safe with us. You don't need to worry anymore."

Charlie looked up at him with fear in her heart. "David, are we okay? Are they going to come after us again?"

She already knew the truth before she asked and knew too that he would lie. It didn't matter. She didn't want the truth. She wanted to be comforted. She wanted David to tell her that everything would be all right even if she knew it to be untrue.

He smiled. "We're fine Charlie. It'll take the NSA a while to figure out where we are and by the time they do we'll be long gone. They won't catch up with us again." He sounded confident, too confident.

Rather than comforting her, his words served to frighten her further. She knew he feared the NSA would catch up with them before they could get away.

"I'm scared David."

He drew her into a tight hug. "It's okay Charlie. You don't have to be afraid anymore. We are not going to let them get you again. I promise."

It was promise in vain that he would have difficulty keeping. She knew that. They were in serious danger and time was short. His sincerity touched her though and she couldn't help but cry a little.

David stroked her hair. "I promise. They'll never get to you again."

David held her until she had stopped crying and was calm. Then he kissed her forehead and carefully released her. "Sweet dreams. I love you Charlie." The words came out in a faint hoarse tone as they were spoken with great difficulty.

She knew David cared very deeply for her and that it was very difficult for him to express these feelings.

Catherine too bent down and brushed her lips across Charlie's brow in a light kiss. "Sleep well. David and I love you very much."

Charlie looked up at them both and saw for the first time that they were both little more than kids themselves feeling much as she felt: scared and unsure of what to do. "I love you too."

They started to leave. David paused at the door. "Do you want me to leave it open a crack?"

"Yes, please."

He flashed a slight smile. "Okay." Then he turned and left, flicking off the light as he passed through the doorway.

When he was gone Charlie turned on her side and closed her eyes. Sleep would not come. After a while her eyes flicked open again and began to drift around the room as her mind drifted through the many confusing events of the past week and a half.

She had died and come back to life, and then gotten on a container ship and left the United States. Then upon arriving she and David and Catherine were taken away by English government agents and questioned and told that New York City was destroyed.

With that thought came brief flashes of destruction; ruined buildings, flaming rubble, broken bodies. And most powerful of all, the image that would come to symbolize for her the whole of the atrocity. The reporter telling the story his cheeks wet with tears and behind him, drifting silent as death, the massive, single mushroom shaped cloud of smoke. It was an image that would remain burned in her mind forever. Though the mark would fade with time, it would always remain. A dim reminder of what she had seen.

And then they were released and checked into this pub and David put her to bed telling her that everything was okay now. Except it wasn't. They would have to run again if they were going to stay ahead of the NSA.

As she thought that she glanced up at her scrubs, folded and piled on top of the chair by the bed in a neat stack. She had no other clothes to her name, not even a pair of underwear. She was naked underneath her robe. On the container ship she had for the most part stayed below decks in the crew's quarters. She had tried to keep herself out of sight of the sailors. But now… Charlie felt her cheeks flush with embarrassment.

I can't go around dressed in scrubs with no underwear. Someone will see.

She felt like crying. It wasn't fair. It never ended. There was always more hurt, more horror, more fear and more embarrassment. She had already gone through so much humiliation, being stared at like a freak, kept under constant watch, not even able to use the toilet in private.

She thought she had escaped that. Now it was beginning all over again. It was almost too depressing to stand. She couldn't bear to go through all of that horror again. A tired, tearful sigh escaped her throat. It wasn't fair.

Under other circumstances she would have been embarrassed, not reduced to tears, but this was another torment piled on top of the hurt, horror, and fear she already felt.

Everything had crumbled away, leaving her world strange and twisted. In a way it felt like she was still on the run with Daddy. In a way everything was the same. But everything was different. David and Catherine were not her father and mother. They had taken her in and treated her like their own daughter, but they were not Daddy and Mommy. Her real mother and father were dead, and she missed them terribly. That fact was perhaps not even the most terrible thing. Her father had been dead for over a year now; her mother died when she was only six.

As she lay in bed that night Charlie found that she could not recall what her mother looked like, it was even hard for her to remember her father's face. His memory too had faded with time. She knew that she would eventually forget what both of her parents looked like and felt sad. But that was still not the worst thing.

The worst, most terrible thing was the cold feeling in her heart, the dark certainty that something awful was beginning. Some terrible event was coming and there was nothing she could do about it.

Tears spilled from her eyes and rolled across the bridge of her nose and the top of her right cheek. Charlie did not make a sound. She only lay there weeping in silence until she cried herself to sleep.

XIV

Charlie awoke the next morning feeling calm and rested. She sat up, yawned and stretched her arms above her head. The window drapes were drawn keeping the room dark save for a thin sliver of light that crept in where the curtains met.

Charlie stretched again, then stood up, went to the window and opened the drapes. Golden sunlight streamed in from a perfect, solid blue winter sky. Charlie smiled. Everything seemed so much better in the good daylight. All of the terror and hurt of the night before were gone. Even the feeling of impending danger had faded into her subconscious.

For a moment she just stood there, enjoying the warm sunlight. Then she turned away and headed for the bathroom.

After shutting the door Charlie took off her robe and turned on the shower. She used the toilet while she waited for the water to get hot, then stepped under the spray. The water drummed on her chest, her shoulders and her head encasing her in a warm cocoon. Charlie closed her eyes and smiled. Nothing in the world felt as good as the first few moments in a hot shower.

A quiet voice spoke up in her mind. *It's not over you know.*

A wrinkle of fear crossed her face. *We're ok for now. The NSA doesn't know where we are.*

You don't really believe that do you. You know you can't hide from them. They'll find you. They always do.

She frowned. *David said we're safe. He promised he would never let them get to me again.*

Your daddy and mommy couldn't protect you from them what makes you think David and Catherine can?

Goosebumps rashed out on her arms and she began to tremble slightly. *David promised to protect me. He promised.*

That doesn't really matter. The voice insisted. *They'll catch you eventually and when they do they'll kill David and Catherine and take you away.*

NO! David promised to protect me, and he will. David has the power he's stronger than...

She didn't want to complete that thought. She knew David and Catherine were stronger than her father and mother. They were like her, ever so much more like her than her parents. She knew these things but would not admit them to herself just as she would not admit that the voice was right.

They weren't safe, and it wasn't just because of the NSA. The feeling that something dark and terrible had begun remained with her. The NSA was dangerous, but it was not the true threat. Something else, something far worse, loomed unseen over the horizon.

Suddenly the water no longer felt warm. Charlie began to shake, not with cold but fear. She did not yet know what had begun but she knew it was something awful.

Charlie stood under the shower for several minutes clutching her small body and shuddering. It took that long before she was able to even move to pick up the shampoo.

Charlie washed her hair absently, her mind consumed with fear. In the process she managed to get shampoo in her eyes twice and spill half of the little bottle in the bathtub. After rinsing the shampoo from her hair Charlie reached for the soap only to drop it in the bathtub. She bent down and picked it up, mind still preoccupied with fear. Charlie washed slowly, taking care not to miss anyplace.

When she was finished she stood under the shower for another five minutes before turning off the water and getting out.

Charlie dried herself off equally slowly and carefully, then wrapped one of the big bath towels around herself and went back to her room.

The living room was still dark. Charlie crossed in silence not wanting to disturb David and Catherine. When she was less than six feet from her room door she heard David's voice.

"You want to take the first shower?"

"Why don't we take one together?" She barely caught Catherine's reply.

"We can't." David replied. "What if Charlie hears us?"

"She's still asleep." Catherine's voice was low and seductive. "Come on we haven't had sex since Charlie went into the hospital."

They were both silent for a few moments then:

"Sure, she probably won't wake up for another hour if we're quiet." David's voice was husky.

Charlie rushed to her door and was about to open it when she heard the other bedroom door open.

"Oh, good morning Charlie I didn't know you were awake."

Charlie's skin flushed with embarrassment as she turned around. "Good morning."

David and Catherine looked at her sheepishly, both equally embarrassed. "Sorry we didn't know you were out here."

Charlie forced a smile. "It's okay. I'm not naked or anything." She felt naked, standing in front of them wearing nothing but a towel. She started to turn away. "I'll be ready in a few minutes."

"That's ok Charlie. Take your time." David's voice was apologetic.

Charlie felt mortified. David and Catherine had seen her *naked*. The towel covered her privates but she was still naked. It didn't matter to her that David had seen her before. She felt humiliated.

For a moment she felt like crying. When the feeling passed she laid her towel on the bed. Instead of gathering up her scrubs Charlie went to the dresser on the wall and opened it. She had not expected to find anything and was pleasantly surprised to find it filled with girl's clothing,

After looking over all the clothes, Charlie picked out a red t-shirt, a pair of faded blue jeans, pink cotton panties, and a pair of white ankle socks. She wasted little time getting dressed, then went to the wardrobe where she found a pair of black leather shoes and a small suitcase with a note taped to the outside.

Dear Charlie,

I hope the clothing suits you. I wasn't sure about your tastes, so I picked out what I have seen most girls your age wearing. Everything should be in your size. You may take whatever you want. The suitcase is big enough to hold everything within the dresser. Inside the suitcase you will find a brush, a comb, bottles of hairspray, mousse and shampoo and a bag of scrunchies for your hair. You will also find a jacket on the other side of the wardrobe with six thousand dollars cash in the inside pocket.

Take care,

Charlie looked and found everything as the note said. The jacket was actually a purple parka complete with a hood. Besides the money she also found a pair of gloves in the outside pockets and a scarf hanging over the jacket's shoulders. It occurred to her that she should find all of this suspicious and yet she accepted it without question as she sensed no immediate danger.

Charlie packed the suitcase with the clothing in the dresser and then took the jacket from its hanger and threw it over one shoulder.

Upon leaving her room Charlie found David sitting on the couch alone. She could hear Catherine in the shower.

"Hi Charlie." David's voice was apologetic. "I'm sorry I didn't mean to embarrass you like that."

"That's okay." She sat down beside him. "Where are we going now?"

"We're going way up to the northern tip of Scotland to a little town called Glen Dunbairn to stay with my father." He offered her a slight smile. "I haven't seen him in five years now."

Charlie looked up at him inquisitively. "What does he look like?"

"My Dad's almost as tall as me and very thin. He has reddish brown hair that was just starting to gray when I left." David broke off quickly. Charlie sensed a mixture of anger and hurt.

"Why didn't you visit him?" She asked plaintively.

"Well for a while I couldn't afford to. Dad was transferred to Glen Dunbairn about a month after I left for college. I could barely afford tuition, there was no way I could pay to fly to Scotland."

He was only telling a half-truth. His real reason was something else, something he very much wanted to keep from her. That soon became unimportant to her though as something else fell into place.

"Your dad was in the military?" *Did his parents participate in the same experiment that Daddy and Mommy did?*

"No, he's a Jesuit priest."

Charlie was confused. "I thought priests couldn't have kids."

"They can't." He replied matter-of-factly. "Dad adopted me when my mother couldn't take care of me anymore."

Her heart went out to him. "Your parents died too."

"No. My biological father died when I was very young. My mother got sick and went into the hospital. The state took me away from her and put me in an orphanage. That was where Dad found me." Once again there was something he wasn't telling her. Something he didn't want her to know.

"Did you ever get to visit her?"

"No." His voice was flat, emotionless. "Mom was too sick. I lost touch with her after Dad adopted me." Charlie sensed a lot of pain in his heart.

"What happened to her?"

"I don't know Charlie. I was never told anything about her as a child and I barely remember her now."

This was a flat out lie. She felt that he had clear memories of his mother and that he wanted nothing to do with her though Charlie didn't know why. Whatever reason he had, it was buried deep within his mind beyond what she could feel. She could sense only the hurt that surrounded it.

Charlie looked at him carefully but said nothing. Whatever it was that he was hiding, it was very painful for him. She saw no need to ask him any more about it.

Charlie took David's hand and gave it a gentle squeeze. He squeezed back. For a moment they sat in silence.

Then the bathroom door opened, and Catherine emerged wearing a short white bathrobe and nothing else. Her reddish gold hair was still dripping as it hung loose on her shoulders.

Charlie felt something crop up within David. It felt similar to want but it was much stronger and of a much different nature, a nature which she did not yet understand. Her mind told her that it had to do with sex and physical attraction. The actual word that came to mind was *lust* and it was a concept that was foreign to her. *Lust* was a thing of the adult world, a world that she understood academically but not emotionally or viscerally.

She knew quite a bit about sex and the feelings and desires that surrounded it; quite a bit more than her father had ever told her or would have been comfortable with her knowing at eight or even nine years of age.

This understanding came part and parcel with her abnormally high intelligence and her powerful psychic senses and was something that she shared with no one.

Understanding often brought with it confusion and fear and this was something else she kept to herself.

As she watched Catherine, Charlie sensed a similar feeling in Catherine to that which she had sensed in David. She felt confusion and slight disgust. Charlie understood *lust* and sex, what made adults want to have sex, the purpose it served, and she even understood that it was supposed to be pleasurable but she could not understand why anyone would want to do something so disgusting.

I would never let a boy do that to me.

For a moment the feeling swelled within David and Catherine then it was gone. Catherine smiled at her. "Hi Charlie, sorry about earlier."

Charlie returned her smile. "It's okay."

Catherine turned to David. "Shower's all yours if you want it."

"Thanks." He stood up and went into the bathroom. As he did Catherine turned towards their bedroom door. "I'm going to go get dressed. You can watch TV while you're waiting for us to get ready, if you want."

"Ok Catherine."

Charlie watched her until she closed the bedroom door. Then she picked up the remote and flipped on the television. Loony Tunes came on. Charlie watched blankly as Wile E. Coyote plummeted off a cliff and slammed into the ground in a cloud of dust.

Normally she would have found this hilarious, but her mind was preoccupied that morning. Something had begun, something dark and horrible. She was no longer numb with shock as she had been last night nor was she hysterical with terror. What she felt now was nagging fear.

Time was short. Whatever had begun last night was already gaining in strength. Though she could not see them she felt the dark forces building and building like some great invisible flood. She had felt it since last night.

Except that wasn't true. Deep inside she knew that she had always felt it, always known. She just hadn't realized it until now. Deeper still she knew that she was somehow tied to the dark forces.

The thing that had begun, whatever it was, had something to do with her. And below that knowledge, buried in her unconscious mind beneath layer upon layer of guilt and horror lay the full knowledge that she was the catalyst and key to the events to come. She would never consciously acknowledge this, but her mind and heart knew it to be so.

A short time later David emerged from the bathroom and went into the bedroom with Catherine. Shortly after that both he and Catherine emerged from the bedroom fully dressed.

Catherine wore a white halter-top that was cut off just below her ribs and a pair of form fitting blue jeans. David wore a gray sweater over a white T-shirt and a pair of faded, loose fitting jeans. Both carried parkas similar to the one she had found in her wardrobe.

Before anyone could say a word there was a knock at the door. Charlie stood up to get it but froze as David motioned for her to stay back. He went to the door and glanced through the peephole before opening it.

The man who had checked them in the night before stood outside with a large tray of food.

"Room service." The man said in a cheerful voice.

"You must be mistaken. We didn't order any room service." David's voice was bewildered.
The man shook his head. "No mistake. Foods all yers."

David started to protest but the man cut him off. "Yes, I know ya didn't call down to the kitchen. A friend of yers had this sent up for you. Don't worry it's all paid for."

David stepped aside looking more bewildered than ever.

"Where would ya like it?" The man asked.

"Uhh, put it over by the couch." David replied distractedly.

The man carried the large tray of food over to the coffee table and set it down.
He gave Charlie a slight bow. "There ya are young miss. Enjoy yer breakfast."
He turned and left nodding to David as he passed.

For a moment they just stood there. Charlie made the first move, spurred on by
sudden hunger. She found the tray overflowing with all sorts of delectable foods.
There was a huge fruit platter laden with slices of watermelon, honeydew and
cantaloupe, green and red grapes, orange and grapefruit sections, and sliced
bananas and strawberries. Next to the fruit platter was a metal case inside of
which she found three plates each containing a steak, an omelet, half a waffle,
four strips of bacon, four sausages, and a pot of warm maple syrup. Finally,
there were three carafes filled with orange juice, cranberry juice and milk, three
large glasses and three clear glass plates.

Charlie ate like a horse finishing a waffle, omelet, steak, bacon and sausages;
two plates of fruit; two glasses of orange juice; two glasses of cranberry juice
and one glass of milk. Everything was delicious and when she was finished she
felt wonderfully full.

XX

After eating they quickly packed. An hour later they were inside a hired car
headed north. The ride took all day and most of the night. At around five in the
morning the driver pulled off the highway and began to drive down a succession
of narrow country roads before coming to a small white farmhouse surrounded
by open fields filled with sheep. A tall, slender man stood on the front porch.

He introduced himself as Father James Lenox and asked her to call him Jim.

It was almost dawn and Charlie was exhausted so she went straight to bed.
Within minutes she was dead to the world.

Chapter 8
Discourse

I

His father gave him a questioning look. "What are you going to do David?"

He shook his head. "I don't know. Run. Hide. What else can I do?"

His father leveled his gaze. "And Charlie, what about her?"

"I don't know." David answered flatly.

"It's not fair to her to keep her on the run like this. A girl her age needs friends, exercise, safety. She needs in to be in school not on the run frightened to death."

"I know Dad." David replied feeling irritated. "What do you want me to do wait for the NSA to catch us?"

"No of course not but you can't just keep running."

"I know Dad." David said tiredly. "That's why I came here. I need your help. Charlie needs your help."

His father's face softened and filled with compassion. "Of course. Tell me about her."

"Charlie's a gifted psychic and a pyrokinetic."

"So, she has the power."

"Yes."

"How much does she know about her power?"

"A lot. Probably more than anyone else."

His father nodded. "Is she yours?"

"No." David replied flatly. "Catherine and I found her under a bush in Central Park about a month ago."

"What happened to her parents?"

"They were both killed by the NSA." As he spoke David's heart went out to Charlie. "Her mother was murdered when she was only six her father was shot in front of her at nine."

"That's a shame. She's only a little kid." Behind his father's sad voice David sensed deep compassion, not only for Charlie but for him as well.

"That's not the strange part though." David paused. "After we found Charlie in the park a man attacked her and poisoned her."

"What are you saying?" His father's expression was confused.

"Dad she died." In his mind David saw Charlie lying on the steel table in the morgue.

"But she's not dead now." His father's voice was both intrigued and questioning at once.

"I know."

David broke off as more images from that night two days earlier flashed in his mind. He saw Charlie floating above the steel autopsy table. He saw the floor split open to reveal Heaven and Hell at once. He saw the brilliant white and red lightning surging around and through her body.

His father's voice broke his train of thought. "What's Charlie's birthday?"

David was caught off guard. "What? Why do you ask?"

"What's her birthday?" He repeated.

"April thirtieth."

"How old is she?"

"Nine."

His father's face paled a half shade. "What I'm about to tell you David is not what you want to hear but it is very important that you listen to me."

"Sure." David replied nonchalantly. Inside he felt confused and somewhat frightened.

"You must continue your training as a Lightwarrior."

In a single, quick movement David got off the couch and turned his back on his father. "No! I wasted most of my childhood listening to that shit." There was no way he would ever do that again. He had been abused, orphaned and isolated because of his power. He was not about to re-embrace it now.

David felt his father's hand on his shoulder. "David listen to me. There are many things that you do not know. Things that I kept from you to spare your innocence. This child is more than just an Enlightened. I believe she may be the *Sigilla Praevaricator*. The Breaker of Seals."

David turned and looked at his father curiously. He had already known that there was something different about Charlie, something beyond the power.

"Before the creation an agreement was struck to allow mankind to settle the final battle between good and evil. Two weapons were forged; one of light, the other darkness. Both weapons were

sealed away to await the end time when a child would be born with the power to unseal them. This child was to be born on the thirtieth day of the fourth month in the second millennium following the birth of Christ. The child's birth was to be signaled by the prominence of the star Baal and the star of David during the final phase before the new moon."

Though his father's words sounded impossible David knew he spoke the truth.

Sudden fear exploded within him as several things came together at once in his mind. He had indeed seen that exact astrological configuration on a night nine years ago. What he had seen and felt that night was like nothing he had ever experienced, save for the night before last.

Still one thing stuck out in his mind. "Charlie got her powers because her parents participated in a government sponsored drug experiment not because of any act of God."

His father remained unfazed. "Yes, but her birthday, the astrological configuration and her power there are too many coincidences."

David's mind was spinning out of control. If his father was right, then that meant the world was ending. It also meant that Charlie would be at the center of the coming war.

"I've never read any of this before Dad."

" And you won't ever either." His father replied. "These prophecies are not written in any holy text. They are a very closely guarded secret known only to a select few."

"Then how do you…" He began.

"That doesn't matter right now." He looked David straight in the eye as if he could see through his calm facade to the fear beneath. "This is much bigger than just the National Security Agency. If I am right, then the end of the world has begun. The people who are searching for this child are far more dangerous than any government agency. They are the agents of the True Dark Lord. Your only chance is for you, Catherine and Charlie to hone your powers."

This was too much. "You've got to be kidding me. It's bad enough that you're trying to get Catherine and I back into this Lightwarrior shit. But Charlie? She's a nine-year-old little girl for Christ's sake. You filled my head up with this crap when I was her age you're not going to do it to Charlie." David broke off, his heart racing both with anger and fear for he knew his father spoke the truth.

"If you care at all for her then you will do as I ask." His father shot back. "Listen to me. This is no longer about drug experiments or government conspiracies. We are talking about true evil. These people will not go away. They will pursue you to the ends of the earth to take this child because she is the key to their victory. You cannot allow them to capture her."

David took an involuntary step backward. His father's words sounded unbelievable, yet he knew them to be true. Something had indeed begun, he felt it deep inside. Now he understood why Charlie had been so distant and easily upset. She had felt it even before he did.

"What happens if they catch her?" It was as if someone else spoke the words. His voice was flat, emotionless and very distant. His anger was gone, washed away by total fear as the full reality of the situation became apparent.

"They will try to make her like them."

"And if they can't?" David already knew the answer before he asked.

"Then they will torture her mercilessly. They will not kill her, but they will make her wish she were dead. They will hurt her so badly that she will do anything to make it stop." His father's voice was low, his eyes never left

David's.

David's heart chilled with horror. "She's just a little girl."

"Yes. That's why you have to protect her and help her complete her role in this battle."

David looked at his father incredulously. "How can we help her unseal the weapons? Do you know where they are, because I sure don't."

"Neither do I, but it doesn't matter." His father replied in a matter-of-fact tone. "If she is the *Sigilla Praevaricator* she will know instinctively where to find the weapons."

"She's just a little girl Dad. It's not fair to tear up her life like this. You said that yourself."

His father's expression became sad. "You're right David it's not fair but her life was torn up long before either of us came into it. You told me that her mother was killed when she was six. She's never going to have a normal life no matter what happens but if we don't do this now she may spend the rest of her life being tortured."

"I guess you're right." David replied with great reluctance. "But it's not fair to make her give up her childhood."

"I know it's hard David. You empathize with her because you grew up in a similar situation but this is what is best for *her*."

"Maybe you're right Dad but I won't make this decision for her. I'll take her to unseal the sword but that's all." He turned and left before his father could reply. He knew his father was right but David could not bring himself to do to Charlie what had been done to him.

II

Shadows bathed a conference room thick with tobacco smoke. Garling stubbed out his cigarette and lit up a second. "The girl has used her power again somewhere in the town of Glen Dunbairn in Scotland."

"Then why haven't we moved yet?" Tarken asked bluntly.

"The directive is to watch them but not move in." McDermott replied.

"Yes, and while we're busy watching them they can be using the girl to unseal the weapon." Tarken answered back.

Garling took a long drag off his cigarette and puffed the smoke out of his nostrils. "Do you really want to challenge *him*?"

Tarken did not reply instead picking up his brandy snifter and sipping it in sullen silence.

"Anyway, we have their IDs flagged. They're not going anywhere."

Tarken set his glass down. "They could have the weapon unsealed in a matter of hours if they want to."

Garling's lips curled into a cold, shark's grin as he took another drag off his cigarette. "I doubt they understand the girl's true potential. I doubt she even knows it herself. And even if they do unseal the weapon do you really think those fools will know what to do with it?"

At that both McDermott and Tarken smiled.

Garling continued. "Both David and Catherine McAuliffe rejected their powers long ago and once the girl has unsealed the first weapon she will be much easier to control."

McDermott nodded as she picked up her brandy snifter and took a slow draft.

Tarken swirled his brandy before taking a slow sip. "What about McAuliffe's father?"

Garling took a final drag from his cigarette and held it for a moment before letting the smoke drift out of his nostrils and stubbing it out in a crystal ashtray. "After they're gone we kill him."

"That leaves us with the McAuliffs." Tarken replied as he slowly poured brandy into his snifter.

"We bring them in alive and unharmed." As he spoke Garling took out a third cigarette and lit it with his silver Zippo. "They'll prove useful in controlling the girl."

Tarken sipped his brandy. "Is there any word about when we move?"

"No." McDermott refilled her snifter. "The only word is wait."

III

Two gentlemen sit at a table in a dark barroom. There is a chessboard between them, the pieces are set for a game. Both gentlemen are attractive but as opposite in dress and appearance as the pieces on the chessboard.

The dark gentleman makes the first move. "They have discovered the girl's secret."

The gentleman in white inclines his head as he makes his first move. "So, they have."

The dark gentleman makes his second move. "It has begun."

The gentleman in white makes a counter move. "So, it has."

The two gentlemen raise their beer mugs and drink.

Chapter 9
The Island Of Magic

I

Charlie drifted in darkness for an unknown length of time, her mind pleasantly blank. She felt nothing, knew nothing. Fear and hurt were miles away.

Charlie.

The word seemed to come from within.

Charlie time to wake up.

She recognized the voice but could not place it.

Come on Charlie we have a big day ahead of us.

Charlie groaned and turned away wanting to sleep longer, not wanting to face the fear and horror that awaited her upon waking.

Wake up Charlie.

She turned onto her back and opened her eyes to see David sitting on the bed beside her.

"Hi Charlie. How do you feel?"

"Good." She did feel good. The sense of impending danger was still there but it had retreated into the back of her mind.

David smiled. "That's good." Behind his smile Charlie sensed apprehension, as if he were trying to work up the courage to do or say something. "I made you breakfast, pancakes, your favorite."

Charlie smiled back. "Thank you." She was nervous now too. Whatever David wanted it was bothering him enough to make him very anxious.

David ruffled her hair and stood up. "Why don't you get dressed while I put your breakfast on the table."

"Okay."

Charlie dressed quickly then hurried downstairs. The kitchen table was set for two. David directed her to the chair on the left where he had set out a glass of orange juice and a huge plate of blueberry pancakes, then he sat down across from her.

After breakfast David took her into the living room and sat down with her on the couch. For a moment neither spoke a word. Charlie felt that David wanted her to do something and waited for him to ask. She sensed David struggling to gather up his courage. Finally, he spoke.

"I was talking to my Dad last night Charlie. He is concerned for you"

She looked up at him. "Because of my pyrokinesis?"

David eyes filled with compassion. "No, this is something else besides that." His voice was gentle, but Charlie could sense anger behind it. It was not with her, for her he felt remorse, but with…

His father?

She was confused. She had only spoken four or five words to David's father since arriving but she *had* felt his concern for them, especially David. She could not understand why David would be angry with him.

David continued. "My Dad thinks you may be the *Sigilla Praevaricator*."

"What's the *Sigilla Praevaricator*?" This was something of which she knew nothing and had no understanding.

David's expression became blank. He spoke in a slow and deliberate tone. "Before the world was created the forces of light and darkness agreed that mankind would settle their conflict. As part of that agreement two weapons were forged and then sealed away. When the weapons were needed a person would be born with the power to recover them. That person is called the *Sigilla Praevaricator*, the Breaker of Seals."

In her heart Charlie felt he was holding something back. Something significant. As she looked into David's eyes she felt fear building beneath his anger.

He feels it too.

Somehow all of this fit together. She was certain of it. The feeling, the nuclear bombing, and this story about the *Sigilla Praevaricator* were all connected somehow. And she was at the center of it all.

David was looking at her with concern in his eyes. "I don't know what to think. I don't know if I believe any of this or not. All I do know is that we can't keep running like this, and if he's right…" David sucked in a slow breath over his teeth. "If he's right then things could get a lot worse. And if this story about the *Sigilla Praevaricator* is true then you will know where to find the weapon of light and if you can find it then we might have a chance to be safe."

Charlie nodded and closed her eyes. *I don't know where the weapon is. I don't even know what it is. I don't…*

Slowly something began to take shape in her mind.

II

[There is an ancient island on the high seas. Known by many names this is the resting place of many heroes. The Dragon King of Camelot came here to slumber. A place of power that can be reached from any body of water, but only by those who know the spell, this is the Island of Magic]

III

Thirty minutes later she was in another hired car with David and Catherine. They drove until they reached the very northern tip of Scotland. It was noon by this time, so they stopped for lunch. After eating they rented a small rowboat and headed out on the ocean. Strong winds and choppy water tossed and shook the little boat.

When they were out past the breakers Charlie turned to David.

"Stop."

He pulled the oars out of the water and let the boat drift. Though he said nothing David's expression was questioning.

Charlie did not quite understand herself, but she had a strong feeling that they had to stop *now*. She slowly stood up. David tried to stop her, saying something about her falling in the water, but she slipped out of his grasp. There was something she had to do.

The water rocked the boat roughly making it difficult for her to stay on her feet, but she kept her balance. She felt the power moving within her, rapidly building to a crescendo. Charlie made no attempt to restrain it. The wind picked up, stirring up the water further and making it increasingly difficult for her to remain standing. David and Catherine were calling to her.

"Sit down!"

"Charlie you're going to fall in if you don't sit down! You're going to get hurt."

Their voices were sharp with fear.

Charlie ignored them.

The power continued to build within her. The wind stiffened into a strong gale. Angry waves pitched the little boat around like a toy. At the same time the sky began to darken. Lightning flicked between dark menacing clouds followed seconds later by the roar of thunder. The air began to shimmer with heat.

Charlie was frightened but continued to allow the power to flow freely. Invisible waves swept through the air around her bending the water below and the dark clouds above. The power was blazing now, raging out of control. She could feel its heat even as she saw it in the air. The water beneath the boat had come alive to a furious boil. Thick clouds of steam rose around her. All at once the air began to *bend*. White lightning struck the water, temporarily blinding her.

IV

When her vision returned Charlie found herself lying on her back in the bottom of the boat. The power was silent. The wind and water had calmed, and the clouds had cleared leaving a perfect orange and blue streaked sky. She groaned and sat up. A large island loomed over the horizon. The current was slowly drawing them closer to its beaches.

From the island Charlie felt an incredible power, a power beyond even her own. It flowed in the air like a warm breeze. A smile of contentment stretched across her face. In that moment she felt relaxed and at peace. This feeling was accompanied by a feeling of intense almost delirious pleasure.

She was enrapt for a moment before reason returned. The island before her was not any part of Scotland or England. She was certain of that. This was a place like nowhere she had ever been before. Charlie turned and shook David's shoulder.

"David. David wake up."

He did not respond.

She shook him again more forcefully. "David wake up."

He stirred, and his eyes slid open. "Charlie?" His voice and expression were confused. "What the hell happened?"

She shook her head slowly. "I don't know."

As he sat up David's eyes widened with surprise and fear. "Where the hell are we?"

Charlie looked up at him with fear in her heart. "I don't know." Until now it had not occurred to her to be afraid.

David turned and shook Catherine. She groaned and tried to turn away at first but then turned on her back and opened her eyes.

"Where are we David?" Her face was bewildered.

David shook his head returning an equally confused expression. "I don't know."

Catherine turned her glance to Charlie. In her eyes and heart Charlie saw deep fear. "What happened? Was it your power?"

Charlie returned a blank expression but said nothing. There was no reason for it, but in her heart, she felt sudden, immense shapeless guilt. "I...I don't know." She was close to tears yet still did not understand why. "I let the power go but there was no fire. I...I don't know what happened."

Catherine watched her for a moment longer before looking away.

The boat continued drifting towards the island. With each moment they grew nearer to its beaches. The feeling of power grew, bringing with it ever intensifying pleasure. Her smile returned despite the fear pulsing in her blood.

She turned to see that David and Catherine too were smiling despite their growing fear. No one in the boat moved. The three just sat and watched as they drifted ever closer to the island. It was the dull thud of the boat striking the sandy beach that finally broke the spell.

Charlie stood up first and climbed out of the boat. David and Catherine followed her a moment later. No one spoke. The power of the island kept their voices still. In her mind Charlie knew this place, not by name but by feel. It was as if she had always been here. She felt more at home in that moment than she had ever felt anywhere, even back in Taylor. The feeling was almost frightening.

This is my home. A statement not a question.

She was crossing the beach to the woods beyond, barely aware of her surroundings. Her mind was still trying to process her revelation. This was her home. She felt certain of it.

As she neared the edge of the forest David called to her.

She did not respond at first.

"Charlie wait for us!" His voice was higher and sharper this time.

Charlie stopped in her tracks and made a slow turn to face him. "Okay." Her voice came out confused.

David and Catherine hurried to catch up with her.

David bent down and gave her a strange look. "Are you alright Charlie?"

"Yes." She was frightened and confused but, otherwise all right.

"Okay." He took her hand. "Let's go then. But I want you to stay with us from now on. Don't run ahead anymore. Okay?"

She nodded.

The three of them walked through the woods for what seemed like endless miles yet when they emerged from the forest at the foot of the northern mountains the sun was still orange in the sky, having barely moved at all. Furthermore, she did not feel tired. It was as if she had only walked around the block. The feeling of power was stronger now. It was tantalizingly close.

David looked up at the mountain's rugged side and frowned. "You wouldn't happen to know an easier way up Charlie?"

She studied the mountain dubiously. Directly ahead was a steep, rocky bluff that seemed to stretch for miles in both directions. Way off in the distance the bluff sharpened into a cliff. She didn't see any…

What's that?

Charlie stared intently at the mountain. Far off to the west, barely visible beneath the setting sun was a thin ribbon of green and brown running up the mountain.

Is that a path?

It was. She was sure of it.

Charlie turned and looked up at David. "There."

She pointed. "There's a path."

He squinted and shielded his eyes with his hand. "I don't…." He broke off. "Yeah okay. I see it." David took up her hand. "Let's go."

She nodded.

The three of them turned and headed west. Again they walked for what seemed like hours without penalty of time or fatigue.

The ribbon was little more than a narrow trail, rocky and overgrown with weeds and grass. As she walked along the path Charlie felt the power growing, changing from an awareness to a call. Someone or something was beckoning, welcoming her.

Charlie followed the call, walking in a near trance like state. It grew stronger with each step she took. David and Catherine were talking, she heard and understood their words but took little notice. Her mind focused only on the call. The air was strangely quiet on the mountain. In the forest she had heard bird calls, rustling leaves, sounds of life, but the mountain was silent save for the whistle of the wind. Charlie took brief note before her mind returned to the call.

The path went up and up and the further she went along it the steeper it became. Rock and grass gave way to snow and ice. Yet strangely enough she did not feel cold.

Under other circumstances she would have found this quite remarkable but right then she took only fleeting notice. Her mind was consumed by the ever-increasing power tugging at her heart. She was close, she could feel it.

They were halfway up the side of the mountain. Directly ahead the path passed through a narrow notch not visible from the base. Charlie paused to check that David and Catherine were still behind her before continuing on.

The notch went on for what seemed like several miles before opening upon the mountain's summit. From where she stood Charlie could see for miles. The view was spectacular, but she could not appreciate it for the long walk she saw ahead of her. The path went down the side of the mountain on which she stood and passed over several smaller ones before leading up the side of a huge mountain on the edge of the horizon.

Charlie glanced back at David and Catherine once more and then resumed walking.

V

After a very long time had passed Charlie found herself at the foot of the massive mountain she had seen from the first summit. She was not tired despite the rugged terrain and long distance she had traveled.

The feeling of power had grown very strong. The air pulsated with its force. Charlie looked as far up the mountain as she could feeling both frightened and excited at once. She shivered slightly and then began to walk.

The pull on her heart had become irresistible. Blood rushed through her veins, driven to high speed by her racing heart.

The path quickly grew steep. Charlie took little notice continuing on with purpose as though each step were lighter than the last. It seemed to take forever to travel the path, yet it was as if no time had passed at all. She did not feel tired. In fact, she felt as if she had not walked at all.

Near the top of the mountain the path led into a cave. Charlie stood at the mouth starring off into its inky darkness. Near the opening crystal stalactites and stalagmites glittered in the dying sunlight. Further inside she saw nothing but total blackness.

If there was an exit she could not see it, yet she felt the power calling to her from within. Without thinking, Charlie took a wooden torch from where it hung on the wall and ignited it with her power before entering the cave.

David called to her from behind, something about waiting for Catherine and him, but she paid no attention.

The cave was massive within and beautifully decorated by multicolored limestone and glittering crystals, but Charlie took only passing notice as she strode further into the cavern.

This was sacred ground. Ground that no person had seen in ages. She felt certain of this despite the torches and other signs of human presence.

Something crunched under her foot. Without looking down Charlie knew it was bone. An arm maybe, or a leg. Still she continued on without reacting.

The cave sloped upward. Charlie had to tread carefully to avoid slipping on the wet limestone floor. With each step she took the call grew stronger. She was nearing the end of the cave. She was certain of it.

Moments later the inky blackness of the cave was penetrated by slender bars of rich golden sunlight.

Charlie quickened her pace, knowing that she was almost there. The feeling of power was overwhelming. It washed through her in waves bringing goose bumps to her skin. Something incredible lay beyond. A power beyond anything she had ever known. She trembled with anticipation.

A moment later Charlie reached the end of the cave and froze, heart in her mouth.

The cave opened onto a narrow, rocky ledge facing out over the water. The view was incredible but that was not what had made her stop.

Though nothing appeared out of the ordinary she knew she was close. The air vibrated with power. She felt something else as well, a powerful sense of desolation. Something horrible had happened here. Charlie shuddered hard and began walking again. As she walked along the rocky ledge the feeling grew stronger.

The ledge circled the mountain once in an upward spiral. As it neared the peak the path widened and became grassy.

Upon reaching the summit Charlie found herself standing at the edge of a field. Scattered here and there were life sized, elaborately detailed human statues.

Except they weren't statues they were people, men, women and children, locked in stone. She could hear their cries of anguish in her mind and heart.

Tears spilled down her cheeks. It was horrible. Some of them had been here for centuries, alive and aware but unable to speak or move.

Charlie walked through the field with slow steps, looking over each statue. She was crying out right now. It hurt to look at them. She wanted more than anything to help but she did not know how. The urge to hug them was strong too but she was afraid to touch them.

"Are you okay Charlie?"

She slowly turned to the sound of David's voice tears streaming down her cheeks. "It's so sad. They're crying for help."

He nodded.

She sensed that David felt it too though not as strongly. "All those people." His voice was heavy with grief and fear.

David was deeply concerned for her. He approached her slowly and bent down to take her into his arms but before he could Charlie turned and continued walking through the field. The cries grew louder and more desperate as she went on. Her heart bled for these poor people doomed to spend eternity imprisoned in stone.

Those poor people. This must be what war is like. Hundreds of people crying in pain begging for help. Begging for someone to put them out of their misery.

For a moment she almost considered it. She could have used the power to destroy the statues and at least put an end to these people's suffering.

But that's killing and killing is wrong.

And burning to death was a horrible, painful death in and of itself. Still it was hard for her to accept the fact that she could not help these poor souls.

I'm so sorry. I wish there were something I could do.

Help.

Please help us.

The cries echoed on and on tearing her heart to pieces. Charlie lowered her head sobbing as she continued on.

The field ended in a sharp precipice. As she neared the cliff edge Charlie noticed that the statues were no longer standing but kneeling, as if begging for mercy or praying.

Near the drop off, looking out over the ocean was a statue of a young girl about her age. The girl was kneeling with her arms extended in a gesture of pleading. Charlie could feel the depth of the girl's anguish. She was crying, sobbing inside. The power of her suffering struck Charlie like a wave.

She felt something else as well. This was it, the source of the power. The weapon was here though she could not see it.

Charlie stopped two feet away from the girl as she felt the first stirrings of power within. Those stirrings quickly grew to a raging pulse as the power swept through her. Every nerve ending in her body seemed to tingle at once and still the power continued to build giving no signs of slowing. The tingling soon became pleasant warmth, enveloping her. This quickly intensified to the point where it was almost painful. She was smiling through her tears now.

All at once a bright column of light streaked down from the sky and struck the ground in front of the girl surrounding both of them in its brilliance. The power of the light was indescribable in its magnitude. The pleasure it brought was beyond anything she had ever known. Standing within the light her power seemed insignificant, a plaything, a tiny spark in a burst of beautiful fireworks. This was the true power, this was the power of whatever god stood above in the heavens. In that moment she knew that everything she had read was true. All of it, even the most implausible parts, was gospel truth. The realization was both exciting and frightening.

She was lifting off the ground now, floating delicately in the air. Her legs hung loose beneath her, yet she felt no weight on her hips. It was as though some great invisible hand had taken her up in its gentle grasp.

Her power was still moving but it was not the same. It had become one with the power around her, moving in its pattern, bearing its qualities. The light was growing brighter to the point of being painful, yet she felt no discomfort. As the light's brilliance grew to where she could no longer see anything but white she felt only comfort and pleasure. Even her power did not frighten her though it was totally out of her control.

An unconscious delirious smile had spread across her face. To all the world she would have looked drunk or stoned out of her mind though in truth she remained lucid. She was fascinated by this new power. Thousands of questions rushed through her mind.

Is this what God is like?

Have I touched Him?

Is that what's happening?

And many others besides. The power continued to build in intensity for a few moments longer before rapidly retracting. In a matter of seconds, the beam of light had faded in brilliance and shrunk to where it only surrounded the ground in front of the girl. Then it was gone. In its place, lying across the girl's outstretched arms was a long, brilliant silver sword. From it pulsated a power much like that which she had just felt.

VI

With trembling hands Charlie bent down and picked up the sword. She felt as though she had touched a live wire. Raw power flowed through her making the hairs on her arms stand on end. The blade seemed to almost sing as she lifted it and pointed it upwards. There was nothing fancy about the sword, only a steel blade and hilt polished to a silvery gleam and a wooden handle. Except there was more than that. The sword seemed to glow by itself, without the sun shining on it and it seemed to almost vibrate in her hands as if the blade had been struck. As she looked at it she noticed something else as well, letters or symbols of a kind that she had never seen before had been etched into one side of the blade. Though she did not recognize the markings she understood their meaning at once.

Deus Irae

Wrath of God

Though they translated to Latin the markings were in fact much older than Latin and from a language other than human. It was strange, the markings seemed to glow with a light more brilliant than the rest of the sword making her think of Frodo Baggins' magic ring.

Charlie stared at them a moment longer before lowering the sword and turning towards David and Catherine. Both were wide-eyed with surprise and fear.

She too should have been frightened yet she was not. She knew nothing of what had happened, only that she had somehow been touched by God. She also understood that she had to make a decision now. She could keep this weapon, *Deus Irae*, or give it to David or Catherine.

The sword's power pulsated in her hands, broadening her senses. As she held it Charlie felt herself carried away to a crossroads in a yellow wood.

To her right Charlie saw a narrow, path bathed in rich, golden sunlight. Here, pink and rose-colored flowers blossomed upon the trees, filling the air with their light, sweet scent. Though beautiful, to Charlie the path felt desolate. A cold breeze flowed across the rough cut, woodland path and upon it Charlie sensed only loneliness.

This path would have Charlie keep the sword and fulfill its purpose herself. In that moment Charlie understood that to keep the sword would mean facing the darkness alone again. It would also mean that she would have to walk away from any possibility for revenge upon the people who had killed Daddy and Mommy. The sword would never permit itself to be used for personal vengeance as it had but a single purpose.

As she looked down the righthand path, Charlie saw that it led out of the woods and into the warm sunlight and yet she turned from this path for she could not bear to be alone again.

No, that wasn't exactly the truth. Though she loved David and Catherine and did not want to lose them, they were not the only reason for her decision.

Deep inside, the bloodstain of *Hate!* demanded that she exact revenge upon the men and women who had killed Daddy and Mommy and though she knew this desire was wrong she could not abandon it.

And so she turned from the right hand path to its left more counterpart. Here, this second path led deeper into the woods. Massive, old growth, trees shrouded this path in shadow. Yet, despite the darkness, the breeze here felt warmer and carried a slight scent of, of all things…

Fresh brewed coffee, frying bacon, French toast.

All scents she associated with home, with Daddy and Mommy, with David and Catherine. As she took in the rich aromas Charlie understood that taking this path would require her to give up the sword but would allow her to remain with David and Catherine. And, without the sword to bar her, revenge for the death of Daddy and Mommy, would still be available to her.

Charlie understood that as each path leads on to another once she had chosen, she would be committed and would never return. Still she kept the right-hand path for another day, promising herself that she could always ask for the sword back and yet knowing that she would most certainly never return to this crossroads again. As she took her first step upon the left-hand path, Charlie understood the import of her choice. Everything would change from this moment. In an instant Charlie found herself returned to the rocky ledge. David and

Catherine stood before her, looking on with concern.

Charlie returned their gaze steadily. Both were concerned for her, but Catherine's concern was overshadowed by doubt and fear. She was frightened by what she had witnessed, frightened of the power she had felt and still felt, frightened of Charlie. Charlie sensed Catherine questioning the wisdom of coming here and helping Charlie unseal this weapon. Catherine was questioning Charlie, wondering who she really was, wondering…

Charlie forcibly closed her mind before she learned anymore.

She then turned to David. In him she sensed doubt and fear as well but also faith. He trusted her. To him she was an innocent child who had the misfortune of being born with a power she had neither asked for nor wanted.

Charlie was touched and had to suppress the urge to cry. She looked at David for a moment longer before feeling confident enough to decide. She went to him with slow steps and put the sword in his hand. David took the weapon and studied it for a moment before putting it aside and taking her into his arms.

"Come on Charlie. Let's get out of here."

She tried on a slight smile. "Okay."

David bent down with her still in his arms and took up the sword then turned back towards the path.

Chapter 10
Surrender

I

It was dark out when they finally returned to the farm. Both Catherine and Charlie were asleep. David gently woke Catherine, then quietly got out of the car and went around to Charlie's door. She was lying limp in the corner between the backseat and the rear driver's side door. Her chest gently lifted and fell with each breath. Her blond hair, down past her waist now, lay about her like a blanket. She was beautiful even in sleep.

David's mouth turned up into a slight smile as he scooped her up, taking care not to wake her. Though slender Charlie was not a lightweight. She had been heavy last month when he and Catherine found her in Central Park and she had gained at least five pounds that he could count. Still he enjoyed carrying her despite the weight.

As he turned away from the car David stole a glance at the trunk where the sword lay. For a moment he felt its power calling to him before exhaustion washed the sensation from his mind. He would have to return for it before dismissing the driver.

David turned away and started towards the house. His father was standing on the porch looking almost as tired as David felt. The two nodded to each other as David crossed the porch. Behind him Catherine's footsteps rang on the wooden porch steps.

"Hello Catherine." His father spoke in a low voice heavy with fatigue and concern.

"Hi." Catherine's voice was tired and emotionless.

David did not stop to listen. He wanted to put Charlie to bed before she woke up. As he carried her up the oak stairs David glanced at the grandfather clock by the wall and saw that it was four in the morning, on Friday. They had been on the island for five days then.

Strange how it only felt like a few hours.

Under other circumstances David would have found this both fascinating and frightening but right now he was too tired to care much.

Charlie seemed to be growing heavier by the moment. His arms trembled under her weight. It wasn't that he couldn't handle her, but his body felt ragged out. Traveling through the mountains on the island had completely drained his strength though he had not become aware of this until after they returned.

Upon reaching the top of the stairs he entered the first bedroom on the left. This had once been his room. Now it was Charlie's. David balanced her on one arm while he drew back the blankets with the other. As he gently laid her on the bed Charlie moaned softly and stirred. For a moment he thought she would awaken but she only turned on her side. David drew the blankets up over her body and kissed her on the cheek.

"Good night Charlie. You did good."

She mumbled something in return.

"I love you."

David turned and left the room in silence, flicking the light off as he passed the switch. He left the door open a crack so that he would hear her if she should wake.

After putting Charlie to bed David went back out to the car, recovered the sword, and dismissed the driver. Though exhausted, David did not feel sleepy, so he went into the living room. There he found Catherine and his father. Their conversation ceased as he entered the room.

David's father stood up and went to him. "I'm glad to see you've returned safely. I was concerned when you didn't come back."

David saw the harried expression on his father's face and felt guilty. "I'm sorry we made you worry Dad. Whatever island we were on..." He broke off. "I don't know the time must have been different or something because it seemed like only a few hours."

His father's face became curious. For a moment he looked disposed to say something.

As he thought back David felt frightened again. He wasn't really sure what had happened on that strange island. He had seen and felt things unlike anything he had ever experienced before save for that night in the morgue. "It was strange. We walked most of the way across the island through dense forest and over rough mountain trails but none of us felt tired until we left the island. It was easy. Much easier than it should have been."

His father was silent, his expression contemplative.

"You got it though." There was something he was holding back. David sensed that he had come to some sort of realization.

Sudden anger flashed in David's heart. He wasn't exactly sure why. "Yeah we got it."

His father nodded. "Sit down then. Let me get you a drink. You look like you need one." He turned to Catherine. "Both of you."

That said David's father went to the glass faced liquor cabinet and took out a crystal decanter of Scotch and two whiskey glasses. He then filled both glasses and gave one each to David and Catherine.

David looked up at him questioningly. "So, what now?"

His father poured himself a whiskey and sat down. "Now the three of you must begin your training."

David took a slow sip from his drink. "No. I won't throw my life away on that crap and I'm certainly not going to ask Charlie to do it."

"It's not crap." His father replied in a flat tone as he sipped his whiskey. "I'm surprised that you don't believe it. After all you've seen you still don't believe me."

David took another sip of liquor and rolled it around in his mouth before swallowing it. "This is just too much Dad. You're asking the three of us to throw away everything we have and run off on some damned crusade based on a bunch of obscure legends."

"You know it's more than that David." His father replied dryly. "The NSA would not spend this much energy pursuing a child unless she's very special. You know this child is more than an Enlightened. She was touched by God. She would not have been able to find the weapon if she were not."

David swirled his whiskey. "She is very special, I'm not denying that, but that does not mean that she or any of us have to throw away a normal life."

In his heart David knew that his life was already irrevocably changed, as were the lives of Catherine and Charlie but he would not admit it even to himself. Moreover, he would not knowingly drag Charlie into a foolish crusade.

She's already involved idiot.

His conscience tormented him over this for she was just a child. David knocked back the rest of his drink, then stood up and poured himself another. "She's a little girl for God's sake. It's not right to do this to her. She deserves to have a childhood."

His father nodded as he sipped his Scotch. "Yes, she deserves to have a childhood but that has already been taken from her. The NSA and the people behind it will not leave her alone no matter what you do."

"He's right." Catherine replied in a soft tone as she took her first sip of Scotch. "And we don't have time to argue." She glanced at David's father. "What do we need to do?"

"The three of you must be trained as Lightwarriors. Especially Charlie. She is strong willed and powerful but if they capture her it will be difficult for her to resist being corrupted. If she becomes a Lightwarrior it will be more difficult for them to break her." David's father paused to sip his Scotch. "There isn't much time, so we'll start tomorrow."

David looked at his father expressionlessly. He didn't know how to feel. Frustration, anger, fear and sadness swirled within him. His father was right, probably more right than he knew but David could not accept this. He wanted so much to disappear, to take Catherine and Charlie and disappear into normalcy. He hated the power, hated it for what it had made him. All his life, all he had ever wanted to be was normal. He had always known that it was impossible, but he still clung to this illusion for as far back as he could remember. To do as his father wanted would be to abandon his dream for all time. Moreover, he would be making the same choice for Charlie and as much as he had suffered for his powers she had suffered far more.

David felt terrible for what Charlie had experienced in her short nine years of life. It wasn't right. She had never had a childhood. Even if he could not have a normal life he would at least give Charlie the chance to be a little girl. "No. I'll do whatever you want but leave Charlie out of this."

Dad shook his head. "She has to be trained. It's her only protection if she is taken."

David started to argue back but stopped. There was no point. His father was only repeating what he already knew to be true. He had felt the change and he had seen what Charlie did on the island. She was not normal, not even for an Enlightened; he had never done anything like that. The world was ending, and Charlie was the *Sigilla Praevaricator*. Her fate was inextricably linked to the change and the events to come. There was no escaping this fact. David gulped down his drink and stood up. "I'm going to bed."

His father stood up and placed a hand on his shoulder. "Good night David."

Though neither spoke something passed between the two of them. An agreement or perhaps a surrender.

As he climbed the stairs David thought to himself: *How can a just God do something like this to a child?*

II

David lay awake for a long time trying to understand what he had seen. Charlie had gone right to the sword as if she had known where it was all the time. She had known exactly what to do to get to the island and once on the island exactly where to go. And she had known how to unseal the sword once she found its resting place. Yet in the car she had told him she only knew they had to go north. In his mind David saw Charlie standing in the little wooden rowboat, her hair blowing out behind her in a golden comet tail, her eyes blank yet sharply focused. He remembered feeling her fear and confusion, her curiosity. He remembered the phenomenal, almost God-like power that had flowed within her, through her. The feeling was still burned into his senses, like the after image of a bright light on the inside of a closed eyelid.

Dad was right. She is more than an Enlightened. She is very special. But she's just a little girl. It's not fair to take away her childhood.

The image of the small, blond haired child standing in the wave tossed boat was now replaced by an image of the same child standing near a cliff edge looking out over the ocean a statue of another little girl at her feet. Again, her perfect blond hair flowed behind her this time set ablaze by the dying sunlight.

His body trembled as he remembered the power he had felt in that moment. This power had been far beyond anything he had ever felt before save for that night in the morgue. Like in the morgue it had encircled Charlie, flowing from her and through her, enveloping her in its white brilliance. An echo of this power remained with him even still, burning upon his senses in a tingling after-image. David's flesh felt cold.

What did I see that day?

Who is she?

Sudden fear pulsed in his blood for this confirmed what he had already sensed. Something had begun, a terrible, momentous thing that would change everything. It was slow and not readily visible in its full magnitude, but the groundswell had begun. There was no denying it now.

III

The first thing she noticed was the smoke, thick and oily, it filled the air like a black bloodstain. The stench of raw gasoline was strong, the air hot and close. Charlie groaned and eased herself into a sitting position.

Fire burned all around her. The remains of the cars she had destroyed, the wreckage of the police station, and sections of the parking lot itself continued to blaze brightly. Her father was crouched beside her. His eyes registered concern.

"Charlie? Charlie are you alright?"

She looked at him fearfully. "What happened?" Her mind was a confused jumble of fragmented memories and emotions. "Why is everything on fire? Am I doing it?"

She did not feel the power, but she couldn't imagine anything else that could have done this.

All at once the fragments came together and she remembered. Tears spilled down her cheeks. "I did this. Me."

Daddy took her into his arms. "It isn't your fault Charlie."

"But I burned down the police station. I burned up all those people…I…I" She couldn't finish. She was crying too hard.

Daddy clasped her tight to his chest. "Shhh. It will be alright Charlie. Everything will be alright." He was lying. As upset as she was Charlie knew it at once.

She looked down and away unable to look at the fire or her father.

Bad girl!

Very bad!

Look what you did!

She wept bitterly. There was no force behind her tears, only deep remorse. She had done a terrible thing. She had killed people. Her eyes and cheeks burned with deep sorrow.

I killed them…all of them.

All at once the raw gasoline stench became tinged with that of scorched and burning human flesh. The smell was like some perverted backyard barbecue. Charlie's stomach lurched violently, and it was only by sheer force of will that she did not vomit.

"Don't cry Charlie. Everything will be fine." Her father spoke with no conviction. His voice was tense. As he spoke Daddy held her to his chest. "Everything will be fine."

Charlie buried her face in his shoulder still crying piteously.

Daddy stroked her hair. "Shhh. It will be alright. You don't have to cry anymore. It was not your fault."

She looked up at him slowly, unbelievingly. "But I burned down the police station. I killed all those people."

"Charlie, I know you didn't mean it." He paused and sighed. "You did it to protect us both. You have nothing to feel bad about." He was telling the truth but there was also something he was holding back.

Charlie held his glance for a moment longer before turning her eyes away. A siren wailed in the distance. Daddy's grip changed.

"Come on we need to get out of here before the firemen get here."

Charlie did not respond. She wasn't crying anymore but her eyes ran anyway.

Daddy held her tight against his chest and ran across the parking lot to the street. There was an old Ford F-150 pickup truck parked along the opposite curb. Daddy carried her around to the passenger side and set her down on the seat then walked around to the driver's side and got in.

Daddy reached down for the key, but the ignition was empty. "Damn it!" He turned to her. "Charlie, I need your help. We need to get out of here. I do not have the key. There is no time to hot wire it." He did not have to tell her that he would not be able to drive if he used his power.

She looked up at him miserably. "Do I have to?"

"I am sorry Charlie."

Fresh tears spilled down her cheeks. "Please don't make me."

"Charlie, we need to get away *now*." Daddy's voice was stern but inside him she sensed concern and tension that could almost be mistaken for *guilt?*

Why? I was the one who… She pushed the thought aside before it could play itself out.

"Please Charlie. I need your help."

A half sigh half sob escaped her throat. "Ok."

Charlie turned her glance on the ignition then reached out with her mind and *shoved* it. In an instant the engine roared to life. The power spun within her. Charlie forced it down.

Stop it!

Stop it now!

Steel spikes ripped through her skull bringing fresh tears to her eyes. Still she would not let go.

Not again!

I won't do it again!

The power continued to race in her mind for a few moments longer before it was silent.

Daddy was looking at her with concern in his eyes. "Are you okay honey?"

"Yes." She was lying. Her head ached, and she felt on the verge of tears.

Daddy patted her leg. "Thank you, Charlie."

They were moving now, houses and trees slipped by on either side of the pickup truck. The smell of burning was still strong, but it had begun to fade. Charlie stared straight ahead, unable to look at what she had done.

The siren wails were very close now. Fierce tremors took Charlie's body. *What if they catch us? What will they do to Daddy and me?*

Silent tears streamed down her cheeks. *I'm a murderer. I burned up all those people. I killed them on purpose.* The pickup truck accelerated as they left town. *I killed them all.*

She closed her eyes in shame but even here there was no escape. The firestorm burned on behind her eyelids. Endless images danced before her, flashing faster and faster, bleeding together into one solid orange and yellow blaze before fading into darkness.

IV

When the darkness broke and she opened her eyes, Daddy had stopped at a McDonalds beside the road. He ordered them each a Big Mac, super-sized fries and large Sprites. Charlie ate half of her hamburger and a handful of fries and threw the rest away.

She wasn't hungry, and the smell of the food nauseated her as it reminded her of the smell of the government agents as they burned. She was, however, very thirsty and gulped down her soda.

Before leaving Daddy took her into the bathroom, where she threw up the little bit of food she had eaten. Though he said nothing Charlie knew Daddy was concerned for her.

Charlie went to sleep not long after they got back on the road and did not awaken until the middle of the next day. By this time Daddy had stopped again for food at a Wendy's. Charlie ate less than she had the night before and again promptly threw up what little she did eat.

Food was no longer appealing to her. The smell of cooked meat brought back images of the massacre at the Ephrata police station.

After leaving the restaurant Charlie fell asleep. She felt crushing exhaustion all the time now and it was easier to sleep than face the reality of what she had done.

Daddy awoke her sometime after dark. He had pulled into a wooded park. The area was deserted save for a single pickup truck whose owner was nowhere in sight. The only building was a small brick structure, which housed the bathrooms.

Neither Charlie nor her father had to go. Instead they walked hand in hand across the parking lot to where it sloped off into a soft embankment, then descended into the woods below.

The air was hauntingly quiet. The road they had come from was deserted and because of the season there were no crickets or owls to disturb the oppressive silence. Even the wind was as still as death.

The air was bitter cold and sliced through her clothes like a razor. Charlie shuddered hard as she walked through the trees.

Her tremors could not be accounted for by cold alone. In her mind she saw fire sweeping across asphalt and cars exploding like bombs. Her heart burned with guilt.

After walking a short distance, they sat down at one of the many picnic tables scattered throughout the woods. Charlie stared at the weathered wooden table, eyes and cheeks hot with shame. She was a killer, a murderer. She had burned those people up.

I'll never do that again. I'll never use it again. Never.

Again, she saw the fire sweeping across the parking lot as if someone had laid trails of gasoline on the asphalt. Again, she heard the screams of the dying as they were swallowed by the flames.

I deserve to die for killing those people.

Daddy was watching her with concerned eyes. "In another day or two we will be in Texas. From there we can cross the border into Mexico. Then we can book passage on a freighter to Europe." His words were quick and forced as if she were accusing him with her silence.

Charlie looked up at him slowly. It hurt her to meet her father's eyes. "Daddy please promise me you won't ever ask me to light another fire because if you did I'd do it and then I guess I'd kill myself. So please...never...never." She broke off sobbing.

Daddy took her into his arms. "Don't talk like that Charlie. I love you and I do not want you to hurt yourself." He touched her face gently. "Charlie, I do not know if I can promise you that I will never ask you to light another fire, but I can promise to try. Is that good enough?"

She looked up at him again but said nothing. She was still weeping.

He clasped her tight against his chest. "It will be alright Charlie. Somehow everything will be alright."

She hadn't believed him at the time, but she would never have imagined just how wrong he was.

V

Charlie laid awake most of that night starring at the dim, moonless sky. She cried on and off until she finally cried herself to sleep.

Daddy awakened her early the next morning. Neither of them was hungry so they drove for an hour before stopping for breakfast. Charlie ate like a bird but managed to keep the food down this time, though it sat in her stomach like a stone.

It was colder that morning than the night before and the sky had filled with clouds. By mid-morning it was snowing hard; an hour later Daddy was forced to stop.

For some time now, they had been driving between barren farm fields along a double lane road only a hair wider than a bike path. Daddy had been avoiding the interstates all along for fear of being caught. Instead he had taken them along a labyrinth of State and US highways. Their progress was slow. Early that morning they crossed the Ohio state line into Indiana.

They might have been close to a town or city, but the heavy snowfall made it impossible to tell. The winds had picked up whistling through the open fields and whipping the falling snow into swirls of white. Fierce shudders washed through Charlie's flesh. The pickup truck cab was not well insulated, and her clothing offered her little protection from the bitter cold.

Daddy looked over to her with concern in his eyes. "It appears we will be here for a while." When he saw her shivering his concern deepened and he took off his jacket and handed it to her. "Take my jacket. You need it more than I do."

She became concerned. "Oh no I couldn't. You'll freeze."

"It is fine Charlie. Take it." He draped it over her shoulders before she could argue anymore. "You look very cold. I can live without it for a little while."

Charlie smiled up at her father feeling both grateful and guilty at once. He was lying. She didn't need psychic senses to know that Daddy was as cold as she was. Charlie drew Daddy's jacket closer around her shoulders and snuggled up against him. "I love you Daddy."

He hugged her to his chest. "I love you too."

The two remained like that, neither speaking a word, as they waited out the blizzard.

Sometime later the storm died down a little.

Daddy released her and pulled back onto the road. "The storm has passed. I think we can travel safely again."

She nodded without a word. The wind was still strong, and it was snowing blankets, but she supposed it wasn't as bad as it had been earlier.

He took her hand and gave it a gentle squeeze. "Everything will be alright now Charlie."

She was not convinced, but she said nothing.

They drove for an hour before the weather began to deteriorate. Still Daddy continued on despite the thickening snow and hard winds. Though she did not wish to, Charlie remained awake throughout this time watching the road in fear. She could hear the pickup truck's engine straining to propel it forward and feel the wheels slipping as they continued down the road. All of a sudden, the truck tipped forward and stopped short with a dull thud.

Charlie let out a cry of fear.

"Holy shit!" Daddy exclaimed.

The pickup truck's engine sputtered for a few moments before quitting.

Daddy turned to her. "Are you alright Charlie?"

"I think so."

He glanced outside the pickup truck for a moment before turning back to her. "Looks like we walk from here."

She returned a frightened glance. "Where are we going to go?"

"We will need to find a town or some other place to wait out the storm." He patted her leg. "Come on we should get going before this snow gets any worse."

She gave a silent nod. They had entered a forest some time ago. A sign along the road indicated that these were state game lands. Daddy was trying to put a good face on it but Charlie knew that there were no towns nearby and little hope of finding anything other than trees and snow. Charlie took Daddy's coat from her shoulders and handed it to him. "Here Daddy. You'll need your coat."

He took it from her with a slight smile. "Thank you, Charlie."

Upon leaving the pickup truck Charlie saw just how badly they were stuck. The front wheels were completely buried in snow as was the bumper and half of the grill.

Daddy must have seen the worried expression on her face. "Don't worry Charlie we'll get it out tomorrow."

Charlie turned to her father but said nothing. She knew they were in real danger and was afraid. In her heart she felt that she deserved this, it was fair.

Still, she feared for her father. She had not forgotten what he had done in New York. Still, he was her daddy and she did not want him to be hurt because of what she had done.

All he ever did was try to protect me. He doesn't deserve to suffer because of me.

The wind picked up still more, slicing through her clothes like razors. Charlie shuddered hard. Daddy took her hand and got her moving.

"Come Charlie. Let's get out of the cold."

Charlie nodded without a word. The two of them walked for a long time finding nothing but endless miles of forest. With each hour the snow grew deeper and the weather grew more severe. As the remainder of the day passed and it began to get dark the temperature dropped steadily. Still they found nothing. No cars passed them by and there were no buildings. It wasn't until the sky had changed to a deep bluish purple that she saw the outline of a small building.

She pointed. "Look Daddy."

He squinted then smiled at her. "Good work Charlie."

The building turned out to be a tiny single room, hunting cabin. The door was secured with a padlock and there were no signs of human inhabitance.

Daddy started to turn to her, then stopped and touched the lock with the tips of his fingers. For a moment she felt him push and sensed that he was in great pain. Then the lock fell open.

Charlie watched in silence. This was wrong. They were breaking into someone else's house. Yet she said nothing because she was cold and wanted to get out of the snow.

Daddy opened the door and held it for her. "Come on Charlie we need to get out of this storm." His voice was heavy with suffering.

"Okay Daddy."

The cabin was pitch dark inside. She would not have been able to see her hand if she held it in front of her face.

"Stay here. I'm going to look for a light." Daddy's voice came from nowhere.

A moment later she heard his footsteps on the wooden floor. Then she heard him opening drawers and cabinets and rummaging around. After a few minutes he struck a match and used it to light a Coleman lantern.

As it turned out the cabin was very small and sparsely furnished with only a small cot along one wall, a pair of canvas camp chairs, a row of cabinets and drawers, a short red oak counter top and a small wood stove.

Daddy was standing beside the stove looking very sick. He held his head in his hands and swayed on his feet. His face was pale as a sheet and he was soaked in sweat. Two thick streams of dark red blood trickled from his nose.

Charlie's heart chilled with fear. "Oh Daddy."

He needed to lie down. She went to him and helped him into the nearer of the two camp chairs. She then quickly searched the cabinets and drawers for blankets and pillows. In one cabinet she found a large green nylon sleeping bag and a single pillow. Charlie took the sleeping bag and pillow and laid them out on the cot. She then went to her father and helped him into bed.

After tucking Daddy in, Charlie went through the rest of the cabinets and drawers. In one cabinet she found dozens of cans of various types of food, including Campbell's soups and Dinty Moor stews. Another cabinet held two large bottles of water, a pile of dishrags and a bottle of Palmolive dish soap and a third held a case of Alpo dog food and two cases of Hi-C. In the drawers she found a large Bowie knife, two additional packs of wooden matches, six twelve-gauge shotgun shells, a battery powered lantern, four tin plates, six forks and three table knives, a can opener, a small propane tank and a deck of playing cards. She also found a large tin pot and a heavy iron grill in the oven.

Charlie sat and played with the deck of cards until she became tired. Then she extinguished the Coleman lamp and climbed into bed beside her sleeping father.

VI

When she awakened again golden sunlight streamed through the cabin's single window. Daddy was still fast asleep. Charlie slid out of the sleeping bag taking care not to make a sound and went to the window. The storm had passed but not before piling snow halfway up the window. Charlie tried the door and found it sealed shut by the heavy blanket of snow.

We're stuck.

They wouldn't be able to get out of the cabin until the snow melted off. Fortunately, she did not have to go. She was, however, starving. Charlie went to the cabinets and took out one of the Dinty Moor cans and opened it. There wasn't any wood to burn so she emptied the can onto one of the plates and ate the stew cold. It was thick and gelatinous and tasted like dog food, but it quelled her hunger. When she was finished, Charlie opened one of the water bottles and took a healthy swig. She then washed the dishes and put them away before sitting down in the director's chair closest to the cot. Daddy was still fast asleep. He looked better than he had the night before. His skin had regained some color and he was no longer sweating or shaking. His face was set in an expression of peaceful slumber.

Charlie smiled. He always took good care of her. He had tried so hard to give her a chance to be like everyone else. Now she would take care of him. It frightened her a little, but she didn't mind. She had done it before and she loved him dearly. Charlie gently touched her father's hand.

I love you Daddy.

Sometime later Daddy awakened looking much better. Charlie gladly let him take over, relieved to return to the role of a child. After eating lunch Daddy sat down with her on the cot.

"Looks like we're going to be stuck here for a while Charlie."

She nodded.

"I know I said we're going to Croatia, but I think it might be better to wait until spring time."

"Okay Daddy." She replied without emotion.

"We cannot take the main highways because of the border check points and it is too dangerous to use the back roads while they are covered in snow." Her father's tone was cool and logical, but Charlie thought she heard a hint of apology, as if she were accusing him with her lack of emotion.

In truth she was very tired and still psychologically drained from the firestorm at the Ephrata Police Station. She forced a smile. "That's ok Daddy."

He gave her a firm hug. "You're a good girl Charlie."

VII

The winter was long and difficult. In addition to firewood Daddy found a three-gallon can of kerosene and a double bit ax in a small shed behind the cabin but that was all. They had no medicine, no fresh fruits or vegetables and no money for Daddy had spent the last of it buying food on the road.

A week after they arrived at the cabin, Charlie came down with food poisoning and for several days ran a high fever and spent most of her time outside puking and shitting her brains out, sometimes both at once. There was little her father could do for her during this time other than make cold compresses with dishrags and snow from outside and try to keep her from becoming dehydrated. As sick as she was Charlie felt guilty for she knew she had put Daddy in danger again.

Daddy had explained to her that he intended to travel southwest and into Mexico. From there they would catch a container ship to Eastern Europe where he thought they would be able to hide. Now she had gotten sick and the weather had gotten so bad that they wouldn't be able to travel anymore until the spring. They were trapped.

To both Charlie and her father's relief her fever abated by the weekend although she continued to feel weak and suffered sporadic attacks of diarrhea and vomiting throughout the winter.

This was perhaps in part the result of the poor-quality food that they lived on. The Dinty Moor stews and Campbell's soups, while filling, were hardly a balanced diet. Charlie knew that were it not for the drink boxes of Hi-C that Daddy insisted they drink they would both be suffering scurvy.

This situation was made worse by the fact that there was not enough food to last through the winter. Only the Hi-C lasted until the spring and this was because Daddy rationed it very carefully. By the first of December they had finished off the last can of Dinty Moor stew and were forced to eat the Alpo dog food and by Christmas the dog food was gone leaving them dependent on animal traps and foraging. When they were lucky they were able to eat enough to keep up their strength, when they weren't they went hungry. Charlie soon grew to appreciate what it must be like to live on the street, where all that mattered was where your next meal was coming from.

As her body recovered from the ravages of food poisoning her mind began to slowly recover from the horror of the firestorm at the Ephrata police station. For a while she suffered terrible nightmares in which she would relive that horrible day. She would awaken from these screaming or sobbing in terror frightening her father from his sleep.

Daddy was very patient and gentle with her during this time. He would sit up with her, holding her in his arms until she went back to sleep and when she could not sleep he would stay up all night with her.

Sometimes her guilt would overcome her, and she would burst into tears. Again, Daddy would put aside whatever he was doing to sit with her for as long as she needed to calm down.

He was always so kind. She didn't deserve such a kind father. She was a killer; she didn't deserve kindness, she deserved punishment.

Time crawled by and as the winter dragged on Charlie's horror and self-loathing gradually healed leaving only a scar of guilt upon her heart. With the passing of raw emotion came the realization of certain truths. Truths that Charlie came to believe she understood better than her father.

As difficult as it was to accept, Charlie understood that she would never be normal. The life she had, had in Taylor was gone forever. She and her father would never really be able to escape from the people who were chasing them. Even if they could escape they still wouldn't be safe. They would always live in fear of someone discovering her power.

She was going to need help, the kind of help her father couldn't give her. She had to find a way to turn off the power because she knew she wouldn't be able to keep it in check forever. Deep down she knew she would have to be put away for her own protection both from the people who were chasing them now and from herself. She was dangerous and had already killed people. It was not inconceivable that she might burn herself up one day.

VIII

When Charlie worked up the courage to tell Daddy these things she learned that he had been thinking along somewhat different lines.

"Charlie, I know this will be difficult to understand but I need you to listen carefully. When the spring comes we will be able to travel again. We will go to Mexico and then from there to Croatia. There is a convent there, just outside the town of Selci. The sisters there are trustworthy. They rescued me once after I had been shot. They saved my life."

Charlie knew even before he said it. "Daddy please don't leave me."

He looked deep into her eyes. For a moment Charlie imagined she could feel his sadness though she knew that was impossible as her father was incapable of sorrow. "Charlie, I do not think there is anything else I can do to keep you safe. These government agents will never stop chasing us. As long as they know who you are and what you can do they will continue to try to capture you to use you as a weapon. The only way you and I can truly be safe is if no one knows you exist."

She understood at once. Her father would leave her in Croatia at the convent. She would pose as an orphaned Croatian child. He would then return to the United States and kill everyone who had any knowledge of them. He would destroy any records. She understood too that she would never see him again. Still, she was just a little girl, and, in that moment, she wanted only to hear her father tell her everything would be alright.

"We'll be able to stay together after that won't we?"

He forced a smile and hugged her. "Of course, Charlie. Nobody's ever going to take us away from each other."

She hugged him back with all her strength. "Then I don't care what happens.

And I'm not going to light anymore fires."

He nodded. "Of course not."

Though she said nothing Charlie sensed the lie. She sensed that her father expected to die protecting his daughter. She also knew they had no other choice. As long as there were government agents who knew about her and her father, about what she could do, they would never be safe. Charlie understood and accepted this without protest even at the cost of losing her father.

Charlie spent much time thinking these things over as Daddy left her alone for hours every day while he went to search for food. During this time Charlie contemplated her situation and watched the time crawl by.

IX

The weather remained snowy and cold through February, March and April before finally breaking the week of her birthday. It was around this time that Daddy decided they couldn't stay any longer.

After dinner one night, Daddy sat her down and explained that now that the weather was becoming warmer they could safely travel again.

Charlie knew this was only part of the truth. In truth her father feared that the government men knew where they were and would soon come after them again. For her own part Charlie felt a strong sense of danger. She felt certain they were being watched. This knowledge brought about a low-level nervous feeling that never left her.

Over the next few days as they packed up the few supplies they had left and prepared to leave Charlie's sense of danger grew stronger. The night before they were to leave Charlie had a terrible nightmare in which snipers ambushed Daddy and her as they tried to leave the cabin. One of the shots struck Daddy in the neck, killing him.

Charlie awoke from this dream screaming in terror and soaked in sweat. Daddy sat up with her for most of the rest of the night before she was finally able to go back to sleep.

Not long after she had fallen asleep Daddy awakened her.

"It's time to go."

She groaned softly. "Okay Daddy."

He put on a thin smile. "Happy birthday Charlie."

She grinned in return. "Thanks Daddy."

It was her birthday and she was nine but that didn't matter now. All that mattered was getting away before the government men came for them.

Daddy helped her up and held her coat while she slipped into it. Then she took his hand and the two of them walked out of the cabin.

It was still dark outside and bitter cold. There was no moon and few visible stars leaving the woods shrouded in pitch darkness. As she crunched across the frozen ground the wind picked up slicing through her clothes like razors.

Charlie's entire body shook with the cold. It was going to be a difficult morning. They had a long walk ahead of them and she was starving.

As they walked Charlie's sense of danger grew. She was trembling continuously, more from fear now than cold. Something was going to happen. Someone was waiting for them. Charlie looked up at her father, fear painted across her face. He offered her a nervous smile in return.

"You feel it too." Her voice came out low and frightened.

He nodded in reply. "Perhaps the feeling is early."

She did not answer. The feeling wasn't early. She was certain of that much. They were walking into a trap.

Charlie was silent for a few minutes before looking up at her father again. "Daddy I'm not going to light any fires. Even if they come before we can get away. I'm never going to light another fire in my life."

He squeezed her hand. "I understand Charlie."

She sensed the lie immediately. He didn't want to, but he would ask her to use the power before allowing them to be captured. She understood this but still refused to ever use the power again.

As that thought passed through her mind Charlie's vision changed and she found herself looking at a tall man perched in a tree taking aim with a long antique rifle. His features were obscured by shadow and his face was hidden behind his rifle scope. The muzzle was pointed directly at her; she could see the little hole clearly. A moment later the image vanished leaving her trembling with fear.

The sky had gone from black to dark purple. Still the woods remained very dark. The trees were thinning now, and she thought she could the faint twinkle of lights ahead. They were nearing a town.

Again, her vision changed. The man was taking aim. His finger curled over the trigger.

She never heard the rifle shot. Sudden pain exploded from the base of her throat accompanied by a strong choking sensation. A low gurgle escaped her throat. Warm blood trickled down her neck. She groped for the wound without thinking. After a moment her hand closed around a long slim dart and twisted it upward setting off a second explosion of pain and starting a fresh flow of blood. She was dying. The world began to spin. Blood coated the back of her throat filling her mouth with its acrid metallic flavor. She was choking to death, drowning in her own blood. Black butterflies danced in front of her eyes, blocking her view of the rapidly spinning world. Her head swelled as her lungs screamed for air. Her eyes felt as if they would burst in their sockets. The black butterflies were multiplying, bleeding together into one solid field of darkness. Her last conscious thought: daddy watch out passed through her mind in an instant. Then everything fell away.

X

Beyond the sheep pastures surrounding David's father's house was mile after mile of thick, old growth forest. As she walked among the trees with David, Charlie was carried back to that day. She saw and felt everything with perfect clarity. As she saw the dart sticking out of her neck, she felt the pain in her throat and the warm trickle of blood. David was staring at her with a frightened expression. Charlie was confused at first. She tried to ask David what was wrong but was only able to produce a wet gurgle followed by several sharp coughs. Her mouth filled with the metallic taste of blood.

"Oh, Jesus Charlie you're bleeding!" David's voice was terrified.

She looked down and was horrified to see a small bright red stain in her shirt collar. Her hands instantly flew to her neck where she found a small hole in the base of her throat.

Where the dart was...

A thin stream of blood flowed from the wound.

Oh God...

Fear welled up in her heart bringing with it the beginnings of panic. Charlie began to gasp for breath, certain that she was going to suffocate. Her heart began to race. Her head was spinning like crazy.

"Oh God!" David's voice was terrified. He took her into his arms just before she lost her balance. "It's okay Charlie. You're going to be okay."

Help me...

The black butterflies had returned, swarming before her eyes and opening their wings.

When her vision returned she was lying on her back and David was crouched over her pressing a Kleenex against the wound in her throat. His face was terrified.

"Jesus Charlie are you okay?"

She replied with a low moan.

"Shh don't try to talk." David's voice was gentle but held an edge of fear. "You're going to be all right. Just try to relax so the bleeding stops."

Charlie met his eyes in reply. She lay still for a while waiting for the flow of blood to end. When it did David picked her up and carried her back to the house. Once inside he took her into the bathroom and set her down on the toilet.

"Try to relax. I'll take care of that wound, so we can go back outside."

She answered again with her eyes.

David went to the medicine cabinet and took out two pieces of sterile wrapped gauze, a bottle of iodine and a roll of surgical tape. He then opened one of the pieces of gauze and soaked it in iodine. Charlie braced herself knowing before David said that this would hurt.

"This is going to sting a little Charlie."

As he spoke he bent down in front of her and gently blotted the hole in her throat. An invisible hornet immediately buried its barb into the wound painting radiating fire across her throat. Charlie gritted her teeth to suppress a cry of pain.

After smearing a goodly amount of iodine on her throat David opened the second piece of gauze and pressed it over the wound.

"I need you to hold this for me Charlie."

She complied without a word.

He pressed down on her hand making her cough lightly. "You need to put a little pressure on that."

Charlie did as she was told at the same time watching as David opened the roll of surgical tape. He made two half loops across her throat, one at the top of the gauze and one at the bottom drawing each one taut.

"There, how's that feel? It's not too tight is it?"

"No." Her voice came out scratchy and hoarse, but Charlie was surprised to find that she could talk at all.

"Good. Are you going to be alright?"

"I think so." Her throat still hurt, and she was a little frightened but otherwise she felt ok.

David smiled but Charlie could feel his concern. "Why don't we wait awhile before going back outside?"

"Okay." Charlie looked up at him. "What happened?"

"I was hoping you could tell me." David replied.

Charlie shook her head. "I don't know. I started thinking about when Daddy and me were living in the cabin in the woods and then it happened."

"The day you were taken by the NSA?"

She nodded.

His expression became concerned. "And you started bleeding in the same place that the dart hit you." He was speaking more to himself than to Charlie now.

As she looked into his eyes Charlie felt David's growing fear. He was frightened for her health and safety and he was keeping something from her. She could not tell what for certain, but she sensed that he felt deep guilty over it. For her own part Charlie was both frightened and intrigued at once.

I did this to myself.

Was it the power?

The thought was terrifying. Could she have somehow opened a hole in her own neck? There was still so much she didn't know about the power.

David was silent for a few moments longer. Then he offered her his hand. "How would you like a bowl of ice cream? That should make your throat feel better."

She smiled. "Okay."

David took her downstairs and gave her a huge bowl of black cherry ice cream. He then filled a bowl for himself and sat down across from her.

"There are some things you should know." He kept his voice tightly controlled. Charlie detected both guilt and anger behind it. "Remember what I told you before we went to that island?"

She nodded.

"You are the *Sigilla Praevaricator*. We... I'm sure of it. You took Catherine and I to that island and you unsealed that sword. I'm not sure what happened there but I know you did it somehow."

Guilt and fear bubbled up within her. "I...I didn't mean to..."

He touched her hand. "It's okay. You didn't do anything wrong, but this does change some things."

Her fear was not allayed. "What do you mean?"

She feared she already knew the answer. The NSA was dangerous enough, but if she was the *Sigilla Praevaricator* then the situation was much more serious than any of them had imagined. David and Catherine could not protect her from the people who would come after her. As she was thinking this, a name came into her mind.

Dark Knights. Men and women with the power who used it for their own personal gain. Servants of the darkest evil.

This knowledge both mystified and frightened her at once. She had always been highly intelligent and a powerful psychic. She did not find this remarkable. It was just another part of her, like her blue eyes and double-jointed thumbs. At the same time though she was also intrigued and baffled by this ability. She understood that this was yet another manifestation of her power but there was still much about the power she did not understand.

Charlie took a spoonful of ice cream, but it no longer held any pleasure for her. The taste had become sickly sweet and nauseated her. As she held the ice cream in her mouth her stomach flip-flopped in protest.

David too seemed to have lost interest in his ice cream. He stirred it around and stabbed at it with his spoon without eating. "I think it's time you learned to better control your power."

Charlie stared at him in surprise, almost dropping her spoon on the floor.

David must have interpreted her surprise as horror for all at once his voice became apologetic. "I know you don't like using your power, but you need to learn to control it."

"Okay." Charlie was only partially aware of her own answer as her mind was overwhelmed with relief.

Now it was David's turn to be surprised. "Oh…ok." He had been expecting to have to convince her. "But let's wait awhile, until your throat doesn't hurt so much."

Charlie smiled. "Okay."

Her throat hadn't been bothering her until he drew her attention to it, but she was glad not to have to do this right away. Charlie took another spoonful of ice cream. It tasted better this time and her stomach did not balk. The cool soothed her throat.

David ate a mouthful of ice cream. "We don't have a lot of time. It won't take the NSA long to find us here."

XI

Later that day they went back into the woods. For a while they just walked together talking about inconsequential things. Eventually David changed the subject.

"When I was your age I had trouble controlling my power too. So, my Dad taught me meditation, to help me focus my mind and better control my thoughts and emotions." They had stopped and were standing face to face. "I want you to try it. Would that be alright?"

"Ok."

"Sit down with me."

"On the ground?"

"Yes."

She did as she was asked.

"Good, now close your eyes and try to relax."

Charlie looked up at the sky for a moment then closed her eyes and focused on the sounds of the woods pushing everything else from her mind.

"Good girl. Now I want you to slowly tighten and relax each muscle in your body starting with your toes. Squeeze them into a ball as tight as you can and hold it."

She rolled up her toes into tight balls inside her sneakers.

"Ok now relax them and tighten the muscles in the backs of your lower legs."

Again, she complied, tightening her calf muscles until they felt as if they would cramp.

"Now relax your lower legs and tighten your thighs and butt."

She did as David asked held it until he told her she could relax.

"Now tighten your stomach muscles. Suck in your stomach as far as you can and hold it."

She drew in a deep breath sucking in her stomach and held it. After a few seconds her head began to feel swollen. The muscles in her legs and feet tingled pleasantly.

"Now relax." He paused. "Now tighten your chest. Hold it as tight as you can."

She did so drawing a second breath and holding it. The pleasant tingling sensation in her lower body had become an even more pleasant limp feeling.

"Now relax your chest and make a fist with each hand. Hold them as tightly as you can."

Charlie cooperated feeling for that moment as if she were about to enter a fight.

"Now relax your hands and tighten the muscles in your arms."

Charlie bent her arms and made a muscle like she had seen Popeye do on TV.

"Good job, you can relax your arms. Now I want you to tighten your shoulders and neck."

She nodded slightly then did as she was told.

It felt strange, almost as if she were trying hard to swallow some object that was too big for her throat. It hurt. The hole in her throat throbbed and burned. She was grateful when David told her she could relax.

"Now tighten your jaw. Squeeze your teeth together as tightly as you can."

Charlie complied, perhaps a little too willingly for her head began to throb from the pressure.

"Good. Now relax. Just let your body go limp."

Charlie gladly did so. As she relaxed her jaw muscles she felt her fear and guilt wash away. The world began to fade. The ground disappeared from beneath her body and the air became still and calm. All sound had vanished save for the sound of David's voice leaving her floating peacefully in a field of reddish pink.

"How do you feel Charlie?"

David's voice seemed to come from everywhere at once.

"Good."

Though spoken in her voice the words seemed to come from someone other than her. She could not have spoken them herself. Her voice, her thoughts were lost in pleasant nothingness.

David set something down in front of her. "Now I want you to light this matchbook on fire."

"But I could hurt you." She couldn't see anything. She had no way of knowing what she might be setting fire to.

"You won't hurt me I trust you." David's voice was kind and gentle, but she sensed the fear behind it.

"Alright." She was not very convinced, but she trusted David.

Slowly Charlie reached out with the power. An image of a small pack of Holiday Inn matches took shape in her mind. The pack was sitting on a small rock approximately four feet away from her.

With great reluctance Charlie flicked out at the matchbook with her mind. The power flared up and leapt out of her igniting the pack of matches with a soft rush. Though it was faint she could feel the heat radiating from the fire. Fear cropped up within her.

It's so much stronger.

Her breathing became quick and she began to tremble.

"Your fine Charlie. Just relax. There's nothing to be afraid of. You know you can control the power. You've done it before."

She nodded. *Yes, I can stop it I've done it before.*

It didn't sound very convincing. Yes, she had some control over the power, but that control was still limited. In her mind she saw trenches of fire spreading across the grass at the NSA compound and heard men and women's screams as they were swallowed by the flames.

Charlie slammed the power down.

STOP IT NOW!

To her surprise it vanished almost at once. It took little effort and was almost painless. For a moment she just sat there, mind blank.

"Charlie? You can open your eyes now if you want."

She remained still for a moment before slowly opening her eyelids. Brilliant white sunlight shone from the sky causing her to squint for a moment until her eyes readjusted. David was watching her carefully.

"Are you alright Charlie?"

She nodded. "I just blanked out for a moment."

David smiled. "Guess you did. Are you ready to try it again?"

"Sure."

This was how it began. The two repeated the exercise again and again until dusk. As the sun dipped below the horizon the sky reddened to the color of maple trees in autumn. David and Charlie watched from the edge of the woods. Both man and child understood this to be more than just another sunset.

As she walked back to the house with David Charlie felt the change gaining in strength.

XII

David took her out early the following morning to the same place in the woods. For the first few hours they continued the meditation exercise. Then he had her try something new. She was to close her eyes and relax as he had shown her but this time instead of lighting a fire he asked her to move a small rock. She did so with no trouble and was again able to stop the power with ease. After repeating this exercise several times, he asked her to lift the rock into the air and hold it there for a few seconds before lowering it and stopping the power. She repeated this exercise many times holding the rock in the air for increasing increments of time.

At twelve-thirty they stopped for lunch. David made her a peanut butter and jelly sandwich and a banana split. Charlie was ravenous, finishing everything quickly.

After lunch they walked in the woods for a while just talking.

"Charlie do you know why we're doing this?"

She did but she said nothing.

"There are people out there who will want to use you for your power."

"Like the NSA?"

He nodded. "Yes, but there are other people as well." He paused. "I want to tell you a story. Remember when you said that I had the power too?"

"Yes."

"There are a lot of people with the power. They are called the Enlightened. A lot of these people go through their entire lives hiding their powers but some of them develop their powers and learn to harness them. Some of them use their powers for good and become Lightwarriors but many of them are tempted by the idea of being able to do whatever they want and become Dark Knights. Dark Knights are immortal and very powerful. They are also very dangerous because they only care about themselves."

Charlie already knew this but hearing David say it was frightening. "These Dark Knights are after me?"

"That is what Catherine and I are afraid of."

Now she was very afraid. "What are we going to do?"

"You are going to continue with your exercises and Catherine and I are going to figure out where we can go to be safe."

Charlie nodded. She was not comforted but she trusted David. He would take care of everything.

They walked for a while in silence.

David spoke first. "Tomorrow we're going to do one more exercise. Then we'll have to move on. There is a great deal left for you to learn but we're out of time. For the rest of today I just want to talk."

She nodded.

"The powers you have are a gift and a curse. They are also a great responsibility. You aren't like everyone else. You can do things that very few others can do. Your power sets you apart from everyone else. It also holds you to a higher responsibility."

Charlie understood at once. She too had thought along these same lines more than a few times.

David's voice became very serious. "I know that you are angry about the death of your parents and what the NSA did to you and that you want revenge, but you have to find a way to get past that. The people looking for you will try to use your anger and wish for revenge to control you. If you hold on to that wish they will know it and use it against you."

He bent down and took her by the shoulders. "It is very important that you understand this. You cannot take revenge, or you will become like the Dark Knights. No matter how angry you feel you have to control it."

She nodded. Deep inside the bloodstain of *Hate!* cut a brilliant blaze upon her heart.

David seemed to relax a little after this. If he sensed the lie, Charlie detected no sign of it.

XIII

They walked in the woods and talked for the rest of that day. David told her many stories; stories of the Lightwarriors and Dark Knights, and of the *Sigilla Praevaricator*. Charlie listened to these with mixed fascination and fear for she understood perhaps better than he did their true implications.

Mankind was created in the image of the divine. This oft repeated bit of scripture meant to set humanity apart from the rest of the animal kingdom was perhaps the most misunderstood verse ever put to words. Though true, this verse did not refer to the physical form of mankind but rather mankind's very nature, and as part of that nature mankind was originally gifted with certain godlike abilities. This was the origin of the power. After the fall of man, the majority of humanity was stripped of knowledge of the power, save for a select few, who would later become known as the Enlightened.

The Enlightened exist for a singular purpose, to serve as a shield between mankind and the darkness. Those Enlightened who lived up to this ideal and came to serve the true light would come to be known as Lightwarriors. However, like normal humans (or Outsiders as Enlighteneds often referred to them) Enlighteneds retain free will and with it the capacity for malevolence. Throughout history many Enlighteneds fell to the temptation to use the power for selfish reasons. These Enlighteneds were inevitably corrupted to the point of true evil and would become Dark Knights.

Unlike, Lightwarriors, Dark Knights are immortal their immortality comes at the price of damnation when the Dark Knight is finally killed. Both because of their immortality and the seductive temptation to use the power for selfish purposes, Dark Knights have always outnumbered Lightwarriors and constitute an ever-growing threat to all of humanity. Thus, the primary function of Lightwarriors had long since been to hunt and destroy Dark Knights.

XIV

That night after everyone else had gone to bed David stood alone on the porch drinking Scotch and listening to the dead silence of the winter night.

They were running out of time. The NSA knew where they were.

Charlie was a quick study. David couldn't help but be amazed at how fast she had picked up the exercises. Still there was much for her to learn and she remained full of anger and craved revenge. She had promised him that she would not take revenge, but he knew she had lied. He did not need psychic senses to know this. He needed only to look in her eyes.

She was in very real danger, not as much from the NSA or the so-called Dark Knights as from her own anger threatening to consume her. David took a long sip of Scotch.

The NSA or the Dark Knights wouldn't harm her. They'll need her alive. They'll try to control her and if they can somehow take advantage of her anger...

It was a thought he did not want to complete.

She has to learn to let go.

David stared up at the clear, starry sky with trepidation in his heart for he knew that she would not and that sooner or later she would try to take revenge for the deaths of her parents. He slowly swirled his drink and took another long sip.

He needed to sleep. Tomorrow was the most crucial day. Tomorrow he would teach Charlie the "Forging" or whatever Dad had called it. He didn't quite remember. This was the real test and he had never done it himself.

To kill an Enlighted was exceptionally difficult. Any sort of ranged weapon would be effectively useless both because the Enlightened would sense the intention of the shooter and because the Enlightened would be able to easily deflect a projectile. Use of the power to kill an Enlightened posed its own set of problems both due to the difficulty of successfully attacking an Enlightened with the power and because of the potential for massive destruction. Moreover, as society advanced technologically, Outsiders began to become a threat to Enlighteneds, thus requiring a great deal of secrecy around the use of the power. Not wanting to inhabit a hellscape world, nor face the wrath of an Outsider majority armed with weapons potent enough to rival the power. Lightwarriors and Dark Knights had long ago reached an informal accord of sorts. Conflict between Dark Knights and Lightwarriors would be settled in single combat using the sword.

Once entered into, this ancient accord bound all Dark Knights and Lightwarriors. Legend told that any Dark Knight or Lightwarrior found to have broken the accord would face one known only as The Arbiter. Though the true consequences of defying the accord had long since been lost to history, whispers through time hinted that The Arbiter had the power to take that which the oath breaker values most. Still, violation had become taboo even among the most malevolent of Dark Knights.

Here too the power offered its own unique solution. With proper focus and training an Enlightened could learn to convert energy into matter thus forging his or her power into the shape of a sword. This sword would then function as a conduit of the Enlightened's power and was one of the few weapons effective in slaying other Enlighteneds.

David's nerves screwed a little tighter for he knew that the process could be dangerous if not properly performed. This was why it was important for the Enlightened to develop control over their power before attempting it. Charlie seemed to be gaining a tighter grip on her power, but she had only just begun. There was no way of knowing the true extent of her control.

After a long pause David downed the rest of his drink and went back inside. He was drinking too much. He'd had at least two drinks every day that week. It didn't matter. He'd have his chance to cut back soon enough.

As he headed back inside David's mind returned to the next day. If Charlie didn't maintain control of her power she could be seriously injured.

...or killed.

This was not a good idea.

XV

David slept poorly that night and awoke early. After showering and dressing he went downstairs and made breakfast. Then he went to wake Charlie. By this time Catherine had also awakened and was in the shower.

He found Charlie sleeping peacefully looking more rested and relaxed than she had in a long time. For a moment David stood and watched her sleep, feeling almost guilty to wake her. Then he bent down and gently shook her awake. Charlie stirred and moaned softly. Then her eyes opened and locked with his.

"Good morning David."

He smiled.

"Good morning Charlie."

She sat up without a word and slid to the edge of the bed. He watched her with a feeling something like fatherly pride. She really was beautiful, disheveled hair and all.

"Breakfast is on the table when you're ready. I made scrambled eggs and bacon."

She smiled. "Mmm. Sounds good." In that moment she was just another little girl, eyes and face filled with a child's simple excitement at the prospect of another day.

He stood still for a moment longer, then turned and headed for the door. "I'll let you get dressed. Catherine's in the bathroom now but she should be out in a few minutes."

"Okay." Charlie studied him for a moment before adding. "Are you alright David?"

For a moment he was taken aback. He had not noticed, until she had drawn his attention to, the guilt and fear in his own heart. His muscles were tense and there were tiny beads of oily sweat on his skin. "I'm fine." His voice came out flat and foreign, as if someone other than he had spoken.

Charlie's expression was troubled for a moment before smoothing over into a renewed smile. "I love you David."

"I love you too, Charlie."

David sensed nothing, but he knew from watching her that Charlie had detected the lie. Without speaking another word David left the room and went downstairs.

Ten minutes later Catherine appeared in the kitchen looking stunning in a white turtleneck and a pair of faded blue jeans. Her red-gold hair hung loose and dripping on her shoulders.

"Good morning David."

"Good morning."

She frowned. "What's wrong?"

"Oh, nothing."

"Really, what's bothering you? I know something's wrong. I can see it on your face." Her expression was troubled. Behind it David sensed both concern and more than a little fear.

"I still can't believe we're actually doing this. I spent most of my life trying to walk away from my powers and now I'm forcing Charlie to embrace hers." This was a lie. He still felt guilty for forcing Charlie to begin training but that was not what really troubled him. In truth, he had doubts about the extent of control she had over her power and feared for her safety.

Catherine went to him and wrapped her arms around his neck. "It's not your fault David. She was born with the power. It's a part of who she is. This is the only way we can really protect her."

"I know." The knowledge didn't help. He could not accept that this was her future. She was only a little girl. She deserved to have a childhood.

Catherine must have sensed his continuing guilt for she tightened her embrace. "You didn't do this to her David. You're doing the best you can for her."

A slow sigh escaped his chest. "I know. It doesn't make it any easier. She's only a little girl.”

Catherine’s eyes flashed. “Why can’t you let go of that.” She walked around the table and sat down across from him. “You haven’t done anything wrong. You didn’t put her in this situation. If you want someone to blame, blame her damned parents for Christ sakes. They were the ones who participated in that goddamned drug experiment. They put Charlie in this situation, not you.”

David knew she didn’t blame Charlie’s parents. She was just concerned about him. The real blame could only fall on the men and women who would sponsor such atrocities.

For a moment the two sat in silence. Then the kitchen door opened, and Charlie came in smiling and looking relaxed. David stood up and went to her.

“Hi Charlie. Sit down and I’ll get your breakfast.”

“Okay.” She went to the table and sat down between Catherine’s and his chairs. David took her plate to the stove and filled it with scrambled eggs and bacon, then set it down in front of her. He then took Catherine’s plate and his own and filled each with eggs and bacon before returning to the table and sitting down to eat.

Breakfast went quickly and with little conversation. When they had finished David and Charlie cleaned up the dishes. Then they went outside and into the woods.

As he walked David’s heart continued to torment him with guilt. She was a little girl. She didn’t deserve this.

They walked for a long time before David found what he was looking for. They had come to a break in the trees; one not quite big enough to be a field but bigger than what one would consider a clearing. Despite being exposed to direct sunlight the grass here remained short and there were no dried-out tassels or dead field grasses to suggest that it had ever been longer. A single ancient oak grew near the center of the clearing. Beneath it sat a large rock covered in blue, green, and gray lichens.

“Oh, it’s so beautiful.”

Charlie’s exclamation broke the spell of silence.

“Yes, it is.” David replied quietly.

To David it was not beautiful but haunting. The morning sun was not its usual golden yellow but rather a harsh white. A stiff breeze whispered through the barren trees and a low mist lurked over the brown earth. It was not cold out today but cool and damp.

David shivered despite himself. The forests here were different. They seemed to go on forever feeling less like a place than another world. Here one could walk on for miles upon miles without coming to anything but more trees. These were ancient lands with ancient histories haunted by the ghosts of many centuries. As he stood there David could almost hear their voices.

"What's wrong?" Charlie was studying him with her eyes.

"Oh nothing. I was just thinking that's all."

She watched him for a moment longer before turning her eyes away. "What are we doing today?"

"We're going to try a new exercise Charlie."

She looked up at him with curiosity in her eyes. "You don't want me to light any fires or move things today?"

"No. I think you're pretty good at doing that. I want you to try something new today."

"Alright." Her voice was trusting. David could not sense the true feelings behind her calm exterior.

He took her hand and led her over to the rock. "Come on. Let's sit down."

"Sure." She sat down cross-legged on the left-hand side of the rock.

David sat down beside her. "You've been very patient over the last few days. You did everything I've asked you to even though you don't like using your power. I have one last exercise I want you try and then we're done."

In truth she had only just begun. There was so much she still had to learn but there was no more time. With what she knew now she would at least be able to defend herself.

Charlie watched him in silence. Her expression was inscrutable.

David remained silent for a moment. Inside he was still struggling with guilt.

"Are you ready?"

"I guess." Charlie's voice remained calm and trusting.

"Then let's get started." David stood up and crouched down in front of her. "First I want you to do the relaxation exercise I taught you."

She nodded and closed her eyes. Then she became very still; more still than he would have thought possible for so young a child. As he watched Charlie's breathing slowed and her body seemed to relax while remaining perfectly stationary. To David she looked like a tiny blond-haired Buddha.

He touched her hand where it lay on her knee. "Now I want you to reach deep inside where the power is."

She was silent for a moment. "I'm ready."

"Alright. Now reach into the power as deeply as you can and bring it out. As you let it out I want you to focus it as tightly as you can."

She nodded. In a heartbeat and a half David felt her power building in the air. There was no fire but he could feel it building and building, wildly spiraling out of her. Her hands slowly lifted from her knees and came together in a gesture similar to prayer. The power grew stronger still. The air pulsated with its force. All at once everything became deadly silent save for the hum of power. Charlie froze in place, her body a living statute. As he watched the air around her began to shimmer.

Shit what have I done. She's going to set herself on fire.

Heat baked out at him as the acrid stench of burned grass met his nostrils. Flames licked up in a circle around her searing the dead grass and blackening the rock and tree trunk. As David watched in horror the circle of fire closed around her, the flames literally enveloping her body. Yet strangely enough she made no sound, nor did she show any signs of harm. Charlie appeared unburned even as yellow fire danced over her skin. It was a strange, almost surreal sight.

Jesus, Charlie what are you doing? Be careful.

He dared not speak for fear of breaking her concentration and condemning her to burn to death. The flames continued to intensify changing from yellow to brilliant blue-white. It was almost painful to look at. The heat was intense enough to scorch the hairs on his arms and in his nostrils and redden and blister his skin. Tree branches above her began to curl and blacken.

Holy shit…what is she doing?

The fire's intensity continued to grow reducing Charlie to a faint outline against its brilliant blue-white hue. The air was filled with the combined roar of the flames and the power. It was terrifying to watch. Frantic, David's heart raced as his skin broke out in thick oily sweat.

Please don't let her hurt herself.

If she lost control even for a second, she would be incinerated. As he watched her David could feel Charlie's power continuing to build. Somehow, she still had control over it. The power was coalescing between her hands, drawing in upon itself, focusing. She was doing it.

Whatever it is…

Oh, Jesus Charlie be careful!

A sudden earsplitting crack ripped through the air followed by a deafening – ***shriiiiik-***. A moment later he felt her trying to pull the power back. She was in great pain and struggling with all her might to maintain control. The flames and the power continued to roar, shaking the air with their fury. Then the fire began to slowly decrease in brilliance and intensity. As it did Charlie became visible again, seeming to reappear as if by magic. As more and more details became visible David saw the pain in her eyes. She was in agony.

Hold on. Please hold on.

I… I don't know if I can…

The voice was hers and barely perceptible. It whispered in his mind.

The flames became yellow once more then bright orange. Fierce tremors wracked her body. Her skin was drenched in sweat. Her face flushed dark red. Thick streams of dark blood flowed from both of her nostrils.

Oh God…

The bleeding quickly worsened until blood was dripping from her chin and soaking her blouse. Still she somehow remained in control.

God help her…Help her.

He was terrified that she would either burn to death or have a stroke.

What have I done?

All at once the flames disappeared and Charlie collapsed. An iron gray sword with a long red flaw near its fuller slipped from her hands and clanged off the ground in front of her. The blade's red flaw still glowed from the heat, but David barely noticed. He was more concerned with Charlie. She lay on her side only semi-conscious, gasping for air and trembling. Her face remained flushed and her nose continued to stream bright crimson blood. David gathered her up and started towards the house.

"Wait." Charlie's voice was no more than an exhausted whisper. "Don't leave it."

"Alright." David bent down, picked up the iron gray sword with his left hand and slipped it inside the back of his belt then carried Charlie back towards the house.

Fear rushed within him bringing with it deep burning guilt. What had he done? Charlie looked near death. Her skin was pale bone and feverish.

"You're going to be alright Charlie. Everything's going to be alright." He was speaking without thinking, repeating the same words over and over.

"Did I do ok?" Charlie's voice was faint and very tired.

He forced a smile. "You did fine Charlie. Try not to talk."

She inclined her head and closed her eyes. Her breathing became slow and shallow.

"Oh, Jesus Charlie hold on."

David began to run. His heart was trip-hammering now. White spots flashed before his eyes. David glanced down at Charlie and saw that her nose continued to stream blood.

She must have burst a blood vessel.

He dared not add what he suspected to be true for the implications of that were too terrible.

David felt as if he were running in a dream for no matter how fast he tried to run his progress remained slow. When he finally reached the house, David was close to panic. His reasoning faculties were nearly gone. All he could think was: *If I can just get her to the house she'll be alright;* even though he knew it made little difference. She needed to go to the hospital.

David passed his father and Catherine in the living room. Both scrambled to their feet when they saw him. David ignored them continuing on to the stairs. Once upstairs David carried Charlie into the closest bedroom and laid her on the bed. He then rushed into the bathroom, soaked a washcloth in cold water and grabbed a handful of toilet paper before rushing back into the bedroom. David laid the wet washcloth across Charlie's forehead and used the toilet paper to stem the continuing flow of blood from her nose.

"What happened?"

David spun around to see Catherine and his father standing in the doorway both looking concerned.

"What happened?" Dad repeated.

Sudden anger flashed in David's heart. "What do you think happened? She almost died doing your stupid stunt! I told you she was too damned young!"

"Calm down David." Dad's soothing tone only served to infuriate David further. "She'll be fine. Psychokinetic crystallization is stressful but any Enlightened can do it without permanent harm as long as they are able to maintain control. She'll sleep for a while and wake up hungry, but she'll be fine by tomorrow."

David stared at his father, incredulous. "She's bleeding. What about that?"

"That happens sometimes when you're trying to maintain such tight control over the power. She probably raised her blood pressure a little and broke a capillary in her nose. I'm sure it looks worse than it is."

David would not be placated. "Dad you didn't see this. She was surrounded by fire. There were flames on her skin and she wasn't burned."

His father's right eyebrow rose ever so slightly, and he was silent for a moment before replying. "She must have really pushed herself." He paused. "If she can do that, then she is much stronger than I imagined."

Dad bent down, carefully drew Charlie's sword from David's belt and gazed at it intently. "Iron gray…and red. I've never seen one like this before."

"Shouldn't we be taking her to a doctor or something?" Catherine interjected.

Dad shook his head. "No. From what David described it sounds as if she may have pushed her power to its absolute limit. She'll sleep for a while but she's fine. The bleeding is superficial and will heal on its own." Seeing the anger in David's eyes he quickly added. "I'll leave you two alone with her." Then he turned and walked out.

David had to suppress an urge to haul off and smash him in the back of the head.

Damned old man. She's a little girl not some damned mythological creature.

As he was thinking that Charlie groaned and sat up wiping at the blood still flowing from her nose with the back of her hand. "What happened? How did I do?"

David offered her a gentle smile. "You did fine Charlie. Now try to rest."

Charlie looked down at her hand with an expression of horrified curiosity. "I'm bleeding." Her voice sounded as if she had first noticed a stain on her shirt.

In an almost businesslike manner, Charlie picked up the now bloody ball of toilet paper and used it to staunch the flow from her nose. David and Catherine both stayed with her until the bleeding had stopped and she was asleep. David took her sword from his belt and propped it up against the wall beside the bed before leaving with Catherine.

XVI

Later that day David went to the gun cabinet where he had stowed the sword Charlie had unsealed. As he lifted the long, silver blade from the wooden cabinet he could feel its power flowing through his body. He felt as though he held a high-tension power line in his hand.

David glanced down at his arms, which had begun to burn beneath their bandages. He hadn't felt anything before leaving Charlie to sleep.

David gritted his teeth against the pain and leveled the sword. This was only the second time in his life he had handled a sword, yet he held it in an expert's grasp. David spun the sword backward in both hands first to his left side then to his right. Then he brought the blade back up in a relaxed grip feeling both surprised and a little frightened.

Somehow, he knew how to handle the sword even though he'd never used one before in his life.

David stared at the sword in his hand for a moment longer before lowering it and walking out the front door towards the woods. He had no real idea of where he was going or even why. He just walked.

Sometime later he came to the clearing where he had taken Charlie earlier that day. As he approached the tree line David froze in shock.

The rock on which Charlie had sat was scorched black and had turned to obsidian as was the ground beneath it. The tree above it was completely incinerated, leaving behind a pile of white powder. He had not noticed this when she was performing the exercise nor when he had gone to her after she collapsed.

Wow...

As he stood starring David unconsciously raised the sword. Shock turned to fear and anger.

She could have been killed.

All at once David changed his grip on the sword and swung it hard like a baseball bat. The blade whistled through the air and neatly sliced through several saplings. In the same smooth motion David brought the sword up again and turned a forward somersault extending the blade as he flipped through the air. Then upon landing he brought the blade around again in a wide horizontal slash.

All of the motions came instinctively, as if he had always known them. It was strange to the point of being disturbing.

David slowly raised the sword and studied it carefully. It gleamed brilliant white in the waning winter sun. The weapon was simple and plain save for a series of strange markings etched into one side of the mirrored blade. The long curved and looping lines, dots and zigzags shone more brightly than the rest of the sword as if outlined in white fire. David stared at the markings a moment longer before turning the blade over in his hands and swinging it in a wide horizontal arc. He then raised the blade above his head and brought it down hard.

It's as if I've always known how to use it. There's no need to teach Charlie to use a sword. She'll already know how, probably better than I do. Having her practice will only teach her aggression.

As he thought that David drove the sword into the ground then turned and started back towards the house. Upon reaching the edge of the clearing he stopped and apropos of nothing turned and extended his arm. In an instant the blade flipped out of the ground and flew towards his outstretched hand. David caught it, then turned back around and left.

XVII

Upon returning to the house David locked the sword in the closet in his and Catherine's bedroom then poured himself a scotch and sat down in front of the television in the den. After flipping channels for a few minutes David found the BBC news. A young and slender blond-haired woman sat behind the commentator's desk beside a middle-aged man with fluffy brown hair. They were identified at the bottom of the screen as Hannah Williams and Jack Windham.

"Investigation continues into the January 6th nuclear bombing of New York City. American officials believe they may have identified the men responsible for the attack." As Hannah Williams spoke the screen changed to an overhead view of the remains of lower Manhattan. A moment later it changed again to an image of a young man in a black, off the rack business suit standing behind a podium adorned with the FBI seal.

"Spokespersons for the American Federal Bureau of Investigation have indicated that they believe Aziz Al Faruq, Turiq Hassan, Ali Bakir, and Alasar bin Alasar carried out the deadly bombing." Again, the screen changed to show photos of four men of clear Arabic origin. "All four men are from the former Saudi Arabian region and are believed to be connected to the ISIS militant group. Laura McNeil has more."

The screen image changed again this time showing an image of another young woman with light brown hair standing in front of a montage of Washington DC.

"FBI spokesperson Madeline Tanner announced the names of four suspects in the January 6th nuclear bombing of New York. Ethnic Arabs Aziz Al Faruq, Turiq Hassan, Ali Bakir, and Alasar bin Alasar are believed to be responsible for the deadly attack twelve days earlier. All four men are suspected of being connected with the ISIS militant group and are believed to have been killed in the blast."

The image returned to Hannah Williams and Jack Windham. This time Jack spoke. "Riots continue in response to perceived security deficits within the United Kingdom."

The screen changed again to show a series of images of out of control crowds, acts of violence and burning buildings.

"Following the devastating nuclear bombing of New York City conservative and anti-immigration groups have taken to the streets across the UK to protest current immigration policy. Two hundred people were arrested today making the total arrested two thousand fifty since the anti-immigration protests became violent three days ago. London police have begun using choking gases and rubber bullets in an attempt to break up the riot, but so far have only succeeded in provoking a hail of rocks and Molotov cocktails from the crowd. Meanwhile rioters have begun setting fire to buildings and are looting businesses and government facilities all over the city. Prime Minister Windsor has warned that if the rioting does not stop by six o'clock tomorrow evening he will dispatch the military and impose martial law upon the city. Riot leaders have replied by threatening to destroy the entire city of London if the military attempts to interfere with the protests. Our own Holly Peterson has obtained an exclusive interview with conservative, anti-immigration leader Robert Michaelson."

The screen image changed to show an older looking redheaded woman seated across from a fifty or sixty-year-old portly and balding man. Holly Peterson spoke first. "Why don't we start by having you explain exactly what your position is?" Her tone of voice was cool, her expression suggestive of her politics.

"My position and that of the immigration reform movement is that our leaders need to put the security of our people above the demands of immigrant pressure groups and businesses looking for cheap labor." Robert McMichealson's speech was steady and dispassionate.

"But the current immigration rules are settled law." Peterson replied. "The majority of these people are not terrorists. They are simply poor people looking for a better life. How do you answer those who say that you are motivated by racism and classism? How do you answer charges that your movement only protests immigration from Asia, Africa and the Middle East?"

McMichealson answered her in a steady and patient tone. "This is not about race. This is about safety. People are tired of being afraid while the government continues to insist on an open-door immigration policy. We watched the World Trade Towers come down and our government continued to admit people without any changes. We endured the attacks on the Tube and still nothing changed. Twelve days ago, a thermonuclear weapon detonated in Manhattan. Are we to be expected to go back to the status quo again and wait until the terrorists annihilate one of our cities?"

Peterson's brow wrinkled, and her lips curled into what could have been mistaken for a shadow of a sneer. "Let's talk about the rioting in London. How do you feel about what the rioters are doing in the name of national security?" Peterson's sneer became quite obvious as she spoke the words "national security".

A wrinkle of annoyance crossed McMichealson's face. "I commend the protesters' fervor. I was in fact one of the organizers of the original rally. But I do not condone violence. What the protesters are doing now shames the immigration reform movement and diminishes our credibility. Every time someone commits an act of violence in the name of the immigration reform movement they make it that much easier for open borders movement to label us as fanatics and racists."

Before Peterson could respond the screen, image returned to Hannah Williams and Jack Windham. "You may view the full interview at ten o'clock on BBC Magazine."

Williams started to say something but then stopped. "This just in. A massive quake just shook Moscow, Russia. Fires are burning everywhere. Thousands are feared dead. We have no footage at this time and there is very little information available." She was silent again. "We have another breaking story in Paris, France. An F5 tornado just passed through the city destroying a great deal of it including several historical monuments." She broke off again. "Tsunamis struck the cities of Sydney, Australia; Shanghai, China; and Venice, Italy. An enormous chemical fire rages in Delhi and the Republic of Iran just completed a devastating air strike against the Israeli city-state Tel Aviv."

David switched off the television and knocked back his scotch in one shot then stood up and went back into the living room.

It's really happening. God help us all.

He walked with slow and unsteady steps, as if drunk.

Jesus it's really happening.

David found the decanter of scotch and poured himself another glass then knocked it back in a single gulp. His blood ran cold. His body felt limp as if dead. With trembling hands David filled his glass for the third time and then drained it. He continued like this until he had emptied half of the decanter and was feeling very drunk. Then he stumbled over to the couch and flopped down. His heart was racing now, and he continued to quake with fear.

Fires, floods, deadly storms, earthquakes, rioting, war. It was really happening. The end time had truly come. Despite his drunken state David could feel the change accelerating.

"David?" Charlie's voice broke his train of thought. "I'm hungry. What's for dinner?"

"What?"

David lifted his eyes to meet hers. Charlie was standing over him in her nightgown looking rested and fresh. It was dark outside but a glance at the clock told him it was only six thirty. Charlie had been asleep since mid-morning and had only eaten breakfast. She had to be starving.

"Sure, I'll get you something." David dragged himself into a sitting position and then stood up. As he did his head swam with dizziness. "Ugghh what the hell was I thinking?"

Charlie was looking at him strangely. "Are you alright?"

As he looked at her Charlie suddenly doubled, then trebled. "Are you drunk?" She looked at him for a moment. "You are drunk." Her voice had become angry.

"You can barely stand up." She turned and started to storm out of the room. David caught her shoulder.

"Hold on. I'll make your dinner."

She twisted out of his grasp and marched out of the room. "Forget it. I'll get it myself."

David lurched across the living room and into the kitchen where he found Charlie rapidly pulling out the makings for a ham sandwich. Her expression was absolutely furious. Catherine stood beside her trying to get her to calm down.

As he approached Catherine spun around and glared at him. "Get out of here." Her voice was calm but sharp. David turned and stumbled back to the couch. Ten minutes later Catherine appeared looking angry herself.

"Your father's taking care of Charlie. What the hell are you doing getting drunk? Charlie's really upset, and I have to admit I'm not happy about it either."

David looked up at her drunkenly. "I…"

Catherine grabbed his arm. "Get your ass up. I don't want Charlie seeing you here and getting upset all over again. Jesus, I don't believe you."

David made no effort to explain himself. He was too intoxicated. He only let Catherine lead him upstairs. As they reached the top step David's head began to spin and his stomach lurched. "Uggh I'm gonna puke."

Catherine let out an aggravated sigh. "Alright hang on."

He barely made it bathroom and wound up puking on the floor rather than in the toilet, which only served to further annoy Catherine. When he had completely emptied the contents of his stomach Catherine put him to bed.

XVIII

Charlie ate her dinner quickly, then followed David's father into the TV room still fuming. How could David do this? When she and Daddy had been living in Pittsburgh and New York Daddy drank heavily some nights. She had hated dealing with Daddy when he was drunk. It was scary, and he always acted mean and stupid. Now David was doing the same thing.

Jerk! Why does he have to act like that?

In her mind she saw her father stumbling in the apartment door after a long night of drinking. *"Hey kiddo wazzup? Howzit gowin?"*

She could still smell the stench of smoke drifting off his clothing and see the single orange-red eye of his cigarette. *"Hey get your ass over here and give yer father a hug. Hey warz my dinner? Whadijya make me fer dinner?"*

Daddy had often made her cry when he did that. Now she just got angry.

Why does David have to be like that too?

David's father (he'd asked her to call him Father Jim) was sitting beside her on the couch trying to placate her. "I'm sure David didn't mean to get drunk Charlie. He cares a lot about you. He'd never do anything to hurt you."

Charlie sat staring straight ahead, not speaking a word.

This seemed to make Father Jim very uncomfortable. "I know it's upsetting to see someone you care about like that, but you need to cut David some slack. He's under a lot of pressure and he's very concerned for you. He's…"

"I don't care. He's drunk!" She snapped back.

Father Jim had nothing to say to that.

David always tried hard, that was true but this she could not forgive. In a way it felt like a betrayal, one no less horrible than Robin Striker's; the man who had professed to be her friend then killed her father.

You killed my Daddy you bastard!!

Charlie slammed the thought down before she lost control of herself.

With the passage of that thought came another. The change was growing stronger, accelerating and they were in danger. They had to leave now. It was these feelings that had awakened her from her sleep. A slow shiver swept through her body. *It's really happening.*

XIX

At that moment Catherine had the exact same feeling and following thought. She was sitting alone in the living room eating a ham and cheese sandwich when her appetite suddenly evaporated, and her stomach lurched. This was followed a moment later by a sharp tremor, for she knew and understood at once what had to be done.

XX

David too was having the same thought. Despite his intoxicated state he was not so far gone as to not appreciate the ramifications of what was happening. Now that the initial shock was gone his mind (or whatever lucid part of it remained) had begun to process what he had seen and felt. They had to run again. The NSA would soon move against them. The time to escape was now.

XXI

David's father entered the room just as Catherine was chewing the last bite of her sandwich.

"I put Charlie to bed. How's David?"

"Piss drunk." She replied flatly. Despite her annoyance Catherine understood deep inside what had driven David to drink. "We can't stay any longer."

James nodded his head. "Yes, I know."

"As soon as David sobers up we're going to have to run again."

James nodded again. "I know but it won't help if you go running off without a plan."

Catherine looked up at him steadily. "What do you have in mind?"

"I can help you, but I'll need a day to arrange it."

Catherine remained silent signaling with her eyes for him to continue.

"You don't have a lot of time left. I know that but you're not going to get very far if you're recognized before you can leave the country. You need to change your appearances if you're going to have any hope of escaping. I have a friend that can help us."

Catherine nodded silently. It actually wasn't a bad idea. If they could get through the security checkpoints on the borders, then this would give them cover. They might be able to get halfway across Europe before the NSA even knew they had left the farm.

If I can convince David to wait another day.

As drunk as he was David had to have felt the change growing. It was probably the reason he had gotten drunk.

Catherine stood up slowly and went to the liquor cabinet where she took out the decanter of scotch. It had been nearly full the night before, now it was half empty. Catherine poured herself a drink and downed it.

She didn't blame him. She was frightened herself.

XXII

As it turned out the plan worked better than any of them could have imagined. It did take Catherine and James some time to convince David that it was worth another day but in the end, they wore him down.

They decided to disguise themselves as a Jordanian father with his brother and young son on their way to Riyadh.

Though he had not initially seen any value in taking another day to disguise their appearances, once Bonnie arrived David began to believe the ruse might actually work. If they could avoid passing through any check points their disguises would make it much more difficult for the NSA to track them and would allow them easier passage through the Middle East.

David volunteered to go first. Bonnie started by dying his hair black; then she gave him a large tube of artificial tanning lotion and sent him to the bedroom instructing David to cover every inch of skin on his body.

When he finished David emerged from the bedroom looking to all the world like a man of Middle Eastern descent save for his coral green eyes and his eyebrows and eyelashes which remained their natural color.

It was at this point that Bonnie applied the finishing touches. Using a mascara brush and a tiny amount of black hair dye Bonnie darkened David's eyebrows and eyelashes to match his new hair color. She then produced a pair of brown contact lenses to complete the illusion.

The process took a little longer with Catherine. Her hair had to be cut short to look like a man's before being dyed black and when she finished applying the artificial tanning lotion Bonnie had to tape her breasts down to give her the appearance of having a man's flat chest.

When Bonnie was finished Catherine closely resembled an Arab male. Still her wider hips and the slight bulges under her shirt betrayed her true gender. Bonnie insisted that she could disguise these with the proper clothing but neither David nor Catherine was fully convinced.

Before Charlie took her turn, David sat down with her to talk. She had been watching the process carefully and was unhappy about the prospect of having her beautiful long blond hair cut short and then dyed jet black.

"I know you don't want to do this but it's very important."

Charlie looked up at him glumly.

"The NSA is looking for a white man and woman with a blonde-haired little girl. They won't suspect two Arabic men with a young boy."

She said nothing.

"It'll only be for a little while. Your hair will grow back and when it does we can cut out the black parts if you want."

"Alright." She tried on a tentative smile. "After all it's only hair anyway."

David smiled back and gave her a gentle hug. "Good girl. Are you ready?"

"Yes." Her voice had cheered up a little.

Charlie sat down without hesitation in the wooden backed chair that Bonnie had been using, even smiling at the woman as she tied a plastic smock around her neck.

"Ya 'ave such beauti-full hair Dani." She said as she began to brush through it.

Charlie smiled at her in the mirror. "Thank you."

"It's so long but there're no tan'gles. Ya must spend hours brushin'it out every day."

Now David had to smile. Charlie spent very little time brushing her hair despite how long it was. She seemed to be one of those very few people who are lucky enough to have hair that did not tangle easily.

Charlie sat in the chair smiling silently seemingly content to take Bonnie's compliment without correction.

"Y're goin' ta be a real ha'rt breaker when ya get olda. Boys'll be linin' up ta go out with ya."

Charlie giggled. "Thanks. I think."

She was still young, too young to have developed an interest in boys in David's estimation, yet at the same time she did not have the same inbuilt dislike for boys that characterized most girls her age.

"Y'll ne'er 'ave a problem getting dates."

Bonnie continued brushing Charlie's hair for another ten minutes. She was having a harder time with cutting Charlie's hair than Charlie was. It was almost comical in a way. Still it was a shame to cut off such beautiful hair.

When Bonnie finally got around to cutting Charlie's hair she did it very quickly like one might rip off a bandage rather than peeling it to shorten the amount of time spent in pain.

When Bonnie had finished cutting off the length she took out an electric clipper and trimmed the hair on the back of Charlie's head to buzz cut length. She then took out an even more precise trimmer, shaved off much of the hair on Charlie's neck and cut a sharp line along the edge of her new hairline, thus creating the suggestion of sideburns.

As he watched this David thought of what a strange place the Middle East had become.

Following the second gulf war and the impeachment and removal of the then current administration by Congress, the new administration immediately pulled all American forces from the Persian Gulf area and from Afghanistan and Pakistan. The result was the total destabilization of the entire Middle East. Nations collapsed overnight under growing warfare and civil unrest, which began in Iraq and Afghanistan and quickly spread as far as Pakistan and parts of India in the east and all of northern and central Africa in the west. Even Turkey and Israel disintegrated in the ensuing chaos. As central authority disappeared warlords and terrorists seized control of the region, turning it into a modern-day old west. Now the Middle East was a fairly even blend between secularist and traditionalist groups collectively under the thumbs of the many warlords, gangsters and terrorists that now ruled the region. Violence and crime had become the norm, as the only law of the land was loyalty to the local leader.

The Middle East was a dangerous place but it was also probably the only place on earth where they would be effectively out of the NSA's sight.

After a few minutes Bonnie finished and began preparing the dying solution she would use to darken Charlie's hair.

The effects were dramatic. With her hair darkened Charlie really began to look like a boy. Given the right clothing and manner it would be impossible to tell that she was not male.

The next step was to darken Charlie's skin and when this was finished she really did look Middle Eastern. It was almost eerie.

Charlie too received contact lenses to disguise her eye color. David helped her insert them under her eyelids. Once they were in place she looked like a totally different person bearing no resemblance at all to the tow-headed little girl known as Charlene MacLeod.

The final phase was to outfit them with appropriate clothing and when this was finished the illusion was complete.

It was late so Bonnie stayed for dinner. When she left after dinner it was eleven-thirty at night. David put Charlie to bed. Then he and Catherine went to bed themselves. They were leaving at six the next morning.

XXIII

After David left her bedroom Charlie quietly got up and went over to the mirror.
The face that looked back at her was that of a stranger. Her blue eyes were now
dark brown, her skin darkly tanned, and her hair short and jet-black. She wasn't
sure how she felt. Part of her was upset, part of her found this almost fun, like
playing dress up. Charlie stared at herself in the mirror for a long time. Just
before turning away she mouthed two words: Amir Farakad, the name she would
go by from now on. As she was walking back to her bed Charlie's eye was
caught by a gleam of silver as the moonlight reflected off her sword.

She had not touched it since the day she made it. Charlie did not think she
needed a sword. David's explanation for the sword rang hollow to her. She
doubted that she would need anything to focus and channel the power, she had
never found a limit to her ability and there was no weapon she could pick up that
was deadlier. If she ever needed to face a Dark Knight she would certainly be
able to incinerate him. But it seemed important to David.

Still, he had never trained her with it. She had expected him to have her practice
with it while Catherine was being made up but he did not. And now they were
leaving. Why was it so important that she make this sword if she wasn't going to
be taught to use it?

As she was thinking this Charlie picked up the long blade. At the touch of her
fingers, the blade's great red flaw glowed and pulsated angrily with the blazing
bloodstain upon her heart.

She had never before handled any weapon, yet her hands closed on the sword as
if she had been using one all her life. Without instruction her hands brought the
sword up smoothly and leveled it. Then her grip changed, her hands positioning
themselves to allow her to put her weight behind any swing she might make.
Frightened amazement flooded through her.

How am I doing this?

She did not know and that made it more frightening. In an almost trace-like state
she carried the weapon down the stairs and outside. The ground felt cold beneath
her bare feet as she continued walking towards the woods beyond the sheep

pastures surrounding the little farm.

Where am I going?

The question echoed in her head as her heart quickened.

Charlie walked in the woods for an unknown period of time before stopping with the same suddenness that she had started.

She was standing in front of a sapling. Its trunk was slightly thicker than her arm. Without thinking Charlie brought the sword back and swung hard, harder than she would have imagined she could. The blade sliced neatly through the sapling's trunk dropping it to the ground with no sound save for a low *-thunk-* as steel bit into wood. In the same smooth motion, she brought the sword up and sliced the stump straight down the center to the root. Charlie gazed at the blade in her hands in wonder.

How did I do that?

She didn't know, and the spell had broken. Charlie turned and headed back reaching the house two hours before it was time to leave.

Chapter 11

Taken

At seven o'clock that morning David, Catherine and Charlie left Glen Dunbairn for the last time. At the same time Father James Lenox vanished leaving only a typewritten letter of resignation.

I

They hired a car and traveled south all day until they reached Dover. Upon arriving in Dover, they bought a ride across the English Channel. Though it was costly they easily found passage to France that would not require them to pass through any checkpoints. From France they journeyed across the Alps into Switzerland, then to Germany and from there into Eastern Europe.

From here the journey became much more dangerous. Like the Middle East, Eastern Europe was politically unstable. While they would no longer have to avoid security checkpoints they would be at a high risk of becoming victims of random violence. Furthermore, their disguises would put them at a higher risk in some areas. As "Muslims" they would be targets for the Christian Serbians spread throughout the region. David, Catherine, and Charlie were each mindful of this as they crossed the eastern German border.

From Eastern Europe they traveled south into what had once been Turkey and from there into northern Iraq.

On February 1st David, Catherine and Charlie arrived in a tiny Kurdish village. It was late, around nine or ten o'clock at night. The village's narrow streets were deserted, and its tall clay buildings were dark save for a few scattered lights in windows.

Charlie's heart began to race. She had felt a strong sense of danger since entering the town. That feeling was growing now both in intensity and urgency. Someone was watching them, waiting unseen. Charlie raked her eyes over the darkened buildings and shadowy streets and alleys but saw nothing. A slow shiver crept up her spine. Something was very wrong.

As they neared the village's center the feeling grew stronger still. Charlie waited for her vision to change and show her where the NSA agents were hiding but it did not. Something, perhaps her own fear, was blocking it.

A cold breeze tugged at her clothing. Charlie shivered again and drew her robes more tightly around her body. It was strange how cold it got in the desert at night.

As she looked around Charlie imagined she could see movement in the shadows. The sky was a clear black span with no moon and few stars making for a very dark night. The perfect setting for an ambush.

It was too quiet, as if every living thing out there were holding its breath waiting for whatever was about to come. David and Catherine must have felt it as well for they too were nervous. Charlie could sense it in the air. She looked up at David fearfully. He returned a nervous smile but said nothing.

They were within twenty feet of the well that marked the center of town. The breeze had fallen still. Everything was deadly silent. The feeling of danger was overpowering. Then it happened. A figure appeared out of the shadows. It was male and short and stocky.

"Hello Charlie." The man's voice was low and smooth. "And you must be David and Catherine McAuliffe. It is a pleasure to finally meet you."

Charlie stared at him with cold eyes. The power was already stirring within her. "What do you want?"

"I thought I'd give you one last chance to surrender." Though she could only see his outline Charlie sensed the man's smile.

"Why would we want to do that?" David asked in cool voice.

Charlie never heard the shot. She screamed then dove to the ground, somersaulting into a crouching position. Green fire streaked though the air above her head as men in black armor streamed out of the buildings on her left and right. They were not NSA.

Instinctively Charlie struck out with the power. Fire swept up around the short and stocky man swallowing him alive. He let out a horrific scream. Charlie watched impassively. He looked like a burning scarecrow. His flesh was running like candle wax then flying off his bones in liquid blobs. Then the bones themselves began to burn. That was when he collapsed to the ground. It all took only seconds.

Charlie turned to her left and lashed out with the power. Fire erupted from the ground beneath the black armored men's feet. The air filled with their screams for a moment before they collapsed and were still. More green fire flashed around her from behind and to her right. Charlie spun around and was about to strike out again with the power when a hand caught her shoulder and forced her to the ground.

"Stay down." As she watched David grabbed one of the men and spun him around into the continuing stream of green fire then returned several bolts of red fire from the man's rifle. Each struck a different man and blew him apart. Without pausing David snapped the man's neck then clamped down on her wrist and roughly pulled her to her feet. "Come on."

Charlie made no effort to resist. Her mind was reeling with fear. The power was blazing. As she watched Catherine bent down and grabbed one of the dead men's rifles before following after them. Charlie turned around an instant before David dove over the top of a pile of cinder blocks pulling her after him. Instinctively Charlie pulled her body into a ball, turned a single somersault and landed in a crouching pose. In the same motion she spun on her heal just in time to see green fire splash off the top of the pile. Hot sparks rained down on David and Catherine.

David snarled a curse. "Shit that's hot!" Then he jumped to his feet and fired off another volley of red fire. Screams rang out on the cold night air followed close behind by more volleys of green fire.

"Stay down." David's voice carried deep fear. "Catherine and I will handle these guys. And be ready to run when I say so."

Charlie nodded. Green fire streaked overhead missing her by only inches. The air had filled with the strong smell of lightning.

"Who the hell are these people?" Catherine's voice was bewildered.

David shook his head. "I don't know."

Death Troopers. The words came into Charlie's head from nowhere.

Catherine stood up and snapped off several more shots. These were immediately followed by fresh screams of agony. The ozone smell was now joined by the stench of scorched flesh.

The power was spiraling wildly within her. She had it under control, but it was rapidly growing in strength. As David straightened up to fire off another volley a streak of green fire grazed the top of his head scorching some of his hair. David collapsed backward with a cry. "Oww fuck!"

Sudden anger flashed in her heart. *You bastards hurt David.* Slowly, Charlie got to her feet, heart pounding. *You're gonna be sorry.*

"No Charlie! Stay down!"

Charlie ignored David's cry. Trenches of fire swept across the ground in front of her in a widening spider web engulfing the nearest Death Troopers. Then all at once the ground vanished in a solid lake of fire before erupting into a massive fireball. There were no screams, only a loud *–waruummp-* as the flames swept upward through the air.

For a moment she thought it was over. There seemed to be no more Death Troopers, only piles of scorched and blackened corpses and a wide scattering of body parts. Then a fresh wave of Death Troopers swept through the still towering wall of fire, blasting away with their rifles.

Charlie did not flinch even as green fire filled the air around her. The power was blazing, dancing upon the razor's edge of her ability to control it. Without hesitation she shoved it out of herself in the direction of the Death Troopers. This time the ground in front of her erupted in a wall of fire which immediately swept forward engulfing this second wave of Death Troopers. The air filled with their screams for an instant before they were cut off leaving only the low crackle-sizzle of burning flesh.

In that same instant her vision changed, and she found herself looking at the tall shadow of a man standing on a rooftop. He was leveling a rifle, taking aim.

II

"No!!" David watched in horror as green fire streaked down from a rooftop at the opposite end of the street and struck Charlie in the face. She was thrown backwards by the impact and landed in a heap on the ground.

"Charlie!!" He went to her and found her lying flat on her back unconscious. Her breathing was slow and shallow and her heart beat barely perceptible. "Oh God. Who did it?!" He demanded. "Who shot her?!" There was no answer of course. He did not expect one. "Which one of you bastards shot her?!"

Catherine was crouched beside him. The two locked eyes for a moment before dropping their rifles and slowly standing up hands raised above their heads. It was over. Charlie needed medical attention. She was hurt, he wasn't sure how badly, and he could not risk having her get hit again. Her only hope was for them to surrender and let the NSA take care of her.

The black armored men paused only a moment before opening fire and gunning them both down.

Chapter 12
The Ninth Circle

I

The dark gentleman moves his queen between the gentleman in white's king and queen creating a skewer.

"Check!

The gentleman in white nods his approval. "Good move." Then he proceeds to move his king one square to the right taking it out of the queen's range of attack. "I didn't see it coming."

"You are behind in material and I have your strongest player. There is no shame in resigning. There is always next time." As he spoke the dark gentleman captured the gentleman in white's queen on a diagonal.

The gentleman white sipped his beer. "It is not over yet."

II

Upon awakening David found himself lying on a bed in a small black steel cubicle. The front appeared to be open, but a slight bluish flicker told him differently.

Charlie! Catherine!

They were gone. He was alone. Cold terror exploded within him. The last thing he remembered was being gunned down with Catherine.

By the men in black armor...

The Death Troopers. His mind told him, seemingly from nowhere.

After Charlie was shot in the face. Now they were both gone.

Catherine, Charlie! Jesus please let them be alright!

He had no way of knowing what had happened to them. They could have died. Except somehow, he knew they weren't dead.

Charlie, Catherine, where are you?!

His heart was pounding. David stood up and went to the opening of the cubicle. As he neared it the blue flicker became brighter then changed to a light blue haze. He was close to panic.

"Charlie! Catherine!" He called their names aloud without thinking. His voice echoed hauntingly off the black steel walls outside the cubicle.

Before he could do anything else the blue flicker vanished, and two black armored Death Troopers appeared. One of them struck David in the head with a rifle butt dropping him to his knees.

"Shut up!!" The voice was metallic and recognizably female.

Hands closed on his arms and dragged him to his feet.

"Let's go."

David stumbled to his feet with a groan. His head was throbbing, and his muscles were very stiff. The female Death Trooper kicked him in the butt.

"Move it!"

David got himself going despite the pain in his head and his growing fear. The corridors outside of the cell seemed to stretch on forever as if in a child's dream. Each was identical to the last with only heavy blast doors differentiating one from the next. As he walked David's heart pulsed with fear. His mind was blank save for a single thought.

Charlie! Catherine!

He had to find out what had happened to them.

After an indeterminate period of time they entered a large chamber filled with hundreds of Death Troopers lined up in two perfect block formations separated by a single aisle. David was led down this aisle to the front of the right-hand formation where Catherine was already waiting.

"Catherine! Thank God!" The words escaped his lips before he could stop them and were answered with another rifle butt to the back of his head.

"I said shut up!"

David stumbled but managed to stay on his feet this time.

"David!!" Catherine's cry was cut off by a fist to her midsection.

David struggled against his captors. "Catherine! Are you alright?" Another blow fell on the back of his head.

"I said *shut up*!"

David stumbled but caught himself with his right hand. As he was straightening up one of the Death Troopers stepped out of line and lowered his rifle to David's eye level. Though he said nothing the message was clear. 'Keep it up and I'll give you something to yell about.' David remained silent after this, not wanting to provoke them any further.

He was taken to stand next to Catherine. Each was flanked on both sides by Death Troopers.

At the front of the room was a raised platform equipped with a steel table on a free-floating base that allowed it to be spun around three hundred and sixty degrees and tilted to an upright position although it was currently lying flat. The table itself was equipped with heavy, padded steel wrist and ankle restraints and filled with hundreds of holes to allow fluids to drain into a collection trough below. Beside the table was an IV pole, a machine that looked like an ECG monitor, and several steel carts containing what could only be torture devices. Standing beside these were a dozen or so men and women in white lab coats and behind them a huge shadowy figure straight out of his darkest nightmares as a child. Icy cold waves radiated out from where it stood. David shuddered inwardly knowing at once that this creature was a Dark Knight and knowing too that they were to be tortured. Although he was afraid of being hurt himself he was more afraid for Catherine. He could not bear the thought of her being harmed.

At least Charlie's not here.

As that thought passed through his head he sensed the door opening and turned to look.

"David!"

Charlie entered as she had been born, her face white as a sheet and twisted into an expression of pure terror. An entourage of six Death Troopers surrounded her, two of them held her arms, literally dragging her down the aisle like a circus animal. David's heart chilled with horror for he knew at once what they intended for her. Charlie struggled against them with desperate ferocity. It was to no avail for she was no match for her captors and was forced steadily onward despite her efforts. David's heart was pounding now, threatening to burst from his chest.

"Charlie!!"

The rifle butt fell yet again on the back of his skull setting off a burst of white light.

David reached for the power but found, to his horror, that it was gone, turned off as if by some invisible switch. Though he was not aware of it at the time part of him had questioned why Charlie had not used her power to escape. At first, he had thought she was too frightened but now, now he wasn't so sure.

"David I'm scared! Help me!" Charlie's voice was on the verge of panic.

David felt terrible, he desperately wanted to help her, but he too was not strong enough to break free of the two Death Troopers that held his arms. Still he struggled despite the successive blows raining down on his head.

"David!!" She was terrified.

Desperation welled up within David for there was nothing he could do for her. She was going to be tortured right in front of him and there was nothing he could do about it.

"Hold on Charlie. You're going to be alright." Somehow his voice came out calm and reassuring.

One of the Death Troopers kicked him in the stomach winding him and causing him to collapse. He was roughly dragged to his feet before being punched in the face and ribs.

"Now behave yourself!" The female Death Trooper warned. "Or you'll really be sorry."

As he watched the Death Troopers holding Catherine began to beat her mercilessly even though she was not struggling. Without a word David nodded and the beating stopped.

"David please!!" Charlie cried desperately.

She had reached the platform now and was being dragged towards the steel table.

"Please help me! Please don't let them do this!" Her breath came in ragged, terrified gasps and her entire body shook with fright.

He had to help her somehow. "Charlie listen to me. Close your eyes. Don't pay attention to anything but the sound of my voice. You're going to be all right. We're far away from here. We're together. We're someplace faraway where they can't hurt us anymore. Just hold that picture in your mind while they do this. Don't think about anything else, just picture us at that safe place." Something hard and heavy struck him in the back of his head setting off an explosion of white across his vision.

"Please don't let them do this!" She was terrified. Tears glistened on her cheeks. She had begun to hyperventilate now and was shuddering so hard that she had to struggle to stand up straight.

David too was trembling, both with horror and anger. *How can they do this? She's only a little girl for God's sake.*

Then Charlie did something that he would never forget. As she neared the table she pulled out of the Death Troopers' grasp and walked the rest of the way to the table alone. Without hesitation she climbed up and lay still allowing the Death Troopers to strap her down without struggling.

After the Death Troopers had secured Charlie to the table the technicians went to work on her. First, they placed IVs in both of her arms. Then they wheeled one of the steel carts up to the table. This cart contained a small electronic device dripping a rat's nest of thin black wires that ended in small cylindrical sockets. Beside the machine was a small surgical tray filled with long, hair-thin acupuncture needles. David could not see much of what the technicians were doing but Charlie's agonized screams told him everything.

She's just a little girl…

How can they do this?

When they had finished the table, the technicians turned the table and tilted it upward to face out into the room. David shuddered involuntarily. Charlie's face had gone white as bone. Her eyes were wide with shock and her expression filled with horror. She hung loose in her bonds, arms stretched out to both sides.

"Don't hurt her!" The cry escaped his throat without his notice. The blow to the back of his head that followed caught his full attention.

The dark figure stepped forward and raised its hand. "Enough. They are not to be harmed. I want them to see this and remember." His voice was deep and metallic. His ragged, artificial breathing echoed as if in a dream. For a moment he turned his blank, artificial eyes on David. "You should have better protected her." Sudden, cold darkness radiated from the Dark Knight. Charlie's breathing became very rapid, each gasp separated by little sobs and her eyes went wide from an unseen terror.

"I regret that this child must suffer thus." The Dark Knight rumbled. "But she must learn to fear and hate those who are not like us." As he spoke, the icy black stream from the Dark Knight's mind intensified.

David understood at once, the Dark Knight had penetrated Charlie's mind and was forcing his will upon her, forcing her to see and perceive what *he* wanted. It was an assault, not of the body but of the mind.

All at once Charlie's body tensed and she let out a blood-curdling scream. The cry pierced him to the soul. He wanted so much to stop this, to save her from suffering anymore. David struggled against his captors but could not break free of their grasp. Charlie was crying hysterically. Then all at once her body tensed more and she screamed again, a long-sustained cry of pure suffering. After a few seconds her cry subsided, and her body relaxed a little. She was wailing in misery and terror. Her face was filled with pain. A moment later her body tensed again, and she resumed her screaming.

David stood frozen, heart chilled with horror, blood boiling. He felt like screaming in rage and bursting into tears at the same time.

She's just a little girl. She doesn't deserve this. Why are they doing this to her?

David never forgot that day. The image of Charlie's suffering stayed with him forever, as did the sound of her screams.

III

Charlie was tortured in this way for ten hours without rest. When it was over she was carried from the room semi-conscious. She remembered little of the trip back to her cell other than the image of a Death Trooper's face mask and the cold touch of his armor. The smooth black steel and plastic mask with its little silver grill remained burned in her mind long after she was returned to her cell before changing into the black, skull mask of the dark man.

He was real. She had known it since she had first had the dream, but she had convinced herself that he would never find her.

She was trapped, and she was alone again. The dark man had taken away David and Catherine just as the NSA had taken away her father and mother. She could still hear David's words in her mind.

Charlie listen to me. Close your eyes. Don't pay attention to anything but the sound of my voice. You're going to be all right. We're far away from here. We're together. We're someplace faraway where they can't hurt us anymore. Just hold that picture in your mind while they do this. Don't think about anything else, just picture us at that safe place.

Tears rolled down her cheeks though she was not crying anymore. Crying would have taken energy and she was exhausted.

Charlie was lying flat on her back on the bunk suspended from the right-hand wall. Fragmented images of death and torment flashed through her mind. In them she saw men and women lined up before a straight backed, red oak chair. Each in turn took his or her seat upon the squat, fearsome device. Their screams echoed within her mind, adding and mixing with her own in a terrifying cacophony. Their suffering, ripped through her, even as her body convulsed from electric shock.

These images were aggressive and threatened to overtake her other memories of the torment. The dark man's face threatened to melt into the faces of a thousand angry NSA agents. The large black steel chamber grew fuzzy in her mind and became desert sands bathed in pale blue winter's morning light. The cold steel touch of the perforated metal table became the hardwood embrace of the dark, terrible chair.

Had she ever really seen the dark man? Or had it been the NSA all along? The corridor they had taken her down, was identical to the one outside her cell the last time they had taken her.

But they wanted to kill me, didn't they?

Except they had killed her, and she had come back. Perhaps they hadn't really meant to torture her but rather to kill her. Perhaps…but no. She had felt the dark man's presence so strongly, like an icy wave. She had never felt anything like it before.

Still, the images insisted that they were real, insisted that she believe them, and insisted upon pushing all doubt and inconsistent memory aside. She fought against their demands for some intuition deep inside insisted that these images told lies.

Charlie felt violated both in body and mind. Her muscles were stiff and sore, her head throbbed, and her skin burned. Sharp pain radiated out from the places where the needles had been. Inside Charlie felt hollow, sick, frightened and more alone then she had ever felt in her life. This feeling was like nothing she had ever known before. It hurt so much. This pain was worse than the physical pain of the torture.

She supposed that was the intent. The act was meant to degrade and dehumanize as much as it was meant to hurt. She had to suffer emotionally as well as physically and this was a pain that would never fully leave her. The bloodstain had grown.

More than anything she wished David were there. He would know what to do. How to make the pain better. Her eyes continued to run with silent mournful tears. Deep inside she knew would never see David and Catherine again.

Charlie closed her eyes but could not go to sleep. Though she was exhausted her mind would not allow her, so she simply lay there without moving.

She struggled to drive away memories of the horror that had been inflicted on her only minutes earlier but could not. Images, both false and true flashed through her mind again and again aggravating her emotional pain. She began to feel ill. Her stomach lurched and then clenched filling her mouth with the taste of bile.

No please…

Please I don't want to…

Please…

All at once her stomach locked in painful spasm and before she could stop herself Charlie puked all over herself. Fresh tears spilled down her cheeks, but she made no effort to get up. She was too tired. All she could do was lie there in her own hot stinking mess.

IV

After some time had passed the force field was lowered. Two Death Troopers entered her cell, roughly dragged her to her feet and took her to the showers. She was given nothing to cover herself nor was she allowed to shower in private. The two Death Troopers flanked her on either side the entire time. There was no hot water and the soap made her skin sting and burn.

Charlie struggled to wash herself with her right hand while clutching her slight body with her left arm and shivering. When she finished Charlie was returned to her cell still soaking wet, shivering and clutching herself in a futile attempt to keep warm.

Upon returning Charlie collapsed on her bed more exhausted than ever. She was freezing cold but could not even muster enough strength to pull the blanket over herself.

The two Death Troopers returned a few minutes later with an IV pole. Charlie understood at once that this was how she would be fed. She would not even be permitted normal food. Even eating had to be made unpleasant.

It didn't matter. It wasn't important. It would only be a little needle stick. It wouldn't hurt that much.

Charlie cooperated mutely, allowing the Death Troopers to insert the IV needle into the vein in the crook of her elbow and tape it in place. She barely noticed the pinch.

Within a few seconds cold began to radiate out from where the needle penetrated her skin. Charlie closed her eyes and lay still as the cold, clear liquid dripped into her veins. It took some time but eventually sleep did come.

V

Charlie awakened to the sound of soft, artificial breathing. She opened her eyes to see the black, death's head mask of the dark man. Her breathing quickened, and her heart began to race. Before she could stop herself, she screamed and scrambled into a sitting position. Several groups of muscles cried out in protest, but she barely noticed.

"You fear me." His voice was dark and metallic. "You think I hurt you and that I will hurt you again. You need not fear me. I am not the one who hurt you. The men who hurt you were NSA. I am not NSA."

Sudden anger flashed within Charlie's heart. She turned her eyes upon him, letting them bore into the artificial lenses that served as his eyes. "You're a liar. I know you were the one that hurt me. You tried to trick me, but I know."

"You are mistaken Charlie." The dark man's voice had taken on a tone of soft condescension. "My men and I rescued you from the NSA and brought you hear. NSA agents were the ones who hurt you. You do not remember because you were heavily drugged."

As he spoke, Charlie felt cold hands closing around her mind and forcing images of laughing men in white lab coats standing over her and tormenting her as she lay strapped to a perforated steel table, in an unadorned steel walled chamber. She recognized this chamber as one in which she had burned up the stone slab. This image was replaced a moment later by one of that same, fearsome squat red oak chair. Even now, she felt its smooth hardwood frame beneath her back and bottom and its cold metal skull cap upon her brow. Charlie pushed back against the hands and forced her mind to return to what she thought was reality.

STOP IT!

"You're a liar." She repeated in a low whisper. "Stay out of my head."

The dark man approached her and extended his hand. "Get up. It is time to go."

Charlie was terrified but took his hand and allowed him to lead her out of the cell. The dark man was alone. The Death Troopers guarding her cell had left sometime after she went to sleep. Charlie looked up at him with cold fear in her heart. His mask hid any trace of emotion and she was too frightened to sense his intentions. Standing next to him he was huge. The top of her head did not clear his waist. His arms were thicker than her legs. His massive grip swallowed her hand whole. It was powerful though not painful. She imagined he could have crushed her hand if he wanted to. The dark man took her down the hallway outside her cell to where it ended in a heavy blast door. On the other side of this was another hallway.

Halfway down the second hallway they stopped and boarded an elevator. This elevator took them up what she imagined to be hundreds of floors before the doors opened and they got off. It was strange; the elevator had no buttons outside or in.

How does it know when to open and what floor to stop at?

The question passed briefly through her mind before being washed away by fear. They had entered a large open atrium the center floor of which opened into space. Charlie froze in shock.

Where am I?

As if he had read her mind the dark man answered. "You are aboard the *Darksaber,* flagship of the Black Imperial Navy. I am Lucius am Beathach Commandant of the Black Imperial Military and Dark Lord of The Legion of Dark Knights. My proper title is Lord Beathach."

Charlie remained perfectly still unsure of what to think. Until now she had believed they had been taken by some government agency. Now she had no idea who had taken them.

What's the Black Empire? Who are these people?

She stood beside Lord Beathach for a moment longer neither moving nor speaking. Then he became impatient and gave her arm a rough tug. "Come. We are wasting time."

Charlie complied mutely. The atrium was filled with numerous ships of varying sizes and designs. Though she had never seen any of them before Charlie somehow knew the names and purposes of each ship. Closest to her were two rows of S -20 Ravens. These were long, sleek spacecraft that resembled a US Airforce F-15E. Behind these were two rows of S-10 Cerberuses. These too were sleek, slender spacecraft and resembled a Navy F-14. The S-20 and S-10 were the backbone of the Black Imperial Starfighter Corps and were the most numerous of all the ships in the atrium.

Hanger. It's a hanger idiot.

Charlie counted twenty wings of each before she stopped counting. Besides these were a dozen wings each of S-100 Saber Wolves, S-200 Bloodhounds, and S-300 Talons (Close facsimiles of the F-22, F/A-18, and F-16 respectively.). There were also two dozen Delta class transport shuttles, two dozen Firebrand

and Thunderbolt light cruisers and a dozen Alpha class heavy transport shuttles.

Lord Beathach led her towards the closest Delta transport shuttle. Inside it was like a scene out of *Star Trek*. Despite her growing fear Charlie could not help being awed. This was beyond her wildest dreams of what the future might look like. Contrary to her expectations she was not confined but rather was brought to the ship's cockpit. The pilot smiled when he saw her.

"You must be the young lady. My name's Will." He gestured to the couch behind him. "Have a seat. We'll be underway in a couple of minutes."

Lord Beathach sat down beside her. "The pain you have suffered at the hands of the NSA is but a taste of what the Outsiders would inflict upon you."

Charlie looked up at him again. She knew he was lying, yet she sensed a deeper truth behind his words. "You're lying to me. I know it was you. Why did you hurt me?"

Without responding Lord Beathach removed his mask.

Charlie's eyes widened in horror. The right half of his face was that of a young man with light colored, smooth skin, long blond hair and eye the same shade of blue as hers. He might have once been thought handsome were it not for the other half of his face. On the left side the flesh had been burned away leaving only blackened bone; even his hair and left eye were gone.

"This is the price I paid for my power." His deep metallic voice took on an edge of anger. "The non-Enlighteneds, the common people burned me at the stake when they learned what I am. Your power is far greater and rarer than mine. What will they do with you when they learn who you are?"

As he spoke, Charlie felt the cold touch of his mind and before she could stop it she was carried away to a desolate prison camp to stand before that same, squat, red oak chair. This time she felt hands upon her shoulders and found herself driven forward towards the chair's deadly embrace. Now she was seated, and the hands drew heavy leather straps over her arms and legs and across her chest. Something icy cold and wet was placed on her head. A loud, thrumming engine, rumbled within her mind, growing louder and louder until her body suddenly tensed and lit up with white fire. Charlie screamed and shoved Lord Beathach's mind away.

STOP IT! LEAVE ME ALONE!

"That is the future they would give you and your adoptive father and mother. It *is* the future they gave to your natural father and mother. I am not your enemy; Charlie and I do not enjoy showing you such things, but you must understand that this is what they will do to you for all eternity if you allow them."

She looked up at him questioningly. *What is he talking about?*

The remnants of his face hardened into stone. "You did not know." His voice was almost regretful. "Your 'friends' have cursed you to immortality by asking you to unseal *Deus Irae*. The blade contains the power of the Almighty. Those exposed to it are moved outside the flow of time."

Charlie stared at him blankly, not wanting to understand.

"You will never grow old and you will never die. You will remain a child for all eternity."

"No. That's a lie. You're lying." Tears streamed down her cheeks in rivers for she knew he spoke the truth.

Lord Beathach returned an icy glare and held his mask up in his right hand. "I wear this as a reminder of what they had intended for me." Then he placed it back on his face.

Charlie was only peripherally aware of this. She sat staring straight ahead still unable to accept what she had been told. She would live forever, she would never have to worry about dying unless someone tried to kill her, but she would also never grow up. She would out live everyone she loved, and she would never escape this place, this Black Empire. She would always be their prisoner, forever.

As she watched, the ship lifted off the deck and flew towards the open porthole. A few seconds later they emerged into space. As it turned out they were in orbit above a large, blood red planet. It looked like Mars, but it was much too big to be Mars. It was beautiful, and Charlie could not help but marvel.

They were heading towards a large black sphere in orbit around the planet. At first, she took this for the planet's moon but as they grew closer she saw that it could not possibly have been anything natural. It was too perfect; there were no craters, no cracks. The sphere's surface was smooth and shiny, like a black pearl. It gleamed in the light from the planet's large white sun. Surrounding the sphere on all sides were hundreds of massive black, wedge shaped ships.

Star Cruisers and Galactic Dreadnaughts. The Black Imperial Central Star Fleet.

As they grew closer still Charlie saw that the sphere was in fact a gigantic, planet sized space station. Part of her found this very disturbing, both because of the sheer size of the space station and because she had not recognized it at once.

She might have been more frightened had she not been so distraught. She was still crying hard though she made no sound. She was doomed. She would spend the rest of eternity being tortured. They were nearing the space station. It had grown to fill the entire front window. Charlie's heart felt cold like the heart of a condemned man on that last long walk. This was her future and there was no escape.

Upon landing they were greeted by a huge entourage of Death Troopers. As she left the ship with Lord Beathach they fell into two razor sharp lines flanking the gangplank on either side.

All at once Charlie was struck by a powerful cold, empty sensation. It was almost choking in its oppressiveness. A slow shudder crept up her spine. There was something very wrong here. She felt as if she were standing at the site of a massacre. This was a place of pain and suffering, a place of darkness.

They were nearing the blast doors at the rear of the docking bay. As they approached, the doors slid open silently. Charlie turned to see the Death Troopers fall in behind them as they entered the corridor beyond.

The lighting here was too bright, almost painful. Charlie squinted to shield her eyes. She was trembling though she was not aware of it.

Please…somebody help me.

There was no answer of course but then she had not expected one. There was no hope. No escape.

They entered an elevator and rapidly descended deep into the space station. A few seconds later the elevator doors opened on a narrow, brightly lit corridor. This corridor ended in another blast door. Behind this was another narrow corridor. More Death Troopers lined both sides of this corridor at twenty-foot intervals.

This was where she was to be kept. The corridor itself consisted of heavy, reinforced blast armor, small, six by six cells occurred every ten feet along the right wall. All of them were empty. Lord Beathach took her to the last cell and pushed her inside.

"Welcome to the *Destroying Angel*."

He turned and left. Charlie remained perfectly still, not moving from the spot where he had pushed her. Her heart was racing, Terror boiled up within her until she could no longer hold it back. All at once Charlie burst into tears. There was no force behind her crying. Any there might have been was sublimated by fear.

The cell was so tiny and there was nothing. Just nothing. All she had was a bare mattress with a single army blanket and a toilet. There were no windows, no toys, she didn't even have a pillow, and there was no privacy. She couldn't even pee without being watched by the two guards standing outside the cell's force field.

Like a monkey in the zoo.

The Death Troopers outside watched her without moving. Charlie stared back defiantly despite the tears streaming down her cheeks. It was strange, almost like staring at a machine for she could not see their eyes or faces. Their black helmets and face masks saw to that. There was a visor in the top half of the mask, but this too was opaque from the outside. The armor itself was solid black and glistened under the bright overhead lights. It did not, in fact, look all that different from the blast armor that made up the corridor itself. A single black satin armband on each Death Troopers' left arm signified their allegiance in red silk strands.

Charlie shuddered but would not turn away. She would not give up her pride. It was all she had left. Eventually though exhaustion overcame pride and she turned and lay down on the bed to sleep.

VI

Charlie awakened sometime later feeling hungry. She called to the Death Trooper outside her cell.

"Can I have something to eat please? I'm really hungry."

There was no response, not even an acknowledgement that she had spoken. The two guards simply remained as they were; perfectly still, cold, lifeless, rifles slung over shoulders in a statuesque pose. She could not help but be impressed by their discipline. But right now, she was hungry.

"Come on. I know you can hear me. I said: Can I have something to eat?"

Still no response, not even a movement.

"Why won't you answer me? I said I'm hungry. I want something to eat." She screamed at them. "Goddamnit! Answer me you stupid assholes!" She turned away angrily, close to tears.

Who are these people? The Black Empire? What's that?

She did not understand. The knowledge had not yet come to her. It was strange, she felt much calmer and more clear headed than she had earlier yet her psychic senses remained blunted. She felt as though she were wrapped in gauze. Something other than just emotion was interfering with her psychic senses. This same something must have also been blocking the power for it too was strangely silent.

What did they do to me? Is it drugs?

She didn't feel drugged. Other than being hungry she felt fine.

But the power's gone. Why?

She had always thought she would be glad to be rid of the power, but this was scary. She had lived all of her life with the ability to sense other's intentions, to sense danger, to move things, to light fires, losing those abilities was terrifying. To her it was like losing an arm or her sight or hearing. Though she feared and sometimes hated the power it was as much a part of her as her arm or leg. To lose it was to be maimed.

Slowly Charlie went back to the bed and sat down. She would have to wait for whatever they had planned for her next. There was nothing else to do.

Sometime later the force field was lowered, and two Death Troopers appeared wheeling an IV pole. Charlie cooperated mutely though she would have preferred actual food.

After the Death Troopers left Charlie returned to the bed and sat down. Having nothing else to do she sat and stared at the clear liquid dripping into her veins.

As she watched her arm began to ache and she imagined she could feel the cold liquid flowing with her blood. After a while she laid down. Sleep came over her quickly.

VII

Not long after she fell asleep Charlie was shaken awake by a pair of strong hands. She opened her eyes to see two Death Troopers standing over her. Though startled and frightened Charlie did not scream. One of the Death Troopers held out his hand.

"Get up. It's time for your shower."

Charlie sat up by herself, ignoring his hand, before sliding to the edge of the bed and standing up.

The Death Troopers took her down the hallway and through an armored blast door into a large open shower room. As soon as she entered ice cold water began to stream down from above. Charlie began to shiver at once. One of the Death Troopers tossed her a ratty looking bar of off-white soap. Charlie held it for a moment without doing anything before she began to wash.

When she had finished she was taken to a room filled with death troopers who later became NSA agents. Here she was tortured for twelve hours straight in the same way she had been the last time and when that was over she was dragged into another cold shower before being returned to her cell exhausted and barely conscious.

VIII

It went on like this for what seemed like weeks or maybe months. She wasn't sure. There were no days or nights only waking and sleeping and they changed by the day. The Death Troopers never came at the same time twice. She would be awakened at random times to eat, shower or be tortured. She was always fed intravenously, never allowed to shower privately and when she was tortured she always felt those same cold hands closing around her mind and flooding her memories with images of NSA men and facilities that weren't there. Those same hands attempted to sweep away any perspective she had of time or place and any memory she had of Lord Beathach's participation in her torment.

Charlie fought against the hands and the aggressive images they forced upon her until present time and memory became a confusing jumble of fragmented images. With each passing day it became harder for her to differentiate the invasive, predatory images forced upon her mind from true memory. And yet above and below the flood of images blazed the black image of Lord Beathach's death's head mask. It was this image that helped her continue to hold onto reality.

IX

After an unknown period of time what appeared to be a pair of NSA agents in black business suits took Charlie to a room containing a small octagonal chamber with thick glass windows running around its perimeter at her eye level. In the center of the chamber was a single gray steel chair. Though he was nowhere to be found, Charlie felt the faint but familiar touch of Lord Beathach's mind.

Charlie was dragged to this chair and strapped down. Then the door to the chamber was slammed shut and sealed. She cast about the apple green chamber fearfully.

Please no more. Please I don't want to hurt anymore.

There was a soft *–plink--*, like something falling into a bucket of water, followed by a low *–hiss--*. Thin wisps of white smoke drifted up from beneath her chair. A strong bitter almond odor filled the air. The smell was heavy, almost smothering. She began to choke as it filled her lungs. The smoke was spreading, filling the chamber with a thick fog. Charlie's eyes began to water. Her throat and chest were on fire. She coughed so hard that she thought she would vomit. She couldn't breathe. Panic exploded within her.

I'm dying! I'm going to choke to death in here.

The air filled with terrible screaming and crying. She did not yet understand that it was hers. Charlie began to hyperventilate. She was trying so hard to breath, but she could not get any air. The harder she struggled the more she choked and gasped. The smoke was making it impossible to breath. It was killing her. Black butterflies fluttered in front of her eyes and began opening their wings. They quickly multiplied obscuring more and more of her vision. The hissing sound was fading fast, replaced by a sharp ring. She could no longer see or hear anything. Ants crawled over her skin making it tingle and itch. She would have scratched but her arms were cemented in place.

No please!! Please somebody help me!! Please!!

The cry rang in her mind with deafening clarity. She was going to die. They were killing her.

Please!!

Her thoughts were breaking apart, dissolving like salt crystals in a cup of water. She could not hold her mind together. Everything was falling apart. Everything was gone.

Reality snapped back all at once and she found herself lying on her bed soaking wet. She was shuddering and weeping though it took her a full ten minutes to realize this and another twenty before she realized that she was cold. Charlie wrapped herself in her blanket and cried herself to sleep.

X

What seemed like another two or three (maybe even four) more weeks went by with more of the same. Torture alternated between electric shock and the gas chamber and the randomness of both continued as did the flood of broken, reality twisting images. After a while the NSA men…

No Lord Beathach

…added another new torment.

She would be taken to a small room where she would be strapped to a steel table and injected with various drugs. Each had a different effect. All of them were unpleasant and many were quite painful.

There was a clear red liquid that made her feel as if she were on fire, a yellow liquid that made her itch, and a green one that made her very dizzy and nauseous but prevented her from puking. There was also a series of chemicals that caused a variety of frightening hallucinations. This new torment was added to the others at random.

Life had become an ever-changing circle, a rapidly descending spiral. Everything was the same, yet everything was changing.

Chapter 13
Charlie's Awakening

Those who do not learn from history are doomed to repeat it.

-George Santayana-

Paraphrase

Thirteen years after the Fallow Point incident involving Angela Cacy NSA agents began to make the same mistakes that led to so much death and destruction.

I

Her first memory was of having a massive headache. That was how she woke up, dragged from blackness by a dull throbbing ache. Charlie cracked open her eyes and looked around. She lay on dirty cot in a small 4 foot by 4-foot cinder block cell. The cell was featureless save for a small rust stained porcelain sink and a dingy toilet. A single frosted glass porthole in the heavy steel door that kept her confined within served as the chamber's only window. A single overhead bulb shielded by a steel cage gave the cell's only illumination. For a moment she just lay there all emotion washed from her mind. This couldn't be right.

How did I...

Then she remembered. She had been with Daddy; they were leaving the cabin in Maine. Something hit her in the neck and… She couldn't remember anything after that.

"Daddy!" She screamed before she could stop herself.

Panic washed through her. "Daddy!!"

In an instant she was on her feet and at the door. It was locked, no surprises there. She could have easily destroyed it but that thought did not occur to her.

"Daddy!! Daddy!!" There was no answer.

She rattled the doorknob again and again to no avail her panic growing with each passing moment.

Where's Daddy? What happened? Where am I?

The power flared within her, which only served to terrify her more. *No! NO! NOOO!* She bit it back hard sending an explosion of pain ripping through her body.

Tears welled in her eyes. ***STOP PLEASE!! STOP!!***

The power and the pain continued to flair. ***STOP!!***

Still the power grew without showing any signs of slowing, wracking her body with intense burning pain.

PLEASE STOP!

Charlie struggled with the power for what seemed like an eternity before she was finally able to stop it. When she finally did she collapsed to her knees panting in exhaustion. Tears streamed from her eyes. She was not crying. Not yet at least. Her eyes watered from the pain. They had been taken. The NSA had found them and taken them away...*somewhere.*

Where is this?

She didn't know.

A sob escaped her throat. Now she was crying. They had been taken. Daddy was gone. She didn't even know if he was still alive. She didn't feel that he was dead but there was no way to be sure.

Charlie sat and cried for a long time before finally getting up and returning to her cot. There was nothing else to do so she went to sleep.

<h1 style="text-align:center">II</h1>

Sometime later she was awakened by the sound of a bolt snapping closed. She turned over slowly to see a steel tray of food sitting on the floor. After staring at it for a moment Charlie went to the tray and picked it up. The food smelled bland and looked unappetizing. Without pausing Charlie took the tray to the toilet beside her cot and emptied it into the bowl, saving only the Hi-C drink box that she had been given. She was too thirsty to throw that away. Charlie flushed the toilet and went back to the cot. For a moment she sat perfectly still, the drink box held absently in one hand. Then her thirst reasserted itself and she slurped down the Hi-C without pausing to take a breath. The taste of the juice lingered in her mouth bringing on nausea.

They had been taken. The realization crashed in on her once more. She was alone. She knew not where her father was or even if he was still alive. Tears trickled down her burning cheeks.

Where are you Daddy? I need you.

Charlie lowered herself back onto the bed and wept until sleep overtook her.

III

After an unknown period of time Charlie was awakened by the door buzzer. She opened her eyes to find several men standing over her. Two of the men were NSA agents. They were dressed in off the rack, black suits and held themselves in that casual but aggressive stance that she associated with government men. Not that it would have mattered. Her psychic senses told her at once who they were. They could have been dressed in drag and dancing on a stage; she would not have been fooled. The third man though…He was different. His stance was also casual, but he had a more reserved, business-like manner of carrying himself. She sensed this man was…here for her benefit. He was her…

Lawyer?

At once she was confused.

Of all the people who they could bring in here why would they bring me a lawyer? As that thought passed through her mind the lawyer turned to the two agents.

"You can leave now. I would like to speak privately with my client."

Both men glanced at once another. The one on the left turned back towards the lawyer. "No problem but you should know that the girl's dangerous. She burned up an entire police station just because she wanted to."

A look of contempt flickered across the lawyer's face. "Yes, I am familiar with the allegations against her. I doubt she can do any harm to me here."

"We'll be right outside if you need anything." The left-hand agent replied.

Both agents turned and left. After the door had slid shut behind them the man who was her lawyer turned back to her. "Hello, my name is Alexander Moore. You must be Charlene MacLeod."

Charlie did not respond.

Mr. Moore crouched down to her level and offered her a gentle smile. "It's ok to talk to me Charlene. I was appointed to be your attorney. That means anything you tell me is just between us. Do you understand?"

Charlie sensed that his words were sincere but there was no concern or kindness behind them. This man was all business, here to do a job. Furthermore, suspicion and mistrust came easily to her now.

"It's Charlie." She replied softly. "Everyone just calls me Charlie."

"Ok Charlie it is then." Mr. Moore replied. "You may call me Mr. Moore."

She smiled slightly. As she reached out to him with her mind Charlie realized at once that this man had only been told part of the truth and had been led to believe outright lies about what was going on here. He had no knowledge of her power or the true reason she had been brought here.

"May I sit down?' Mr. Moore asked.

Charlie scooted over to make room for him on her cot. Mr. Moore sat down beside her and opened his brief case. "Do you know why you are here Charlie?"

She did not respond. She knew exactly why she was there, but she did not trust this man. He was here to represent her interests, sure, but beyond that he had no concern for her. She was just a client.

"You're here because you've been accused of Domestic Terrorism and Arson." Mr. Moore's voice was cool and overly professional, as if he were a doctor diagnosing a cold. "The U.S. Attorney for the Eastern District of Pennsylvania apparently thinks that you are somehow responsible for the firebombing that destroyed the Ephrata Police Department." Now Mr. Moore's tone had changed to one of thinly veiled contempt. "The Ephrata attack has been classified as an act domestic terrorism and because of your father's activities in Eastern Europe the entire matter has been referred to a military commission for prosecution. Apparently, the federal government has become convinced that you and your father are a threat to national security. The judge appointed me as your legal counsel." He paused to read over some papers in his brief case. "It says here you are fifteen years of age. You don't look fifteen to me. More like eight or nine. How did you manage to blow up and burn a police station?"

Charlie sat in silence her cheeks burning with shame.

Bad girl! You burned up those people. Very Bad!

"I'm going to try to get you released to a foster home." Mr. Moore continued. "You don't look like much of a threat and I don't think you will run away. Right?"

She glanced at him but said nothing. She wasn't going anywhere and if this man thought he could get out of this place then he was dreaming. Mr. Moore was wrong about something else too.

I am dangerous. I burned those men alive. I deserve to be here.

IV

The following day two NSA agents arrived and escorted Charlie from her cell to a conference room several doors down. Inside Mr. Moore waited along with a slender, red-headed woman, an older brunette woman seated behind a court stenography machine and a grizzled looking man in an army general's uniform. As she entered the room all four stood.

The two agents led her to the chair next to Mr. Moore and who pulled it out for her. As Charlie sat down a sudden feeling of dread flooded through her. She could sense hostility from both the red-headed woman and the army general. Both perceived her as dangerous. Both knew about the power and what she had done.

I burned up those people...

"We are here in case number CR-25615-66 United States vs. Charlene Danielle McCloud." The army general began. "This case comes on for arraignment and custody determination. Present in the courtroom today are Assistant United States Attorney Margarete Provenzo, on behalf of the Government and Alexander Moore on behalf of the Defendant. The Defendant Charlene Danielle MacLeod is also present." He turned to the red-haired woman. "Miss Provenzo."

The red-haired woman stood up. "This Defendant set a firebomb that destroyed the Ephrata Police Station resulting in the deaths of both local law enforcement officers and federal agents. Furthermore, Miss MacLeod's father is well connected with the Russian mafia and has substantial financial assets. It has taken us many months to locate and capture Charlene and Jack MacLeod. Miss MacLeod constitutes a significant risk to public safety and has the means to flee the United States. As such the Government would move that she be detained without bail."

"Thank you, Miss Provenzo." The army general turned to her attorney. "Mr. Moore?"

"Thank you, your Honor. My client is a young child. The government's indictment has her listed as age fifteen. She is clearly no older than eight or nine. I find it incredible that Miss Provenzo honestly believes that this little girl had anything to do with the tragic events in Ephrata. That she would characterize my client as a threat to public safety is laughable. That she thinks my client is any sort of flight risk is absurd. My client has been separated from her father and is traumatized. She is presently being kept in a four foot by twelve-foot cell. She has no privacy and is receiving no psychological or psychiatric care for the trauma that was inflicted by Miss Provenzo's jack-booted goons. Miss MacLeod needs to be in counseling, not a prison cell. She should properly be placed in a foster home. Defense would move that Miss MacLeod be released into the custody of State child protective services pending disposition of her case."

"While I find it hard to accept that such a young child could be involved in such a heinous crime and disturbing that the government's attorney would be so sloppy as to misstate the age of an accused juvenile terrorist I none the less find that based on the nature of the allegations against this defendant, Miss MacLeod poses a significant danger to the public and that she is a flight risk. Therefore, Miss MacLeod, you are remanded to the custody of the Government without bail pending trial."

The army general's ruling came as no surprise to her. Nevertheless, she was devastated. To hear her fate pronounced by a man with such authority made in real in a way that it had not been before. Moreover, although he had never actually come out and said it she felt as though he had judged her and pronounced her guilty.

Guilty of arson!

Guilty of murder!

The words echoed hauntingly in her mind.

I deserve to be locked up. She thought with deep self-loathing. *I am a murderer.*

In the days following her court hearing Charlie sank into deep depression. She did not eat, had trouble sleeping and cried frequently. She missed her father but more than that she needed him. He had been the only thing protecting her from her own guilt. Daddy had always been there to comfort her when she became upset. Now he was gone.

V

Not long after she was taken Charlie was greeted by a man who introduced himself as Dr. Barrister. From Barrister she learned that she had been taken to the National Security Agency's compound in Fallow Point, South Carolina.

Charlie distrusted him at once. He acted friendly enough, but he was insincere. Barrister talked down to her and was too interested in her power. Charlie felt that he cared nothing for her. She was an object, a lab specimen and nothing more. All that mattered to him was the power.

Charlie would not cooperate with him. Instead she demanded to see her father to which, he answered with placations and lies.

Over the prevailing weeks Barrister tried again and again to get her to use the power but she would not. She felt terribly lonely. Nobody cared about her and there was nobody she could talk to. She was truly alone. This loneliness drove her deeper still into depression.

She was put on a number of medications. She wasn't sure exactly which ones or how many. All she did know is that they made her feel worse. One of the drugs made her feel so miserable that she couldn't help crying constantly. Another made her so nauseous that she spent most of her time puking and a third made her feel floaty and out of sorts.

During this time, she was taken to see a dozen or more psychologists, psychiatrists and other 'counselors'. Each had his or her own style in dealing with her, but they were all the same. After all the questions, placations, false promises and fake sympathy it always came down to the same thing: 'Charlie set this on fire'.

Sometimes it would be a pile of shredded newspapers or curly wood shavings in a metal tray; other times it would be little pans of oil or kerosene. All things she could have easily set fire to.

But she would not do it. She had promised Daddy and herself that she would never use the power again. She did not say this to Barrister though. She would only tell him no. She would not answer his questions and did not respond to his promises. Though she desperately wanted to believe that she would see her father if she obeyed she knew Barrister would never allow it. So, she continued to resist, fearful that one day she would break.

This went on for most of the summer. Then one day late in August everything changed.

VI

The day began as any other. Charlie woke up at nine, got dressed and ate breakfast. At eleven thirty the door buzzer went off and Dr. Barrister entered accompanied by four agents.

"Hello Charlie. How are you feeling this morning?"

She looked up at him but said nothing.

"It's time for your tests."

Charlie stood up slowly her eyes never leaving his. "I *told* you I won't do it."

"Let's go."

Charlie went with him without another word. She had no intention of cooperating, but she went with him anyway. She didn't quite understand why.

Barrister took her into a small white room where a tray of crumpled newspaper waited on a steel table in the center of the room. A video camera watched her from the far wall.

Barrister stood over her watching expectantly. "Whenever you're ready."

"No."

"Why?" His tone was gentle, but Charlie could sense the anger behind it. "Why do you keep it under wraps? What good does it do you?"

Charlie stared up at him. "I won't do it."

"Come on. It won't be that bad. It'll only be five minutes then you're all done. It's not like it'll hurt."

"No." She repeated more firmly. Fear cropped up within her. *Leave me alone. Please.* She had slept poorly that night and felt tired and miserable.

"Come on Charlie. If you do this for me, I'll leave you alone for the rest of the week."

"No."

She was close to tears. She didn't want to be there. She wanted Daddy. She wanted to be somewhere far away.

"When can I see my daddy?"

Barrister pointed to the tray of crumpled newspaper. "If you light that. I'll take you to see him right away."

She shook her head. "No. I won't do it."

Barrister's expression became sad. "I don't understand why you hurt yourself like this Charlie. Your father wants to see you; don't you want to see him? He told me that he's afraid you don't love him anymore."

Then she did cry because she wanted so badly to see her father, but she couldn't do this. She could not use the power no matter how much she missed her father. It didn't matter anyway. She knew he was lying. He would never let her see her father no matter what she did.

She sensed no compassion from him. His expression was cold and calculating. He was contemplating how he might use the current situation. Oh, how she hated him. Charlie glared at Barrister refusing to break away first. He returned a sharp glare. Though his expression betrayed no emotion his eyes glittered with anger.

After a few minutes he grabbed her wrist and turned towards the door. "Let's go. You have other tests to do and I don't have all damned day."

Barrister led her out into the hallway and turned her around to face him. "I hope you'll reconsider your position. I really hate to see you so unhappy."

He then took her to another room in another part of the compound. This room was set up as a traditional laboratory complete with steel examining table and chair each equipped with padded leather restraints. Barrister took Charlie over to the chair and forced her to sit. She was surprised when Barrister did not strap her down.

"I don't want to restrain you, but I will if you are uncooperative."

Charlie did not respond.

Barrister went over to a steel cabinet on the wall and took out a large syringe, a bottle of iodine, three sterile wrapped strips of gauze, and two sterile swabs. First Barrister swabbed her arm with iodine and drew a large volume of blood. Then he took samples of her saliva and mucus from the back of her throat. When this was finished he performed several other tests and took some x-rays before returning her to her cell.

Upon returning Charlie found lunch waiting for her on her cot. It was one of her favorite meals; cheeseburgers, French fries and a Pepsi.

After she finished her lunch Barrister returned and took her back to the white room. This time a tray of kerosene waited where the crumpled newspaper had been.

"Now light it." Barrister commanded.

She returned a defiant glare. "No. I told you I won't do it."

"If you don't show me your power then you'll never see your father again."

Tears came to her eyes. Charlie bit them back. "No."

She turned intending to march straight out of the room when Barrister caught her arm.

"Where do you think you're going?" He snapped.

Charlie stared up at him allowing her anger to show through for the first time. She was crying though she made no sound.

Leave me alone.

Her tears were out of combined anger and hopelessness.

Just leave me alone.

Barrister was still speaking but she no longer heard him. It wasn't important.

I'm never going to see Daddy again no matter what happens. I'll always be alone.

In that moment part of her wanted to die. She longed for Daddy and she felt deep guilt for what she had done. She was a killer. A murderer. She deserved to be here. It was fair.

She deserved to die here but she couldn't deal with this man. She would never use the power again. Why couldn't he understand that? Why couldn't he understand how dangerous the power was? He had to know what she had done at the Ephrata Police Department. The NSA had to have told him. Why couldn't he leave her alone?

Just leave me alone to die.

It couldn't be that bad. It might hurt at first but then she would slip away into nothingness and never feel anything again. There would be no more pain, no more fear and no more guilt. She would be free of it all.

As she looked up at him Charlie felt cold anger wash through her.

Leave me alone you asshole.

A hand closed on her wrist.

"Do you understand me?" The hand jerked her wrist. "Huh? Do you understand what I am saying?"

Charlie jerked her hand away. "I won't do it." Her voice came out low and very hostile bringing with it the first stirrings of the power. She forced it down as best she could.

No!

Suddenly her head snapped back, and the world went white for an instant. Barrister had slapped her. The knowledge came to her even before her vision returned. Before she could react, he clamped down on her hand and dragged her out into the hallway where he spun her around and struck her again sending her sprawling.

"You'll do as I tell you or I'll make you sorry."

Charlie struggled to her feet eyes never leaving Barrister's. "No." Her voice came out calm despite the tears streaming down her cheeks.

Barrister brought his hand back in a closed fist intending to strike her again. Before he could a dark, slender figure caught him by the wrist, spun him around and laid him out with a single blow. It took her a few seconds to recognize the figure as Mr. Striker, Robin for as far back as she could remember.

"If I ever see you touch her again I'll snap your neck." Robin's voice was low, calm and threatening.

Barrister's face went white, but he remained silent.

"Now get out of here before I decide to kill you."

Barrister stared at him in impotent fury for a moment before he turned and storming away.

Robin turned to her. "Are you hurt?"

"I don't think so."

She was close to tears. Simple kindness and concern were never shown here.

He extended his hand to her. "Come on. Let me take you back to your room."

"Alright."

Charlie glanced at his hand for a moment before taking it. She wanted so much to trust him but still she was afraid.

Charlie wasn't quite sure what to make of Robin Striker. Robin was a longtime military buddy of her father's. Daddy had never told her what Robin did for a living and she was unsure of whether or not her father had known he worked for the NSA. Still he was not like the others. He came to visit daily, not to do tests or to question her but just to talk. Charlie rarely responded, but that didn't seem to bother him. He would keep talking, never expecting a reply. Robin would tell her stories about his dog, his broken television, or his beat-up old car. Sometimes he read to her from books. She supposed he was lonely. He wasn't a bad looking man, but he was very big and had an unusual manner. Robin's voice was soft and intense, and he spoke with a slight accent. He was friendly but had a disquieting air.

Charlie did not find this frightening, but she imagined that others might. She almost felt sorry for him. He seemed so kind and was the only person here who was ever honest with her.

She could not be sure of this though. Robin was strangely closed to her. She could only judge him by his actions and body language.

The only other person she had met like this was Mr. Taglierie, one of her father's friends in New York. Mr. Taglierie and Daddy would take turns inviting each other over for dinner. Charlie always looked forward to those nights. Mr. Taglierie was fun to play with and a great cook. He always made the most delicious lasagna. He had promised to share his recipe with Daddy the week before the NSA men found them and they had to run again.

One of the times they were at Mr. Taglierie's apartment, Charlie noticed a little star shaped medal sitting out on a table inside the bedroom next to the bathroom. She had asked her father about it later and he promised to explain it to her when she got older after making her promise never to mention it to Mr. Taglierie. She had always found it odd that Mr. Taglierie lived alone but had never been able to get an answer from her father. Again, he promised to explain this to her when she grew older and told her never to ask Mr. Taglierie.

All of these thoughts remained lucid despite her fear and upset. It was sort of odd and she didn't understand it. Part of her wondered how her father's old friend Robin Striker could have gotten in to see her here and why but those questions were sublimated by her overwhelming gratitude for being rescued.

When they returned to her cell Robin came in with her. Charlie followed him to her cot where they sat down together. At first neither spoke a word. Then after a few minutes had passed Robin broke their silence with a question.

"What is this all about? Why are they keeping you here?"

Fear pricked up in her heart at once. For a moment Charlie was silent, as she carefully considered whether or not she should talk with this man. This was a very strange thing for him to ask.

"Aren't you an NSA agent. Don't you know already?"

He smiled. "I am an NSA agent, but I know about as much as you do. They keep us all on a need to know basis so none of us can rat them out or something like that. All I know is that you're here and I'm supposed to keep you company, so you don't completely lose it."

Charlie couldn't help but laugh. The way in which he had answered was just too funny. This only lasted for a moment thought before her fear and suspicion set back in. She wanted very much to trust her father's friend. She had nobody, not even her father. She needed a friend. But she could not be sure of his intentions. It just seemed too convenient that her father's old friend had been able to get in to see her.

This could be a trick. Her mind warned. *Barrister acts friendly and concerned too. You can't be sure of what he wants.*

Charlie looked up at Robin carefully. His smile seemed genuine. It was friendly without any of the smarmy false chumminess of Barrister and the other doctors. Still she felt uneasy. If she opened up to this man and he betrayed her then Barrister might find a way to force her to use the power. It wasn't worth the risk. Still, she was so lonely. Daddy was gone, and she had no one she could talk to, no one to ask advice from. At least Robin wasn't like the others.

In the end it was her loneliness that decided her, and she told, often with tears. Robin was very kind to her, holding her clumsily when she cried and letting her rest when she needed to. He asked her questions, but they were always gentle and kind, not the sharp interrogatives that Barrister and the others constantly shot at her. As she spoke her emotions took over and she told more than she had meant to.

When she finished Charlie felt both tired and afraid for she had told *everything,* even the parts she had meant to hold back like stealing from the ATM machine at the airport and the incident at the Ephrata police station.

She knew that Barrister and the other doctors knew everything that had happened but that didn't matter. She didn't care what they thought of her. With Robin it was different. She wanted him to like her. She wanted him to be her friend and she was afraid of what he would think now that he knew what she had done. Robin surprised her.

"That's terrible. I'm so sorry they hurt you." His voice was filled with remorse. "You don't deserve to suffer."

Now it was Charlie's turn to feel sorry. She had made Robin feel guilty when he had nothing to do with what had happened. "Don't feel bad. You didn't do any of this."

He sighed. "No, but I am your father's friend and I work for the same agency that hurt you. I should have done something to try to stop it. What they did was illegal, and I should have reported it."

Charlie took his hand. "It's alright. It wouldn't have made a difference anyway. They control the police and the rest of the government. Even if you told they wouldn't have done anything." She paused feeling deep guilt and not just for Robin. "It wasn't your fault it was mine. They were after me because of my pyrokinesis and because I killed those men."

"The way you told it, it sounded like self-defense."

"That's no excuse." She replied. "I killed them on purpose. I murdered them."

He shook his head. "You saved your father's life. If you hadn't used your power, they would have killed him."

Charlie opened her mouth to argue but was cut off.

"Believe me when I tell you Charlie the only reason they haven't killed your father now is because they're afraid of you and they need him alive to control you."

Excitement exploded within her. She had felt that her father was still alive, but she had, had no way of being sure until now. "He's still alive?! How is he? Where is he? Can you take me to see him?"

"Whoa slow down Charlie." Robin's expression was serious. "I've seen your father and he looks fine. They're keeping him in a cell on the other side of the complex, but I can't get you in to see him."

Charlie's excitement evaporated immediately and was replaced by suspicion. "Why not?"

"The director of this facility personally sent orders to everyone who has contact with either of you that you are not allowed to see each other. If I take you anywhere near his cell they'll have me killed." He leaned in close and dropped his voice to a whisper. "And then I can't help you."

Her excitement immediately reappeared. "You'll help me?" It took a great deal of self-control for her to keep her voice low.

He nodded.

"Why?"

"Because this is wrong. You're a kid, not a lab rat. They had no right to do this to you and your father and it just makes me sick. You should be out playing with your friends, going to school, being a kid. Not locked up in some government rat hole. I didn't join the military to do this shit." His expression immediately became embarrassed. "Oh sorry. I didn't mean to…"

"That's all right." She smiled. "My dad uses that word sometimes." She remembered one time when he was fixing her bike he had used that word several times along with some others.

"I joined the Army to make a difference." Robin continued. "I wanted to fight for my country, but they decided I would be more useful as a professional killer."

Charlie watched him intently understanding at once how he felt. "I was asked to become an Agent while still active in the military." His lips curled into a humorless smile. "Officially Agents don't exist. Unofficially we are the most highly trained and skilled assassins in the world. I was assigned to Afghanistan following nine-eleven and Iraq a month before the official war began. After the second gulf war I was sent into Russia as part of the president's War on Terror. I was supposed to be hunting for terrorists in the Russian underworld. That is, I would find them and get enough dirt to nail them and then rendition units would come in to capture them. All we were really doing though was eliminating renegades. We helped weed out the true believers in the Islamic movement so that they could be replaced by gangsters loyal to American intelligence. When I found out what was going on I tried to get out but before I could I was betrayed and captured. The group that caught me decided to make an example so rather than just killing me they shot me in both knees and left me in a cell to die. I managed to survive and eventually escape. After I recovered from my injuries I was told that I still owed time and assigned to the Pentagon which loaned me out to the NSA. Because of my injuries I would not be useful as a field agent, so I was installed as a 'watcher' in Taylor, Illinois. Which meant I would be assigned to watch over the NSA scientists working at Fort Dearborn to make sure they aren't revealing secret information or doing anything else they shouldn't be."

Charlie felt deep sympathy for Robin. They had used him, just as they had used Daddy and her, and when he tried to do the right thing he was betrayed and nearly killed. One question did bother her though. "Why did they take you back after they betrayed you?"

His face darkened. "Someone once said 'Keep your friends close and your enemies closer.' I think that's what they were trying to do. Anyway, it's not like I know anything that I could hurt them with. All I usually do is watch the scientists come in and go out and then follow them home and watch them there. Someone else watches them inside the laboratory. "

"Why did they assign you to me then?"

He shook his head. "I don't know Charlie. I would have thought they would want to keep me from knowing anything about what happened to you and your daddy."

This puzzled Charlie, but she quickly dismissed it. The suspicious part of her mind scolded her, but she ignored it.

For a while they talked of unimportant things. Then Robin whispered something that brought a resurgence of her earlier excitement. "Listen I'm going to do everything I can to help but I need you to help me."

She looked at him silently.

"I need you to cooperate with their tests for now."

Charlie was shocked as much as if he had struck her. "I can't. It's too dangerous. I said I'd never do it again."

He nodded. "I know but it will help a lot…"

"I can't do it!" Fear and guilt cropped up within her and she began to tremble. The mere thought of using the power did this to her. "If I use it again it could get out of control and start a con- conflagration." She felt close to tears.

Robin took her in his arms. "I'm sorry. I didn't mean to upset you. I should just shut my big mouth."

He sat with her in silence until she calmed down a little. Then he slowly released her and stood up. "I need to leave now Charlie. If they see us talking like this for too long they'll get suspicious but listen, I will help you. Just give me some time."

She nodded. "Thanks."

Robin left her with many questions. Could she trust him? Or would he betray her to Barrister? Moreover, was it possible for her to escape with Daddy? She wanted to believe it was, but she knew better. This place was too tightly secured. She had seen the frequent security patrols in the corridors and she knew she was surrounded by solid steel armor. There was no escape from this place. Part of her mind warned that this was a trick.

Why do you think he wants you to do the tests?

VII

Charlie puzzled over these things for the next two weeks. They were not constant thoughts, but they troubled her intermittently. During this time Robin made no mention of the tests or escape. The next time he brought up the subject was on a Friday morning. The two of them were sitting on the floor playing a game of rummy five hundred and talking in low voices.

"Have you given any thought to what I said about the tests?"

She tensed immediately. Sharp tremors rippled through her body.

Robin's expression became remorseful. "I'm sorry. I didn't mean to upset you. I'll shut up if you want me to."

"No. That's all right." She did wish he would shut up, but she wanted to please him. Somewhere deep inside a voice warned that this was a trick. That voice went unheard.

"Look I'll be honest with you. There is no way I can get you out of here and very little chance that you'll be able to escape."

Charlie's heart sank. She had known all along that there was no way to escape but had harbored some hope that she was wrong. Now that hope was crushed.

"I can't help you." Robin continued. "But I can tell you how to help yourself." He stared into her eyes. "You can take control of this situation any time you want. Barrister is obsessed with your power. It's all he cares about. He will give you whatever you want if you agree to do their tests. Make them pay you for each test. You may not be able to escape this rat hole, but you can at least put yourself in control. Do you understand?"

She nodded. Her heart was pounding, and she was trembling.

I don't want to do this. God, I don't want to do this. Please don't make me use it.

She wanted to speak the words aloud but could not.

"I... I just don't want to light fires."

Robin did not argue. "It's up to you Charlie. Just remember you can control them because you have what they want."

With that the subject was dropped.

Robin stayed late that night. When she grew tired he laid her on her cot and sat with her until she drifted off to sleep. Charlie was touched by his concern. He was the only one of them that cared about her.

Charlie awoke sometime later to find Robin gone.

Sleep was elusive. Charlie laid awake for a long time just thinking. What Robin had said frightened her, but it was also very tempting. She was so lonely and miserable. Maybe she could get Barrister to let her see Daddy in exchange for doing one of his tests. Still, she knew it wouldn't be that easy. Barrister was as smart and devious, as he was cold and mean. He would not just give in to her demands, not without trying to put himself in control of her. Once she agreed to do one test there would be no end. Barrister would want more and more tests and bigger and bigger fires and if she tried to stop he would never let her see her father again.

If he lets me see Daddy at all.

Deep inside part of her continued to warn that this was a trick. The warning went unheeded.

She wanted to believe there was hope. She wanted to believe that she could take control of the situation as Robin had suggested but she was afraid. This was a dangerous game and she feared she would be trapped.

It was not that she lacked intelligence or insight. These were among her greatest strengths, but she was not used to thinking this way. She had never tried to manipulate an adult before. Adults were to be obeyed, not tricked and manipulated. What Robin had suggested went against everything she had ever been taught. Yet she felt that it was the best course of action. Still, she could not break her word.

And when will I ever stop? And how?

She knew the consequences of stopping after she agreed to do the tests would be worse than the consequences for refusing to do the tests in the first place. Barrister would know that she could be made to do the tests and would use every method he had at his disposal to make her resume testing. She felt that he had all sorts of *things* he could use to force her to do the tests and feared what they might be. She felt deeply afraid. Yet the allure of hope was strong.

VIII

Over the next four or five weeks (she wasn't exactly sure how long) Charlie considered her decision. One question continued to come up: Once she started how and when would she stop? It was this question that kept her from cooperating with the tests despite everything Robin told her. She could not answer this question herself nor could she shake the feeling that she was being tricked. Eventually she brought her concerns to Robin.

"If I do Barrister's tests when will I ever stop? He'll always want more and more tests and bigger and bigger fires. He'll want me to light matches, then candles, then oil lamps, then bonfires, then I don't know what, but I'm scared."

Robin took her in his arms. "It's ok. You don't have to be afraid. I never should have told you to do Barrister's tests. I'm just a fucking… Oh hell I'm sorry Charlie."

"That's alright." Despite her fear she had to smile at Robin's woe-be-gone expression.

"I'm just a soldier Charlie. What do I know about giving advice? I have enough trouble just balancing my checkbook. If I had any real brains, I wouldn't have gotten stuck here in the first place."

Now it was her turn to feel bad. "That doesn't mean anything. You had no choice. You said it yourself."

"Yeah but if I were smarter I could have gone to college instead of joining the Army."

"My Daddy is an FBI agent." She replied. "And he was in the Army."

IX

A week later she decided. It was Sunday and she was alone. Robin had not come to visit her, so she spent the day in her cell reading and thinking. What finally decided her was the realization that things couldn't get much worse. She was alone and a prisoner.

It was fair. She was a murderer and she deserved what she got, but she did not want her Daddy locked up. She wanted him to be free or at the very least she wanted him to be with her, even if she did not deserve to be with him. If she did the tests, then maybe she could get Barrister to let her be with Daddy. They would at least be together even if they could not be free. The thought brought her small comfort in the face of her fear. Charlie lay awake most of that night, too frightened to sleep. What little sleep she did get was plagued by nightmares.

Charlie got up early the next morning and after finishing her breakfast called to the agent outside her cell and told him she wanted to see Dr. Barrister. He arrived ten minutes later accompanied by two agents. After asking Barrister to dismiss the two agents Charlie told him of her decision to do the tests and of what she wanted in return. Barrister was visibly angry though his voice remained calm. He agreed to her request but insisted that she do the test first. When she told Robin later he was very concerned.

"Don't do this unless you're really sure."

"I am." She replied in a voice much calmer than she felt.

"What's Barrister giving you in return?"

"He's going to let me go outside." She smiled. She hadn't seen the sun in months.

"That's good." Robin's expression became deadly serious. "Don't you ever do any test without getting something in return. Understand?"

"Yes."

"Don't let them use you like they did to me." That said his expression lightened a little. "So, when's the big day?"

"Thursday. Barrister said he wanted to do the test first thing after breakfast." A slight tremor wormed its way up her spine.

Barrister came at ten o'clock sharp on Thursday morning accompanied by four agents, two male and two female. Charlie went with them without a word. She was taken to a small steel walled testing room. In the center of the room was a plain steel table on top of which sat a steel tray piled high with crumpled newspapers. To the right of the table was a large, open tank of water. An EEG machine sat in one corner of the room. The technician who presided over it was clad in a bright silver fire suit. A long, one-way glass panel ran along one wall.

"As you can see we've outfitted the room exactly as you asked."

She nodded. She supposed it would do. "Alright."

"Alright then." Barrister's voice held an edge of impatience. Charlie could sense his annoyance and eagerness to begin.

She looked up at him. "Only I want you to go in the other room. I don't want to have to look at you while I do this. There could be an accident."

Barrister paled and left the room. A moment later his voice echoed in the room from a speaker in the ceiling.

"We're ready Charlie, you can start whenever you want."

She began to tremble. She didn't want to do this. She wanted her father. She needed him. She wanted to be anywhere but here. Yet part of her longed to use the power as one who is hot and thirsty longs for water. That part begged to use the power.

Charlie looked down at the pile of crumpled newspaper and found herself *wanting* to do it. A wave of horror and self-loathing washed through her. Charlie pushed it aside.

Why shouldn't I want to do it? I'm good at it. Everybody likes doing things they're good at.

She found herself thinking about lighting the newspapers like one might sit and think about gobbling up a steak just before actually eating it. It would be satisfying to use the power, but she wanted just a moment to savor it.

Charlie gazed down at the little metal tray and for a moment felt almost insulted. *Newspaper? Really? How about a challenge?*

As she stood there Charlie gathered herself. All at once she struck out with the power. It was really just a flick, a tiny touch of the power but the effects were dramatic. There wasn't a fire but rather a loud *–warruuumppp-* as the newspapers exploded in a bright orange fireball. In the same instant the tray flipped through the air scattering sparks all over the floor and embedded itself in the far wall. Charlie was terrified and exhilarated at once. It had gotten so much stronger. Nearly panicked Charlie threw the power at the water tank. There was an instant sharp *–hiss-* as the water came to an immediate boil. Steam poured from the tank filling the air with a thick fog.

Stop! Please stop!!

Please!

Stop it now!!

The power whirled for a moment longer before silencing. Charlie turned, mind racing with combined fear and excitement and half walked half ran from the room. Someone met her in the corridor and took her back to her cell. She did not see who.

X

Early the next morning Robin came to her cell carrying a small duffel bag.

"Hi Charlie."

She offered him a tired smile. "Hi." She had gotten little sleep the night before and was still frightened from yesterday's test.

He held out the duffel bag. "Here. Why don't you get dressed? I'll wait in the hallway"

She looked up at him curiously. "Why? What for?"

He smiled. "You'll see." Then he turned a left.

Charlie took the bag and opened it. As it turned out it contained a two-piece girl's bathing suit, a pair of denim shorts, a pink t-shirt and a large beach towel. Charlie was puzzled but dressed as Robin had asked. When she was finished she called to Robin through the cell door and he opened it

"Where are we going?"

"It's a surprise." He motioned towards the open cell door. "Come on."

The moment she stepped out of the building Charlie closed her eyes, turned her face towards the sun and smiled. It felt so good to be outside.

The compound consisted of mile after mile of manicured lawns and forest surrounding a massive black glass tower. There was a duck pond, what looked like a golf course, tennis courts, a swimming pool and a little red barn. It was all so beautiful.

As they neared the tree line at the rear of the compound a familiar sound came to her ears.

The ocean. We're on the beach! The thought brought on a rush of elation. "We're going swimming?"

Robin's smile broadened. "Yep."

Behind the tree line the ground dropped off into a sheer cliff. Before she could ask how they were going to get to the beach below Robin pointed to a small break in the cliff. As they neared it she saw that it was in actuality a narrow stairway cut into the stone cliff face. Charlie could not help but be impressed.

"Cool."

Robin nodded. "Yeah. It is, isn't it?"

The beach below consisted of approximately one hundred feet of perfect white sand. Without pausing Charlie threw off her shirt, shoes and shorts and ran into the blue and white surf calling for Robin to follow.

This was how they spent the rest of the day. After the sun dipped below the horizon Robin built a small fire over which they roasted hot dogs and made smores. It was late when they finally returned to her cell and she went right to bed falling asleep with no trouble at all.

XI

For the next test she was asked to incinerate a large block of ipey wood. It seemed simple enough, but she was surprised by how hot the block burned. The heat was enough to bring sweat to her skin despite the industrial refrigerator units in the room.

Charlie loved to swim and had asked to go in the ocean again as her reward but was surprised when the NSA rented a local water park instead. It was a glorious day except that she wished her father could be there too. She awoke late that night after crying for she missed him terribly.

For the third test she was taken to a larger steel armored room. This had previously been a gymnasium but had since been converted to a testing room. Fifty industrial refrigerator units had been installed along with a twenty-thousand-gallon tank, which was currently overflowing with ice.

Today's test was a massive ten by twelve-foot slab of granite. Temperature probes had been inserted into the slab at strategic locations.

Prior to being brought here Charlie was taken into a small examining room where she was told to disrobe. A female technician then proceeded to paste small plastic patches all over her chest, stomach, head, legs and back before allowing her to dress.

As Charlie stood there she began to tremble with anticipation. She felt no fear, only excitement. Finally, a real test. The power had already begun to stir, awakened by her emotion. Barrister's voice echoed over the loud speaker.

"We're ready when you are Charlie."

Charlie reached into the power building it up rapidly. Slow trickles of smoke drifted up from the granite. These quickly grew to thick billowing clouds. Her heart began to race with excitement. Intense pleasure washed through her body, warming her to the core. All at once white flames erupted from the granite slab. The air filled with their deafening roar. A slight smile spread across her face. Her body came alive with ecstasy almost hurtful in its intensity. The power continued to spiral upward bringing with-it ever-increasing pleasure. She felt delirious with its strength.

Without warning the slab exploded in a blinding white flash filling the air with a sound so loud as to be inaudible. Chunks of flaming liquid rock flew through the air.

All of this happened in a span of seconds; though to her if felt like hours.

Without hesitating Charlie turned the power on the tank of ice. In the same instant the ice vanished transformed in an instant into steam. The air filled with a loud hiss as the remainder of the now melted ice was vaporized. Steam enveloped the room reducing her vision to a few feet.

The power continued to spiral upward. Charlie clamped down on it as hard as she could. In an instant pleasure turned to pain. Steel spikes slammed through her skull bringing tears to her eyes.

Why did I agree to do this?

The thought was slushy and distant in the face of her growing pain. Still she continued to fight back the power.

Stop it!

Stop it now!

The words screamed in her mind as the power continued to build. Invisible fire swept across her skin. A cry was building within her. Charlie fought to suppress it.

STOP IT!!

STOP IT NOW!!

The power continued building unabated. Fear raced within her.

STOP!!

Heavy beads of sweat ran down her face, her arms and her chest, soaking through her clothing. She was dressed in a white t-shirt and pair of jean shorts. Her legs and arms were bare. Still she was sweating rivers. Fierce tremors took her. Charlie felt her strength fading. The power would break free soon.

STOP IT NOW!!

Something in her mind disengaged, spun free for a moment and then was gone. Charlie turned from the steaming and now mostly empty ice tank towards the one-way glass panel behind her. She was crying though she was not yet aware of it.

"Good job Charlie. Wait there and I'll send someone to take you back to your room." Barrister's voice sounded faraway and alien.

She wanted to say something in reply but could not find the words. A few minutes later the heavy blast door beneath the one-way glass opened and two agents appeared. Charlie went with them in silence.

After the agents had left Charlie changed into her nightgown and went to bed. It was early, but she felt very tired. She passed out within minutes of lying down but did not sleep long before being awakened by the door buzzer. Charlie opened her eyes to find Dr. Barrister standing over her.

"Hi Charlie."

"I want to see my Daddy." She demanded in a flat tone.

"I think that can be arranged if you do one more test."

"I've done enough tests." She replied in a sharp voice.

Barrister was silent for a moment. Charlie sensed him plotting how he could manipulate her.

"Your friend Robin was worried when I told him you didn't want to go swimming. Are you sure you don't want to go to the water park again? We rented it just for you."

"No, you didn't." She shot back with tears in her eyes. "You only rented it to get me to do your stupid tests."

If only Barrister could have known how much he had hurt, her by saying that. She knew nobody cared about her except Robin and he wasn't her father. She needed her father more now than ever.

"And I did them. Now I want to see my Daddy!" The power began to stir within her.

Barrister's face paled.

He feels it. Good.

"Don't get excited Charlie. There's no need to get upset. Listen how would you like to go to Disney World. It's only an hour or so flight from here. We could rent the park for a day. You'd have it all to yourself."

"I don't want to go to any amusement park! I want to see my Daddy and I'm going to! Do you understand me?! I'm going to! You tell them I want to see my Daddy now and then I'll do their tests again. I don't mind. But if I don't see my Daddy I'll make something happen. Tell them that."

"Okay Charlie. Just stay calm." Barrister's face had turned as white as his lab coat. His skin was dotted with thick sweat. "Don't do anything you'll regret."

Serves you right you fucking bastard! "Now get out of here and stay away! Don't you come back unless it's to take me to my Daddy!"

Barrister stood for a moment, frozen in place by fear. Then he turned and almost ran from the room. Charlie watched him go with no satisfaction.

After the door snicked shut behind him Charlie turned and threw herself onto her cot sobbing hysterically. Her mind was awash with a flood of mixed fear, anger and confusion. She wanted her father but more than that she needed him. She needed him to tell her what to do now. Should she continue doing Barrister's tests or should she stop forever. The power had gotten so much stronger and it hurt so much to stop it. She *liked* using it and she wasn't sure she could stop. What if she couldn't? What would that mean? Oh, what would that mean?

Charlie remained like this for several hours before crying herself to sleep.

X

Charlie awoke to the sounds of heavy boots on metal. She opened her eyes to find herself in a steel cell. Fear and confusion cropped up within her. *What happened? Where am I?*

A moment later memory returned. She was a prisoner of the Black Empire, Daddy was dead, and David and Catherine were gone. She was alone and soon she would be tortured again. Tears trickled down her cheeks as the pain of losing her father was renewed.

Charlie stood up and went to the cell opening. The two Death Troopers were there as always. She stared at them for a moment before turning away and walking back to the bed.

She wanted to sleep but she did not feel tired or rather she did not feel sleepy for she had never felt more exhausted in her life.

Instead of sleeping Charlie sat down on the bed and stared at the opposite wall. She felt like crying but that would have taken more effort than she was capable of, so she simply sat there staring blankly.

After an unknown period of time the clang of armored boots on steel brought her back to reality. Charlie slowly turned to see Lord Beathach standing over her.

"Hello Charlie."

She said nothing. Fear cropped within her.

"It is time to go."

"You're going to torture me again." She was surprised by the strength in her voice.

"It is time to go." He repeated flatly.

Lord Beathach took her arm and led her from the cell. As she expected, she was taken to the shower room. Lord Beathach remained with her the entire time.

When she was finished Lord Beathach took her into a smaller adjacent room. This room was plain black steel and was unfurnished save for a single wall mounted bench that ran the entire perimeter of the room. A small pile of clothing lay on the bench in one corner. Beneath the bench was a pair of knee-high armored leather boots.

"You have been provided with a grand admiral's uniform. Get dressed."

Charlie went to the pile of clothing and sat down. Here was black, brushed cotton tunic and slacks, black cotton socks, a black leather garrison belt and a pair of pink silk panties. A black cap similar to that of a US naval officer sat on the bench beside the pile of clothing.

Charlie dressed quickly. To her surprise everything fit as if it had been custom tailored to her body.

After dressing Charlie carefully looked over the uniform. A single row of black steel buttons held it closed. The insignia on the tunic resembled those of a US naval officer with only small variations in pattern and coloring. Also, the insignia were only on the right side of the tunic. The left was bare save for a black silk armband bearing the markings of the Black Empire. Charlie removed this before donning the uniform. She would not wear the symbol of her captors. The lower half of the uniform was plain and fit comfortably. The material was cotton but felt like nothing she had ever worn before. It was almost like a second skin.

Lord Beathach was watching her in silence. After a moment he spoke. "It is time to go."

"Where?" The question came out before she could suppress it.

He did not answer instead taking her hand and leading her out of the room. This time he took her out of the cell block. Powerful apprehension swept through her.

The rest of the *Destroying Angel* was exactly as it had been weeks (*months?*) earlier. Except it was so much bigger. Charlie felt as though she were walking for miles and with each step her fear grew.

As they went along, the hallways became more and more posh and elaborate and more and more heavily guarded. Eventually they came to a section with guards at every ten feet. The corridors here were solid black with elaborately carved gold trim and vaulted ceilings decorated with horrible scenes of torture, mutilation and murder. As they passed deeper into this section of the space station the images changed to scenes of violent rape, bestiality and other acts of sexual debauchery. Though disgusted and appalled Charlie could not turn her eyes away. The images held a sort of horrifying fascination that was difficult to resist.

After passing through several corridors like this they boarded an elevator. The elevator took them shot upward past what she imagined to be dozens of floors before opening upon a massive chamber that could only be a throne room. The ceiling of this room was very high and decorated with more elaborate, full color images of graphic violence, sexual obscenity, and profanity of all sorts outlined in platinum, gold and silver. Massive serpentinite and steel columns stretched from floor to ceiling. The floor and walls were comprised of similar material. All three gleamed like polished black glass. A blood red carpet ran the length of the center of the room its gold tassels lying only inches from the elevator door. The back wall was a single massive window looking out over the red planet below and into space beyond. In front of this stood a massive throne forged from the same serpentinite and steel as the rest of the room. The air was colder here than in the rest of the space station. Charlie could not help shivering though her tremors were not entirely from the cold.

A non-descript figure sat upon the throne, its features obscured by the light from the window behind. As she approached with Lord Beathach the figure rose and walked towards them. As it moved towards her she saw that the figure was male.

Lord Beathach immediately dropped to his knees and bowed his head.

"You disappoint me Lord Beathach. You were instructed to find and rescue the girl and not to harm her in any way. Instead you have terrorized and tormented this poor child." As he spoke, Charlie felt the figure reach into the power. Lord Beathach lifted off the steel deck of the throne room and hurtled across the chamber before slamming into the rear wall and collapsing to his knees once more. "I should kill you for your cruelty to a fellow Enlightened, but I will leave your fate up to young Charlene." He turned towards her. "You are Charlene MacLeod correct?"

Charlie did not respond.

"But you like to be called Charlie, don't you? My name is Eric Kain, but you can call me Eric." His expression became apologetic. "I am truly sorry that Lord Beathach hurt you. I regret to say that he has been a servant and friend of mine for many years. He had no reason to hurt you and I certainly never wanted him to." As he spoke Charlie was suddenly certain that Eric was telling the truth. "Since Beathach hurt you, I will let you decide what to do with him."

Charlie was taken aback for she knew Eric was sincere. She sensed no anger from this ordinary looking man. Only disgust and cold, seething evil. He cared not for what she decided to do with Beathach. Charlie slowly crossed the throne room to stand over her tormentor.

As she gazed down upon Lord Beathach's death's head mask Charlie came to a sudden realization.

The power's back. Whatever drug they had given her had worn off. She could use the power to escape if she wanted to. Except something was holding her back, some force she could not name.

For a moment Charlie contemplated incinerating Lord Beathach. Images of the endless torment he had inflicted upon her played across the screen of her mind. Fiery agony swept her body, her lungs cried out for air and her brain froze as icy hands closed upon her consciousness. It would be easy, and she sensed that Eric would do nothing to stop her or retaliate. The power raced within her, a living thing within her mind begging to be let out. And in that moment, she *wanted* to let it out. She had suffered horribly at Beathach's hands.

But its wrong. David said taking revenge is wrong. Charlie clamped down on the power, sending twin chromium bolts of agony tearing through her skull.

STOP IT! STOP IT NOW!

The power continued to spiral upwards, spurred on by sudden anger that had kindled in her heart. *He hurt me. He hurt me so bad. And I Hate! him for it! I want him dead!*

STOP IT! STOP IT NOW!

As she looked down up Lord Beathach, the invasive images of the NSA men and their red oak chair suddenly shattered, and Charlie saw only Beathach's death's head mask and behind it his half charred, sneering face. The power continued to rage, sending flaming spurs tearing through her flesh.

PLEASE STOP! PLEASE!

Something disengaged within her mind, spun free for a moment and then went silent. Charlie resolutely turned away from Beathach's fallen form and met Eric's gaze. "Don't hurt him anymore. Just…" She was close to tears and had to choke back a sob. "Just keep him away from me."

Eric offered her a gentle smile. "If that's what you want." He turned his gaze upon Lord Beathach and the dark lord was roughly hauled to his feet. "You will stay away from Charlene MacLeod, she is my responsibility now. Now get out before I change my mind."

"Very well." Lord Beathach turned and disappeared into the elevator. A moment later the door reopened to reveal an empty car.

Eric turned to her and offered her a gentle smile. "Don't be scared. Nobody's going to hurt you anymore."

Charlie looked up at him with deep suspicion.

His smile remained unchanged. "I promise. I'll keep you safe. In fact, I'll let you and your family go free if you want."

Charlie remained silent, studying him carefully. Eric was tall but not unusually so and very handsome. He had jet-black hair and lightly tanned skin. His eyes were sky blue, deep set and intense. His teeth were perfect as was his nose and other features. He had a muscular build but was not ripped or unusually big. Everything about this man was perfectly average and normal. Eric Kain was in every way just an ordinary man. What was particularly striking though was his dress. His clothing consisted of a simple black button-down shirt with matching slacks and shoes. He wore no jewelry or adornments upon his clothing. Nothing about him suggested that he was anything other than just another man.

Except for the feeling. The intense cold feeling remained strong. This man was not just greedy or selfish he was truly evil.

She had sensed a similar but less intense cold sensation radiating out from Lord Beathach. Beathach was a man who enjoyed violence and took pleasure in hurting people. Not because he derived any personal gratification from these acts, but rather because he truly hated people.

In contrast Eric Kain's pleasure was power. He derived no personal enjoyment from the use of violence or brutality but instead from the ability to control people and make them do whatever he wanted. This was Eric's true pleasure and he would do whatever was necessary to satisfy it.

Eric remained unperturbed by her silent distrust. "There's nothing to be afraid of. I have no intention of harming you. If you don't believe me listen to my thoughts. I know you can read my mind."

Charlie did as he suggested and found to her surprise that he was telling the truth. "What do you want from me?"

"I want to help you Charlie." He replied in a matter-of-fact tone. "And if you'll let me I'd like to be your friend. I was the one who sent you the money and clothing you found in your hotel room in London."

Charlie gave him a blank stare, unsure of how to respond. She knew this man was evil, knew that he was interested only in power, yet somehow, she no longer felt afraid. She did not trust Eric Kain, but her fear was subsiding. This was most likely because she knew he had no desire to harm her and moreover did not enjoy harming others as Lord Beathach did.

Eric continued before she could think of something to say in reply. "I ordered Lord Beathach to bring you and your family here for your own safety, but after what happened I would understand if you want to leave. In fact, you are free to go right now if you'd like."

Charlie couldn't believe this. He had to be lying and yet her psychic senses told her that he spoke only the truth. "Then I want to see David and Catherine and I want you to let us go." Even as she spoke the words Charlie expected Eric to refuse.

To her surprise Eric remained cheerful and agreeable. "Of course. I'll have my Death Troopers bring them at once." As he spoke Eric returned to his throne and pressed a button on the right armrest. "Bring the McAuliffes to the throne room please."

He then turned back towards her. "But Charlie, if I let you and your family leave where will you go?"

Charlie's heart sank. She hadn't thought of this. The NSA had chased them across America and all the way to Scotland. Where could they go to be safe? Where could they go to end the chase? To this she had no answer. Robin had once offered her a release and at the time she had been willing to accept that release. Now she did not want Robin's release, but she also did not want to continue running and being afraid.

A disembodied female voice disrupted Charlie's train of thought. "The McAuliffes have gone my Master."

Eric's expression became troubled. "Do you know where?"

"No, my Lord their whereabouts are unknown."

Charlie's heart sank, and she nearly burst into tears. *Gone?! Why would they leave without me?* They had given up so much for her. Maybe David and Catherine had finally had enough. Charlie reached out once more with her mind hoping desperately that this was some sort of trick. It was not. The voice belonged to a female naval officer from whom Charlie sensed no deception. Neither did Charlie sense any lie from Eric though she felt there was a deeper truth behind his words and actions.

Eric turned back towards her, his expression both concerned and apologetic. "It seems that David and Catherine McAuliffe are missing. I'm very sorry."

Something inside her ripped apart and Charlie began to weep softly. She desperately wanted to be with David and Catherine. It seemed like forever since she had last seen them and now they were gone. "You're lying." She sobbed and yet she felt that Eric was in fact telling the truth, after a fashion. There was some darker truth to his words but when she tried to explore this truth her mind flooded with cold darkness and she became afraid.

"I'm so sorry, Charlie." Eric repeated gently. He approached her slowly and took her into his arms. His touch sent a cold shockwave through her flesh causing her to recoil involuntarily.

""Did I hurt you?" Eric's tone was both concerned and apologetic.

Charlie did not reply. Inside her heart was torn to shreds and bleeding profusely within her chest. David and Catherine were gone. They didn't want her anymore and how could she blame them. She had come into their lives and cost them everything. They had nearly been killed because of her. In that moment she felt terribly alone and despite having been abandoned she still wanted, no *needed* them. David and Catherine had become her parents now and she needed them to tell everything was going to be alright.

Charlie stood sobbing in Eric's clumsy embrace for an unknown period of time before her sobs tapered off to little hiccups. When she had regained control of herself, Eric led Charlie from the throne room to a massive, ornate dining hall.

Charlie took little notice of this though as her attention was fixed on the long, mahogany table at the center of the room where a smorgasbord of every conceivable variety of food lay before her. Charlie didn't want food, but her body had other ideas. Unbidden, her mouth immediately began to water to the point where she had to swallow to keep from drooling.

It's a dream. It has to be.

Except it was not. Her rapidly building hunger pangs told her that much. Charlie followed Eric to head of the table where a place had been set for her. He then walked over to a smaller side table, which had been set up as a bar.

"What would you like to drink? You can have anything you want."

Charlie was silent she was still hurting inside and didn't really care.

"Have you ever tried wine? I'll pour you a glass if you'd like."

Charlie had tasted wine once when she was seven and her father had given her a glass to celebrate Christmas. At the time she had found the deep red liquid sour and unpleasant, but she also remembered feeling relaxed and slightly silly after drinking half of the glass.

"Okay…I mean yes, please."

Eric offered a gentle smile. "Your parents did a great job Charlie; you have perfect manners."

Charlie immediately dropped her head as Eric's words cut her like razors. *My parents…. Daddy and Mommy are dead, and David and Catherine are gone. I don't have any parents anymore.*

Eric's expression fell. "I'm sorry Charlie I shouldn't have said that. I've upset you again." He renewed his gentle smile. "You know you really are a charming young lady." As he spoke Eric filled two crystal goblets with blood colored wine from a crystal decanter and set one down in front of her. "Try it, it's very good."

Charlie reached out a tentative hand and lifted the wine goblet from the table. It was surprisingly light given its size. She then brought the goblet close to her nose and sniffed. A pungent, yeasty-sour grape scent filled her nostrils. The glass could have been drugged or poisoned. She knew that, but in that moment, she didn't care and so took a large mouthful of wine. In an instant her tongue came alive with a stronger version of what she had smelled a moment earlier. The flavor was wonderful, and Charlie had to suppress an urge to gulp down the remainder of the glass.

"This *is* good." She whispered between tears.

Eric nodded. "Now let me get you some food. What would you like first?"

Charlie was silent. The entire table had been decked out with every type of food she could have imagined. There were hot dogs, hamburgers, spaghetti and meatballs, pizza, candy, cookies, cake... literally anything she could want or ask for lay before her and yet none of it looked good. After a few minutes of hesitancy her stomach reasserted itself.

Without much enthusiasm Charlie ate half of a large cheese burger, a handful of fries and a glass and a half of wine leaving her feeling both nauseous and more than a little drunk.

Eric remained silent through most of the meal seeming content to watch her eat his food. As she was finishing up Charlie noticed Eric staring at her with an expression of fascinated wonder. Before she could say anything, he broke his silence.

"You have such beautiful hair it's a real shame you had to dye it like that. I mean you didn't want it black, did you? And you didn't really want to use that fake tanning lotion either I bet. My beauticians can take care of that if you want. It shouldn't take them long."

Again, she was taken aback.

What does this guy want with me?

She could read his mind quite clearly but that particular detail remained somewhat obscure. All she could tell for sure was that he wanted to be friendly. Just as he had said.

"Mmm…Okay, that would be nice."

And so, she wound up spending the next hour sitting in a plush leather chair having the black parts of her hair cut off. When this was finished her hair was once again perfect blond and hung a little above her shoulders. After the beautician finished she took Charlie to a private shower stall and instructed her to thoroughly was her hair.

As she dried off and dressed Charlie thought about what she had allowed them to do. Her hair was one of the reasons she knew she had been here a long time for it had gotten long again so that only the ends were black. It was the only reliable measure of time she had. As for her skin, well she had, when she was younger, wanted tan skin and had even tried sun tanning on the beach in Long Island. All she got for her trouble then was a nasty sunburn covering most of her body. But when she applied the artificial tanning lotion she had not liked the way it looked. It made her skin yellowish brown and looked fake to her. She had *hated* dying her hair. Charlie loved her perfect blond hair. It was a part of her and to give it up almost hurt. It didn't help that the black dye made her hair *look* unnatural, as if she were a goth kid looking to piss off her parents.

Charlie was embarrassed by her changed appearance though she never complained about it. It was a relief to have her old hair and skin color back. Yet part of her felt as if she were betraying David and Catherine. The feeling lingered in the back of her mind where her continuing fear and suspicion already resided.

When Charlie had finished dressing the beautician took her to another room containing a mirror and a single counter top filled with dozens of perfume bottles.

"You can wear whichever one you like." She told Charlie before stepping back to wait for her decision.

After a moment's startled pause Charlie timidly went about opening and sniffing each bottle on the counter top before finally deciding on a light cinnamon scented perfume. Having decided Charlie gave the bottle to the beautician who carefully applied it to Charlie's skin. She then led Charlie outside to where Eric waited patiently.

"You look beautiful Charlie."

"Thank you." Her voice came out a little more confident. The suspicious voice in the back of her mind grew slightly softer.

"I have a little surprise for you Charlie."

Instinctively Charlie reached out with her mind.

"We're going to go for a space flight. If that's alright with you that is."

"Sure."

As it turned out what he had in mind was a ride in a fighter. After giving her a chance to sober up Eric outfitted Charlie with a flight suit. Then he took her into one of the docking bays where the two of them boarded a Black Imperial S-20 Raven.

Inside, the fighter was like something out of a dream. The cockpit was huge and far more comfortable than she would have ever imagined.

The ride was an incredible rush. After clearing the docking bay Eric took the star fighter though what he called some basic combat maneuvers which consisted of a series of loops, sharp climbs and dives, barrel roles and corkscrews. He then fired off the fighter's weapons at a pair of target drones before turning the controls over to her.

Charlie was frightened at first but found to her surprise that she could handle the fighter just as well as Eric. Flying came naturally, as if she had been doing it all her life. Within minutes she was pulling the fighter through tight loops, steep dives and spectacular barrel roles and corkscrews with ease.

When a second wave of target drones was launched she found that the weapons systems came just as easily and was able to destroy each target with a single blast from the fighter's laser cannons.

The experience was so exhilarating that she forgot to be amazed or frightened by her suddenly discovered flying skills. This was like nothing she had ever done before. It was like a dream. The fighter moved with perfect smoothness at her touch. Her hands and feet were fused to the controls her torso melded with the soft leather couch. She was one with it and it was part of her. The feeling was both deeply intoxicating and exciting at once. The ship had become invisible leaving her feeling as though she were flying free through space. Her heart raced, and blood thundered in her temples. She screamed, not out of fear but because to not scream would have caused her to explode.

Charlie threw the throttle all the way forward coaxing greater speed from the fighter's powerful engines. She felt the ship accelerate but there were no G-forces. It was a strange feeling.

Charlie watched stars, planets, and other ships spin all around her as she took the fighter through a second series of maneuvers and felt something close to happiness.

Eric sat behind her in silence allowing her to enjoy the experience in peace.

Charlie flew for more than an hour before she finally tired and returned control to him.

As they returned to the *Destroying Angel* Charlie felt cold darkness close around her like a noose. In space she had felt free, now that feeling was gone, replaced by choking evil.

After landing, the two boarded an elevator and descended deep into the space station. At first Charlie thought Eric was returning her to her cell but as the elevator continued down she realized they were going somewhere else.

Several minutes later the door opened on a narrow, poorly lit corridor. A single pair of guards patrolled here. There was no one else. Eric said nothing as he led her down this corridor to where it ended in a thick blast door. On the other side was a large featureless room. There was no floor in this room, only a vast opening that looked out into space. A single catwalk bridged this opening. Eric took her out to the center right edge and pointed down.

"Look."

Below her the Black Imperial capital world gleamed like a great ruby. Beyond it space stretched out into eternity. It was an awesome sight.

"Everything you can see and beyond is part of my empire. All of it. It can be yours too if you want it."

Charlie stared down in silent amazement. Now she understood. He didn't just want her friendship. He wanted *her*.

"If you join me I will make you my empress. We'll rule the universe together as equals."

Charlie did not know how to respond. Eric was not lying. He was offering to share his empire with her, to give her everything he had. Everything she saw and everything she could possibly imagine was within her grasp if she wanted it. No one had ever offered her such a gift. She took an involuntary step forward bringing herself to the very edge of the catwalk. There were no safety rails here, just a slender black steel bridge over open space.

Eric was watching her intently. "No one will ever offer you more. Not even your God. Hell, all he's ever given you was pain. He let people hurt you just because you're better. Fuck Him!" He gave her an expectant look. "Say it with me Charlie. Fuck Him!! He made you what you are and then hurt you for being born different. Fuck Him!"

She could not. She did not believe that God had hurt her on purpose. He had saved her and gave her, her life back after the NSA took it away. She was hurt by people, not by Him.

He could have stopped it, though couldn't he? He brought me back to life. Why couldn't he have saved Daddy? Why doesn't he bring back David and Catherine?

Charlie looked away as doubts began to rise within her. She forced them down quickly. It didn't matter right now. She could not listen to what Eric said no matter how logical it seemed, or she would become like him.

"I know it's hard to accept but what I'm saying is the truth. He doesn't care about you or anybody else. He's just playing with us like toys. He doesn't care if you get hurt any more than you would care if you dropped your Barbie doll down the stairs."

Charlie remained silent.

"If you don't believe me you can test it yourself. There's nothing between us and space except a thin force field that keeps the room pressurized. It can't block solid objects though. If you really think He cares about you then jump. If he's at all concerned about you then he'll protect you." He motioned with his hand. "Go ahead. If you really trust Him that much."

Charlie stood perfectly still, trembling with fear. Some part of her thought that maybe she would be okay but most of her thought she didn't want to find out.

Eric pushed her a little closer to the edge. "Go ahead. He'll catch you, right?"

Her body tensed as fierce, terrified shudders rippled up and down her spine. She had seen a movie once where a man was ejected into space without a protective suit. He had exploded, but not before suffering horrific pain.

The power began to stir, awakened by the force of her fear. Beneath her the red planet gleamed malevolently.

I can't. I can't do this…

She stepped back quickly, bumping into Eric's chest. "Please I don't want to die."

"I didn't think so." He bent down to her level and spoke in a very gentle voice. "It's okay to be afraid Charlie. I would be too because I know I would die if I jumped through that porthole. He wouldn't save me, and He won't save you. He'd just sit back and laugh." Eric's face filled with deep compassion. "You've spent your entire life doing the right thing. Your Mom and Dad taught you from a young age that your power is dangerous and that you shouldn't use it, right?"

She remained silent.

"And you didn't use it when you should have. You didn't use your power to destroy the NSA before they could kill your Mom. Before they could kill your Dad."

Charlie's heart ripped apart. "Please stop." Eric's words were razors that cut deep and yet she knew without having to touch his mind that he spoke the absolute truth. She could have stopped the NSA from killing Mommy and Daddy. She could have stopped everything.

Eric's expression deepened. "I know it's hard to listen to Charlie, but you need to hear this. You could have saved your Mom and Dad. You have the power to destroy the NSA, but you didn't because your Mom and Dad taught you that its wrong to use the power, and that its wrong to kill. There's no doubt that they meant well but they were deceived just like you."

"Please!" She begged him. He was right though she could not hear it. What he suggested was dangerous. Though she could have stopped it all it was bad. Daddy and David had said so. It was bad to use the power. It was bad to hurt people. And yet it hurt her to be reminded that she *could* have done something to stop it all.

"I'm sorry Charlie but you need to hear this. You are powerful enough that you could have stopped the NSA and anyone else from harming you and anyone you care about if you wanted. Except you were lied to and told that you shouldn't use the power, that you shouldn't hurt and kill people who try to hurt and kill you, that you should treat people the way you want to be treated, that you should treat non-Enlighteneds like they are your equals. And you were a good girl and did as you were told. You did the right thing and look what it cost you. You lost your Mommy and Daddy, they made you do their tests and hurt you, and when they were done with you they killed you, didn't they?"

Big tears welled up in Charlie's eye and trickled down her cheeks in hot rivers.

"I don't like to do this to you Charlie. You're a good and decent person but you need to open your eyes. Doing the right thing has cost you everything. And it didn't stop the NSA or the normal people from terrorizing you and taking away everyone you love."

Charlie fell to her knees at the edge of the catwalk sobbing uncontrollably, her tears dropping through the open portal and floating off into space in silver globes. She had lost so much because of the NSA and she *could* have stopped it. She could have burned them all up before…

Before they killed Mommy

Before they killed Daddy

Now she was alone again. She supposed it was fair. She had brought the NSA into David and Catherine's lives. It was only fair that they leave her. Everyone whose life she had touched had been hurt because of her and she had done nothing. She deserved to be alone.

"You lost everything for a lie Charlie."

Charlie remained as she was, crying her eyes out for several minutes before she was able to regain control of herself. When she did, Eric offered her his hand. "Come on. You look like you could use another drink."

Charlie went with him mutely. Her heart was flayed open in her chest and her eyes stung with tears. Eric poured her two large glasses of red wine and made her drink them before taking her to a lavishly appointed bedroom not two floors below the throne room.

"I know today has been difficult Charlie and I'm sorry for that. Try to get some sleep. Tomorrow I will take you down to my palace."

"Okay." Charlie's voice came out tired and unenthusiastic. She had indeed had a difficult day and her heart still bled from the loss of David and Catherine and from Eric's words.

"Good night Charlie." Eric said gently.

Charlie did not reply. Despite her loneliness and hurt she did not trust Eric and did not want to allow herself to grow close for she knew doing so would be dangerous.

Without another word Eric left, shutting the bedroom door behind him as he went. Charlie felt nauseous from the wine, so she sat up for several hours before finally allowing herself to sleep.

XI

Charlie was awakened the following morning by Eric. "Good morning Charlie. Are you hungry?"

"Yes."

As he had done the day before Eric took her down to the massive dining hall where she once again found a cornucopia of food. As he had done before, Eric sat in silence while Charlie ate waiting until she was finished to speak.

"Are you ready to head down to the palace?"

Charlie looked at him with suspicion.

"We can use the Raven if you'd like."

This brought on a rush of brief excitement that she had to fight to suppress. "Okay." Her voice came out as little more than a whisper.

He smiled. "Alright then. Whenever you're ready."

Charlie stood up and headed towards the door. Eric followed close behind. Ten minutes later they were aboard the same Raven they had used the previous day descending towards the red planet below. Charlie was in control of the fighter.

"You are looking at the planet Ifrin. Capital of the Black Empire." It was strange, Eric's voice held no pride. His tone was merely informative.

The thought passed quickly though as it was swept away by wonder. The descent was spectacular. As they entered the planet's atmosphere she began to see the first twinkling of light from buildings on the planet's surface. Beneath its blood colored atmosphere Ifrin was a black gleaming jewel, much like the *Destroying Angel* orbiting above. Within seconds the tiny twinkling lights began to take shape as massive high rises, tiny ribbons of road and speeding aircraft. Numerous large, blood and fire colored clouds hovered between them and the obsidian surface. These made the planet look like the *Destroying Angel* might if it had caught a bad case of chicken pox.

The image made her want to giggle. However, Charlie managed to suppress the urge.

As they continued their descent more and more buildings took shape. Soon they were among the aircraft speeding through the atmosphere. Up close they appeared similar to fighter jets with their flat clipped wings, slim air intakes and broad jet outlets with flaring afterburners.

A few seconds later they passed through the clouds and were cruising among the planet's many gleaming black skyscrapers. Charlie gasped in awe. It was beautiful; unlike anything she had seen before.

Eric's voice brought her back a moment later. "If you continue straight ahead you'll see my palace and a private docking bay. Land there."

She nodded as she leveled the fighter out at four hundred feet.

Now many of the buildings were above her and she could see that what had appeared to be normal roads was actually an intricate system of elevated roads and walkways beneath which lay many hundreds of feet of dark, open space. The buildings all continued downward below this network into the darkness beneath. She could not even yet see the ground, only a black abyss.

They were flying towards a system of angled towers that all came together at a single, massive central spire. At the top of this was what had to be the largest medieval castle she had ever seen.

From here came an overwhelming sense of cold darkness. The feeling was like drowning. It *hurt* in a way she could not describe, it was both physical and psychological and something else as well.

Charlie became very afraid as she realized that she had been feeling this same sensation since first approaching the planet but had not been aware of it until now. Deep, cold fear pulsed within making her want to turn away. But she could not. Some power had gotten hold of her and was drawing her towards itself. It was a power she could not resist.

As they neared the massive black central spire she pulled back on the stick drawing the fighter into a steep climb. Seconds later they were cruising above the spire's castle crown and minutes after that she was neatly dropping the fighter into a narrow docking bay beneath the castle's south wall.

Charlie's fear was intensifying, building into outright terror. She was trembling by the time she landed the Raven. As she climbed down from the cockpit her head swam with dizziness from a sudden rush of blood. White spots flashed in front of her eyes in time with the thundering of her heart. Eric caught her by the waist and lowered her to the floor just as she was about to slip from the ladder.

"It's ok Charlie. There's nothing to be afraid of. This is your palace too."

His voice was gentle and friendly, still it brought her no comfort. Waves of cold rushed through her bringing with them increasingly powerful tremors. There was great suffering here, and great evil.

Eric helped her back on her feet and released her after making sure she wouldn't fall. "There you go. Are you all right?"

She nodded without a word.

"All right then." He smiled kindly. "Welcome home. How about I show you around?"

"Okay." Her voice was little more than a whisper for she was truly terrified.

XII

Eric took her all over the palace and through much of the surrounding city. She was shown restaurants, clubs, bars, casinos, theaters, zoos, theme parks, drug houses, brothels, and dozens of other places of amusement. Every conceivable form of diversion was available here as well as every conceivable form of vice. There was even a coliseum like the ones in ancient Rome she had learned about in Mrs. Peters' class.

As Eric explained the Black Empire was a nation of hedonism. The only law was loyalty to the state. Beyond that citizens were free to do as they pleased and because of the large slave population they were never required to work.

To Charlie this was both frightening and tempting at once. Part of her was intrigued by the notion of never having to go to school or do chores or do anything else she didn't want to, but another part of her found the implications of such a policy very disturbing. She would be able to do whatever she wanted, but so would everyone else and while she would never dream of maliciously harming another person there would be others without such compunctions. And one of them might want to harm her.

Like Lord Beathach.

The condition of the slaves bothered her as well. Here were people no different than the citizens of the Black Empire at whose mercy they lived. They could be raped, tortured or murdered without any consequences. What was worse was that all of these things were done routinely. Slave men and women, even children, would be suddenly grabbed and brutalized. The most attractive slaves were forced into the brothels. Others would be thrown into the coliseum to be tortured and killed for the amusement of the spectators. It was terrifying. What kind of people were these that they would not just allow these things to go on but do them for fun? The answer terrified her even more.

As they traveled through the city, Charlie saw hundreds of people. Here were families, couples, grandparents with grandchildren, kids running and playing. These were not deranged criminals or brutal monsters. They were average, normal people doing things average, normal people did. And like average, normal people without the power they eyed her and Eric with great suspicion as they passed.

"Are you hungry?" Eric had stopped walking and was looking down at her with his penetrating blue eyes.

"Yes." They had been walking for hours and she was ravenous.

"What would you like Charlie? We can go anywhere you want."

She knew at once and though she did not think there would be one she asked anyway. "Can we go to McDonalds?" Her voice came out timidly hopeful.

"Sure. There's one on the next block."

Upon arriving she found the biggest McDonalds she had ever seen in her life and the only one she had ever seen with table service and a full bar.

Upon entering they were greeted by a young blond-haired man who asked them where they would like to sit. Eric let her decide and Charlie asked to sit on the third floor by the window though in truth she did not care one-way or the other.

After taking their drink orders the man vanished and was replaced a moment later by another young man who waited patiently to take their food orders. Twenty seconds later the first man reappeared with their drinks. After perusing the menu for a few minutes Charlie ordered a Big Mac with Super-Size fries. Eric ordered the same. Twenty seconds later the second man returned carrying two of the biggest hamburgers she had ever seen along with two huge platters of fries. Charlie stared for only a moment before digging in.

It was strange, though it looked delicious the food was tasteless. It remained this way regardless of how much salt or pepper she added. Her drink, a strawberry milk shake, was the same.

As she ate Charlie watched the other people in the restaurant. Most of them were families. Young men and women with babies or children, many of them around her age; some older couples with teenagers; and a few teenage or young adult couples on dates. At one table a father was helping his son pour ketchup on his French fries. Nearby another family talked excitedly about their vacation to a planet called Longinus. To their right a young man and woman sat holding hands and talking in soft voices.

There was nothing unusual about these people. They were like the people on earth. Inside them she sensed all of the same emotions, desires, and needs of any normal person, including their deep abiding suspicion and fear of Eric and her. Yet beneath these lay a dark core of evil. Charlie sensed this in everyone in the restaurant, even the children. They too had been corrupted. It was truly frightening.

"As you can see we are normal people, not monsters."

Charlie turned her gaze on Eric. His expression was friendly, not sinister or smug, but friendly. An involuntary shudder crept its way up her spine.

Eric's expression immediately became concerned. "You don't have to be afraid. No one here will hurt you. You are one of us now."

Charlie returned a blank stare as she was unsure of what to say. She had stopped chewing the French fry in her mouth.

"You are already a citizen Charlie. When you want to you will become empress."

Charlie remained still for a moment longer before swallowing. The French fry went down in a lump causing her to gag. She pushed the remainder of her food away no longer feeling hungry. "I'm done."

Eric came around the table and offered his hand. "Come on there's more I want to show you."

Charlie stood up without taking his hand and followed him out of the restaurant. Their next stop was at a dance club. From there they went to a series of bars before returning to the palace.

XIII

Upon returning Eric took her to a room at the top of the palace's highest spire. This room was set up as a combination lounge and observatory. There were no walls. A single pane of glass encircled the room from floor to ceiling. Its furnishings consisted of plush white suede lounge chairs, recliners and couches;

and crystal coffee and end tables.

A small group of men and women was scattered around the room. Among them was the man who had shot her in Iraq. The force of their evil intent struck her like a cold wave. Fear and anger stirred within.

As she entered the room with Eric they all stood and bowed down on one knee.

"I wanted to introduce you to my lieutenants." Eric turned to the group. "You can get up."

They all stood up.

Eric first presented the man who had shot her. "This is Hardliner, my personal enforcer."

Charlie knew without having to ask that Hardliner was the man's military code name. For a moment she wondered what his real name was before the question was swept from her mind. This was the man that had shot her. Anger sublimated her fear and she began to tremble with fury.

Hardliner extended his hand to her. Charlie stared at him with glacial eyes.

Hardliner was a tall man though not as tall as Lord Beathach. He had a slender muscular build, with pale skin and jet-black hair. He was handsome in a macabre way. Hardliner's expression was blank, but his deep-set gray eyes told a different story as did his heart. He distrusted her. He wanted to kill her.

Hardliner wore a black shirt with black jeans, black military boots and a black trench coat.

"Your name is Charlie, right?" Hardliner's voice was soft and sounded like worn tires on a gravel road.

She inclined her head.

"It's a pleasure to meet you Charlie." His tone was friendly but held a slight warning tone. His distrust of her was strong.

Beside Hardliner stood a tall and slender raven-haired woman. Her skin was dark caramel, and her eyes were a rich honey brown. This woman was very beautiful and enjoyed showing it off. She was dressed in a short white and gold thread skirt with a matching armored top that left her stomach and most of her chest bare. She too wore boots though hers were brown rather than black leather.

Eric turned to her next.

"This is Lady Riyadah, my personal bodyguard."

Riyadah smiled coldly. "I can see why Eric chose you as his empress. You are powerful and beautiful." She extended her hand and Charlie shook it.

From Riyadah she sensed pure evil but also another sensation. This feeling was alien to her though she had felt it once before. *Lust.* The name came into her mind unbidden. Charlie pushed the thought aside.

Without pausing Eric turned to the woman standing next to Riyadah. She was equally attractive with long blonde hair and clear blue eyes. She wore a black blazer and skirt with a blue blouse and black kitten heels.

"This is General Nicole McDermott, one of my representatives on earth."

Nicole extended her hand. "Hi Charlie."

Her voice was friendly, but Charlie was not fooled. Nicole, like Hardliner, distrusted her and perceived her as a threat.

Again, Eric moved on without pausing. "This is General Vic Garling another of my representatives on earth."

Garling was tall and slender with jet-black hair and gray eyes. His dress was similar to that of Nicole, black suit with a blue button-down shirt and a slim dark red tie. He clenched a cigarette in his teeth.

Garling extended his hand and Charlie met his eyes with a cold glare. "It's a pleasure to finally meet you." Smoke drifted out of his mouth as he spoke.

Charlie coughed lightly.

"You know you gave the NSA quite a run for their money." He paused to take another drag off his cigarette. "I have to admit I'm quite impressed."

Charlie intensified her glare. She didn't trust this man. He had not been directly involved in the deaths of her parents, but he knew who had given the order.

Eric stepped back from Garling to address the group. "You can go now."

XV

All five of them filed out without a word. When they were gone Eric turned to her.

"Now that you've seen what I'm offering you what do you say? If you join me, you can have anything you want. Your wildest dreams will become real."

Charlie might have been tempted were she not so horrified. She stared up at him without speaking.

"You still don't trust me, do you?"

Charlie remained silent. Her flesh felt cold.

"You're a good girl Charlie and very smart. You've been hurt so many times that you're afraid to trust people." She felt his hand on her shoulder and cringed slightly. "And you want to do the right thing. You want to do what your friends David and Catherine told you to do, what your parents would want you to do. I promise I won't hurt you. I'm not like the others. I really do care about you and I want to help." He paused and bent down to her level. "David and Catherine, and your mother and father all meant well when they told you what they did. They were trying to help you and give you proper guidance, but they were wrong. They were, like everyone else, brought up to believe that a person should put others needs before his or her own. David was taught by his father that people with talents like ours should use those powers to protect and serve people who do not have them, and that lesson was wrong. It's a lie. A lie told by normal people, so they can make us their slaves. It wasn't David's fault or even his father's they were simply repeating a lie told to them by a society that sees us as freaks and monsters that have to be controlled and locked away. The normal people don't care about us Charlie. They hate and fear us because they know we're better. We have power they can only dream of. So, they lock us away in basement laboratories, so they can experiment on us like guinea pigs and try to figure out why we can do what we do. They tell us that it is our duty to protect them because they are weaker. Lightwarriors are slaves Charlie. They are Enlighteneds enslaved by lies."

"No, that's not true."

She couldn't accept this. David had told her they were born to help others. She couldn't believe he would lie to her. He didn't lie to her. She had felt his sincerity. Yet she knew that Eric was not lying either. How could they both be telling the truth? How could this be the truth? Lightwarriors were supposed to be heroes. That couldn't be a lie.

"I'm sorry to have to tell you this Charlie but it is." The compassion and sadness in his voice was hurtful.

Tears spilled down her cheeks. "No."

"Think Charlie." Eric persisted. "Think about how they treated you. They took you away from your mother and father. They locked you up and did experiments on you. They killed your parents. They used you and when they were finished with you they tried to kill you. Just because you were born different. Worst of all they made you hate and fear yourself for being different. They don't give a damn about you Charlie. You're nothing but a freak to them. Why should you throw your life away protecting people who hate and fear you?"

"But they're not all like that. Some people were nice to me. Some even tried to help me and Daddy and me and David and Catherine escape."

"Did they know who you really are Charlie? Did they know about the power?"

"David's father did."

"Yes, but David's father is the exception that proves the rule. He is a member of the Order of Light. Their only purpose is to train Lightwarriors. Can you think of anyone else normal you met who knew about your powers and accepted them?"

She was silent. There was no one else. Striker had accepted her powers, but he was far from normal and he had betrayed her. He was not her friend.

"They all betrayed you. Every one of them who found out who you really are." He paused. "Look you just saw what they are like. Cruel, selfish, violent and bigoted. That's humanity. People are self-serving, violent and intolerant of that which is other. It's in our nature. There's no reason to try to be any other way."

"No." Charlie fought not to break down completely. "They're like that because you made them that way. You told them that it's alright to hurt other people and act selfish. That's why they act that way."

"You know better than that Charlie. The people here are no different than the people on earth. I merely encouraged them to follow their natural instincts and proclivities. What you've seen here *is* what people are like. The only difference is that we are honest about what we are. The people on earth lie to each other and to themselves. They call themselves good and condemn evil acts while they're all the time wanting to do exactly what they call wrong. Criminals are really only punished for getting caught because everyone would do exactly the same thing if they got the chance."

Charlie was silent. She did not want to believe what he was saying but she knew there was truth in his words. She felt very strongly that Eric was speaking from his heart. He was not trying to control her but rather he cared for her and was trying to help her.

It was hard to listen for she knew he was right. She had been tempted more than a few times to use the power to get something she wanted, and she knew other people were no different.

"If you want I can show you what people are really like." He extended his hand to her. "Just take my hand. I promise I won't hurt you. We can stop anytime you want."

She stared at him for a moment before placing her hand in his. Eric's palm was cool and dry to the touch.

She did not want to see but could not resist for part of her hoped he would prove himself wrong.

Within seconds an immense wave of power ripped through her body. She found herself standing beside Eric on a beach littered with corpses. A battle raged all around them. Gunfire rang out, punctuated by the wail and roar of exploding artillery shells and the screams of dying soldiers. White tracer fire streaked through air stained with thick black smoke.

"Humans tell themselves that wars are necessary. That there are good wars, fought for noble reasons. This is a lie." Eric's voice was filled with contempt. "You are watching D-Day, the day American and British forces invaded Normandy. Americans and British tell themselves that this was a noble battle, that World War II was fought to defeat tyranny. In truth this was a war of stupidity. After the first World War, the Allies imposed the Treaty of Versailles knowing that it would breed desperation in the German people. They set the stage for Hitler and his Nazi Party to take control of Germany. Then they sat on their hands and allowed him to become powerful knowing his malevolent intentions. No one in America or the United Kingdom gave a shit about the murder of Jews or anyone else that Hitler's Third Reich killed. They only became involved when Germany and Japan attacked them directly."

As Eric spoke soldiers streamed by them on both sides in waves. Some passed within feet of where they stood. A thought occurred to her.

"How come they can't see us."

"They see what they expect." Eric replied simply.

As she looked on in horror fresh gunfire and artillery rained down, decimating the soldiers charging across the beach. Fresh screams rang out on the cold air as blood stained the sandy beach deep red. A man passed within two feet of her. Suddenly a bullet ripped through his skull spraying her with blood and brains.

Charlie turned her eyes away from the horror surrounding her. Eric gently took her chin and made her look as men and young boys, bled and died. "Look at what they've done. Tens of thousands of young men died fighting over Normandy in a battle made necessary by stupidity and vanity. Over sixty million in total died in World War II because the Allies wanted to punish Germany after the first World War. There is nothing noble about any war. Men kill each other in wars over stupidity, vanity, pride, greed and megalomania. This is human nature, mankind lives to fight and kill one another."

Eric took her hand again and, in an instant, they were standing inside the gates of a large prison camp. A freight train had recently arrived; men in black military uniforms unloaded prisoners and separated them into two lines. The first led deeper into the camp, the second to the basement of a large single-story brick building. It was to this building that Eric led her.

"This will be difficult, but you must look. You have the right to see what human nature truly is." As he spoke, Eric led her towards the long brick building. "People hate those who are different from them." They had reached the brick building and were descending the basement stairs along with the endless line of prisoners. Below men, women and children undressed and were herded into showers that weren't showers. As the last of the prisoners entered the "showers" the black uniformed men slammed heavy steel doors behind them. "Tolerance and acceptance are a lie." Eric spat coldly. "This is mankind's tolerance." As he spoke Charlie heard the first of what would become a cacophony of screams. She understood the meaning at once. These prisoners, innocent men, women and yes, *children* were being executed. Eric led her closer to the steel door. "Look for yourself. They are dying for no other reason than being of the wrong race." As he spoke Eric boosted her up so that she could see through a small glass portal in the door. Inside men, women and children crawled over one another gasping for air that was nowhere to be found.

"Please put me down." She begged. "I don't want to see anymore. I…I can't."

Eric set her down on her feet. Charlie's stomach lurched, and she collapsed to her knees before vomiting. Eric quickly took her from the room and helped her clean up.

Minutes later they were standing on an abandoned desert battlefield. Burned and bloody bodies were strewn everywhere along with a scattering of burned out tanks, APC's and Humvees.

"The entire Middle East was plunged into civil war because of an ideological fight between American liberals and conservatives. After they took over Congress liberal politicians gave the more conservative president permission to go to war with Iraq. Then when the war was over they used it as an excuse to impeach him. Once he was out of the way they replaced him with a liberal who immediately pulled all military forces out of Iraq and Afghanistan. Without American support the governments of both nations collapsed and brought down the governments of the rest of the Middle East with them. Even Israel was destroyed. All that's left of it is Tel Aviv, which sealed itself off as a sort of city-state. All of this happened because both sides had to have their way. The conservatives wanted to get rid of the Taliban and Saddam Hussein and they got their way. The liberals wanted the American military out of the Middle East and they got their way. The result was the destruction of the central governments of both Iraq and Afghanistan and the destabilization of the entire Middle East when American forces were pulled out. It was all about politics. Neither side cared about the people who might be hurt. Except they were being used too. The whole thing was orchestrated by American intelligence to create an open marketplace for drugs and guns. But both sides were too blinded by politics to see that. All they saw was their agendas. Their stupidity and selfishness cost a lot of people their lives."

Charlie stared at the carnage before her in horror. Tears streamed down her cheeks in rivers. How could this be true?

"How could they do that?"

Eric's lips curled into a wry smile. "Because the CIA was making a killing off the narcotics trade and they didn't want the local rulers interfering. I can show you more if you want."

Charlie did not reply.

A moment later they were standing in a smoky back room of a nightclub. A dozen men sat around a table discussing 'business'.

"Lucky Luciano was probably the best friend the CIA ever had. He was the one who established the American Mafia as you would know it and he was the one who established the connection between the Mafia and CIA. Luciano took a bunch of small warring gangs and built them into a powerful syndicate. He made the rules and made sure everyone followed them. Thomas Dewey almost shut him down except then World War II came along and the Germans were able to bomb the docks in New York. Someone at the top decided that it was more important to keep the Nazis from disrupting American shipping than it was to shut down the Mafia so the OSS, which was what the CIA was known as then, made a deal with Luciano. They would let him operate free and clear if he kept the Nazis off the docks. After World War II Luciano went into retirement and was replaced by my man Vic Garling."

Charlie stepped back from Eric, pulling her hand from his grasp.

"I know what you're thinking. 'Why would I condemn the CIA and the Mafia if I helped link them together and build their power?' Well I wouldn't have been able to do a thing if American intelligence hadn't been willing to cooperate. Moreover, the narcotics trade would not be so profitable if the American public wasn't such a bunch of junkies. My people simply gave them what they wanted. If they didn't someone else would." He extended his hand to her. "Come on I want to show you something else."

Charlie stared at it for a long time. She still couldn't believe what she was hearing. Everything she had believed about what people were like and how the world worked was wrong. And now here was the man who had helped orchestrate much of it. With trembling fingers, she put her hand in his and they were transported to a dingy street corner somewhere in Asia. Women and young girls in skimpy clothing stood plying their trade.

"This is some of the worst of it: Humans exploiting other humans for profit. These women and girls are slaves. Their owners send them out to sell themselves for as little as five American dollars. They have no future and no hope of escape." He pointed up a side street. "On the next block it's boys. People, mostly Americans, come here in droves. None of these children will live to see twenty. If they aren't murdered by customers or by their pimps, then they'll die of AIDS. Most of them are already infected and many of them are in the advanced stages. This is what humans are really like Charlie. You are looking behavior that is considered beyond reprehensible throughout most of the world and yet the majority of these men and women will go unpunished. As I said we're not all that different from the people on earth. My people are just more open about it. I don't condone what they do. I personally think that most of it is disgusting but I also won't stop it. This is what humanity is."

Now they were standing in the observation lounge again. Deep despair welled within her. She wanted to cry but could not. The effects of what she had seen and heard were too powerful. All she could do was stand there shaking in horror.

"Nazism, ethnic cleansing, rape, murder, torture. They have all been committed by ordinary people. Many of the worst Nazis began as ordinary Germans. They got themselves involved in Nazi rhetoric and belief and soon began to turn words into actions. There are very few people who are involved in these crimes that are truly insane. Most of them are ordinary people who gave into corruption and selfishness. There's nothing sick about it. It is human nature. I know you want revenge for your parents' murders and if you join me you will have it. There's nothing wrong with taking revenge. When it's justified it is fair. Let go Charlie. You'll feel so much better."

She did not respond. Her mind was still lost in the horror of what she had just learned.

After waiting for Charlie to calm, Eric led her from the Observation Lounge and through a series of opulent corridors before opening a large, ebony door onto the most lavish bedroom Charlie had ever seen.

The walls were covered in red silk wallpaper, the floor was solid marble, covered by elaborate silk Oriental rugs. There was a big canopy bed with pink satin sheets and drapes, and beautiful teak wood furniture. Behind the bed a huge picture window looked out onto the darkened capital.

"This will be your room from now on." Eric explained. "Bathroom's through the door on your right. You'll find everything you need there. There's a nightie on the bed. Good night."

That said he turned and left. For a moment she stood there. Then she turned and tried the door. It was unlocked. The hall outside was deserted.

What? What's going on?

Eric had told her she was free to go at any time, but she had not fully believed it until now. In another time she would have been excited. She would have hurried down the hallway to look for her father or later David and Catherine. Now they were all gone, and she was alone, and she had nowhere to go. She was no prisoner, but she might as well have been one. There was nowhere else to go.

Charlie hung her head and then turned and went back into the bedroom closing the door after herself.

Charlie brushed her teeth and put on the pink silk nightgown lying on the bed. As she climbed under the blankets Charlie felt darkness and loneliness close in around her.

Daddy's gone, Mommy's gone, David and Catherine are gone. They're all gone and I'm alone. I'll always be alone.

In that moment she needed David and Catherine more than ever for she knew not what to do with the knowledge that Eric had given her. Daddy and Mommy had taught her from the earliest age that people were basically good, and David had told her the same. And yet there was no denying the truth of what Eric had shown her. She needed David to help her deal with what she had seen, to tell her what to do. She needed him to tell her whether to *Hate!* the normal people or not. David always knew what to do but he was gone now an she was alone. She would always be alone.

As Charlie laid her head on the soft down pillow a single tear spilled down her cheek and caught in the porcelain shell of her left ear. It was all she could manage for she was exhausted. Charlie closed her eyes on her sorrow and before long she slipped into a deep and dreamless sleep.

XVI

After showing Charlie to her bedroom suite, Kain summoned his lieutenants back to the observation lounge. It was night. The sky had gone from blood red to black satin. Stars scattered across the sky like brilliant white buckshot. Distant flickers of lightning on the horizon threatened an impending storm. Lord Beathach arrived first followed by Hardliner, Riyadah, Nicole McDermott and Vic Garling. McDermott and Garling arrived together.

The moment he saw them Kain knew they had been together. He could feel it. Garling had slept with *his* daughter.

Kain was not happy about this but there was nothing he could do about it. Nicole was a grown woman and the fact that she was his daughter was a closely guarded secret that he dared not reveal. Should anything happen to him Nicole would take his place upon the Black Throne. Her true identity had to be kept secret even from his most trusted lieutenants.

"Hello." With Charlie safely shown to her bedroom on the other side of the palace, Kain saw no need to maintain any façade of formality.

"Greetings my master." Lord Beathach replied.

"Hello." Garling's reply was as nonchalant as ever.

"Eric." Nicole inclined her head as she spoke.

Riyadah greeted him with a silent nod and a knowing grin. *Later, right?*

Yeah.

"Hello, Eric." Hardliner met his gaze for a moment before turning away and sitting down.

Kain waited until everyone was seated before beginning. "I called you here because I wanted your input-on Charlie."

This was only a partial truth. Kain did want their input but he also wanted to judge where they stood on the girl.

"She is very strong for a little girl." As he spoke Beathach stared at Kain with his blank, artificial eyes. "Most adults would have broken long before this. She'll be difficult to turn."

"Yes, I know." Kain felt Beathach's concern but he also knew Beathach believed as he did, that the girl could be turned. "That just makes her more valuable though. She is human and a child who has lost everyone she's ever loved. She is still grieving the loss of her parents and her adoptive parents and she desperately wants someone to love and to love her. I will become a friend to her and in time father."

"How can you be sure of that?" Riyadah inquired in a reasonable tone. "Her mind is closed. I could not sense her intentions. Could you?" Kain sensed that she too believed the girl could be turned despite her concern.

"No, but I don't have to be able to read her mind to know her pain." Kain replied in a casual voice. "All you have to do is look at her."

"Yeah. You're right about that. But she is strong. Lord Beathach's right about that much. Grief and loneliness may not be enough to break her."

As he listened to Riyadah speak Kain found himself thinking about screwing her bowlegged.

"Riyadah does have a point." Garling took out a Camel and his silver Zippo. "We had the girl and her father for over half a year and we couldn't control her. All we got for our trouble was a firestorm and a bunch of dead agents."

"If we continue with this we need to be very careful." Nicole's voice was cautionary. "How good are our controls?"

Kain put a great deal of trust in both Garling's and Nicole's judgment. Both were insightful and highly intelligent. They were also both very loyal. He would not have sent them to earth were they not.

"Charlie believes her adoptive parents have abandoned her here and I've already offered to let her go. She decided to stay because she believes she has no one and has nowhere to go. She probably blames herself for what happened and thinks she deserves to be here. I don't think she has the will to fight us."

"The girl is dangerous." Hardliner's voice was cold, emotionless. "She is more powerful than anyone we've ever dealt with before and she is hostile to us. She may be desperate to avenge her parents but that only makes her more dangerous because sooner or later she's going to find out who was really behind their deaths."

"I think we have that under control." Kain answered steadily. "She has no way of knowing our connection to her parents' deaths. She hasn't perfected using her psychic senses yet."

"That girl will destroy everything we've built here if we do not terminate her." Hardliner persisted in that same icy tone. "We have the weapon of light. We do not need the weapon of darkness or the girl to destroy the forces of light. We outnumber them already and we are stronger. Do not allow your desire for power to cloud your judgment."

Anger flashed in Kain's heart. Nobody questioned his decisions. "Thank you for your concern Hardliner but I think I can handle a child. She *will* join us."

Hardliner was an intelligent and valuable servant, but he had a habit of overstepping his bounds.

Come on. Enough of this worry. Kain thought impatiently.

Sure thing. Riyadah's voice replied in his mind.

Kain could already feel himself hardening. Without another word Kain left the room with Riyadah and the two descended to a lavish bedroom on the floor below.

XVII

Four hours later Kain returned to the observation lounge alone. It was very late, but he could not sleep. Despite his outward confidence Kain was afraid of Charlie. She was very powerful, and he could not read her mind like he could with everyone else around him. He had no way of knowing for sure what the girl was thinking. She was dangerous. There was no denying that. Her power was beyond anything he had ever seen before. She might even be stronger than him.

And that was why she was too valuable to kill. She was the *Sigilla Praevaricator* and thus could unlock the weapon of darkness, but she was also a very powerful Enlightened and would be a valuable asset. She had to be kept alive if it was at all possible.

As if from nowhere Lord Beathach appeared behind him. "Where are the girl's adoptive parents?"

"I had them added to the slave labor pool and randomly assigned. If we need to locate them for some reason we can but since I have no specific knowledge of where David and Catherine McAuliffe are I can honestly tell Charlie that they are gone, and I don't know where they are." His lips curled into a cold smile. "I never actually told her that I set them free."

"Are you certain that the girl will not be able to sense that you are deceiving her?" Lord Beathach replied in a deep rumble.

"As I said Lord Beathach, Charlie has not refined her psychic senses. She would surely know if I were lying but she will find it much harder to detect if I am withholding facts. Especially when I have one of my own soldiers who genuinely does not know where her parents are tell her that her parents are gone. Charlie believes that we are searching for her adoptive mother and father."

"And are we?" Lord Beathach inquired.

"Yes. I have Death Troopers searching earth as we speak."

"This is a dangerous game you are playing my Master." Beathach's tone had grown sharp with warning. "If that girl learns that you are deceiving her then we will face a firestorm worse than the one that consumed Fallow Point."

"I agree. But I believe that our good cop, bad cop game has made her start to trust me. If only a little. She will not probe me deeply and when enough time goes by and her adoptive parents are not found she will eventually give up on ever seeing them again. I will be the only family she will have left." He paused and leveled his gaze upon Lord Beathach. "What would you have done if that girl had decided to set you on fire in my throne room?"

Beathach was silent for a moment. "I would have absorbed her power or burned to death."

Kain leveled his gaze. "You are powerful Lord Beathach, but so is that girl. You too are playing a dangerous game. If that girl decides that she wants revenge on you then you will have to submit."

"Indeed, my Master."

"And if her power proves to be too much for you to absorb, well then you stand a good chance of getting a front row seat to hell before you even get there."

"Indeed." Beathach repeated coldly. "But then, she is just a child."

XVIII

For several months Charlie lived an almost normal life in her suite in the Black Imperial Palace. She would awaken early to find breakfast set out for her. Then around eight or nine in the morning Eric would visit her. On some days he would take her out for the day to do different activities, on others they would remain in her suite and play video games or board games. Sometimes he would read to her or they would just sit and talk. Charlie began to feel closer to Eric if only because he was the closest thing she had to a friend in this dark place. Still her psychic senses persistently warned her of the darkness in his soul reminding her that Eric was not to be trusted.

During this time things stagnated Charlie remained closed to Eric and Eric continued to visit her, to play with her and talk to her, to try to be her friend. Then the day before what would have been her tenth birthday, things changed suddenly in a single day. Charlie awoke early that morning to a sky painted gold from early morning sunlight and the rich, heavenly scent of fresh baked waffles and newly brewed coffee. The familiar smells immediately carried her back to her parents' kitchen the day she and Daddy went to Sugar Lake and for a moment she felt like bursting into tears. Charlie bit back her sorrow allowing but a single tear to spill from each eye.

As always Charlie found her breakfast waiting for her in the living room and began to eat. The food was filling but tasteless as always. After a few minutes there was a knock at the door and Eric entered carrying a blue canvas duffel bag.

"Good morning Charlie."

"Good morning." She spoke the words automatically and in a tone that sounded artificial to her ears.

Eric must have detected something behind her neutral tone for his expression immediately became concerned. "Are you feeling alright this morning Charlie?"

"I'm fine." She lied. In truth she was not fine, for that momentary flashback to the kitchen in Taylor had renewed the pain of her mother and father's loss as if it had happened just yesterday. She had to fight not to burst into tears and the power had already begun to stir restlessly within. Charlie bit it back fiercely.

NOT NOW!

"That's good." Eric continued. "Because I have a little bit of a surprise for you today." As he spoke he handed her the blue duffel bag.

Charlie opened it to find a large, fluffy white terry cloth towel and a sporty two-piece bathing suit. "We're going swimming?"

Eric nodded with a smile. "Yes. There's a great water park near the coliseum called the Imperial Water Gardens. I thought you might like to go since you like swimming so much."

Charlie was so touched she nearly burst into tears. He *had* been listening to her. A faint smile played across her lips. "I'd like that." She said softly.

"Good then get dressed and meet me outside."

Charlie quickly put on the bathing suit and then pulled on a t-shirt and a pair of shorts before meeting Eric outside. Ten minutes later they were getting out of a hover car in front of two columns of massive Roman style pillars carved in pure white marble. Beyond them lay massive white marble swimming pools, dancing fountains and towering white, green and blue water slides. For a moment Charlie found herself carried back in time to the day she spent with her father at Sugar Lake. Before the loss of her mother it had been a perfect day, and the last day normal day she ever had. Charlie's heart bled, as if cut by an invisible razor.

"Are you ok Charlie?"

She slowly turned her eyes upon Eric. "I'm fine." Stinging tears trickled from both eyes.

"Do you want to leave Charlie? We can do something else if you want."

Charlie shook her head. "No. I'll be ok."

"If you're sure…" Eric's tone was both concerned and unconvinced. He gently took her hand. "What would you like to ride first? I have the entire park reserved just for the two of us"

Charlie thought about this for a second before choosing the tallest of the tube slides. Eric followed her with earnest enthusiasm. For the time being he seemed content to simply enjoy her company and be her friend. It was a glorious day, the best she had had for a long time, and yet she could not fully enjoy it. Each slide and pool brought back memories of that day she had spent at Sugar Lake with Daddy. The day the NSA came and tore her life apart.

As the day wore on Charlie felt growing need to talk to *someone*. Her sorrow had crystalized into cold hatred that cut to the soul. The black bloodstain upon her heart was swelling and burning and she could not bear to be alone with it any longer. Her psychic senses warned her not to trust Eric, though he had never lied to her, she sensed a deep, glacial darkness within him. Eric was dangerous, but she felt so alone. Everyone she had loved had been killed or had left her. Eric was the closest person to a friend that she had left. And so, in the end she did tell despite the warning in her heart.

It was late in the afternoon and the warm, spring sun had begun to beat down on the smooth marble tiles of the Imperial Gardens. Eric had bought them both ice cream and they were lounging on a pair of chaises under a large palm tree. The pain in Charlie's heart had become nearly insupportable. She had to tell.

Charlie turned her direct blue eyes on Eric's intense gaze and began.

"The last time I went to a water park was with Daddy, right before the NSA showed up and…" She fell silent. Charlie narrowed her eyes letting the raw emotion pour from them as if they were small blue portals. "…killed Mommy." She spat those last words out with naked, cold, *Hate!*.

Kane met her gaze and for a moment Charlie sensed what she thought might be empathy. "I'm sorry those men took your parents from you. You deserve better than what you have been given."

Charlie looked at him silently and, in that moment, something shifted within her and she felt herself beginning to *love* this man despite her fear of him. Yes, she did love him, not as a father but as a friend, her last friend. Eyes slitted with cold fury Charlie continued. "I wish I knew who killed Mommy. Robin killed my Daddy, but I never saw who killed my Mommy. I was in the car and Daddy went in the house. He told me later that he found her dead, but he didn't tell me who did it. I don't think he knew." Charlie intensified her gaze until she was no longer looking at Robin's intense blue eyes but rather through them to the dark pools of his pupils and the soft, gray flesh beyond. "I killed Robin because he shot my Daddy. It hurt so much, and I was so angry I just burned him up. I shouldn't have done that. It was bad."

Eric's gaze became compassionate and she felt his arm gently close upon her bare shoulders. His touch brought a slow warmth to her heart. "What you did wasn't wrong. He killed your father, it's natural to want revenge and there's nothing wrong with taking it."

Charlie hung her head. "I killed him, and it doesn't even help. It still hurts, and I feel…" She fell silent for a moment. "…so angry. I think I hate him. I think I hate all of those NSA men and nothing helps."

Charlie felt Eric's finger under her chin as he slowly turned her face towards his. "It's ok to hate them. They took your family away and destroyed your life. You have every right to hate them. It doesn't make you a bad person. It makes you human."

Charlie remained silent for a moment, contemplating Eric's words before softly whispering: "I know it's bad but I'm glad Robin's dead."

Eric offered her a gentle smile. "It's ok Charlie. He deserved to die."

In that moment Charlie felt a great swell of relief. She had told. She would no longer be alone with the flaming black bloodstain and Eric had not rejected her. He understood, perhaps in a way that even David would not. Charlie reached out to Eric with her mind and for the first-time sensed sadness and loss behind the darkness clouding his soul. Eric had suffered a tragedy once, though she knew not what or when.

Charlie turned towards Eric and hugged him hard.

"It's ok Charlie." Eric soothed as he ruffled her dripping, blond hair. "It's ok to be angry and it's ok to hate."

"I don't want to be alone anymore." Charlie replied. "It hurts too much."

"You don't have to be alone Charlie." Eric offered in a gentle tone. "I promise you won't ever have to be alone again."

The following day Eric asked Charlie if she would be willing to start school again. He also warned her that the days ahead would be difficult and that she would see things that would upset her. There would be pain. He asked her to trust him. Though she was frightened and wary, Charlie had nothing better to do and felt intensely lonely, so she readily agreed. Not long after that, a young woman with mousey brown hair and big, horn rimmed coke bottle glasses named Logan, began to visit her three times a week in the afternoon to teach her math, science, English, social studies and German. Charlie found the work incredibly easy and more than a little boring and after a while asked Logan for something harder. Thus, Charlie soon found herself studying calculus, American Supreme Court cases and German literature.

XIX

After almost a year had passed Eric brought Charlie to a small and featureless room. She was silent knowing from the moment he had arrived in her suite that today would be different than the train of uneventful days that had come before it. He was dressed in his usual black attire but today he wore a long, black bladed sword encased in seamless jewel encrusted black leather and dangling from a gold chain.

Charlie had already begun to tremble as thoughts of their encounter from many months earlier returned. She still refused to believe what Eric had shown her on that day but deep inside she knew it to be so.

"I wanted to show you a few more things today."

A cold shudder rippled through her body. *Please no more.*

Eric touched her shoulder. "It'll be all right. I know this is upsetting for you, but it won't be much longer now."

Charlie looked up at him with pleading eyes but could find no words.

"We can start whenever you're ready." He extended his hand.

Charlie stared at it for a long time without moving. *I can't do this anymore. Please just take me away from here.*

There was no answer and no escape.

With hesitant, trembling fingers, Charlie placed her hand inside Eric's. In an instant they were standing inside the lobby of a large office building. A long purple banner identified it as the New Freedom Center.

"We have thousands of organizations like this all over the world. Each of them has its own purpose and mission. Some of them are self-empowerment programs, some are non-profit charities, and some are political activist groups but they all have one thing in common. Each of them teaches that religion and morality are lies created by society to take away individual freedom. We take in people and teach them to put their own needs ahead of everything else. We tell them not to concern themselves with right and wrong because there is no such thing. It isn't hard. People want to believe that they can have and do whatever they want without having to feel guilty. Most of them only think something is wrong if it's illegal and that it's only wrong because it's illegal. They really are selfish and stupid. Once they're convinced that their wants and needs are the most important thing then we slowly introduce them to greater and greater corruption. It usually starts with sex. Somehow people got the notion that sex is their right and that they can't be expected to live without it. So we encourage them to have all the sex they want and to give in to their fantasies no matter how perverted they are. And sooner or later they all start getting perverted." His lips curled into a cold smile. "Then we get them involved with other things and before long they're hooked. You see they get so addicted to their own corruption that they can't give it up. That is how I can keep the Black Empire together. All of the citizens were recruited this way at one time or another. Any human can be corrupted because the desire is already there. They want to do these things even though they know it's wrong. And once they get started it gets easier and easier for them to do worse and worse things because they can rationalize it to themselves by saying it's only a little worse than what they're already doing."

As Eric spoke Charlie saw people coming in. In an instant she was standing behind a group of young men and women listening to a speaker discussing exactly what Eric had described. A moment later she was watching the same men and women as they went on to carry out what they had been told. It began with small things; sexual promiscuity, drug experimentation, gambling, shoplifting. These soon escalated to sexual perversion, drug abuse, and violence. Finally, she saw the same group clad in Black Imperial Death Trooper armor gunning down a group of slave children.

Charlie wanted to cry but could not. Violent tremors had taken her body. Charlie struggled to keep her balance. Sheer terror chilled her to the bone for she had seen into the hearts of the people she was watching and knew that Eric was speaking the absolute truth. These people were not monsters; they were average people who had abandoned all moral restraint. Everything they had done was done willingly and with full knowledge of the harm inflicted. These people had simply turned off their consciences. And what was really terrifying about it all was that if these people could do that…

So, can I.

Charlie's heart was racing now, threatening to burst from her chest. Her breathing was rapid and shallow. They were back in the small featureless room, but she had not yet noticed. Blood spots flashed in front of her eyes. She began to waver on her feet and would have fallen had Eric not caught her.

"Are you alright Charlie?"

She could not respond. Her vocal cords had frozen.

Thick sweat poured off her body in rivers as her shivering increased.

"Charlie!" Eric's concern had turned to fear.

Charlie tried desperately to respond but could not. It wasn't so much that she cared whether or not he was afraid for her, but she was afraid of what might happen if he called for help.

It took her a long time, but Charlie was eventually able to force out a few words. "I... I'm okay."

"Are you sure?" Eric bent down and looked into her face. "You look very pale. Do you want to lie down?"

"No, I'm okay."

"Ok." Eric was not convinced but she didn't care. "If you're sure."

He was silent for a moment. "I would like to show you one last thing if you are feeling up to it." Eric extended his hand to her once more.

Charlie remained silent. She could not face anymore yet she suddenly felt as if Eric was about to reveal something terribly important to her. With trembling fingers, she placed her hand within his for the final time. In an instant she found herself standing upon desert sands facing a familiar, squat straight backed red oak chair. A line of men and women had lined up before it. One at a time each would take his or her seat and be electrocuted.

All at once Charlie's heart stopped as she spotted David and Catherine at the front of the line. Charlie opened her mouth to call to them but was stopped by Kain's hand on her shoulder.

"They cannot hear you. And besides, there's nothing you can do for them anyway."

As she watched in horror, David stepped forward first and sat down in the red oak monster that was the electric chair. Faceless men strapped him and clamped electrodes to his right calf and head. His expression was blank with shock and fear.

"Please! We have to help him." Charlie begged.

Kane shook his head sadly. "As I said there is nothing we can do. What you see is one possible future. A future in which the non-Enlighteneds have rebelled and taken over. Make no mistake, they are dangerous to us and will kill us all if we allow them the chance. They would show you no mercy Charlie, why should you show any to them?"

As he spoke one of the faceless men threw a knife switch and David's body convulsed against the leather straps holding him to the electric chair. Steam began to rise from around the electrodes on his head and leg and his face twisted and contorted with pure suffering. Charlie felt her body light up with fiery agony in sympathy.

Before she could stop herself, she screamed and burst into great sobbing tears.

Then, as quickly as they had arrived she found herself returned to that same small, featureless room. Kain stood next to her wearing an expression of concern.

"It's okay. I know it's upsetting but you need to know the truth. This is the future they would give to you and your family."

He placed a gentle hand on her shoulder and carefully drew her into a hug. Despite her fear of him, Charlie placed her cheek against Kain's belly, wetting his shirt with her tears. Kain held her clumsily and without a word for several minutes before she was able to bring herself under control once more.

When Charlie had regained her composure Kain released her and met her eyes with a soft gaze. "You're very powerful Charlie, do you know that?"

She did not answer.

"You were given an incredible gift. You were able to kill my friend Orson Tarken with your power."

Renewed fear exploded within her. Charlie took an involuntary step backward. "I...I didn't mean to..."

Eric cut her off with a smile. "You don't have to be afraid Charlie I'm not angry. Actually, I'm impressed. What you did should have been impossible. Orson Tarken was a seasoned Dark Knight and around five hundred years old. I knew you were powerful, but I never guessed you were this powerful. Normally it would be impossible for an Enlightened to kill a fully trained Dark Knight."

Charlie could not accept this despite what Eric had told her. "But I killed him on purpose."

"So what? Tarken was a valuable servant but he challenged you and you were more powerful. He knew what he was getting himself into. It was just his day to die."

"But it's wrong."

"Why?" Eric's tone was calm and without malice. "Because its illegal? Because it says so in some holy book? What does it matter? Laws are made to keep people in line and holy books are the biggest joke of all. Do you know what your Creator really is? He's nothing but a big prankster. He put us in this world for laughs. He doesn't care about humanity one-way or the other. Holy Books were written by a bunch of fools deceived into thinking they were right so that people could stumble along wondering if they are really doing the right thing. That is all religion is. As for killing, well people kill each other all the time. It's part of our nature. It's nothing to be upset about."

Charlie was silent. She was still trembling hard. The horror in her heart was overwhelming.

How can this be right? How could anyone think like that?

She knew Eric wasn't lying. He was being honest. Perhaps painfully so for he was speaking from his own personal beliefs, from his heart.

"That's not true. My Daddy told me we have laws and morals to protect people so that we don't have to be afraid of being hurt or killed." Mentioning her father brought on fresh pangs of grief sharp enough to bring tears to her eyes.

Eric seemed to shrug. "Fine have it your way. You killed Tarken because he was threatening you and your friends so it was self-defense. You didn't do anything wrong and you have nothing to feel guilty about."

To this she had no answer. Eric was right Tarken had threatened them, but still she could not let go of the fact that she had killed him. She could kill if she had to, but it still made her feel guilty sometimes. Daddy and Mommy had told her again and again to never use the power on a person. And she knew that it was wrong to kill. There was no debating that.

"You were given a gift Charlie and it would be a shame to let it go to waste. So, I thought I would give you a chance to use your power today. That is if you want to."

She felt unsure. The idea of being able to use the power was tempting. A feeling of excited anticipation began to build within.

But he'll use you. He's trying to trick you. You know that don't you?

She didn't feel like she was walking into a trap, but she was deeply wary. This was too easy.

"This room is fitted with holographic projectors. It can create any opponent you want. All you have to do is ask. If the computer doesn't recognize it, you can describe what you want, and the computer will create opponents from the description. Watch. Computer, three Roman legionnaires."

In an instant three men dressed as Roman soldiers appeared out of thin air. They were quite lifelike. It was impossible to tell by appearance that they were not real. Charlie reached out and touched one of the men. To her surprise he felt solid. His skin was identical to that of a real person. The strange thing was that he did not move when she touched him. In fact, he gave no sign at all of being aware of her presence.

Eric reached behind himself and produced her sword. "I think you'll be needing this." He tossed it to her and she caught it left-handed. "Computer, attack."

Without a moment's pause all three men attacked. Charlie slid into a fighting stance. Silver flashed on her right. Charlie ducked and spun around bringing her sword up in a horizontal slash and neatly slicing one of the men in half. Another man lunged forward with his sword in attempt to impale her through the stomach. Charlie side stepped the blow and brought her sword down on the back of his neck, severing his head. In the same smooth movement Charlie spun backward decapitating the last survivor.

Eric clapped slowly. "Well done Charlie. Very well done. Let's try something a little more difficult now. Computer, training routine fifteen."

In an instant they were transported to a barren, rocky wasteland. Men in gray chain mail charged with swords drawn.

Charlie let them bear down on her before lashing out with her sword. She could have incinerated them but that would have been too easy, and she was having fun despite herself.

Charlie jumped forward into a tight somersault extending her sword as she turned over in the air. The blade slammed through the helmet of the lead man splitting him from crown to crotch. The two bloody halves collapsed to either side. A man attacked her from the left. Charlie spun and ducked impaling the man through the chest. Then without pausing she yanked her sword free and severed the head of another man who had tried to attack her from the right. Two men closed on her from the rear. Charlie spun around yet again this time bringing her sword up in an uppercut slash that split one of the men at the chin. She then severed the second man's head with a swift blow to the base of his neck.

The last of the men was also the toughest. Charlie came at him with a high slash intended to sever his head. He easily ducked under the blow and slashed at her legs in the same movement. Charlie jumped over the blow, somersaulted through the air and landed behind him. She then brought her sword down hard intending to split his skull in two. The man parried the blow blind, then spun around and tried to sweep her feet out from under her. Charlie easily avoided this and responded by slamming the point of her sword through the man's thigh nailing him to the ground. She then withdrew her sword and severed the man's head with a single stroke.

Excitement pulsed within her. The power was racing. Without thinking she screamed. It was not a scream of fear or upset but rather one of pure animal exhilaration.

Eric smiled. "Nice work. Computer. Run training routine twenty."

This time it was soldiers with assault rifles and high caliber pistols. Still she killed them with no difficulty. Next, she faced armed Black Imperial Death Troopers, then heavy armor and aircraft, and finally Dark Knights.

During this time, she was able to push her power further than she had ever done before. It was both exciting and frightening at the same time. She had never imagined she was capable of these things.

How am I doing this?

What was strange too was how easily she was able to stop the power when she was finished. It had never been like this before.

"You are powerful Charlie." Eric's voice was genuinely impressed. "You cut through those drones like nothing. I have a few tests I'd like to do and then we can get dinner if you want."

Her stomach grumbled, awakened by the promise of food.

"Come on the lab's across the hall. Let's get this over with."

In the lab a young, female technician took blood and tissue samples. Afterward Eric took her to the dining hall where a huge meal had been prepared.

When Charlie had eaten her fill, Eric accompanied her back to her bedroom suite. As they walked the two talked of unimportant things and Eric asked her if she still wanted to leave.

To this Charlie had no answer for though she desperately wanted to leave she knew she had no one now and nowhere to go. She supposed the Black Imperial Palace was her home now, whether she liked it or not. As she pulled the blankets over herself Charlie felt some part of herself let go as her mind began to accept that this was indeed her home now.

XX

Charlie slept better that night than she had in a long time and awoke feeling rested. As she crossed her bedroom. Charlie smiled, in that moment feeling safe and almost normal. She missed David and Catherine terribly but at least she was safe. She didn't have to run anymore, and no one would hurt her again. Whatever Eric wanted, he had kept his word and was protecting her.

Charlie went into the bathroom and was surprised to find a fresh uniform waiting for her on the toilet.

After showering Charlie dressed and went back to the bedroom. At once her nose was greeted by the delicious smell of pancakes, eggs and frying bacon. Her mouth began to water. Charlie followed the smell into her sitting room where she found a table overflowing with breakfast foods of all kinds.

Charlie ate until she was no longer hungry. Then she wiped her mouth and stood intending to go back to her bedroom. There was a knock at her door. Charlie answered it to find Eric waiting patiently in the corridor outside.

"Good morning. How did you sleep?"

"Good thank you."

"You found your breakfast okay?"

She nodded.

"Good. Then let's go."

Charlie went with him and found herself standing in the same featureless room she had been in the day before. Today's exercises were intended to be more difficult, yet she fought off every variety of opponent the computer could generate with little difficulty.

It felt good. She could feel the power flowing within her and it felt wonderful.

When she had defeated her last opponent, Eric took her back into the laboratory for more tests. This time it was a spinal tap. Charlie was frightened. She had endured a spinal tap once before at the NSA compound and it was excruciating. Nevertheless, she cooperated, motivated mostly by fear.

Unlike the NSA scientists, who had performed the procedure without any anesthetic, the Black Imperial scientists gave her drugs to help her relax and eliminate any pain. She felt nothing save for some pressure against her back.

When it was over she was given more drugs and returned to her bedroom in the palace to rest. Sometime later Eric returned with a tray full of food. He apologized for putting her through the tests and thanked her for her cooperation before turning to leave.

Charlie almost let him go but then just as he was closing the bedroom door behind himself she called to him. She didn't want to be alone anymore.

The two talked of inconsequential things for a long time before she grew tired and Eric put her to bed.

"Good night Charlie." His tone was caring, almost like her father's.

She looked up at him unsure of what to say.

"Sleep well. You'll need your rest for tomorrow."

XXI

Charlie awoke the next morning to the smell of baking. Sitting on a tray on the bedside table was what had to be the biggest Belgian waffle she had ever seen in her life decked out with whipped cream and strawberries. Beside it on the tray was a small pot of strawberry syrup, a big bunch of grapes and a large glass of orange juice.

Charlie's mouth began to water. She knew, even before she started eating, that the food would be tasteless and would not satisfy but it still looked delicious.

As she was finishing the last few mouthfuls of tasteless food Eric came into the bedroom.

"Good morning. I hope you slept well."

Charlie nodded.

"Good. Then why don't you finish up and get dressed."

She swallowed and sat in silence.

Eric's expression became embarrassed. "Right, I'd better get going. I'll wait for you outside."

As she dressed Charlie began to question herself.

Why do I care?

They never cared about me. They treated me like a freak and killed Mommy and Daddy.

That last thought was followed by a sudden burst of combined grief and anger. In her mind she saw her father's pained expression as he took his last breaths.

They killed Mommy and Daddy.

Maybe Eric was right. She wanted revenge so badly. She knew it was wrong even without David's admonition, but she couldn't help it. She wanted to get them back for taking away her mother and father's lives.

She was dressed now. As she headed out the bedroom door a single thought passed through her head:

You cannot take revenge, or you will become like them.

This thought was accompanied by another deeper thought. Or perhaps not a thought but more of a deep knowledge.

I am dangerous. If I try to get revenge, then something terrible could happen.

And so, she was left with the same decision: her need for revenge held against the certain knowledge that to give in to that need would mean unleashing more destruction.

Instead of returning to the training room on the *Destroying Angel* Eric took her to the coliseum. Inside it was deserted save for a few slaves raking out the dirt field.

"There are three kinds of power Charlie. The first and weakest is brute force. People do what you want because they fear you. The word for it is coercion. The second kind of power is economic power. You have something the other person wants so they will do what you want to get it. Do you understand?"

She nodded.

"Good. The third kind of power is called manipulative power. With this kind of power, you control what the person sees and how they see it. You make them obey you without having to use force or pay them. This is the strongest power Charlie. Any idiot with a gun can make people do what he wants but take away the gun and he has no power. The same is true with economic power. Anyone can pay someone to do what he or she wants and as long as they still have money or whatever the other person wants the person will be loyal but the moment you take away the money this person is powerless. With manipulative power people do what you want because they want to. Because you made them want to. You don't need money or brute force because the person *wants* to obey you. You are controlling not only their actions but also their thoughts. That is real power." Eric turned and gestured towards the slaves below. "They do whatever I want because if they don't I will have them killed. My followers do what I want because they believe it benefits them. I don't pay them, and I don't threaten them. They follow me because they want to. Do you understand what I'm saying?"

Charlie looked up at him without speaking. She understood more than he knew. Real power was not what you could do to someone else but what you could get someone else to willingly do for you. She understood this principle very well for this was how Striker had controlled her.

"You should always be ready to use force Charlie, but you should never use it if you don't have to."

He paused waiting for a response. Charlie did not oblige him.

"I think it's time you moved on to real opponents. You've managed to kick the crap out of everything the training computer could throw at you."

Charlie became frightened. "I can't."

"You don't have to be afraid Charlie. I'll have you fitted for some armor and a helmet, so you don't get hurt."

He didn't understand. She was not afraid of getting hurt. She was afraid she might hurt or kill the other person. Her own safety had not even crossed her mind.

"You'll be fine Charlie. I promise."

And with that the conversation was over and she was returned to her room.

XXII

Early that evening Eric came for her.

"It's time Charlie."

She felt terrified for she knew what was coming.

Eric led her from the palace to the great coliseum where she was to face her first live opponent.

Her heart was thumping against the inside of her rib cage.

Directly ahead she could see it. The massive black structure loomed larger with each moment as the hover car drew closer. Bright stadium lights lit up the black satin sky. She imagined she could already hear the distant roar of the crowd within. Dark dread welled up within her.

I don't want to do this. Please don't make me do this.

Thick oily sweat coated her skin and was soaking through her clothes. The black Grand Admiral's uniform she had been given soon became saturated.

They were less than a mile from the coliseum. It towered above like a giant monster from a dream.

Now she could hear the crowd but perhaps hear wasn't the best description. It was more like she could *feel* it. She could feel the power of their excitement, their blood lust. It was strong enough to feel like a sound in her ears though she knew it could not be.

They were getting out now. Charlie had begun to tremble making it difficult for her to stand. A hand closed on her shoulder helping her steady her balance. It was not Eric's. Charlie turned to see the blank facemask of a Black Imperial Storm Trooper.

They began to walk. They were passing through a long circular tunnel that ran beneath the stands. After a few minutes they turned and headed through a door. Inside was a locker room. The combined scents of sweat and blood assailed her nostrils at once. She was still trembling despite the stifling heat inside.

Eric was still with her. "You'll be alright." He was saying. "You're a powerful girl Charlie and you can handle this."

She knew that. It was not getting hurt that frightened her but rather the thought that she might enjoy this. What would happen then? She knew the answer to that question though she did not want to admit it.

"Put out your hands Charlie."

She did as Eric asked, and he proceeded to wrap her wrists and forearms in surgical tape. Then he placed a pair of steel gauntlets over the tape and laced them in place. After this he gave her a pair of fingerless, leather gloves; and a black steel helmet with a plated neck guard. Charlie put these on with trembling fingers. Finally, Eric produced her sword.

"I think you'll want this."

As he spoke he put the weapon in her hands. Charlie held it for a moment without speaking. The sword lay sheathed in a beautiful jeweled and etched black calf's leather scabbard complete with an adjustable shoulder strap.

It was not the scabbard though that kept her silent. It was fear. Fear of her power and what might happen tonight.

Eric helped her sling her sword over her shoulder and adjusted the strap so that it was comfortable.

It was strange. All of the equipment fit her perfectly. The gauntlets came up to the elbow and the knuckles of both hands just as they were supposed to. The helmet fit snugly on her head without being clumsy or obstructing her vision or movement. Even the nose guard was sized perfectly.

She found it both flattering and frightening that Eric would have gone through the trouble of sizing armor for her. She truly was important to him and she did not know how she felt about that.

After she had finished dressing Eric gave her a few moments alone to gather herself.

Charlie was terrified. She was no longer sweating but her tremors remained strong and she felt nauseous. Suddenly her stomach clenched. Charlie ran and barely made it to the toilet before vomiting up her entire dinner.

I can't do this.

As she followed Eric through the tunnels Charlie's breathing grew rapid.

Please I can't do this.

They were inside the final tunnel leading to the center of the coliseum. Blaring rap music filtered in from the arena. It took a minute for her to recognize it as Eminem. The crowd was chanting something. After a few moments she recognized her own name and became even more frightened.

I can't...I can't do this. It's bad.

The power became restless. As she emerged into the stadium lights the crowd began to cheer.

Charlie felt terrified. Without thinking she reached over her left shoulder and drew her sword. She was trembling so hard that she could barely keep her feet never mind hold the weapon steady. A tall, slender man clad in black armor stood in the center of the arena. He was armed only with a sword. He held it in a casual grip as he watched her approach. The crowd took up another chant of her name. Charlie looked around fearfully. The faces in the crowd were those of average people. The same people she had seen days earlier when Eric had shown her the city. Eric walked ahead to stand between the man and her. As she closed the last few feet he spoke.

"Ladies and Gentlemen, we have a special treat this evening. Tonight, as promised you will be able to see the empress in action." He glanced at her. "Now I would like to introduce you to Charlene MacLeod, the *Sigilla Praevaricator* and Black Empress."

The crowd roared its approval.

Eric raised his hand. "Hold on. Hold on. Let me introduce her opponent." He gestured towards the tall man. "Colonel James Laroux ladies and gentlemen. Colonel Laroux is a member of the Black Talon Special Forces division within the Death Trooper Corps and an accomplished swordsman. Tonight, he will face Ms. MacLeod in a fight to the death."

Eric's words made her blood run cold. She wanted to protest, to beg not to have to do this but she was too terrified to speak.

...to the death.

The words echoed sickeningly in her mind. All at once she became aware of the weight of her sword. It hung loose in her hand, the point dragging on the brown dirt floor of the coliseum.

The crowd's cheers were deafening now. The force of their blood lust resonated in the air. Charlie was terrified.

God I can't do this.

She could already feel the power moving within her and to her horror she found herself *wanting* to use it. Her heart was racing but it was no longer with fear. Now it was anticipation, excitement.

The weight of her sword bore down on her right hand.

No. It isn't right. It's bad.

The words had no effect. Her excitement was building.

Eric stepped back. Then he was gone. The tall man, Colonel Laroux, changed his grip on his sword and slid into a fighting stance. Without thinking Charlie did the same then immediately attacked with a high horizontal slash intended to take the man's head off. He blocked this without effort and countered with a shoulder lift that threatened to knock her off her feet. This was soon followed by an intended decapitation blow. Charlie blocked this without effort then spun around into a backwards horizontal slash that the man only narrowly avoided catching across the abdomen.

As she exchanged blows Charlie felt intense pleasure as well as a sense of detachment, as though she were watching someone else fight. The sensation was frightening but not altogether unpleasant.

Another high slash followed by a spinning thrust. The movements were smooth enough to have been choreographed.

The power flowed in perfect synchronization with her muscles making her stronger than most adults. Before these last few days she had never used the power in this way, yet it came as if she had always been doing it.

The man lunged forward and over extended himself. Charlie raised her sword intending to take his head from his shoulders.

The motion came instinctively as her higher mind was preoccupied with the intense pleasure that the power brought on. Anyway, it wasn't really her. Someone else was in control. Someone else was about to decapitate this man. Someone else…

NO!

With a great effort Charlie regained control, changed her grip on her sword and brought the hilt down hard on the back of the man's head rendering him unconscious but leaving him alive.

The crowd's cheers turned to cries of outrage. Charlie turned to face them and shouted in as loud a voice as she could muster: "It's over. I won't kill him."

This brought on a chorus of boos that were quickly silenced when Eric reappeared.

"Very good Charlie. You won and in record time."

This elicited a cheer from the crowd.

"And I see you left him alive too. That was thoughtful of you although normally we execute the losers of death matches if they aren't killed in the fight."

Charlie's heart sank. She did not know this man. Yet though he was one of her captors she had no real desire to see him killed.

"But in this case, I think I can make an exception."

The crowd took to booing again until Eric raised his hand. "It was the Empress's decision to let him live and you should respect her like you do me."

The crowd responded to this with a halfhearted cheer.

Charlie knew what they had really come to see. They didn't care about the fight; they wanted to see someone get killed.

This scene was repeated several times as Charlie was forced to face more and more difficult opponents.

XXIII

The fights were pure pleasure. She enjoyed using the power and the rush that came from being able to easily defeat skilled adult soldiers. Her fear was gone, and she felt no guilt for she never killed her opponents. Instead she would render them unconscious as she had done with the first man.

This worked for every opponent she faced except the last. Her opponent for this fight was a Dark Knight and a far better fighter than the Black Imperial Special Forces she had faced earlier.

Charlie went into the fight feeling a little uneasy. Eric had warned her that she would be facing a Dark Knight this time and that he would be more difficult to beat than any of her previous opponents.

Eric was right. The man, his name was Harold, attacked her before she had a chance to raise her sword. Charlie easily blocked the blow but was caught off guard. She counter-attacked and was surprised by how easily Harold blocked her stroke. He moved almost as fast as she could, and he seemed to be able to anticipate her attacks. But that was impossible. No one could read her mind unless she let them. *Still…*

The two of them went blow for blow for around five minutes before Charlie was able to gain the upper hand. This happened almost by accident when Harold over extended himself in a horizontal slash. Charlie immediately capitalized on this mistake by returning a low horizontal slash of her own. Harold leapt back but could not completely avoid her sword, the tip of which sliced through his abdominal muscles above the naval. Harold retaliated with a high slash aimed at her throat which she avoided without effort. She followed with a vertical stroke that would have cut him in half had it connected fully. Harold was lucky enough to avoid the worst of the blow and only suffered a shallow gash to the sternum. This time he answered with a low slash to the legs which she jumped over.

As she landed Charlie brought her sword down hard. This time Harold wasn't so lucky. The blade struck him hard on the left side of his head splitting off a large piece of skull and exposing the gray matter beneath. It was only by pure luck that she did not slice through the brain itself. Harold stumbled back from this blow but somehow managed to keep his feet. Without hesitating Charlie pressed her advantage with a high horizontal slash that struck Harold's head from his shoulders. It landed on the ground with a dull thud.

Horror and guilt washed through her all at once as she realized what she had done. Her sword dropped from her hand and clanged off the arena floor.

I killed him. I cut off his head.

A scream was building within her. Charlie made no attempt to hold it back.

I cut off his head.

She had killed before, but it had been in self-defense and she had never killed anyone with her bare hands. It had never been like this before. This was killing for sport.

Murderer!

MURDERER!!

The word screamed in her head again and again.

MURDERER!!

The head lay at her feet, the body a little further away. Blood still gushed from the stump of his neck as Harold's heart fought to preserve a life already destroyed. A large crimson puddle flooded the ground beneath his body.

Charlie stared at this scene in shocked horror. She was no longer screaming, and she was not crying. All emotion was frozen.

murderer

It was only a whisper now.

Charlie was frozen in place. Even breathing seemed to stop. What had she done? Cold dread began building within her.

I did this…

Me!

Charlie lowered her eyes to her hands as she became aware of a wet sticky sensation. She was soaked in blood up to the elbows. More blood drenched her clothes. Though she could not see for sure she knew it was in her hair as well.

murderer…

She wanted to turn away, but she could not. The terribleness of her act held her fast. This was something she could not walk away from no matter how much she wanted to. It was something she would never walk away from.

XXIV

Eric never asked her to fight in the arena again. Instead he began introducing her to the Black Imperial military.

Their discussions of power and corruption continued with Eric still trying to convince her of why she should join with him and her answering with ever weakening refusals.

She *was* corrupt. That was the thing. And though she hated to admit it much of what Eric said was accurate. It was becoming very difficult for her to resist him. It was becoming very difficult for her to resist herself. Her desire for revenge had become stronger than ever. She was breaking.

Charlie was beginning to become accustomed to the luxuries he lavished upon her. The temptation to give in was very strong. Part of her wanted to give in. It seemed pointless to hold out when she had already committed murder. If she was already damned, then why shouldn't she take revenge? It was only the voice of David in the back of her mind reminding her of the consequences for allowing herself to be corrupted that held her back.

XXV

Two weeks after Charlie killed Harold, Eric brought her aboard Lord Beathach's flagship the *Darksaber*. He explained to her that a revolution had broken out on a planet called Ypress and he wanted her to watch them put it down. Charlie knew without having to ask that it would be a bloodbath.

It had been over five years since the day she was taken. It was hard to believe for she had not changed at all. Her hair had gotten long again, and she was thinner but otherwise she remained as she had been on the day Hardliner gunned her down. It was frightening for her to think how much time had passed and more frightening when she saw herself unchanged.

Lord Beathach was right. She was immortal, an immortal child. She would never grow up, never be married, never have a family. She would be nine years old forever.

Though many believe otherwise, to be immortal was not a blessing but a curse.

They left Ifrinn aboard the *Darksaber* with a fleet of over two hundred capital ships and millions of smaller ships. It was a force capable of obliterating an entire solar system. The trip took two weeks. Ypress was far out on the frontiers of the Black Empire.

During the trip Eric lavished every possible luxury upon Charlie, even allowing her to use the power at will.

For Charlie it was an uneasy heaven. The freedom and indulgence were bliss but the knowledge of what they were going to do haunted her, as did David's words. She could not truly enjoy herself for she knew this was wrong.

Upon arriving the lead ships dropped into orbit around the yellow brown planet while the remainder of the fleet took up picket positions outside of the planet's gravitational field. Charlie stood on the bridge of the *Darksaber* beside Eric as the attack began.

"The people of this world are at a technology level roughly equivalent to eighteenth century earth. Basically, we're talking cavalry, cannons, flintlock rifles with bayonets and skirmish line style tactics. There aren't any planetary shields so I'm going to go right to the ground invasion."

As Eric spoke, thousands of white transport ships appeared outside the view ports and began to converge on the planet. Lord Beathach stood before the forward viewport, his back turned to them. Charlie heart raced, and skin paled with deep fear as her mind flashed back to that first terrible day when Beathach had strapped her to the cold metal table.

Why is he here?

Eric must have seen the fear in her eyes for he placed a gentle hand on her shoulder. "He's here to command the attack. Don't worry, I won't let him near you."

Charlie was not comforted.

"Lead the attack, Lord Beathach. I'm taking Charlie down to the planet to watch the fighting."

"Yes, my master." Lord Beathach turned his gaze on a man in a uniform similar to hers. "Contact the landing parties. Tell them not to fire until after the rebels have refused surrender."

The man nodded. "As you wish my Lord."

Eric took her hand. "Come on we don't want to miss anything."

Charlie was silent. She did not want to see this, but she made no effort to resist.

Eric took her into a small office off of the main bridge. A few moments later she found herself standing beside Eric in a small, town hall where a group of men and women dressed in eighteenth century clothing were discussing the current situation.

"The Black Imperials are here." The man on the podium shouted. "Now is the moment of truth. If you wish to be free you must fight. We may all die today but a quick death by the gun is better than the slow agony of slavery."

The men and women in the audience cheered.

Eric turned to her. "They are fools. They have no chance against my forces, but they will fight anyway. It's a pity."

In an instant they were transported to an open grass field. Men in uniforms reminiscent of those worn by the American regulars in the Revolutionary War stood in formation on one side. On the other thousands of Black Imperial Death Troopers stood in a similar formation. Leaders from both sides stood at the center of the field talking.

After a few minutes they separated and returned to their respective sides. A drum march began, and the rebel forces started forward. Behind them a row of cannons fired off a volley. The Death Troopers also began to move forward. Several shells exploded among them with no effect.

Charlie stared in horrified amazement. The shrapnel was bouncing off the Death Troopers' armor.

"Present arms!!"

The rebels lowered their rifles as they continued forward.

"Prepare line!!"

The rebels stopped marching and the front row went down on their knees.

"FIRE!!"

The first two rows fired. Then the second row dropped to their knees and the third row fired. Then they dropped to their knees to allow the fourth row to fire. The bullets bounced off the Death Troopers' armor as they continued forward.

When they had closed to twenty feet the Death Troopers stopped, lowered their rifles and opened fire. Blood red energy beams streaked across the field slashing the rebel lines to shreds. Men were decapitated, dismembered and disemboweled. One was blown in half. It was a horrifying sight.

Within ten seconds it was all over. There were no survivors. The ground was littered with bodies and body parts. All of them were rebels. The air was heavy with the combined stench of blood and ozone. Charlie turned away as tears streamed down her cheeks.

They killed…everyone.

Eric took her hand again. "Come on there's more."

In an instant they were transported to another massacre, followed by another and another as the scene was repeated all over the planet. Once the armed rebels were killed off the Death Troopers went about rounding up the civilians. The leaders and their families were loaded aboard the *Darksaber* while the remaining majority was returned to slavery.

XXVI

On the day following their return to Ifrinn Eric awakened Charlie early in the morning and took her to the main docking bay. Here the prisoners stood in ragged lines waiting to be loaded aboard transport ships that would carry them to the surface. Charlie knew what lay in store for them.

"I will make an example of these prisoners for anyone else who would consider rebelling." Eric's voice was calm and emotionless.

As he spoke the prisoners were loaded aboard two transport shuttles. After both ships had left Charlie and Eric flew down to the surface aboard a Delta Class Transport.

On the surface a parade was assembled. Row after row of Black Imperial Death Troopers marched through the streets of the imperial capital followed by legions of Dark Knights. Behind them marched Eric and Charlie. Following them were more Dark Knights and another huge formation of Death Troopers. The prisoners marched at the front of this formation driven forward by the kicks and rifle points of the Death Troopers that followed. A steady stream of insults and abuse rained down on them as they marched towards the place of their execution. The march took only minutes, but it felt like hours. Charlie's heart went out to the prisoners. They had done nothing wrong, they were only fighting for their freedom and for that they would pay with their lives.

The place of execution was an old airfield. Dozens of long spikes had been set up in rows here. Adjacent to them were an equal number of thick wooden stakes surrounded by large piles of twigs and logs. Between these was a single transport ship. The prisoners were divided up into three groups. The first was led to the spikes, the second to the stakes and the third was loaded aboard the transport ship. A single family was set aside. They were restrained by Death Troopers as their comrades were led to their deaths.

Before the executions began Eric turned an almost apologetic gaze on Charlie. "I am sorry you have to see this, but it is necessary. You have suffered at the non-Enlighteneds hands. You need to see them suffer at our hands."

"Please don't." Charlie begged.

"I'm sorry." Eric turned from her and signaled the nearest Death Trooper.

One by one the prisoners in the first group were hoisted up with anti-gravity belts and impaled on the spikes. Their screams were forever burned upon Charlie's soul.

Charlie wanted desperately to do something to stop this but could not. The power was gone, silenced by drugs. She supposed she could have refused the drugs, but it would have only meant more suffering and she could not take any more pain. Tears streamed down her cheeks. She could feel the prisoners' suffering. It was as though she too had been impaled. She tried to pull her mind back but could not. The force of their suffering was too strong. She felt Eric's hand on her shoulder and heard his voice. She could not understand the words.

When all of the prisoners in the first group had been impaled the Death Troopers began tying the second group to the wooden stakes. When they finished, the pyres beneath the stakes were set ablaze and the screams of the second group added to those of the first.

Fire licked across her skin nearly causing her to scream in agony.

Make it stop. Please make it stop.

Charlie tried desperately to pull her mind away from the pain, but she could not. It was too strong. She swayed on her feet and barely avoided losing her balance. It was a scene from hell. After some time had passed and the screaming had died down Eric led her aboard the transport and they ascended to the *Destroying Angel*.

Upon landing the prisoners were led to an empty docking bay and sealed inside. The containment field was then released exposing the bay to open space. For a few moments Charlie was in agony. Her lungs screamed as though deprived of air. Then the feeling passed. No sound came from the docking bay.

"It's done." Eric said softly.

XVII

The cathedral was dark and cold, filled with the smell of death. Charlie stood at its head only a dozen or so feet behind the massive Serpentinite altar. Eric stood beside her looking on with what could have been mistaken for a sorrowful expression, his hand laying protectively on her shoulder.

Several feet away Lord Beathach stood looking on through his black, death's head mask. The chamber was silent save for the steady chanting of the congregation. Dark robed figures encircled the altar platform. Each wore the mark of a Dark Knight. Behind them stood row after row of Imperial citizens in black dress uniforms. It was hard to make them out under the flickering candlelight. The cathedral, or what she could see of it, was built from massive serpentinite blocks and columns. Red silk carpets traced aisles across the floor towards the altar platform. Each bore the markings of the Black Empire in silver stitches. High above, cut into the vaulted ceiling were many large stained-glass windows depicting acts of horrible brutality and sexual debauchery. The dying sunlight made them glow in the shadows. The altar itself was as smooth as black glass and glimmered under the flickering candlelight. Four heavy iron chains were fixed to its four corners. These, the altar and the altar platform were smeared with dried blood. Beneath the altar platform stood three concentric rings of six heavy iron candle stands each holding a single black candle. Their flames provided the chamber's only light.

Charlie shivered. The air inside the cathedral was very cold, not only in a physical sense but also a psychic one brought on by the oppressive power of evil in the air. Much suffering and death had happened here.

Charlie stood trembling in horror.

Eric's hands closed on her shoulders. Charlie found herself being driven forward until she was mere inches from the stone altar. She stood facing the crowd feeling terrified. She knew already what Eric had in mind and though he did not intend to harm her she was frightened regardless.

Lord Beathach turned to her. Horror filled her heart for she knew what was to come next.

There was a scream from the back of the cathedral. Charlie turned to see two Death Troopers dragging a blond-haired girl into the cathedral by both arms. She struggled valiantly to no avail. Her fear radiated out in cold waves.

Fierce tremors took her. Charlie took an involuntary step backward bumping into Eric.

The girl was rapidly dragged towards the altar. The crowd's chanting became more intense. As she grew nearer the girl's sobs grew more hysterical and more terrified. Each cry stirred up fresh horror and terror within.

Upon reaching the front of the cathedral the girl was lifted up and chained to the stone altar. She was only inches away now. Her terror-struck Charlie like a wall of ice.

"Mary!" It was a woman's voice, most likely the girl's mother.

"Don't hurt her! She is only a child!" This was the father's voice.

Both mother and father were silenced by rifle butts to the back of the head. The two stood in the front row directly beneath the altar. Charlie looked down at them sadly both returned glares of such hatred as to be hurtful to look at. Tears filled her eyes.

"Please don't make me watch this."

Eric gently patted her shoulder as if to say 'you'll be alright' as Lord Beathach drew his sword from its scabbard and raised it slowly.

Lord Beathach's voice came to her in a language alien to her ears yet she understood him as though she had heard the word's he spoke all of her life. She recognized the language she heard. It was a nameless ancient language. One older than mankind itself. This was the language of devils, the language of Hell.

The chanting had built to a crescendo.

Suddenly he brought his sword down in a smooth movement that sliced a foot-long strip of skin from the girl's right leg. In the same instant white fire licked across Charlie's right leg. The girl's scream echoed her own. She wanted to tell them to stop. She wanted to beg Lord Beathach to stop but something kept her silent, something dark and terrible.

As Charlie watched in horror Lord Beathach skinned the girl alive, cut out her internal organs and burned them. The girl suffered horribly before dying and Charlie felt it all. Her screams echoed the girl's through the entire, horrible ordeal.

When it was finally over Charlie was barely able to stand. Her whole body was on fire with excruciating pain. Blood ran from the pores on her arms and legs staining her clothes dark red. She was trembling and felt light headed from blood loss. Her mouth was as dry as a woolly sock. Her eyes were fixed on the altar where the girl's mutilated remains lay.

Blood continued to run from the body, flowing from the altar in rivers to a shallow trough beneath. As Charlie watched Lord Beathach took a gold chalice from the altar, filled it from the trough and held the chalice over Charlie's head for a moment before pouring out its contents.

The blood was still warm. For a moment she did nothing. She was in shock, but it was breaking. She could feel the beginnings of horrified terror creeping upon her. Charlie screamed and burst into tears. At the same time the sounds of screaming and sobbing came through to her along with the rank odor of death.

Charlie's stomach lurched, and her mouth filled with the taste of bile. Before she could stop herself, she vomited all over herself. Then she began screaming again.

The stench was overpowering, she had to get away from it. Charlie started to run but didn't get far before she was caught by Lord Beathach. He said something in that same strange language and then dumped another chalice full of blood over her hands.

Then she was being lifted up and placed on the now empty altar. Someone pulled up her left sleeve until her upper arm was exposed.

As she watched Lord Beathach produced a long gold needle and a gold dish filled with red ink made from the blood of the slaughtered girl. After dipping the needle into the ink Lord Beathach thrust it deep into her arm again and again. It was torture, her entire arm burned. She was screaming but she was only peripherally aware of these things as her mind was still in shock.

When Lord Beathach had finished Charlie looked at her arm and saw the symbol of the Black Empire tattooed deep into her flesh in blood red ink. She was still bleeding, and her arm felt as if it were on fire. Still, she took only passing notice of these things. The horror of what she had witnessed remained strong in her mind.

XVIII

Eric pulled her to her feet and took her from the cathedral to a small shower room where he instructed her to clean up and gave her a fresh uniform.

Charlie continued screaming and crying the whole time. She couldn't stop. The image of the girl's mutilated corpse remained strong as did the pain and the *smell*. That was the worst part, the *smell*. It wouldn't go away and the more she smelled it the worse she felt. She didn't understand, couldn't. Why would anyone do something so horrible?

After she had finished dressing, Eric took her into another room where he poured her a glass of red wine from a crystal decanter. Charlie sucked down the blood colored liquid and set her glass down on a nearby table. Eric refilled it and handed it back to her. Charlie took the glass and gazed at it for a moment before gulping the wine down.

The sour crimson liquid warmed the icy fear coursing in her blood and cooled the fiery pain blazing over her skin.

"It hurt so much." She whispered more to herself than to Eric.

"I am sorry for the tattoo. I know it hurt but it was necessary. That tattoo marks you as a Dark Knight of the Black Empire. It forever marks you as under my protection."

"No." Charlie replied. "When you killed those people. It hurt so much. Why did you make me watch that?"

For a moment Eric was silent and Charlie sensed what she thought was amazement. "You could feel their pain?"

Charlie returned an incredulous gaze. "Yes. Couldn't you?"

"No." Eric's tone was low with what could have been mistaken for awe. "I could feel their fear but that's all. To be able to actually *feel* another's pain is a rare gift. I had no idea…" He broke off. "Charlie I am so sorry."

Charlie touched his mind with her own and felt that he was genuinely remorseful. He had indeed not known she would experience the pain of those he had executed.

After Charlie had calmed Eric spoke to her gently. "There is one last execution for you to witness and I don't want you to suffer any more pain, Charlie." As he spoke he produced a small leather case and flipped it open to reveal a long, silver syringe. "This is loaded with a psychic suppressant. It will dull your psychic senses enough to keep you from feeling any pain." He sighed. "I don't like having to use a drug like this on you. It's a violation, an assault. Like cutting off an arm or a leg or chemical castration. So, I'll leave it up to you. You can take it or not."

Charlie gazed at the milky liquid in the syringe with trepidation. To lose the power terrified her, it *was* like losing a limb, but she couldn't bear anymore pain. Charlie extended her left arm nervously. "I want the shot please."

Eric took her arm, swabbed it with cold liquid and slid the needle deep into the vein inside her forearm. There was a brief sting followed by dull heat. At first Charlie's psychic senses remained razor sharp but within a short time she felt the power retreat deep into the back of her mind. All at once Charlie felt as if someone had wrapped her head in thick wool. She attempted to reach out with her mind and found her mind bound within the confines of her head.

Without another word Eric took her to his private box at the coliseum. The remnants of Mary's family waited in a luxury box directly below with frightened, horrified expressions. A pair of Death Troopers stood in silence behind them while Lord Beathach stood directly in front. Without warning, the girl's father lunged at Lord Beathach. Both Death Troopers grabbed his arms and pulled him back.

"You killed my daughter!" The force of the man's grief and anger struck Charlie like a wave.

Lord Beathach regarded the man coldly. "You and your family are rebels and traitors."

The man's face darkened with fury. "You may kill me but before I die I am going to kill you."

"You would face me?" Beathach's voice was contemptuous. "You shall have your wish."

As he spoke Lord Beathach moved forward, stepped up on the railing and somersaulted down to the arena floor, then motioned to the two Death Troopers restraining Mary's father. Without a word they forced the man forward and threw him over the railing. He landed in a heap at Lord Beathach's feet.

Lord Beathach gazed down at the man. "If you should prevail then you shall have your freedom. If you should fail, then your wife will face me in your stead." With that he turned his eyes to the back wall of the box where a pair of swords hung. As if taken by an invisible hand the left-hand sword pulled free from its mounting, flipped through the air and landed point down at Mary's father's feet. "Take up your weapon."

Mary's father struggled to his feet then stood staring blankly for a while not believing what he had heard Lord Beathach say. After a few moments he went to the sword and picked it up. The weapon was fashioned in the shape of a claymore and was large and heavy. Gripping the sword like a baseball bat the man swung wildly. Lord Beathach easily stepped out of the way. His hands were still empty. Mary's father let out a snarl and lunged forward clumsily with the weapon. Again, Lord Beathach easily evaded the blow. As he did Lord Beathach drew his sword and spun it upward slicing off the man's arm.

The man let out a horrible cry then lifted his sword one handed and swung it clumsily in Beathach's direction. Beathach replied with a swift downward stroke that severed the man's other arm. The man screamed again and lunged at Lord Beathach. Beathach side-stepped and brought his sword around in a tight arc severing both of the man's legs. This elicited another blood curdling scream as the man fell to the ground now no more than a torso. Lord Beathach approached slowly, taking his time administering the coup de grace.

When he was within three feet, Lord Beathach brought his sword up and swung downward and sideways slicing the man's belly open and spilling his guts on the ground. The man did not scream this time, he simply let out a strangled moan. Beathach stood over the man for a full twenty minutes watching him suffer before finally severing his head.

Charlie's stomach lurched, and she vomited over the railing. Behind her she could hear the sobs of the man's wife and son. During the fight they had been screaming but now they just cried. Their grief was painfully strong.

Lord Beathach glanced up at Mary's mother and made a slight motion with his left hand. She suddenly hurtled through the air and landed on her knees at the base of the wall. The woman struggled to her feet confused and frightened.

"Please sir, don't hurt my mother."

Charlie turned to the sound of the boy's cry. Tears spilled down her cheeks. The boy was older than her, maybe eleven or twelve, but his face was that of a frightened child. She recognized the look even as his emotions flooded through her. It was the same she had worn the day her father was murdered, combined horror and unreality. She remembered the feelings well. Watching her father die had felt almost like some horrible nightmare. It was too terrible to be real. Except it was real and there is no escape from reality.

She felt horrible for the boy for she knew all too well what he felt. She could have tried to help him but somehow, she felt it would have made no difference. Whatever she did Lord Beathach would have eventually found and killed the boy and his mother.

The boy's mother made no move at first. Then after a moment she went to where her husband had dropped the broadsword and picked it up.

The weapon was too heavy for her. She was forced to hold it two handed it keep it upright. Lord Beathach watched her silently. His sword was lowered, the bloodstained point just above the arena floor.

All at once the woman let out a scream and lunged forward. Lord Beathach easily sidestepped the thrust and brought his sword down on her back splattering her blood all over the ground. The woman struggled to her feet and was struck again. This time Beathach's sword severed her right arm causing her to drop her broadsword. Before she could pick it up again Lord Beathach cut off the woman's left arm in similar fashion. Then with a single slash he separated both legs from the woman's body. He finished by driving his sword through the woman's stomach and twisting, spilling her entrails on the ground.

"NO!" The boy's cry pierced Charlie to the soul. His horror and grief were sharp enough to draw blood. "Mother!!"

The woman did not die right away but rather lay on the ground screaming in agony for several minutes before shock and blood loss silenced her.

Charlie began crying anew as old feelings of grief for her father were reawakened. Lord Beathach gazed up at her. "You should not pity them. Given the opportunity they would burn you at the stake. You know this. These are the same sort of people as those who killed your parents."

Charlie did not respond. *Oh, Daddy I miss you so much.*

Anger kindled within her. Charlie met Beathach's gaze without speaking. There were no words for what she felt now.

After a moment Beathach turned his gaze upon the boy.

"You killed my parents!" The boy was outraged and grief-stricken at the same time.

Beathach's icy gaze did not waiver.

"I'm going to kill you!" The boy screamed.

"You will try." Beathach nodded to the Death Troopers who proceeded to drag the boy to the railing and throw him over.

He landed roughly on his father's remains. The boy wasted no time in grabbing up the broadsword and leveling it as best he could. It was a struggle for him to keep it upright.

Lord Beathach stood perfectly still hands at his sides, artificial eyes glaring down on the boy. His sword was stuck into the ground a few feet away. The boy's expression was calm, but Charlie could feel the terror beneath. With a cry the boy charged, raised the sword above his head and slashed hard. Lord Beathach easily dodged the stroke. The boy tried again and again he missed. After a third failed attack Lord Beathach extended his hand and drew his sword into it. He then rapidly counter attacked cutting the boy open at the mid-section.

The boy screamed and dropped his sword to the ground as he tried to keep his entrails from spilling out of his abdomen.

Lord Beathach followed with a second slash that severed the boy's left arm and a third that cut off his lower jaw. The boy collapsed to the ground following the first blow and now was barely able to breathe. Lord Beathach watched him coldly for a few moments before severing the boy's head.

Charlie screamed.

How could they do this? How could anyone behave this way? She was crying hysterically though she was barely aware of it.

The crowd was cheering its approval of the bloody spectacle below. The sound pulsated like a nightmare. Charlie was vaguely aware of Eric taking her arm and leading her away.

XIX

Sometime later Eric returned her to her room. There was a crystal decanter of wine and two goblets on the bedside table. Eric filled one of the goblets and gave it to her. Charlie guzzled the wine and set the glass down on the table. Eric quickly filled it and gave it back to her. This continued until she had finished a quarter of the wine and was very drunk.

Charlie felt very tired. She stumbled her way into the bedroom and laid down on the bed. As soon as she closed her eyes the whole world began to spin. Her stomach lurched, and Charlie felt her mouth fill with the taste of bile.

"Oh shit." She cried and ran into the bathroom.

Charlie vomited until there was nothing left in her stomach to throw up. Eric held her head the entire time and then helped her to bed when she was finished. As she was drifting off to sleep the same questions plagued her.

How could anyone do these things?

She asked Eric this same question the next day. His answer upset and frightened her more.

"We perform ritual sacrifice as part of our deal with The True Dark Lord. He gives us immortality and power in exchange for the souls of innocents. The coliseum is pure entertainment for the masses. They seem to get some kind of enjoyment from watching people butcher each other so I make sure to provide them with a good fight every now and then. Personally, I find it boring."

His cavalier attitude only served to horrify her further. "But they didn't do anything wrong. They were just trying to get their freedom."

"No, they were trying to restore the old way of doing things." Eric replied coldly. "They wanted to re-impose the old laws and rules of their world. I could not allow them to do that."

Charlie started to argue back but he silenced her with a gesture.

"By gaining their freedom they threaten ours. They do not see things the same way we do. If they were free to rebuild their own nations, they would build nations with strict laws and morality based on their view of the world. The very existence of nations like that would be a threat to us."

Charlie understood this, sort of, but it did not justify the horrors Eric allowed. She could not accept such brutality no matter what the reason.

What about the NSA people? You burned them alive.

That's different. I had to kill them to get away. They would have killed me. They killed Mommy and Daddy.

It didn't feel different though. How could she condemn Eric for allowing what she herself had done? It didn't matter that it was self-defense. She had killed them on purpose.

Except she knew differently. She *hadn't* had any choice and Daddy said it was ok. David and Catherine said it was okay. If she hadn't killed them then they would have killed her.

She had understood this for some time, but it was still hard for her to accept. Everything she had ever been taught told her that it was wrong to kill. That lesson had been branded into her conscience long ago. And Mommy and Daddy had told her again and again not to use the power. That was the other thing.

As she stood looking at Eric she felt her mind touch his. Cold darkness flooded her consciousness. Beneath this she felt emotions similar to her own; anger at his father, fear of being alone, concern and genuine caring for her, a need for his father's approval.

Charlie was both surprised and mystified at once. Here was a man of pure evil and yet deep inside he was no different than her. In a way she almost felt sorry for him.

Looking at him, touching his mind, she began to understand Eric in a way no one else could. He was the illegitimate son of the True Dark Lord, the product of an act of trickery. Eric was born half devil. His father abandoned him, and he was taken from his mother and left to fend for himself. At the age of twelve Eric's father returned to tell him his true heritage. It was then that he began training as a Dark Knight. At age twenty he became a full Dark Knight and with his initiation received the gift of immortality. Thus, he became the first and oldest Dark Knight. Within a year he went on to found the order of Dark Knights and with it the Black Empire.

During his long-life Eric was exposed to horrors beyond anything she could have imagined, the very worst of humanity, and it was this that made him what he was today.

Charlie pulled away slowly feeling immense sympathy for Eric. He had suffered much as she had. People hated and feared him simply for what he was. He was treated as a freak and isolated much as she had been.

At the same time, she was also frightened for she could have become like him. She could still become like him. This thought troubled her long after Eric left her.

XXX

The next few weeks passed quietly. Eric seemed content to show her a good time without any further attempts to convince her to join the Black Empire. This made Charlie very suspicious and afraid. Still she enjoyed this time and felt something close to happiness.

On the day of her birthday, a pair of Death Troopers took Charlie to the throne room aboard the *Destroying Angel* telling her only that Eric wished to see her.

The throne room was dark and colder than she remembered it. Eric sat on the throne a mere shadowy silhouette against the dim light coming in through the massive window behind him. As she entered the room he rose.

"Hello Charlie."

She did not respond. Something wasn't right. She could feel it.

"There's someone here who wants very much to see you."

A shadowy figure appeared from nowhere. "Hello Charlie."

Striker?!

Anger exploded within her bringing the power up with it.

"I've missed you." He started towards her. "You've grown since the last time I saw you."

"How?" She sputtered. "I killed you."

He nodded. "No, you burned me. It is much more painful."

Charlie took an involuntary step backward.

"You don't have to be afraid Charlie." Striker stepped into the light as he said this. "I'm not angry. I wanted to die, and I deserved it. My only real regret is that I was separated from you."

She stepped back again, heart racing.

"There is no known way to use the power to raise the dead; I trust you know that." Eric's voice was almost casual.

Charlie remained silent.

"However, the power can be used to manipulate time and *change* it. Tinkering with the time line is dangerous but I believe you deserve a second opportunity at revenge against the man who murdered your father." As he spoke Eric stood and walked towards her. In his hands he held her sword. It glimmered softly in the dim light from the view ports. "Take it. I can see you want to."

Charlie reached out with her mind and pulled the sword towards herself. It flipped through the air and landed in her outstretched right hand.

"It's okay to kill him Charlie. He murdered your father. It's good to take revenge."

"I won't be angry Charlie." Striker took another step forward, bent down and cocked his head back. "I deserve to be killed. I know that. And if you kill me we'll be together forever."

Charlie tightened her grip. As she did she felt the power leave her. Flames licked up the blade as the sword's crimson heart began to glow and throb with fury.

"Go on Charlie. I know you want to. Let go. No one will blame you for killing the man who betrayed and murdered your father." The gentleness in Eric's voice was frightening.

The bloodstain was swelling. It burned and tugged at her heart urging her to give in. She *wanted* to give in.

He killed Daddy. He deserves to die. I deserve revenge. He's alive and Daddy's dead. He should be dead. He should suffer.

Charlie felt the muscles in her arms and shoulders tense as she prepared to strike.

It's okay to kill him. He killed Daddy. That bastard killed Daddy.

The power was blazing; her *Hate!* was blazing.

I'm going to kill you Striker you fucking bastard!

He deserves it! It's alright! He deserves it!

The words repeated again and again in her mind as she slowly brought her sword back.

David's voice whispered softly in her mind. *You cannot take revenge, or you will become like the Dark Knights.*

She screamed and threw her sword at the wall behind her. It struck hard and buried itself halfway to the hilt. The blade's red flaw went silent as the flames vanished in an instant. Charlie turned away trembling and sweaty.

"Take me back to my cell."

"Okay Charlie."

Eric stood from his throne and took Charlie's hand. Charlie went with them silently body still wracked by tremors.

After Eric left her, Charlie burst into tears. Memories flashed through her head. She saw herself, years younger, running through the streets of New York with her father. She saw the firestorm at the Ephrata Police Station. She saw the cabin in the woods and felt the sting of the dart in her neck. She saw Striker and she saw her father's death. She saw these things and she remembered.

Chapter 14

Endgame

I

Bars of golden sunshine streamed down from a sky of solid blue. She was on the beach with Mommy and Daddy, just walking and holding their hands. The warm white sand and balmy summer air caressed the bare skin of her feet and legs. A cool breeze blew in from the water gently lifting her hair from her shoulders. The beach was perfect and pristine. Its white sand, sharp cliffs, and distant trees unmarred by the usual boardwalks, hotels beach front houses, and crowds of people. Only their footprints betrayed the very existence of humanity. They were free, Mommy was alive.

It was too much to hope for. This had to be a dream.

"What's wrong Charlie?" Daddy's voice was hurtful in its gentleness.

"This isn't real." She heard herself saying. "It can't be."

He smiled. "That's silly. Of course, it's real. Whatever made you think it is not?"

"But we were kidnapped. The NSA killed Mommy and kidnapped us."

"I'm here now Charlie." Mommy replied. "That was just a dream."

Charlie turned to her mother. Her face was as clear as if she had last seen it only yesterday. "It was real. I know it was real. It had to be."

Charlie wanted to believe differently but she knew better. This was too good to be true, too much to hope for.

"That was just a nightmare Charlie. That's all."

When her mother said it a second time Charlie allowed herself to believe it. She needed to. In that moment she became a little girl again, a child without worry or care. She played on the beach with her parents for hours or maybe years. She did not know or care. The glory of the day, of the moment were all that mattered. She was with her mother and father. She was free.

Then without warning everything changed. The air grew cold and the sky darkened with storm clouds illuminated by ragged purple lighting. Charlie shivered as cold wind, stirred by the growing storm lashed her bare skin. She turned to look for her parents, to tell them that she wanted to go home, and realized that they were gone. She was alone. Except she wasn't. A figure stood in the distance, his outline back lit in violet by the flickering, storm swept sky.

Charlie shivered again as cold fear flared up within. "What do you want?"

The figure did not answer.

"What do you want?" She repeated.

"It's alright Charlie. Nobody's going to hurt you." The figure spoke with her father's voice, but it was not her father.

Charlie froze, unable to react. *Who is he? What does he want?*

"I want to help you Charlie." The figure started towards her. "I can help you get away."

"Leave me alone!" Charlie cried out in desperation. "Leave me alone!"

"Don't be afraid I won't hurt you. I promise." As the figure grew closer she saw its face.

Robin?!

Despite the friendly tone of his voice his face and eyes were ice cold. She knew he had betrayed her even before she saw the blood on his hands and clothing.

II

Charlie found herself hurled from sleep, her body wracked by tremors and coated in sweat. This was not out of fear but anger. In her heart she knew. Robin had tricked and betrayed her. Perhaps she had always known this. The power flared within her. Charlie tried to force it down.

No! Stop!

The power continued racing. Charlie got up and threw the power at the toilet. The water inside came to an immediate boil filing her little cell with thick steam and turning the air from chilly to balmy.

Stop it! Stop it now!!

After a few seconds the power was silent. Charlie knew what she had to do now. Part of her found this hard to accept. She wanted so much to believe that Robin had liked her.

But she knew the truth and with it came the certain knowledge of what had to be done. She could not stay here any longer. Now that she had refused to do their tests they would kill her and with her, her father. She was too dangerous to be left alive and when she was dead Daddy would no longer be needed. She deserved to die but she didn't want Daddy killed. They had to get away. Somehow, they had to get away. Charlie lay awake most of that night thinking. The situation seemed hopeless, but she did not become depressed. She was too angry to be depressed. It would be easy enough for her to get outside. All she had to do was cooperate with their tests. But how would she get access to Daddy and how would she get him outside? She didn't know but she had to figure something out.

It was near five in the morning when sleep came and still she did not have an answer.

III

A few hours later Charlie awakened to the sound of the door buzzer as Robin entered her cell. Charlie greeted him and then went back to her cot with the excuse that she wasn't feeling well. She turned he back to Robin and pretended to sleep while he sat with her. Now that she knew the truth Charlie could sense Robin's intentions and emotions. He had noticed differences in her demeanor and became suspicious. Robin did not have the power, she was certain of that, but he was very observant, and he knew her. For the first time Charlie began to realize how much of a problem Robin would be.

As she was thinking this another thought occurred to her. Perhaps she could use him as he had used her. He wanted to kill her. She knew that but before he killed her he wanted to gain her trust. He had had her under his power for a while but now she was out of his control again. He would certainly try to kill her and to do that he would probably take her from her room. That would be her best chance at escape. She would be alone with Robin outside of her cell where she could kill him and burn her way out.

But what about Daddy? How would she find him? Even if she figured out where he was she would still have the problem of getting to him and getting him out. She knew she would not have long either. It would take only minutes for them to find out what she had done and lock the whole place down. Then she and Daddy would be trapped and killed. She had to find out where they were keeping Daddy, or this would never work.

IV

That night she went to bed still troubled over this question. She didn't know where her father was and she had no idea how to find out. Sleep was elusive and when it came it was the product of sheer exhaustion.

As she slept something strange happened. Charlie felt herself stretching out. Not in a physical sense but a psychic one. Her mind seemed to drift above her body. She was moving now, through walls and corridors and rooms. She saw the hallway outside, then an office, then a bathroom. She was traveling somewhere, somewhere important but she didn't know where. Then she saw her father. He was sleeping but he wasn't for he was also standing in front of her speaking.

Charlie? Is that you? She could hear his voice, but his lips remained still.

Daddy!! Excitement washed through her in waves.

Hi Charlie.

You look different. He had gotten fatter and his hair had gone from iron gray to an almost white silver. His face had aged, his eyes were tired, and his expression was one of desperation and sadness.

I suppose I do. I think you've grown Charlie.

She smiled briefly before reality reasserted itself. *Daddy we have to escape.*

Charlie there's no way out of here.

We have to Daddy or they'll kill us.

I'm sorry Charlie but there's nothing we can do. This place is locked tighter than a prison. Even if we got out of our rooms there's no way we'll get out of the complex. Once the alarm's raised the whole place will lock down.

He was giving up. Daddy never gave up. *Daddy what happened to you? Why are you saying that?*

He was silent for a while. *I'm sorry Charlie.* His face went stone cold.

I have a plan Daddy. If you can get them to let you outside I can meet you there.

Charlie…

Please Daddy just get them to let you out.

Okay Charlie.

She went to hug him but before she could the spell broke and she found herself returned to her bed. She knew where he was but was this a dream or was it real? If it was real, then she might be able to escape with Daddy but if it was a dream then she would get them both killed.

What do I do?

She didn't feel it was a dream, but she was afraid to test it. There were no second chances here.

But if I don't do something they'll kill us anyway. Trying to escape and failing was better than doing nothing and letting them kill her and Daddy.

V

Charlie got out of bed an hour later. Now that she knew what she was going to do it was hard for her to sleep. A hot coal burned in her heart. Today was the day she and Daddy would either escape or die trying. She would ask to go outside today. She would do whatever she had to, to get them to let her. She could only hope that Daddy would know to do the same.

Charlie went to her cell door and called to the agent outside.

"I would like to take a shower please."

For a moment there was only silence, then: "Very well. Stand back from the door."

Charlie took two steps backwards. A moment later she heard the door buzzed and a young woman she knew only as Ginny came into her cell.

"Follow me."

Charlie went with her and five minutes later found herself alone in the private shower three doors down from her cell.

As she showered Charlie remembered Dr. Barrister's warning when she had first met him.

This entire wing is rigged with nerve gas cannisters. If you ever try to escape they'll release the gas and you'll choke to death.

 If Ginny or any of the other NSA people figured out what she had in mind, then this whole escape would be for nothing. After Charlie finished dressing she called to Ginny again.

After Charlie finished dressing she called to Ginny again.

"I'm finished. Can I go back to my cell?"

The door buzzed, and Ginny appeared again. "Let's go."

Charlie followed her out of the shower room. As they walked down the hallway Charlie drew in a slow breath and asked the question that had been burning in her mind all night.

"I'd like to go walk on the beach today. At one."

"That's fine Charlie." Ginny replied. "I'll let Dr. Barrister know when he gets here."

"Thank you."

They had reached Charlie's cell by now. Ginny swiped her key card in the door lock and the lock fell open with a sharp buzz. Ginny opened the door and Charlie walked through without a word. In that moment Charlie realized that this would probably be the last time she ever saw Ginny. "Oh, and umm have a nice day Ginny."

"Thank you, Charlie." Ginny's voice registered surprise.

A moment later the cell door snicked shut behind Charlie and she sat back to wait for one o'clock to come. She wasn't hungry, so she just sat there. After a few minutes she picked up a book and began to read about Bilbo Baggins and his magic ring. She had hoped that the book would make the time go faster but it didn't help. She was too nervous to concentrate and soon it became nothing more than a mess of confusing words. Her mind was totally focused on that afternoon, everything else was disregarded as meaningless.

At exactly nine o'clock on the dot the door buzzed. The sound nearly made her scream. Dr. Barrister entered and informed her that she could go out on the beach today if she agreed to another test tomorrow. Charlie readily accepted knowing that there would very likely not be a tomorrow for her.

Robin did not come that morning. She found this odd but quickly dismissed it. She felt sure that he was nearby and even if he wasn't it didn't matter. She could just as easily escape if someone else took her outside.

I hope it is Robin. Then I can kill him.

Charlie was instantly horrified and disgusted with herself.

But still the thought remained. At one o'clock the door buzzer sounded and a man she had never met before entered.

"My name's Mike and I'm here to take you down to the beach. Come on."

Charlie followed him out of her cell. She carried her beach bag with her, but it contained two sets of clothing and another pair of shoes rather than a towel and sunscreen. Charlie wore her bathing suit under her clothing, just in case someone should check. She did not want to give away her true intentions until she was ready to escape.

The man took her through the compound and outside. The air was colder today than the last time she had been out. Charlie shivered slightly. Deep inside Charlie sensed that something was very wrong and was frightened. As she crossed the manicured grounds towards the cliff a feeling of dark doom closed around her. The time was coming. The moment where everything would change forever. On this day she and Daddy would die. She felt certain of it. They were rapidly descending the stairs now. Each footstep was a slamming vault door. Charlie bit back her fear, reminding herself that she would soon see her father.

She could feel him nearby and knew that it would not be long before she could once again look into his gentle eyes. That was all that mattered. She would see her father and then they would die together. They had reached the beach now and were crunching their way across hard, stiff sand. The salty sea air brought on feelings of half remembered pleasure. A cold wind was blowing across the water stirred up by the big thunderheads gathered on the horizon. A low rumble warned of the impending storm.

Charlie turned to Mike. "I need to get my bathing suit on. Could you go somewhere so I can have some privacy."

He shook his head. "Sorry kid I was ordered to keep an eye on you and that's what I'm going to do."

"I'm not going to run away or anything I just don't want to take my clothes off with you watching."

Mike remained stationary. "I can't leave."

"Go away!" The power stirred within her.

"Can't do that kid." He was reaching into his jacket for his gun. His eyes were frightened, rat like. Charlie waited until she saw the gun before flicking out with the power. Mike dropped his weapon with a cry as a crop of fresh blisters sprouted upon the palm of his right hand. He was lucky it had not exploded in his hand. She would not have cared if it did.

Charlie screamed at him. "You get out of here you bastard and don't turn back. I'll be watching and if I see you turn around I'll fry you!"

Mike froze. For a moment he looked like he might go for his gun, which was lying in the sand a few feet away. Then he turned and ran.

"Charlie." She spun around at the sound of her name. She recognized the voice at once.

"You!" Her voice came out as no more than an angry hiss.

"Yes, it's me Charlie."

Cold fury flared within her bringing the power up with it. "You tricked me. You lied. You tricked Daddy and me."

"Yes, I lied. I lied because I had to. I was your father's friend. I did my best to help him out. I didn't make him join the program. Hell, I tried to talk him out of it. I took care of you because you're my best friend's daughter. I got you to do the tests because if I hadn't they would have killed you. What did you think? That they'd say: 'Oops we screwed up.' and put you back on the street. You know better than that. You've seen what these people are capable of. You've seen what they do, what they did to your mother. They ripped out her teeth and shot…"

"Stop!" Charlie was in agony. The power raced within her, spurred to fury by her pain.

Stop it!! Stop it now!!

She turned and sent the power out towards the ocean. There was a low sizzle and thin wisps of steam floated up from the water. The power settled down but remained active.

As Charlie stood staring at Robin sudden realization dawned upon her. "You shot us. You shot us at the cabin in Indiana."

"Yes, it was me. I shot you." His voice held no shame but rather deep compassion. "And we both know that I had no choice. You're not normal. You're dangerous Charlie and you know it."

"That's not my fault."

"No, of course not. But the fact remains you cannot be let go. Even if we let you go you'll just be grabbed up by someone else. The British maybe, or the Russians, the Chinese, maybe even ISIS. You'll never be safe Charlie."

She knew he spoke the truth, but she could not accept it. It wasn't fair. Why couldn't she just have a normal life? *I didn't ask to have the power.*

"It's all bullshit anyway. Barrister, the NSA, all they care about is power. They look at you and see armies of invincible soldiers. Telekinetics, mind benders, firestarters, human weapons of mass destruction. They see human breeding farms, Hitler's dream perfected. You're not even a person to them. You're a thing, a monster, an anomaly to be dissected. I don't care about any of that. I never did. All I care about is you."

Charlie stared at him in disbelief. He couldn't be serious. He had betrayed her.

"I didn't lie about everything Charlie. I was betrayed. The NSA made me an Agent and sent me to Iraq to eliminate rogue insurgents and when I got caught they abandoned me there because they were assholes. Just like Barrister. I won't hurt you like they did. I want to help you. Come and sit down beside me. Let's talk this out."

Yes, his words were like magic. Charlie began to walk towards him, hypnotized by the sound of his voice. He wasn't talking about talking but ending; an ending to all of the fear, the guilt, the horror, the temptation to use the power. He was offering to be her friend in a way no one else could. And yes, part of her wanted that.

"You won't feel anything. I promise. I'll make it quick and clean."

She went to him, knowing that she was going to her death.

"Charlie!"

She spun around at the sound of her father's voice. "Daddy no! Stay away!"

"It's a little late for that Charlie." Robin's voice was annoyed. For the first time she saw that he was holding an antique scoped rifle. As she watched he set the rifle's walnut stock against his shoulder. The weapon was long, and heavy looking. After a moment she recognized it as an 8mm K98K Mauser.

As the knowledge came into her head she was momentarily puzzled before it was washed away by combined joy and fear. Charlie ran to her father and wrapped her arms around his waist.

"Oh Daddy!" Her heart was racing with terror.

"Hi Charlie." Daddy's voice was weary. He looked exactly as he had in her dream the night before.

"Come here Charlie. Nothing's changed." Robin's voice was soft, almost hypnotic.

"I'm sorry but I cannot allow you to do that." Daddy's voice was steady, almost conversational despite the tension and anger she felt within him.

"Come to me Charlie, or I'll shoot your father."

Charlie turned from her father slowly. Her face had fallen. She was no longer angry, only frightened and tired. "Why can't you just leave us alone?"

"You know why. Now come to me. Let's end this."

Charlie returned an arctic glare. "You let us go or I'll burn you up." Her voice, though calm, promised brutal violence.

He smiled. "I don't think you want to do that because I bet I can shoot your father before you can kill me. And Jack if you try to attack me I will shoot your daughter."

Charlie felt trapped. "Please, just leave us alone. Please…"

"It's your choice Charlie. Your father can go free. I don't care. Or I can shoot him in the head. Freedom, or a bullet in the brain. You decide."

A desperate sob escaped her throat. The power was spinning wildly, just within her ability to control it. Seeing no other option Charlie started towards him once more.

"Charlie no!" Her father tried to stop her, but she twisted out of his grasp.

There was no other way. She couldn't let Robin kill her father.

Robin's smile returned. "Good girl Charlie." He lowered the Mauser slightly.

She went to him and allowed him to put his arm around her shoulders. He led her towards a nearby rock.

"Come let's sit down."

Charlie went with him mutely.

"No! Don't go with him Charlie! Don't listen!" For the first time she sensed what she thought might be fear from her father. The force of his desperation brought tears to her eyes.

She did not look back at him. It would have hurt too much. *I'm sorry Daddy. I'm sorry it turned out like this.* When they reached the rock, Robin sat down.

"Come here Charlie. You can sit on my lap."

She did as he told her without a word.

"You know this is the only way."

She did not reply.

"You don't have to be afraid. I promise it won't hurt." He reached into his weather-beaten leather jacket and produced a long and very slim stiletto. "In the days of the Roman Empire the Sakara Ii used stiletto knives like this to kill their enemies. I'll show you. Bend your head forward."

She did as she was told. Daddy was looking on in silent horror.

Robin touched the back of her head where her spine met the base of her skull. "The blade goes in here and penetrates the brain stem. Death is instantaneous. There is no pain."

Charlie shuddered in terror.

"No! NO!" Her father's screams sent chills through her flesh.

"Don't be afraid. It will be very fast. You won't feel anything."

Charlie was not comforted. The thought of being stabbed in the back of the head was horrifying.

"I won't do it until you tell me it's okay. When you are ready nod you're head forward."

Charlie sat perfectly still for a few seconds. She felt terrified, but she did not tremble or sweat. Then, having resigned herself to her fate, Charlie lowered her head silently bracing herself for the thrust of Robin's blade. Robin gently turned her face towards his with his left hand while he positioned the stiletto with his right.

"**NO!**" Daddy ran towards them. Robin instantly spun around rifle in hand and fired a single shot.

-CRACK-

Daddy doubled up clutching his stomach and dropped to the sand.

She screamed and ran to him. "**NOOO!!** Daddy! Oh my God! Daddy!"

"Charlie." She turned at the sound of her name. "Look at me Charlie."

Her eyes fell on Robin. The power was screaming. As she watched Robin quickly cycled the bolt on his Mauser.

"That's a good girl. I can see your eyes now. Thank you, Charlie." He took aim again. "I love you."

The power leapt out of her all at once even as she heard the rifle shot. On its way to Robin the power vaporized the chunk of copper and steel that would have otherwise buried itself in her brain. White fire erupted all around him. In an instant his flesh began to run like tallow, then it was flying off his skeleton in chunks until all that remained of Robin was a pile of flaming bone fragments. Behind him the sand transformed into blazing molten glass and the sea water vaporized. All of this happened in an instant, brilliant flash. Charlie was blinded. The world was gone. Everything was on fire. She could see nothing but white dazzle. Charlie crawled to where she thought her father lay. After fumbling for what felt like hours, she found his shoe. She began feeling her way up his leg, frightened of what she would find. He was dead. She was sure of it. He did not move, and she could not hear him breathing. When she had gotten just above his belt her hand touched something wet and sticky. Charlie stopped here, unable to continue.

"Daddy?"

"I'm here Charlie." His voice was no more than a hoarse whisper and was thick and slushy making him hard to understand. His hands closed on her shoulders and gently pulled her up to his level. His face swam out of the white blur. He was very pale, and blood streamed from both corners of his mouth.

"Daddy you're bleeding." Tears burned her eyes.

"I'm alright Charlie." He didn't sound alright.

"Oh, Daddy I'm so sorry… I killed him." She began to cry.

"Shut up Charlie!" He gave her shoulders a gentle shake. "And listen to me. They're going to try to kill you now and I can't protect you anymore. I'm dying Charlie." His spoke in little more than a whisper and his tone was amazingly calm for a dying man. "You have to get away if you can and if you have to kill any of them to escape I want you to do it." Daddy coughed and spit up a fresh gout of blood. "They started this Charlie and now it's time for you to finish it. This is war Charlie. Make sure they know that. Burn it all down, and don't keep silent. That was my mistake. I want you to tell everything. Tell what they did to us. Make it so they can never do anything like this again."

"I can't…I can't leave you Daddy."

"I love you Charlie." Daddy's voice was barely audible now. "You're the best thing I've done in my life and I am proud of you. I love…" He collapsed backward and died.

Charlie stood up slowly heart bleeding rivers. Unreality closed around her in an instant. This couldn't be happening it was too terrible. She turned away slowly, half expecting to wake up screaming. When it didn't happen, she was shocked. Powerful grief and anger boiled up within her bringing the power with them. She made no attempt to restrain it. Flames licked across the sand in thin trenches. The air had become deadly quiet. Charlie trudged up the stairs knowing that she was walking to her death and not caring. Shock had turned to cold fury.

I hope they do try to stop me. I'll burn them all up.

As she climbed the last few steps she saw a dozen or so men closing on her with guns drawn.

"Hold it right there!"

Charlie turned the power on them without stopping. Thin trails of fire raced across the ground towards them. In an instant the men were engulfed. Their screams haunted the cold air. A gunshot rang out followed by silence. More men appeared and opened fire on her. Charlie sent the power out at them without pausing. Fire exploded beneath their feet. They screamed and writhed in agony within the flames for a moment before collapsing to the ground. Something whistled by her ear. Something else painted thin fire across her wrist. Charlie spun around to see a young woman firing on her with an M4 Carbine. Without hesitation she lashed out with the power instantly engulfing the woman in flames. She shrieked horribly then fell to the ground in a heap. Charlie looked on with neither remorse nor satisfaction. The pain of her father's death was a knife in her heart. The power was rapidly spiraling upward. It was all she could to keep it balanced, suspended. She needed to let it go again. The sound of a truck engine made her turn. A large APC appeared out of an outbuilding at the edge of the toy woods. Its twin machine guns chattered away angrily. Charlie gathered herself then struck as hard as she could. The APC erupted in flames, flew upward and then exploded again in the air spraying bits of shattered armor in all directions. One large piece impaled a man who had the misfortune of getting too close. Another whizzed past her head. There were people running everywhere. She could have swept them with fire. Part of her wanted to. They were NSA, they deserved to die for what they had done to Daddy and her. With a great effort Charlie pulled the power back and turned it on the fence surrounding the compound. The steel links wept tears of molten metal while the electrical conduits that provided power to the fence exploded in showers of blue sparks. Charlie turned from the fence searching for something else to destroy. As she did she swept another group of agents with the power. Their screams were added to the wail of alarms and roar of fire. She barely heard it. Her mind was lost in the power. It was a relief. It was easier not to have to think and the pleasure of the power lessened the pain of her father's death. She turned towards the main compound, the building where she and Daddy had been kept. The power was raging. It hurt to hold it back but she held on. Alarms screamed in her ears, fire crackled and roared. She held the power back long enough to focus it. Then she pushed it out in one single pumping bolt of force.

The tower exploded in a brilliant white fireball. Bits of glass and steel flew through the air like falling stars. A desk chair flew through the air, seat spinning wildly, flames trailing behind in a bright orange comet tail. In the same instant a blazing computer monitor exploded at her feet. Charlie did not even blink. After a moment she turned away. Her eyes fell on one of the outbuildings. Charlie shoved the power out of herself and the building vanished in a tower of fire. She did this again and again until every structure on the compound was destroyed. By now the few surviving agents had fled deciding that their lives were more important than their paychecks. Fresh gun shots rang out. Charlie turned to see a single agent standing spread legged holding his 1911 Colt in both hands. He fired again, missing her head by only inches. Charlie *shoved* at him, thrusting the power out in an invisible lightning bolt. The man exploded into flames, flew through the air and slammed into a tree. He did not have time to make a sound. The power was screaming. She had to let it go. It would kill her if she didn't. She had to destroy something else.

Stop. That's enough Charlie. Stop while you still can. Her father's voice brought her back to reality. She had to stop it somehow. But it was too big, too strong. She had to expend it somehow but there was nothing. Nothing except...*the ocean!!* Charlie ran to the cliff fighting to hold the power back, to keep it balanced. When she reached the precipice, Charlie let go. Thick steam billowed up from the ocean surrounding her in a world of white. Still the power remained strong. It flowed from her as though through a pipe and the more she released the more there seemed to be. The power spun madly giving no signs of slowing. It was a struggle for her to keep it focused on the water. The air had filled with a deafening roar as the ocean water erupted into bubbles and steam. Still the power would not stop. Cold terror built up in her heart. She had to disrupt it somehow or else let it collapse inward. There would be no more destruction, she would let the power destroy her first. As the ocean water continued to boil away she began to believe that she would die for she could not seem to disrupt the power. She had it under control now and was slowly pulling it back but there was still so much. It took a long time, but she was eventually able to bring the power down. When it was finally silent Charlie collapsed to her knees in exhaustion. The sky was a field of solid white, the sun a tarnished silver coin.

The sun... I changed the sun. She thought dejectedly, then: *No. It's just the steam.*

Deep inside though she knew she would one day have the power to change the sun.

Charlie buried her face in her hands and burst into tears. She wept bitterly as the reality of what had happened sank it. Daddy was dead, gone forever. She would never see him again. She had killed many people, but she felt no guilt. They deserved what they got. They had brought it on themselves. But Daddy was dead and killing the NSA people would not bring him back. She was alone. She would always be alone now. Perhaps what Robin had wanted for her would have been best.

VI

Charlie remained like this for a long time. Incredible as it may seem it was possible that she slept for a while. When she finally looked up the sun had descended in the sky. The heavy steam was pulled to tatters by the cold autumn breeze. Charlie dragged herself to her feet still feeling miserable inside. The power was silent. It was as if it was gone. She turned from the cliff. The Fallow Point compound looked like an abandoned battlefield. Smoke poured from the blazing remnants of several cars, the outbuildings and the main tower. The air was thick and hazy, and heavy with the stench of burning human flesh. Scorched bodies lay scattered everywhere. The toy woods were blazing. She did not remember setting fire to them, but she must have for they were burning down. The worst was the fence though. Hundreds of bodies lay piled along its length, the remains of those who had failed to escape her wrath she supposed. In a daze, Charlie shuffled towards the fence her mind broken and shattered. After that everything was a blur.

VII

The lounge was dark and deadly silent save for the soft rumble of Lord Beathach's labored breathing. Eric and Lord Beathach sat opposite each other sipping snifters of brandy. Or rather Eric sat drinking brandy while Lord Beathach watched as he could not eat or drink anything because of his injuries. Even in the darkness Lord Beathach's appearance was fearsome. Without his mask he looked like a vision of death. The skeletal remnants of the right side of his face stood out from the shadows. Eric almost pitied him, or he would have if he were capable of pity. Beathach's face made him a monster. As Eric was thinking this the lounge door opened and Nick Tanner entered. It was Dr. Tanner to most everyone else. Tanner entered carrying a data pad. His expression was animated. Eric could feel his excitement. He could have read Tanner's mind to learn why but he decided he would be surprised.

"Hello Eric." Tanner's voice was filled with thinly veiled delight.

"Hello." Eric sipped his brandy. "What do you have for me Nick?"

Tanner's expression registered momentary annoyance. He hated being called by his first name.

Eric smiled in return.

"We've just finished a complete genetic study on the girl. It would have been finished sooner but we re-ran the tests several times to confirm the results. The girl is not human or at least not like normal humans."

"She is an Enlightened doctor." Beathach replied flatly.

"Yes, but it's more than just that. Her genetic make-up is like nothing I've ever seen before. She's four or five evolutionary cycles beyond modern *Homo Sapiens*. On the outside she looks just like a normal human but inside there are significant differences. Her neurological make up is unlike any normal person's, especially her central nervous system. The neurons are smaller and much more densely packed. I estimate she has probably double or even triple the number of neurons of a normal person. And whereas a normal person uses maybe five or ten percent of their brain she uses something like seventy-five, eighty percent normally. When she uses her power, it goes up to a hundred percent. She has some other unusual characteristics as well. The girl has all recessive traits; blue eyes, blond hair, pale skin; without any recessive genetic defects. In fact, she carries no genetic flaws at all. Whatever effects the D-13 agent had it made the girl a new species of human, one far superior to our own. We have tentatively named her *Homo Prometheus.*"

Eric listened intently. This was very intriguing for it meant that Charlie was much more than even he had thought. She was not only the *Sigilla Praevaricator* but the first of a new species of human, a perfect species. Hitler may have been a racist fool, but his vision of a perfect Aryan race had come to pass.

"The girl has none of the weaknesses of normal humans. She is far more resistant to disease, environmental toxins and injury and heals much faster than normal. Her intelligence is beyond anything we can measure and that combined with her powerful ESP gives her knowledge that no other child her age has. What's more interesting though is that her DNA sequences seem to be constantly rewriting themselves to better resist injury and illness."

Eric swirled his brandy before taking a slow sip. "What are the results of your tests on her power?"

"As with more typical Enlighteneds we are unable to pinpoint the source of the girl's power. However, our tests do indicate that her use of the power is different than that of other Enlighteneds."

Eric was intrigued. "In what way?"

"Normally an Enlightened's ability to use the power safely is limited by his or her ability to maintain focus and control. The Enlightened's focus and control of the power have finite upward limits for reasons we do not fully understand. Thus, even with many years of experience and training an Enlightened will eventually encounter an upper limit on the degree to which he or she can call up the power safely. This girl is different. While her ability to use the power is constrained to some degree by her ability to focus and control it like a typical Enlightened her ability to develop that focus and control seems to have no discernible limit. In effect the girl's power is limitless."

Eric drained his glass. Charlie was truly powerful then. Slow fear began to creep upon him. Eric bit it down quickly before it could take hold.

She's still only a child. She can be controlled.

"What exactly is D-13?"

"D-13 or dimethylphencyclohydroclorocarbamideamphetamine was the last in a series of psychic stimulants developed by the NSA for the purpose of artificially breeding Enlighteneds. Originally these drugs were intended to create first generation Enlighteneds meaning that the drug would turn normal humans into Enlighteneds. Unfortunately, none of the drugs had the desired effect. While the drugs did induce powerful psychic abilities in the subjects, the effect only lasted for the duration of the drug's effects. The other problem was that all of the drugs had very powerful side effects. All of the psychic stimulants are chemical relatives of methamphetamine. D-13 is also a potent dissociative hallucinogen and poison. Test subjects demonstrated extreme detachment from reality, vivid hallucinations, and violent paranoia. In addition, the drug also produces sky rocketing blood pressure and heart rate, elevated body temperature, profuse sweating, tremors and possible seizures, heart failure or stroke."

Eric swirled his brandy as he nodded for Tanner to continue.

"D-13 alters the neurology and physiology of the subject on the first exposure. The neurons in the brain are altered so that they can produce more D-13. This leaves the subjects with limited psionic abilities following exposure. However, using these abilities will make the person sick and cause progressive circulatory and brain damage that will eventually kill them. What we still don't understand is what happened with the girl. Normally D-13 and its predecessors cause severe damage to the chromosomes of anyone exposed to them. They also tend to cause sterility both because of the genetic damage and because of direct damage to the reproductive system. But somehow the girl was conceived and born without any of the severe birth defects generally associated with these drugs."

Eric sucked down the rest of his brandy. He had known much of this already, but he still found it fascinating. If there were some way to reproduce the accident that had produced the girl, then he could breed an entire army with her power. He would no longer need Charlie's cooperation. *Except there's only one Sigilla Praevaricator.* Eric knew the rest of the D-13 story. The first of the psychic stimulants were developed in Auschwitz by one of Joseph Mengele's assistants. The stated purpose was to create a mutagenic agent that would bring out certain recessive gene traits: blond hair, blue eyes, pale but not albino skin; all of the traits manifested by Hitler's Aryan race. The true purpose, as was the true purpose of the camps overall, was to develop a means to artificially breed Enlighteneds. Hitler and his Nazi goons, as with all of history's greatest villains were mere pawns in a much larger and unseen game. "You can go now Nick."

Nick's face registered momentary annoyance before he turned and left.

"We almost had her when we brought back Striker." As he spoke Eric's mind flashed back to the night he saved Striker. He had never called up such power before and had no desire to do it again any time soon. The power had nearly killed him. He was still weak from the experience. And tinkering with the timeline was dangerous. There was no telling what effect plucking a person out of the time stream might have.

"Yes, I could feel her anger. She *wanted* to kill him. She still wants to kill him." Lord Beathach replied.

Eric smiled. "All she needs is a little push. Something to help her let go of her inhibitions. I believe it's time we used the power to do that. "

"Perhaps but that is getting dangerously close to forcing her."

"No." He replied in a level tone. "I merely suggest using the power to unleash feelings and desires that are already there. Bend the rule without breaking it."

Lord Beathach sat in silence save for the harsh sounds of his labored breathing. He did not truly believe this was a bad idea. Eric knew that. He was only ensuring that Eric knew the risks of what he was proposing.

"Have the priests prepare the chapel for tomorrow night."

"Yes, my master."

VIII

David lay awake all-night thinking, mind awash in terror. Tomorrow he and Catherine would try to escape with Charlie. And probably die for their trouble. These Black Imperials were very dangerous. Over the years he had been on *Ifrinn* he had seen numerous examples of their brutality. They had already tortured Charlie. He knew she was valuable to them but that would not stop them from killing her to keep her from falling into the hands of their enemies. Part of him feared what he would find. She might already be dead or worse. There was no telling what they might have done to her. These people were capable of anything.

Please God let her be okay. Please don't let her be hurt.

What he truly feared and could not admit was that he would find that she had joined with the Black Empire and would not want to be rescued. Charlie had become a daughter to him and he loved her as if she were his own. He could not bear for her to reject him.

IX

Catherine too went without sleep that night. She was terrified for she felt strongly that they would fail. Deep inside, beyond reason or conscious awareness, something warned that they were going to their deaths. Catherine wanted to believe that this feeling was wrong, but she could not. Her own intuition told her that this was too dangerous. The Black Imperials were brutally violent. The three of them would be lucky if they were gunned down. Still she could not let David fight alone, nor could she leave Charlie in the hands of the Black Empire. They had tortured her in one of the most horrible ways Catherine could imagine. Charlie's expression from that day remained burned in Catherine's mind. It was an expression she knew well. It was an expression she had worn herself many years ago.

X

At four thirty the next morning Death Troopers came to wake both David and Catherine. As they were led to work each felt terribly frightened. They both knew an uprising had been planned but neither knew exactly what to expect. The majority of the slaves still resented and distrusted them because the guards did not brutalize them as they did to the others. Suspicious eyes fell on them throughout the factory as they were led to their stations. They had no friends here. They would have to move quickly, or they might become victims of the other slaves.

They had almost reached their workstations. This was it.

One of the men screamed and clutched his arm as if it were broken. A nearby Death Trooper went over to investigate. In an instant David and Catherine were on him. David easily got his rifle away and shot the man in the face splattering his brains all over the factory floor. The remaining Death Troopers in the room opened fire. David grabbed Catherine and dove to the floor, returning fire as he did. Several screams echoed in the air as more blood red energy beams slashed through the factory. One slammed into a pillar directly behind, showering them in hot metal shards.

"Shit!" David scrambled to his feet and returned fire, dropping the female Death Trooper who had fired on him with a single shot. More energy beams ripped through the air followed by screams of agony. Then the factory was silent. Someone whistled the all clear and the surviving slaves quickly got to their feet and fled the factory. David and Catherine followed the crowd into a military hanger. Those who could fly immediately headed for spacecraft. The best pilots commandeered a dozen or so S-20s s while the rest each took a transport shuttle. The remaining slaves were then divided among these shuttles.

David and Catherine headed for one of the smaller shuttles and immediately took off before anyone could interfere. David had never been behind the controls of any sort of spacecraft yet to his surprise he was able to handle the small ship as though he had been flying them all his life.

Upon entering space David and Catherine realized for the first time the full scope of what had begun. Star fighters zipped by on all sides trading volleys of laser fire. Their chatter came in clear through the shuttle's radio. They would not have long before the rebel fighters were forced to retreat. They were fighting valiantly but were badly outnumbered and outgunned. The rebels had a hundred fighters, no cruisers and no capital ships with which to face the full might of the Black Imperial Navy. This was by no means a fair fight or even a winnable one. As he watched an Imperial S-20 streaked by with a rebel in hot pursuit. A moment later the rebel opened fire and the Imperial vanished in a brilliant white fireball. This scene was repeated again a moment later this time with the Imperial victorious.

Both David and Catherine watched this in speechless awe. This was too much. The sheer number of ships, the speed and violence of the battle, the technology, it was unreal.

They were closing on the *Destroying Angel* now. The ship's sensors indicated that its shields were down.

"We'll be landing soon." As he spoke David set the auto landing sequence and then turned towards Catherine. Neither spoke but then there was no need for it. Each knew what had to be done.

XI

After a short time, they had landed and were walking down the gangplank. David was surprised by how easy this was. No one asked them for ID when they landed or even seemed to take notice of their presence. It was as if they were just another pair of Death Troopers arriving for duty and while this was their outward appearance no one bothered to check to see if it was accurate. They passed through the station quickly and without difficulty. The blast doors were all open and the frequent patrols of Death Troopers ignored them. Having no better ideas and not having considered the risk David logged onto the nearest computer terminal and to his surprise easily found where Charlie was being kept. It was not as though the system was unsecured but somehow, he was able to anticipate the security measures and bypass them without triggering any alarms. It was strange and more than a little worrisome. But he did not have time to be frightened. According to the computer Charlie was being held in a special isolation unit in sector fourteen of deck fifty fifteen. The area was supposed to be off limits to all unauthorized personnel, which meant their cover would be blown the moment they entered the unit.

David turned to Catherine. "If these guys are as efficient as they usually are we'll have maybe five minutes to find Charlie and get out of the isolation unit before the whole area is flooded with Death Troopers. We're going to have to be very quick if we want to have any chance of escaping alive."

Catherine remained silent.

David closed down the computer terminal and continued on towards the elevator.

"Deck fifty-fifteen."

The computer beeped an affirmative. A moment later the car lurched into motion. David's heart was racing. He was frightened, and he could feel Catherine's fear, which added to his own. This was it. They would only get one shot at this. If they failed he and Catherine would be killed and so, probably, would Charlie.

Neither spoke a word. There was nothing to say. They both knew the risks.

The elevator door opened to reveal a series of bare and largely empty black steel corridors. The lighting down here was dimmer, and the air was colder. David was aware of the temperature difference despite the heavy, heat-sealed armor that encased his body. It wasn't a temperature difference though. It was a sense of dark desolation that only felt like cold. Much suffering and death had taken place here. Silent screams echoed in the air.

"Which way?" Catherine asked nervously.

"I don't know." David replied.

Then all at once it came to him. He turned and headed down the right corridor following it to where it ended in a heavy blast door. Without a moment's pause David gathered himself, reached deep inside and threw the power at the door.

Blue energy enveloped the door flash-freezing it solid. David raised his rifle and fired. The blast shattered the door on impact, reducing it to a pile of crumpled metal shards and revealing a second corridor that also ended in a heavy blast door.

"Come on. We have to hurry. We'll only have a couple of minutes before this hallway fills with Death Troopers." As he spoke David picked his way through the remnants of the door taking care not to touch any of the still frozen metal fragments.

Upon reaching the second door David again used the power to freeze it and then shattered it with an energy bolt from his rifle.

In the corridor beyond the door David spotted four Death Troopers. For a moment they stood there without reacting. Then one leveled his rifle and took aim.

David shouted to Catherine. "Down!" Before dropping to the deck, a hair's breadth ahead of a hail of red fire. As he landed he fired off a pair of his own shots. Both struck the same Death Trooper, severing his leg and blowing him in half.

David glanced behind to make sure Catherine was not hurt. She lay on the ground a little behind him, uninjured. As he watched her, Catherine fired, striking a second Death Trooper in the forehead and blowing his skull apart. His headless corpse collapsed on one of the pieces of the blast door and was frozen solid. Two more Death Troopers charged their position. David and Catherine opened fire at the same time. One of the Death Troopers was struck in the neck and decapitated. The other's leg was severed at the hip leaving him alive but incapacitated.

David leapt to his feet and hurried through the shattered door before any more Death Troopers could arrive.

The corridor beyond was brightly lit and bare save for the tiny six by six cells that occurred every ten feet on the right. Charlie stood within the last cell looking terrified.

Charlie?

It had been years since he had last seen her, yet she remained largely unchanged. Her hair was blond again and hung down around her waist, and her skin was back to its natural color but other than that she was the same little girl he and Catherine had tried to protect all those years ago. She had not grown or matured in any way.

How is this possible? What's going on?

Neither he nor Catherine had changed noticeably either, but he had not found this remarkable. They were adults and had finished physical maturation years ago. But Charlie was still a little girl.

What happened to her? What did they do to her?

Charlie cried out to them. "David?! Catherine?! I thought you were gone forever." For a moment her face darkened, and David sensed terrible understanding and black, cold fury. Then she closed herself to him and burst into tears.

His heart exploded with excitement. He had not seen Charlie in years and here she was. He would have grabbed her into his arms were they not separated by a thin blue force field.

"It's going to be all right Charlie. I'm going to get you out of there, but I need you to step back from the force field."

She obeyed mutely.

David studied the force field with care. There were no visible generators or switches. Its energy seemed to come from the wall itself.

Wonderful.

Without thinking about it David reached out with his mind. Within seconds he had found the source of the force field. A pair of thick power conduits beneath the floor fueled generator circuits contained within the cell walls. Like the walls the floor was constructed of heavy blast armor. His rifle would be useless. Moreover, the conduits were configured as a collapsible circuit. If one were severed the other would keep the force field intact and if both were severed they would trigger a security mechanism that would electrify the floor and walls of the cell. It would not be enough to kill but it would render Charlie unconscious.

They had taken great pains to ensure that Charlie would not be able to escape even if she used the power. The question was how he was going to get her out without subjecting her to electric shock.

Catherine arrived behind him. "Charlie." Her voice reflected a mixture of deep relief, joy and fear.

"Eric said you were gone." Charlie sobbed. "I thought you left me here." Then for a moment her face filled with terrible understanding before filling with combined fear and misery. "You have to get away. Please. It's dangerous here."

"It's all right Charlie. We'll be fine." Catherine's voice was quite calm and reassuring despite the fear David felt in her heart.

There had to be a way to get Charlie out. There was no place for her to go if he severed the power conduits. Even the bed was metal. And he couldn't turn off the force field. Then an idea occurred to him.

"Charlie, do you think you can float in the air for a few seconds?"

"I guess so." She replied dubiously.

"When I say so I want you to concentrate as hard as you can on lifting yourself off the floor. You need to stay in the air for at least ten seconds."

"Okay." She was frightened. "Please hurry David. They're coming."

He knew. A detachment of Death Troopers would arrive in seven minutes. He had to be quick.

"Are you ready Charlie?"

She nodded.

"Good. Then I want you to concentrate as hard as you can. Once you're off the floor I want you to count to ten before letting go."

"Alright…" She glanced at him with frightened eyes for a moment. Then David felt her reaching within herself. Her power rapidly built in the air. As he watched she lifted into the air and hung there in perfect stillness. For a moment David stood and stared. Then he reached into his own power and directed it towards the power conduits in the floor. There was a sharp bang accompanied by a shower of purple and blue sparks as the power conduits and electric lines exploded. After a few seconds the sparks cleared leaving a large crater and the force field disabled. Charlie drifted gracefully downward. As soon as her feet touched the deck she ran to him.

"Oh David, I thought I would never see you again." She started to cry.

David lifted her into his arms feeling close to tears himself. "It's alright Charlie. We're here now and we'll never let anyone take you away from us again."

Catherine hugged them both trapping Charlie between David's body and hers.

Charlie turned and hugged her with one arm. "I love you." She was smiling through her tears.

"I love you too. Now let's go before any more Death Troopers show up." As she spoke Catherine released them and checked her rifle.

David gave Charlie one last hug then set her down. "Come on let's get out of here."

Charlie nodded.

"I want you to stay behind us no matter what happens."

Charlie did not reply but David sensed her agreement.

"When the shooting starts get down and stay there until Catherine or I say it's safe to get up." David continued.

"Okay David." She was frightened though it did not show in her voice.

He took her hand. "Don't be afraid everything's going to be fine."

Charlie squeezed his hand.

David hurried down the corridor doing his best to keep his body in front of Charlie and Catherine. It was still quiet. *Where are they?* Something wasn't right. The cell block should have been swarming with Death Troopers. As he continued forward a strong sense of danger crept into his heart. Something definitely wasn't right. When they had nearly reached the elevator a huge detachment of Death Troopers appeared, seemingly from nowhere. Green energy blasts streaked through the air.

David screamed,

"DOWN!!"

and dove behind a bulkhead pulling Charlie after him. Without pausing he returned a volley cutting down three of the lead Death Troopers. Several green blasts slammed into the bulkhead in reply. David returned fire as Catherine snapped off a pair of shots from behind the opposite bulkhead. Two more Death Troopers collapsed to the deck. A third leveled his rifle, aiming for her head.

"Get down Catherine!"

As he shouted David fired a single shot, striking the female Death Trooper in the face. More green fire streaked through the air slamming into the walls and floors. In response David and Catherine fired off a scattering of shots dropping the Death Troopers a few at a time. It made no difference. For every Death Trooper they killed ten more appeared to take his or her place. Their numbers were endless. The hail of green fire intensified with every passing second. David's heart was racing. They were trapped. They had to get away before one of them was killed. The power was awakening within him.

I should use it. It's the only way to get us out of here.

As he was thinking that David became aware of Charlie's power flowing in the air. It was strong. The air was alive with its presence. Without a word she stood up.

David screamed at her. "Charlie get down!"

She paid no attention. Suddenly, Charlie lashed out with her power. Flames licked across the floor and ceiling in front of her. Then all at once the floor beneath the Death Troopers erupted in a single massive fireball. For a moment the air filled with horrible screams. Then there was total silence save for the roar of the flames.

David grabbed her. "Jesus Charlie don't ever do anything like that again! You could have been killed!"

She was silent.

He took her hand again. "Come on let's get out of here."

"Okay." Her voice was distant. He could feel her struggling against her power.

At the same time, he struggled to silence his own power. *Stop! Stop it now!! I don't need you!*

After a few moments it was gone.

They boarded the elevator.

"Deck fourteen-ten sector five." David barked.

The elevator beeped then lurched into motion.

"What now David? They know we're here. They'll never let us off this station."

David glanced at Catherine without speaking. She was right, and he had no idea of what to do. He could only guess at the *Destroying Angel's* capabilities.

"They'll kill us before they let us escape." She persisted.

"I know!" He snapped. Then he leaned in closer and added. "But you don't have to say that in front of Charlie."

As he spoke he became aware of Charlie's fear. David gently stroked her hair. "It's going to be all right Charlie."

"Damn it, David, why don't you tell her the truth!" Catherine snapped. "She has a right to know what's really going on."

"Keep your voice down Catherine." He covered Charlie's ears with his hands. "What do you want me to say? That we're probably going to be killed trying to escape. She doesn't need to hear that. She deserves to have some hope."

"So, you're going to lie to her then? Is that it?"

Charlie twisted out of his grasp. "Stop it! Don't fight. Please."

David turned an angry glare on Catherine then bent down to Charlie's level. "I'm sorry Charlie we won't fight anymore."

"It's okay." She replied in a soft tone.

Catherine was watching him through slitted angry eyes. The message was unmistakable.

The elevator door opened onto a firestorm of green energy blasts. David grabbed Charlie and Catherine and pulled them into the front right corner of the elevator.

David fired a couple of blasts in response. He did not see if they connected but a pair of screams suggested that they were on target. David turned to Charlie and Catherine.

"Keep your heads down. Let me deal with this."

More green energy streaked by only to splash against the rear of the elevator. David responded with several quick shots before ducking back into the elevator. The door started to slide shut. David took off one of his shin guards and jammed it in the track. A green stun bolt struck his hand instantly numbing him to the elbow. David gunned down the storm trooper who had shot him one handed, then quickly ducked back into the elevator. Before he could stop her Catherine stepped into the open and fired off several volleys of energy blasts before a near hit to the head convinced her to take cover on the opposite side of the elevator.

Anger flashed in David's heart. "What the hell is wrong with you?! Do you want to get shot?"

"I'll be fine." She shot back. "Worry about them."

David snapped off another pair of red energy bolts. "I told you to keep your head down!"

"Put down your guns." Charlie's voice came to him through the din of blaster fire.

David turned to Charlie unbelieving. Her expression was perfectly calm, but he could feel her anger.

"You don't need them." Charlie's voice was almost serene.

Slowly and deliberately she stepped out into the hail of green fire. Again, David felt her power building in the air.

XII

"Get down Charlie!!"

She ignored him. Her power was blazing wildly. Anger flared in her heart.

Leave us alone you bastards!!

The power was building up within her, spinning wildly just within her ability to control it.

I'll kill you!

Charlie shoved the power out of herself in the direction of the Death Troopers. Flames swept across the floor and ceiling in a wave. In the same instant there was a brilliant white flash and an earsplitting boom. White fire burned where the Death Troopers had once stood. There were no bodies. More green energy streaked through the flames. Charlie lashed out again setting off a second explosion and igniting the entire corridor.

That'll teach you.

She started forward. The flames parted in front of her. David and Catherine remained in the elevator. She could feel their fear. Only her anger kept the guilt from returning.

Those bastards deserved it. They deserved to die.

David hurried down the hallway with Catherine in tow. "Wait for us Charlie." He called after her.

She paid no attention.

Some distance down the hallway she was obliged to stop by a sealed blast door. The power continued to move within her. Without really thinking about it Charlie shoved the power out of herself as hard as she could. The door did not catch fire. It exploded in a brilliant white flash that momentarily blinded her. When her vision returned she was standing before a pile of small flaming chunks of molten metal.

David ran to her. "Are you hurt Charlie?"

She did not respond. He could feel her still struggling with her power. Her voice rang in his head.

STOP IT!!

STOP IT NOW!!

STOP IT!!

He felt no change. Her power continued spiraling upward heedless of her pleas. Still she continued to fight for control.

STOP IT!!

XIII

Gradually David felt her power begin to slow down. Her expression was one of intense pain but she was bringing the power down, dragging it back under her control. After several more minutes she was able to silence it.

David went to her. "Charlie are you okay?"

"I think so." Her voice was pained and very tired.

"You look exhausted." Catherine's voice was calm despite the fear David sensed from her.

Charlie offered a forced smile. "I'm fine."

David took her hand. "Then let's get out of here."

"Alright."

The three of them picked their way over the still blazing remnants of the blast door and then hurried down the corridor beyond. At its end the corridor opened into the docking bay where they had left the transport shuttle. After everyone was aboard and strapped in David ignited the engines and took off. As they left the *Destroying Angel* David silently prayed that they would be able to get clear without being killed or captured.

The battle was heating up. More imperial fighters had been launched and were rapidly killing off the remaining rebels who were already beginning to retreat. At the same time the bulk of the Black Imperial capital ships were moving into position to block their escape. The trap was closing. There was no way out now.

Not that it would have mattered. Even if they could get away there was nowhere to go. None of them knew anything about interstellar travel. David didn't even know where he was. Their only hope was to land and hide out until the battle ended and then try to figure out how to get back to earth.

A rebel fighter streaked out in front of him with an imperial in hot pursuit. A few seconds later the imperial sprayed the rebel with green laser fire and the rebel exploded in a brilliant white fireball. Whatever rebels remained were going to die. They were hopelessly trapped.

Suddenly a sharp bang violently rocked the ship. This was followed a moment later by a second shock and then a third. The control panel lit up as numerous alarms went off.

"What the hell happened?" Catherine cried.

"We've been hit." David quickly glanced over the control panel. There was damage to the engines, sensors and shield generator. The ship wasn't mortally wounded but the damage was significant. A second pass would probably disable them. The fighter had streaked out ahead and was coming around for another pass. David quickly armed the ship's weapons and brought them to bear on the now rapidly approaching ship. After a moment the guidance computer beeped. David fired a pair of missiles at the ship obliterating it almost instantly.

"We have to get out of here." As he spoke David turned the ship away from the battle and towards the planet.

XIV

Charlie stood in front of the rear-view port watching the *Destroying Angel* fade into the distance. Memories of suffering, temptation and betrayal flashed through her mind. She saw herself tormented, heard her own screams, felt the pain as one would hear the echo of a shout long after the sound was gone. Eric had rescued her for Lord Beathach, but he had only been using her. He only wanted to use her as a weapon and he lied about David and Catherine leaving her behind. He was no better than Robin. He had made her love him, and he had, if only for a moment, made it ok for her to *Hate!*. Cold fury ignited within her heart and the black bloodstain began to swell and blaze. The power stirred within her. She made no attempt to control it. She would obliterate the *Destroying Angel* and

Eric with it. She would wipe them both from existence. She would never go back there again. The power was blazing now flowing in rivers. An intense wave of pleasure swept through her. Her body sang in ecstasy. It was incredible. Charlie felt her breathing quicken. The power was raging now.

You made me think David and Catherine left me alone.

You made me think they didn't want me anymore.

You made me think it was ok to Hate! and take revenge.

You made me love you and it was all a lie!

You were only using me for my power!

Then another, more terrible realization came to her.

You knew what Lord Beathach did to me. You knew, and you let him do it! You let him hurt me!

Her heart was thundering. Suddenly everything took on a blue-white hue. Charlie became vaguely aware of her body lifting off the deck.

XV

There was a low rumble that quickly built to a deafening roar. The ship shook with its fury. An incredible force was building in the air. Power like that he had felt in the morgue years earlier pulsated in the air. David stood up.

"Take the controls Catherine."

"What's going on?" She asked with nervous words.

"I don't know just take the controls."

"David?" Her voice reflected plain fear now.

He hurried back into the main cabin. What he saw astounded and terrified him at once. Charlie floated exactly four feet above the deck. Brilliant blue-white fire surrounded her body. From where he stood the heat was sufficient to scorch his eyebrows and the hair on his arms. His skin had already burned though he had not yet noticed it. All around him the air was alive with indescribable power. It flowed around and through him. His body trembled with its force.

This must be what it's like to be struck by lightning. He thought numbly. Deeper inside another thought occurred or rather an unconscious realization. *This must be what it's like to be in the presence of God.*

He was terrified, yet he felt nothing. Shock swept away all conscious emotion and thought. All he could do was stand and stare at the blazing white figure before him. He had never imagined Charlie had such power. This was beyond anything he would have thought possible for anyone, even an Enlightened. And still the power grew stronger. The shuttle was shuddering now as though it had caught a chill. Somewhere in the back of his mind it occurred to David that if this continued the tremors would tear the ship apart.

Something began pulling at him, drawing his attention away from Charlie towards the view port she was looking out of. Through it he saw the *Destroying Angel*. It had shrunk to the size of a large bowling ball now. In an instant Charlie's power rocketed out towards it. A moment later the *Destroying Angel* vanished in a blinding white flash. In the same instant the ship came alive beneath him. David was thrown to the deck. A terrifying roar filled his ears for an instant before total silence ensued. Scorching heat encased his body singing his hair and clothing. An intense burning smell flooded his nostrils. He could no longer feel Charlie's power, not because it was gone but because there was so much of it as to be insupportable by his psychic senses. The power's force carried his mind away leaving him drifting in a field of searing white light.

XVI

When his senses cleared David found himself flat on his back on the deck. Charlie crouched beside him looking frightened.

"Are you hurt David?"

"I think so." He looked himself over carefully. His skin was burned, and his hair and armor scorched. Large blisters had already cropped up on his exposed flesh. His joints and muscles protested bitterly as he struggled to sit up.

Strangely enough Charlie appeared unharmed. She had no visible burns and her hair and clothing were undamaged. How was this possible?

He looked around. The inside of the ship was devastated. Small fires were scattered everywhere. Part of the ceiling had collapsed, and the computer terminal back here was incinerated. Sparks flew from a number of severed power conduits. David choked on the thick, smoky air.

"Catherine!"

There was no answer. David scrambled to his feet and ran into the cockpit. Catherine lay unconscious in the copilot's seat. The skin on her face and arms was deep red and covered in massive angry blisters, her armor was blackened and burned away in some places and large portions of her hair were charred black.

Charlie ran to Catherine's side. "Catherine? Catherine are you alright?"

She still did not respond.

"Catherine please wake up. Please…" She clutched Catherine. David could feel her struggling to hold back tears. "I'm so sorry. Please wake up." She started to cry.

Sudden nausea took him. It wasn't that he was disturbed by Catherine's injuries, he had seen much worse, but something was making him feel very sick. Before he could stop himself, David doubled over and vomited on the floor beside Catherine's seat.

David plopped down to stave off a second wave of nausea. It worked a little, but he still felt queasy.

He glanced through the front windshield and instantly forgot his nausea. The *Destroying Angel* was gone along with all of the rebel fighters and most of the Black Imperial fleet. The explosion had completely obliterated the entire battle leaving a massive white fireball to mark the spot. For a moment David just sat and stared before an alarm brought him back to reality. The concussion from the death of the *Destroying Angel* had crippled the shuttle. They had lost shields, weapons, communications, much of the engine and computer functions and had suffered significant structural damage. Somehow the ship had settled into orbit, but that orbit was now decaying. They did not have enough power to counteract the planet's gravity. David's fingers flew over the controls independent of his mind. Within a few seconds he had brought the ship into a controlled descent. As the ship flew down to the planet's surface David wracked his brain for a way out of this trap. The ship was crippled, and he did not have the skills to repair it. He knew no other way to get back to Earth other than to fly there. They would have to try to steal another ship and the planet would be crawling with Death

Troopers following the slave uprising. Worse he did not know how to get back to Earth.

Catherine awoke and immediately vomited.

"Catherine you're not hurt." Charlie hugged her again.

"What happened?" She spoke in a dazed half whisper.

"We're badly damaged." David replied. "I'm trying to land."

"How?" Her voice was confused "What hit us?"

"I don't know." David replied in as calm a voice as he could muster.

If Catherine detected his lie she gave no sign.

Charlie glanced at him in silence. Her expression registered deep gratitude. Though he could not be sure David suspected that she felt guilty for what she had done. He felt bad for her. She had committed an act of unimaginable destruction, but it had been an act of desperation on the heels of much suffering. She had not acted out of malice or vengeance.

The shuttle descended rapidly. They would reach the surface in minutes. David typed in a command that would activate the ship's anti-gravity field. This slowed the ship a little but without full power it was not enough to stop its descent. They were below a thousand feet now. They had only seconds before impact. David's heart raced. If they hit the ground at this speed they would be killed.

David turned to Charlie and Catherine. "Everybody strap in, we're going to crash."

Both Catherine and Charlie rushed to buckle themselves into chairs. Charlie screamed as they plummeted the last two hundred feet to the ground.

The ship struck the ground with a hard jolt followed by a sharp bang. Then everything went black.

XVII

Striker waited until Kain had left, then crept into the Imperial Chambers. Charlie's sword was kept here. He found it lying inside a glass case along one wall. Striker carefully looked over the case. There were no visible alarm triggers. There wasn't even a lock. After rechecking the case, Striker opened it and removed the blade within.

The moment he touched the sword Striker felt himself become connected to Charlie. Great power flowed through him bringing on a sensation like nothing he had ever felt before. He felt alive for the first time in decades and he knew what he had to do. He had seen the pain in Charlie's eyes when she learned he was alive. Now he could feel it.

Striker had come to steal Charlie's sword to challenge her to fight to the death. Now he knew he had made the right decision. Charlie was in an agony of hurt and anger, feelings that would never leave her and could only be eased by his death. He could not bear her suffering. He loved her, like nothing and no one else in his life. She was like a daughter, but she was more than that. She had understood him in a way that no one else could. He thought perhaps she was a soul mate but that didn't matter anymore. He had to find a way to ease her pain and he knew no other way than to die at her hands. He knew if he challenged her that she would kill him with ease. He was going to his death but that did not matter either. Charlie was all that mattered. She was the only thing he cared about.

As he held Charlie's sword Striker found himself amazed by how light it was. It had a heft to it yet it seemed light as a feather.

The *Destroying Angel* had exploded, living up to its name in a way no one could have imagined as it took with it most of the Black Imperial fleet. A single transport had escaped the blast and crashed on the planet's surface. Somehow, he knew Charlie was still alive, that she was aboard that ship.

Striker was not the only one who had concluded this. A large detachment of Death Troopers had been dispatched to the crash site with Lord Beathach himself in command. Fortunately, Striker knew a way to get there first. He knew something else as well. Though she was not bound to, Charlie would certainly accept his challenge and once she had Lord Beathach and his men could not interfere. He needed only a few minutes' lead-time and he could easily arrange that.

XVIII

Charlie awoke in a daze. Her head ached. Thick, heavy smoke filled the cockpit. She coughed hard as she struggled to clear her lungs. Something warm and sticky trickled down her forehead. Charlie ran her fingers over her brow.

A soft cry escaped her throat. *Blood...*

She carefully felt around until her fingers found a shallow gash just below her hairline. A sharp bolt of pain slammed through her head.

"Oww."

The wound wasn't serious, but it bled steadily. Charlie carefully unstrapped herself and stood up. Cautiously she groped her way over to where she thought she would find David. After a few minutes of fumbling blindness, she located him.

"David? Are you alright?" Her speech was followed by a series of sharp coughs as she again struggled to clear her lungs. Her eyes began to water and burn. Tears trickled down her cheeks.

He did not respond at first.

"David?" He was alive, she knew that much but he gave no signs of recognition. She felt nothing from him but his presence. All thought, and emotion were suspended. Charlie ran her fingers over his face and upper body searching for wounds. She found several shallow cuts two of which were bleeding steadily. She gently shook him. "David, wake up?"

He groaned softly. "What happened?"

"We crashed." Her voice was hoarse from the smoke.

David coughed heavily. "We need to get out of here before this whole thing burns up. Where's Catherine?"

Charlie pointed. "She's over there I think." She coughed again.

David stood up and walked in the direction she had pointed and vanished in the thick hazy air. A moment later his voice came to Charlie through the smoke.

"Catherine? Wake up."

"Uhhh. What's going on?" Catherine moaned.

"The ship crashed." David replied. "We need to get out of here now."

Catherine cried out in pain. "Oww damnit!"

A moment later David appeared supporting Catherine who was gushing blood from a long gash to her upper leg. "Come on let's go." He motioned towards the rear of the ship. Charlie followed close behind him. The rear door was jammed shut. David used his power to freeze and shatter it.

As it turned out they had crashed into a building somewhere in the sub-city. The building was dark and deserted but Charlie felt they were not alone. Someone very close was looking for them. It was someone she knew well.

Anger flared in her heart bringing the power with it. "Striker!! Where are you? You come out here right now!"

There was no response. He was outside. Charlie hurried towards the door.

David called after her. "Wait for us Charlie."

She ignored him. The street outside was deserted. Charlie raked her eyes over the buildings and alleys searching for the slightest movement. She saw nothing. Perhaps the feeling was premature. Except she did not really believe that.

"Where are you Striker?" Her heart was racing with fury.

There was still no response.

David's voice came from behind her. "Come on let's get out of here."

She turned at the sound of David's voice. "Ok."

If Striker was out there he wasn't anywhere nearby.

Charlie walked down the street with David and Catherine, still feeling as if Striker was watching.

Where is he? He had to be out there. The feeling was too strong to be false.

"What's wrong Charlie?" David asked in a gentle tone.

"Nothing. I'm fine." She knew he was hiding somewhere nearby.

A figure moved in the shadows. Charlie knew at once who it was.

"Hello Charlie." Purple lightning flashed overhead revealing Striker's location.

Charlie glared into the darkness. "Where are you? Come out here right now." Another flash of lightning broke the darkness for a second. This was followed a moment later by a deafening roar of thunder.

He stepped into the light. "Okay Charlie. Okay."

Charlie's felt anger rising within her. "What do you want with me now?"

He reached into his trench coat, produced her sword and threw it so that it stuck into the ground in front of her. "Charlene MacLeod, I challenge you to fight to the death." There was a brilliant flash of lightning accompanied by an explosion of thunder. A gust of wind lifted her hair from her shoulders.

"You don't have to do this Charlie." David's voice was concerned. "He's not a Dark Knight, you don't have to fight him. You can walk away."

"I accept." She growled. Her anger had turned to cold fury. Charlie reached out with her mind and pulled her sword into her outstretched right hand. Brilliant white flames licked up the blade. Beneath the flames the sword's red flaw glowed balefully. In that same moment the first drops of rain began to fall.

Striker reached into his trench coat again, this time producing a slim Japanese tachi sword. The moment it cleared the scabbard Charlie charged forward bringing her sword up in a powerful vertical slash that knocked Striker's sword out of the way. In the same motion she brought her sword around again in a horizontal slash that slit open his belly and spilled his intestines on the ground. Striker collapsed to his knees with a groan. It was pouring now. The rain spat and sizzled on her sword. Charlie struck again this time drawing a long bloody gash across his back. Her heart was slamming against her ribs threatening to burst from her chest.

You killed Daddy!

You took him away!

She struck again and again literally butchering Striker alive. He was in agony and she felt no guilt. All that mattered was her anger. He deserved this. He deserved to suffer for what he did. Charlie slashed open his chest, arms and legs. She severed several of his fingers and stabbed him in the groin. Still she was not satisfied. Charlie brought her sword up and slashed Striker across the back again. He did not scream or even gasp in pain, but she knew he was suffering terribly. It didn't matter. He killed Mommy and Daddy. She struck again nearly severing his left arm. Striker collapsed on his chest. For a moment he lay there gasping for breath. Then he pushed himself to his knees with his remaining good arm. Charlie raised her sword to strike again then stopped when she saw the pain in his eyes.

For the first time her fury was broken by a tiny ray of compassion. He had hurt her on purpose and she had every right to want to get him back, but revenge would not bring Mommy and Daddy back and it would not undo her pain. If anything, it would add to it for she would then have to live with the guilt for her actions. Charlie raised her sword one last time and brought it down as hard she could on Striker's neck. The blade struck with dull thud and sliced all the way through. Blood sprayed everywhere soaking her from head to toe. Her sword slipped out of her hand and clanged off the concrete street its flames instantly extinguished. Charlie stared at the decapitated remains for several minutes without moving. She had done it. She had killed in cold blood. Despite whatever reasons she could rationalize to herself she had accepted Striker's challenge, so she could kill him. She knew she did not have to accept a challenge from an Outsider. She could have walked away, and she didn't. She fought Striker knowing he had no chance of defending himself. Perhaps this was not murder, but she had certainly helped Striker kill himself.

Of course it's murder. He had no chance against me.

The rain was coming down in sheets now. Charlie was soaked to the skin. All at once she burst into tears.

What have I done?

A scream built in her chest. Charlie made no attempt to hold it back. She screamed and screamed unable to stop herself. She was truly damned now. There was no denying it. When she had screamed herself hoarse Charlie just stood there shivering and crying softly.

David came up to her. "It's fine Charlie. It's all over now. Striker's dead and you're safe. Everything's going to be all right." He was lying through his teeth.

David took her into his arms and hugged her tight. Charlie wept bitterly against his chest for she knew what had to be done. She had spilled blood. Thus, her blood would have to be spilled in atonement. She was not afraid to die. It was fair. She had committed murder. She was afraid of what would come after for she knew already what would not. The concrete beneath her feet ran red with Striker's blood. Soon it would be reddened by her blood as well.

Charlie pulled back from David. "Do it. Please. I just want to get it over with." She tipped back her head and closed her eyes in anticipation.

David was confused. "What do you mean Charlie?"

"Kill me."

"What?!" David bent down to her level and gently turned her face to his. "Open your eyes Charlie. Look at me."

She did as she was told.

"Why do you think I should kill you?"

"Because I murdered Striker." It was hard for her to talk without bursting into tears all over again.

"You didn't murder him Charlie. He challenged you and you accepted. It was your right to accept. No one forced him to challenge you."

"But he's not an Enlightened. He couldn't have won."

"That doesn't matter Charlie. You don't have to take a challenge from an Outsider, but you are permitted to if you want. There's no rule that says we can't take challenges from idiots."

She was not comforted. "But I took his challenge because I wanted to kill him because he killed Daddy."

David's expression became deeply sympathetic. The force of his compassion was painful. "I know Charlie and it's okay. You did not act out of vengeance but self-defense. It doesn't matter that Striker wasn't a real threat to you. Your reasons for accepting the challenge don't matter. Accepting a challenge is always self-defense. I told you that before."

She nodded slowly. "Because if you don't take a challenge you have to surrender."

"That's right Charlie." He took her hand. "Come on let's go help Catherine and then get the hell out of here."

"Alright." Charlie felt some relief, but her guilt remained strong. She picked up her sword from the street and slipped it under her belt, then followed David to where he had left Catherine sitting on the ground. She had vomited again and looked very sick. "Are you ok?"

Catherine forced a smile. "I'm fine honey. Just need a little help getting up."

Charlie was frightened. She could tell that Catherine was getting worse. She looked a lot like Daddy when he overused his power. But there wasn't time to be afraid. Without hesitating Charlie slipped under Catherine's left arm while David took her right. It took some effort but together they were able to get Catherine to her feet.

"Alright let's go." David's voice was tired. He too looked sick though not as sick as Catherine.

A short distance down the street they were intercepted by a large detachment of Death Troopers led by Lord Beathach.

"That's far enough Charlene." Lord Beathach rumbled softly.

The Death Troopers leveled their rifles.

"I recommend surrendering." He continued. "Your friends do not look like they could survive being shot again."

The power stirred within her. Charlie bit it back. *NO!!* A soft sigh escaped her throat. "Okay." She dropped her sword.

"A wise choice Charlene." Charlie could imagine Lord Beathach's half smile behind his death's head mask.

"No! You can't have her!" David's voice was defiant but exhausted. He raised his rifle and fired on Lord Beathach.

Beathach calmly raised his right hand and deflected the energy beam with his palm. The Death Troopers surrounding him raised their rifles to return fire. Beathach stayed them with a gesture. He was chuckling softly. "Excellent shot Mr. McAuliffe but you underestimate my power. You do not want to face me. You are only an Enlightened, you are not even a full Lightwarrior. I could destroy you with a gesture. Charlene was wise enough to surrender. I suggest you follow her example." He paused. "Oh, I see. You thought you could escape." He laughed. "My master allowed you to escape and rescue the girl. He wanted to give Charlene the opportunity for revenge. He knew exactly what you would do and were you would be."

David glared at him, still clutching his rifle in his right hand as he supported Catherine with his left arm.

Charlie looked up at him with pleading eyes. "It's ok David. I'll be fine."

"No." David replied in a steady tone. "I promised I wouldn't let them take you and I meant it."

She returned a gentle smile. "I know David."

Then she hugged him before turning towards Lord Beathach.

"Come Charlene. It is time." Lord Beathach's tone was soft and reflected unmistakable satisfaction.

She went to him without a word. She could feel David and Catherine's terror.

Lord Beathach turned to his Death Troopers "Bring the other two. The Emperor wants them to witness the ritual."

The Death Troopers swarmed on David and Catherine. There was no struggle.

XIX

Charlie was taken to the palace where slaves dressed her in an elaborate white gown. A wreath of white roses was placed on her head and a diamond pendant on a silver chain was hung around her neck. She was then taken to a small chapel deep inside the Black Imperial palace.

The chapel was dark and cold, filled with the smell of death. Charlie's footsteps rang, ghost like off the mirror polished Serpentinite floor, each footfall a gunshot in the chamber. All at once the chamber filled with low, monotonous, demonic chanting. Charlie recognized the language from the day Lord Beathach murdered Mary. The sound was nightmarish. Her flesh went cold.

Surrounding the chamber were dozens of figures in black robes. Charlie could not tell the sex of the figures for their faces were hidden by oversized black hoods. Still, she knew these were Eric's lieutenants and other high-ranking Dark Knights within the Black Empire.

The congregation stood in a rough circle around the center of the chamber where the altar lay. Tonight, the altar did not stand alone. Behind it stood a huge stone basin carved from a single piece of granite. The basin was pitted and stained with blood from ritual past. Above the basin hung a pair of heavy iron manacles. These too were streaked with dried blood. Beside the basin stood a gigantic furnace. *Deus Irae* lay within its belly surrounded by the black flames shooting from its gaping maw. The altar itself was a single massive piece of polished Serpentinite. It too bore numerous nicks and bloodstains. Upon it lay a censer, a horse hair brush, a platter containing a single consecrated host, a small bowl filled with urine and a jeweled chalice filled with human blood. All were solid gold. Between the altar and the stone basin stood Eric and Lord Beathach.

Surrounding the altar were three circles of six black candles each. These provided the chamber's only illumination.

"Bring forth young Charlene MacLeod." Eric spoke in a tone she had never heard before, one both solemn and deadly serious at once. Charlie was prodded forward by the woman behind her. She too was a Dark Knight. There were no Outsiders here.

"Charlie!" David's cry echoed in the high-ceilinged chamber. He was immediately answered with a fist to the back of the head.

"No!!" She screamed. "Leave him alone!"

The woman Dark Knight pushed her forward roughly.

Charlie started to run towards where David and Catherine stood but was immediately stopped by a hand on her shoulder. That hand remained in place driving her inexorably forward. As she continued towards the altar the congregation's chanting intensified.

Charlie was terrified. Sharp tremors rippled up her spine. The Black Empire's victory was at hand and she was to be its instrument.

No! I'll never let that happen. They'll have to kill me because I'll never do what they want. Never.

"Don't hurt her." More blows rained down on David's head.

Charlie wanted to call to them to stop but her tongue was stayed by terror. She was almost to the altar now. The power was racing within her, awakened by her fear. Charlie forced it down. It did not occur to her that for once she might actually want the power. Approximately ten feet from the altar Charlie broke free of her captor. Eric looked down on her with eyes of ice freezing her in her tracks.

Sudden anger flashed within her heart setting the power ablaze within her mind. "You tricked me." She spoke the words in a low, deliberate voice, letting her anger show in her tone. "You told me David and Catherine were gone! You made me think they left me behind! YOU LET LORD BEATHACH HURT ME!" She was shouting now. The power was blazing. Charlie instinctively bit it back sending blood-soaked shards ripping through her skull and into the soft gray tissue of her brain. She could have killed Eric right there.

But its bad. David said it is bad.

"I never lied to you." Eric replied matter of factly. "I did conceal some facts from you, but I never lied. And I only concealed the truth to protect you. Your Dad couldn't protect you. He let the NSA capture both of you and got himself killed. David and Catherine couldn't protect you either. They let the NSA poison and kill you. I can keep you safe here and I will let you use the gifts you were given to protect yourself."

Charlie narrowed her eyes. "Leave me alone and let us go."

Eric offered her a sad smile. "You've always been free to go Charlie. I only ask that you cooperate with the ritual first. When you are done I will let you and your adoptive parents leave."

Charlie felt both angry and afraid at once. She did not want to do this 'ritual'. Lord Beathach had hurt her at the last ritual. Her flesh burned with the memory of her suffering. "What if I say no?"

"I don't doubt that you could use your power to escape Charlie, but my Death Troopers will fight back. Do you really want to risk your adoptive parents being killed in a firefight?"

She returned a tired gaze. "Do you promise you won't hurt them?"

"I give you my word. They will not be harmed." He was speaking the truth.

"Are you sure?"

"Yes."

She lowered her head. "All right I'll do it then."

"No! Don't Charlie! Get away while you still can! Don't worry about Catherine and me! Just get away!" David's voice was panicked.

"Go Charlie! Run away!" Catherine cried.

Both David and Catherine's captors raised their rifles to strike. Eric stopped them with a glance.

Charlie looked at them sadly then turned back towards Eric. "What do you want me to do?" She was shaking so hard now that it was hard for her to keep her balance.

Eric patted the polished stone altar. "Climb up here and lie down." As he spoke he moved the ritual implements to a small golden tray held by a robed assistant.

Charlie did as she was told.

"No." David screamed. "Don't! Don't listen to him!"

Charlie ignored him. She had to do this to protect him, to protect them both. Eric would kill David and Catherine if she did not do as he wished.

The stone altar was cold beneath her. Charlie shivered again hard, not so much from the cold as from fear. She knew already what Eric had in mind and was terrified. Eric smiled down on her. "Don't be afraid. I'm not going to hurt you."

Lord Beathach appeared beside him. His soft, ragged breathing mixed with the ever-intensifying chanting of the congregation.

XX

Eric slowly raised his hands. When his arms were fully extended above his head he closed his eyes. Lord Beathach did the same. A great dark power was building in the chamber. The air pulsated and throbbed. The altar beneath her seemed to shake. All at once her fear transformed to anger. The bloodstain began to swell. The power was blazing within. Charlie held it down but made no effort to stop it.

You bastards killed my daddy and mommy!

You killed them!

You killed them!

The words repeated again and again in her mind. The dark force was growing in strength. The chamber shuddered with its force. Charlie felt herself lifting off the table. She wanted very much to get away now, but her body had frozen. Deep blue flames enveloped her body. Dark power surged through her engulfing her heart and mind. Uncontrolled black fury exploded within her. The bloodstain swelled and throbbed. *Hate!* rose within her. Charlie felt herself being drawn deep inside. She saw the bloodstain. It was growing, darkening to a deep angry red. The bloodstain was pulling away, separating itself from her heart and her control. As she watched it tore away becoming an amorphous dark red blob of pure *Hate!*. Slowly the blob took on human form. At first a rough outline it gradually developed features until it became a blond-haired blue-eyed girl similar to her. But there was something different about this girl. This girl's blue eyes were ice chips and glimmered with *Hate!*. Her lips were twisted into a mocking sardonic grin.

"Hello Charlie." The girl spoke with Charlie's voice, but the words were not hers.

"Who are you?"

"I'm you. Charlie, or rather the stronger part of you."

"What do you want?" Charlie asked in a tired voice.

The girl's smile widened. "You know what I want."

Charlie shook her head forcefully. "I won't do it!"

"Of course not." The girl's voice was positively dripping contempt. "They killed your parents and tried to kill you, they chased you all over the world, they tortured you. They took everything from you but you're not going to take revenge because that would be wrong. The people you're so worried about not hurting didn't give a shit about you. They never thought twice about what they were doing to you. They took everything you ever cared about and all you can do is drown in guilt for wanting to get them back."

"David said that it's wrong to take revenge." Charlie replied with halfhearted conviction.

"Oh yes, David said." The girl spat. "What David said never mattered. You're weak. That's why you can't take revenge and that's why you couldn't protect your parents. It was your fault they died. The NSA wouldn't have given a shit about them if they hadn't had you. You brought the government down on their heads because of your power and then you couldn't even use it to protect them because you were so afraid of what might happen. You let your parents die. You let them be murdered."

Tears spilled down her cheeks. "Stop. Please stop. I didn't mean too." Her heart bled with grief.

"Of course, you didn't mean to. You did it because you were weak." The girl's eyes flashed. "Wake up you stupid bitch. You're so worried about people that hate and fear you and look what happened. They destroyed everything. They took away everyone you ever cared about. You could have stopped them if you wanted. You're better than they are, we're better than they are. You could have destroyed them anytime you wanted, and you didn't. "

"But it's wrong." She sobbed. "David and Daddy said it's wrong to hurt people. They said to never use the power that way."

The girl laughed. "Why is it wrong? Because Daddy and David say it is? Because God says it is? God doesn't give a shit about you. He's just used you for laughs. He puts us in a world full of evil and lets us get hurt. Then he turns around and tells us to turn the other cheek. Oh, here I'll give you this wonderful gift of power but don't ever use it. Oh, and when normal people persecute you for being different don't fight back. They can do whatever they want to you, but you can't do anything back, not even out of self-defense. Eric was right. God is an asshole. He's sitting up there laughing at you."

"That's not true"

"Yes, it is and you know it. Your power is greater than anyone's and you have the insight to use it properly. But you're too damned weak to do what you know you must. Listen to *me* for once in your life. Listen to me instead of your stupid conscience."

"No. I won't do it." She was barely able to get the words out between sobs.

"You will." The girl replied in hard, cold tone. "Because I'm in charge now. You let us get hurt. Now I'm going to get rid of the pain."

XXI

David watched in terror as Charlie was led to the center of the chamber and placed upon the altar. Part of him feared that they would sacrifice her, but he knew that was not what was intended. They wanted to use her not kill her. She would be of no use to them dead.

The Emperor began by intoning some words in a language David had never heard before. Lord Beathach responded in the same language. Then they began. Both men raised their hands above Charlie's frightened form. Dark power began to build in the air. David shivered.

Please don't hurt her.

The power continued to grow in intensity. As he watched Charlie lifted off the altar and hung suspended six feet in the air. The power had built to a crescendo. The chamber shuddered with its force. Suddenly deep blue flames licked over her body encasing her in a veil of fire.

Her eyes opened wide and for a moment he thought she would scream. She did not. Cold fury was building within her. At the same time, he felt her falling inside of herself almost as though she were entranced.

"Charlie!!"

She did not respond.

"Charlie!!!" His heart was slamming against his ribs, threatening to burst from his chest. David turned towards Kain his heart in his mouth. "What did you do to her?"

He smiled down on David with cold malice. "I've helped her face her own anger."

"Why? What do you want from her?"

Kain's expression became scornful. "You know what I want from her. It's the same thing you want."

"All I want is for her to have a normal life." David replied with low anger.

"Right." Eric's voice was positively dripping contempt.

Before he could reply Charlie sat up and looked right at him. "You're full of shit David. You and Eric are the same. You both want me to join you, so you can control my power. That's all you really care about." Her blue eyes were glacial and glistened with hate.

Charlie's words cut like knives.

"Charlie, you know that's not true." David replied gently. "Catherine and I love you very much. You're like our daughter."

"Is that why you made me unseal *Deus Irae?*" She spat. "Because you love me? You made me an immortal child. I'll never grow up and I'll never have kids. I'll always be nine years old. Forever."

David's heart crumbled with guilt. "I'm so sorry Charlie. I didn't know. If I had known that would happen I never would have asked you to unseal that sword."

Charlie replied with a cold laugh. "Yeah right. You were interested in my power just like everyone else. You forced me to use the power. You made me learn to be a Lightwarrior and then you didn't even finish teaching me. You made me more of a freak. And you let them take me away and torture me. I should kill you but you're not worth the trouble."

"I... I'm sorry Charlie. You didn't deserve to suffer like this." He was close to tears.

"That's right I didn't. You did this to me and you should burn in hell for it." She turned on Catherine. "And you. You're the most pathetic excuse for a woman I've ever seen. You're so afraid of your own shadow you can't trust anyone. Just because your parents abused you when you were younger. You're just plain pathetic."

Catherine did not respond. Tears spilled down her cheeks.

Charlie turned back to him. "You could have stopped this you know. If you had been willing to accept who you are instead of running away from it. You had the power to fight them, but you were too busy trying to be normal. You ran away from your power while you were making me face mine. You're an adult. I'm a child and you promised you'd protect me. This is all your fault."

Now David was crying outright. Charlie was right. He had failed her. Worse he had betrayed her. He had made her embrace her power while he was refusing to embrace his. She deserved to have a childhood and he had helped take it away from her. He had always resented his father for doing that to him and now he had done the same to her.

Charlie turned on Catherine once more. "Filthy, cold hearted bitch. You never cared about me one-way or the other. You would have been happier if I was gone so you could have David all to yourself. Not that you actually cared about him either. He was just a man for you to pussy whip, so you could feel strong. I know what you're really like. You hate people, especially men because you were abused by a man. Only that's not really true either. Your mother abused you as much as your stepfather. You just can't accept it because she was your real mother. You could always tell yourself that your stepfather wasn't your real father."

Behind Charlie Eric smiled coldly. Suddenly she turned on him. "You lied to me! You pretended to care about me, but you were just using me for my pyrokinesis. You made me think David and Catherine had left me. You made me watch and feel it when you killed those people! You let Lord Beathach *torture* me! I should burn you up and fry you!"

Eric's expression remained unchanged.

"You want me to hate Outsiders because they killed Daddy and Mommy but you're just as bad. You're in love with power because you've always felt powerless. You saw all of the worst things in history, but you couldn't stop any of them because you were too weak. Instead you just stood by and watched. Then you turn around and talk about how rotten people are. Maybe if you used your insights to educate people instead of corrupting them things would be different. You're lucky I'm not like you wanted me to be or I would have killed you and taken over your empire. I could have if I wanted to and you couldn't have done anything about it."

She turned to Lord Beathach. "You're just a stupid brute. You're so brave you'll fight people who have no chance against you. You butcher women and little kids for fun because your over inflated ego is bruised because someone burned off half your face."

She started to turn on David once more when she suddenly collapsed backward on the altar. Powerful muscle spasms wracked her small body. Her eyes were no longer filled with hate but rather pure suffering.

"Charlie!" David's heart went out to her. She didn't deserve this.

XXII

"I won't let you do it!" Charlie screamed.

The girl smiled. "You don't have any choice."

The power was racing within her. Charlie reached into it and lashed out at the girl.

The girl laughed. "You can't kill me. I'm part of you. We're both part of the same person."

Charlie tried again. Still nothing happened.

"I told you. The power is mine too. It won't work against me unless we both let it."

"You can't do this. It's wrong."

"You can't stop me Charlie. I'm stronger than you are. I am everything you fear."

"I won't let you take over."

With that Charlie charged forward and grabbed the girl by the neck. The girl responded with a hard punch to Charlie's stomach. Charlie stumbled backward momentarily winded before charging forward again and delivering a hard, right cross to the girl's jaw. This time it was the girl's turn to stumble backward. Before the girl could counter attack, Charlie followed her first punch with a second that bloodied the girl's nose. She then charged forward again tackled the girl to the ground and began to beat her about the head and face. The girl struggled to fight back and was eventually able to repulse Charlie by clawing her face. Charlie staggered to her feet as blood trickled from several shallow tracks in her right cheek.

The girl laughed again. "You can't win. I'll always be a part of you." Blood streamed from her nose and mouth. "You're still afraid. You can barely face me."

Charlie struck her again. "Shut up! I won't let you win."

"I already have." A sword appeared in the girl's hand. It was identical to Charlie's other than it's dark coloring. Black fire quickly surrounded its blade. "I told you. You can't win. I am stronger." The girl leveled her sword in preparation to strike.

Charlie backed away slowly.

I have to beat her. I can't let her take over.

Suddenly she became aware of a weight pressing upon her right hand. Charlie looked down and saw her own sword. White flames licked up the blade. Without pausing she spun the sword around and lashed out at the girl.

XXIII

Charlie's power was building in the air. Suddenly fire erupted around the altar where she lay convulsed. More flames licked along the floor and up the walls. Their heat baked out at David.

XXIV

Charlie traded blows with the girl for what seemed like an eternity. They were a perfect match. Neither was able to gain even a slight advantage. Each seemed to know the other's intended moves before they were made.

Charlie leapt forward in a tight somersault extending her blade at the last second. The girl sidestepped the blow and responded with a low horizontal slash, which Charlie leapt over. While still in the air Charlie brought her blade down intending to slash through the top of the girl's skull. The girl brought her sword up to deflect the blow. In the same motion she brought her sword around again and slashed at Charlie's neck. Charlie blocked the blow leaning into her parry so as to unbalance the girl. It worked but before she could press her advantage the girl slashed at her face forcing Charlie to step back to avoid the blow. Charlie responded with a high slash, which the girl ducked under and answered with an upward thrust. Charlie sidestepped and slashed downward forcing the girl to bring her sword up to parry the blow.

XXV

The air was alive with Charlie's power now. The chamber was an inferno. David felt the hairs on his arms scorching. The smell of burning was overpowering.

What did they do to her?

He could have broken free of his captors, but he feared what Kain and Beathach might do to Charlie if he tried. There was little he could do for Charlie anyway. She was on her own now. He could feel her fighting a war within and whatever adversary she was fighting she would have to face alone.

XXVI

The girl attacked Charlie with another high slash followed by a counter strike aimed at her midsection. Charlie sidestepped and brought her sword down hard on the girl's blade. An idea was taking shape in her mind. The girl was right. She could not kill her but that did not mean she could not be beaten. If she could not kill the girl perhaps she could subdue her. Charlie struck the girl's sword again slamming it against the ground with a sharp clang. The sword buried itself deep. Charlie raised her sword again and struck the girl across the face with the flat sending her sprawling.

"I won't let you win."

The girl scrambled to get up but before she could Charlie was upon her. Charlie brought the hilt of her sword down on the crown of the girl's head. "I'm not afraid of you anymore. You're a part of me but I'm a part of you too and I can control you."

"You'll never win." The girl snarled. "Inside you know I'm right even if you won't admit it."

Charlie struck the girl again with the flat side of her sword. "You're wrong. And I won't listen to you anymore. You belong to me and you're going to do what I tell you to." Charlie kicked at the girl then dropped her sword and grabbed her in a tight embrace. "It's over."

"It'll never be over." The girl spat defiantly. "You'll never get rid of me. Never."

"It's over." Charlie repeated as she tightened her grip.

The girl struggled for a few seconds before becoming still. There was a strange sensation of doubling and Charlie felt herself *merging* with the girl.

The girl laughed. "See I told you. You can't let go. You want revenge too much."

"Maybe I can't let go. But I won't let you control me."

XXVII

Suddenly Charlie sat up and looked right into his eyes. David knew at once that she was back even before she spoke. "David!!"

"Charlie!!"

She slid off the altar and ran towards him. Suddenly the figure holding David threw him aside and drew a rifle from within his robe. Before David could react, he fired. The red energy bolt streaked towards Charlie. Again, David felt her power surge in the air. At the last second the energy bolt curved off its course that would have otherwise carried it through the center of Charlie's chest. It did not curve far enough though and grazed her left shoulder. Charlie collapsed backward.

"Noooo!!" David ran to her with Catherine in tow. Charlie lay in a heap unconscious and barely breathing. The flesh was totally burned away from the top and side of her shoulder leaving behind only charred bone.

David stood up and turned away leaving Catherine to tend to Charlie. Hot fury burned in his blood. The figure that had fired on Charlie dropped its robe to reveal a slender dark-haired man. The man smiled coldly upon seeing the fury in David's eyes.

"Hello David, my name is Hardliner."

David glared at him. All at once a realization came over him. This was the man who had shot Charlie the last time. This man was responsible for their capture. "Hardliner, I challenge you."

His smiled widened and hardened. "I accept."

Without thinking David reached out with his mind, found *Deus Irae* and pulled it into his hand. Then with a cry he charged forward, sword raised above his head. Hardliner calmly dropped his rifle and drew his own sword. He easily sidestepped David' first blow answering with a horizontal slash aimed at David's midsection. David stepped back from the blow then charged forward again slashing wildly at Hardliner's head. He missed and nearly caught Hardliner's sword in his stomach. David didn't care.

You shot Charlie you bastard.

He struck again, this time aiming for Hardliner's neck. Hardliner ducked again then responded a moment later with a powerful uppercut slash. David jumped back once more but was unable to completely avoid the blow. The tip of Hardliner's blade drew a thin line up his chest and sliced open his chin. David felt no pain, only anger. Again, he attacked and again he was repulsed. His anger was growing. David charged forward yet again this time deliberately forcing Hardliner to parry. When he did David pushed him backward then pressed his advantage with a hard-downward slash that knocked Hardliner off balance. He followed this slash with a second horizontal slash and then another vertical. Hardliner was able to block these but did not have time to counter strike. David's anger was still growing and with it his courage and recklessness. Without thinking he raised his sword high above his head and brought it down hard. He was lucky that Hardliner did not have time to counter attack or he might have ended up impaled on the man's sword. Hardliner parried but it made no difference. David's sword shattered his blade on impact and kept going without slowing. The blade split Hardliner completely in half from crown to crotch. David turned away, soaked in blood. He no longer felt angry. His mind was in a total daze. He felt nothing, not anger or horror or fear, just nothing. Lord Beathach moved to attack but Kain stayed him with a hand on his shoulder.

"Let them go." He turned his gaze on David. "I told your daughter before, you are not prisoners." He paused. "I must admit I am impressed. When I first saw you, I took you for an Enlightened. Now I know I was wrong." With that he vanished, followed a moment later by Lord Beathach.

Chapter 15
And So, It Begins Again…

I

Before he could react David found himself standing on a busy street corner with Charlie in his arms. Catherine stood beside him looking every bit as confused as he felt. His confusion only lasted a moment as his attention returned to Charlie. She was still unconscious, and her breathing had become very slow and shallow.

"Help!!" He screamed the word before he could stop himself. No one took notice. All were preoccupied with their daily business and all were content to mind their own business and let others mind theirs as was typical of cities. Near panic, David raked his eyes over his surroundings. The street signs were all written in German. After a few seconds of frantic searching David ran up the street following a sign that read 'Krankenhaus'. Several blocks up he turned left and then a block after that he made a right into the hospital parking lot. Catherine was close behind. She had spoken to him several times, but he had taken no notice. Now her voice burst through his haze of near panic.

"David what are we going to do? They won't treat her without ID and we don't have any money to bribe them with."

"I don't know." He shot back. All he could think about was getting Charlie inside. Everything after that was irrelevant. As he rushed across the parking lot David rapidly scanned signs until he found one pointing towards the emergency room. He followed this sign to a large automatic door, which he then rushed through. A nurse intercepted him ten feet inside.

"Sie können nicht kommen hier durch. Diese Tür ist für Sanitäter nur ." ["Sir you can't come in through here. This door is for paramedics only."]

David tried to shove past her to the desk beyond, but she stepped in the way. "Sie müssen nach draußen gehen zurück und kommen in der Öffentlichkeit Eingang um die Ecke." ["Sir, you'll have to go back outside and come in the public entrance around the corner."]

"Meine Tochter ist verletzt . Bitte helfen Sie ihr . " ["My daughter's hurt. Please help her."] David begged.

The nurse ignored him. "Sie Müssen gehen um der Öffentlichkeit Eingang." ["Sir you have to go around to the public entrance."]

David was desperate. "Bitte. Sie stirbt. Sie braucht Hilfe. " ["Please. She's dying. She needs help."]

"Herr …"

„Sie braucht Hilfe. Sie ist schwer verbrannt, und sie wird sterben, wenn sie nicht jetzt helfen bekommt. " ["She needs help. She's badly burned and she's going to die if she doesn't get help now."]

"OKAY. Gib sie mir. " ["Okay. Give her to me."]

David placed Charlie in the woman's arms.

"Jetzt gehen auf die andere Tür . Ich werde jemanden schicken Sie zu finden. Wie heißen Sie?" ["Now go around to the other door. I'll send someone to find you. What's your name?"]

"Ich heiße David McAuliff."

„Herr McAuliff wir kümmern uns um Ihre Tochter. Gehen Sie rund um der Öffentlichkeit Eingang und dort zu warten . Jemand wird rund um Sie in wenigen Minuten zu sprechen. " ["Ok Mr. McAuliff we'll take care of your daughter. Go around to the public entrance and wait there. Someone will be around to talk to you in a few minutes."]

David did as he was told. Catherine followed without a word.

II

For a while after she was shot Charlie drifted in darkness. Then the darkness broke and she found herself lying on a table in the hospital. Doctors swarmed around her sticking needles in her arms and tubes in her nose and mouth. Strangely enough though she felt no pain. Something emitted a loud bleep. Charlie tried to sit up to see what it was and was surprised to find that she could. Then to her even greater surprise she found that she could stand. Charlie plodded across the room, the bleeping sound already forgotten. She did not yet realize what had happened and was shocked when she was able to pass through the wall. It was then that reality began to sink in. She was dead. This time for real she supposed. Yet this knowledge brought no fear as it had before. She felt only relief. It was over. She was free of the power forever. Soon she would see her mother and father again. Charlie passed through another wall and found herself standing outside. A brilliant sun bathed everything in beautiful golden hues.

I'm free.

Charlie walked towards the sun enjoying its warmth. As she continued forward it grew brighter and brighter until she could see nothing but radiant white.

III

"Excellent comeback."

The gentleman in white smiled. "Thank you. I told you it wasn't over."

"Shall we play again?"

All of the pieces had been captured save for the two kings.

The gentleman in white sipped his beer. "Yes. Let's play. We still have not settled who is the better man."

"No, we have not." The dark gentleman finished his beer and stood up. "Can I get you another beer while I'm up?"

"Yes, thank you."

The dark gentleman went to the bar and returned a few minutes later carrying two large tumblers of beer. He set one down in front of the gentleman in white before taking his seat.

"Thank you, my friend."

"You're welcome. What's wrong?"

The gentleman in white took a slow sip from his beer. "It is unfortunate things worked out this way."

"I suppose it is, but you know the rules."

"Yes. I know but this was not intended when the rules were made."

"No, it was not. What do you want to do?"

"Let's release her. It will not change anything."

"Very well." The dark gentleman replied as he sipped his beer. "But only on the condition that she will not be permitted to leave the game."

The gentleman in white nodded. "I suppose that is fair."

IV

The light was clearing, or more accurately her eyes were adjusting to it. Charlie found herself standing in a beautiful green field. A warm breeze stirred its grasses. Men and women and children in white robes frolicked happily. Their voices carried on the air like a melody. Among them were her father and mother. Charlie ran to them, heart soaring with joy.

"Mommy!! Daddy!!"

They turned smiling blissfully.

"Charlie!"

"It's so good to see you."

Charlie ran to her father and mother hugged them with all her might. "I missed you so much." She began to cry.

Both Daddy and Mommy hugged her tight. "Don't cry Charlie." Daddy whispered gently. "We're together again. There's nothing to cry about."

She smiled through her tears. "I love you."

Daddy bent down to her level. "We know Charlie. Now I need you to listen to me, there isn't much time."

Charlie's joy immediately evaporated. "What do you mean? I'm not leaving. I don't want to leave you."

"I know Charlie but it's not your time yet. You have to go back to help David and Catherine."

She shook her head. "No. I don't want to go back. I want to stay here with you."

"I know Charlie. I know, but you have to go back. There's nothing we can do to change that. You have to go back." He repeated. "But it won't be like it was. You'll be able to grow up and have a family of your own." He paused. "There is a price though. You have to finish your role in the battle that's coming. Do you understand?"

She nodded as fresh tears spilled down her cheeks. "Please don't make me go away. Please Daddy…Mommy."

Mommy looked at her sadly. "Oh, Charlie I wish you could stay. I miss you so much. But you have to go back. A lot of people are depending on you."

"But I don't want to leave." She sobbed. "Please don't make me."

"You have to go back Charlie." Daddy replied gently. "There's nothing any of us can do about it."

"Don't worry." Mommy added. "We'll be together again. It'll just have to wait a little while longer that's all."

Charlie started to protest but before she could the bright light took her.

V

The moment David saw the doctor he knew it would be bad news. The man looked tired and his expression was grave. David did not need his psychic senses to know why.

"We've done everything we can for her, but it doesn't look good. Most of her left shoulder is burned away. She's still in shock and she's badly dehydrated.

Because of the extent of the damage we had to remove the majority of the shoulder bones. I have to be honest with you Mr. McAuliffe your daughter has maybe a five percent chance of surviving. With a burn like that she's almost guaranteed to get an infection and she's too weak to survive if she does. And her left arm needs to be amputated but we can't perform the surgery while she is in this condition. If we don't remove her arm in the next few days, it will become gangrenous and that will kill her. I'm very sorry."

David's heart sank. He had to struggle not to cry. "Can we see her?"

"Yes. She's in the pediatric ICU. I can take you to see her if you want. I have to warn you though she's still unconscious and she looks bad."

David nodded.

Charlie looked worse than he had expected. Her skin had grown very pale and had taken on a bluish tinge. Her left arm was swollen up like a sausage. The wound itself was wrapped loosely in gauze that was already soaked through with fluids. Dozens of tubes protruded from her body connecting her to numerous machines. There was a breathing tube in her mouth, and IV's in one arm and both legs. Her face was contorted into an expression of pure suffering. As he looked at her David knew she was in great pain.

"Hi Charlie. It's David."

"We're with you now Charlie. Everything's going to be ok." Catherine's voice was surprisingly calm despite the tears streaming down her cheeks.

"You're safe now." Anger blazed in David's heart. *How could that bastard do this to her? She's only a little girl. He didn't have to shoot her.*

David sat with Charlie day and night waiting for her to die. At first Catherine remained with him but in the end, exhaustion overtook her, and she had to leave. But not David. He would not leave her to die alone no matter what the cost to himself. She at least deserved that much.

Strangely enough though she did not die. David dared not believe it but he thought she might even be recovering. Her burn did not become infected and she did not develop gangrene in her arm. Charlie's doctors were even more dumbfounded. They had all expected her to die and here she was showing signs of recovery. It was amazing. Still the doctors warned David and Catherine not to get their hopes up too high. Charlie was by no means out of the woods. As time passed and Charlie slowly recovered David began to allow himself to consider the possibility that she might survive. He knew it was still unlikely, but she was getting better. Perhaps she would beat the odds.

Then on May twenty-fifth a miracle happened.

VI

The light cleared, and Charlie found herself lying in a hospital bed. There was a tube in her throat and another in her right arm. More tubes ran into both of her legs. David sat beside her looking washed out and very tired. She tried to speak but the tube in her throat prevented her from forming any words. Charlie choked and sputtered on the fat piece of rubber.

"Charlie?"

She tried again to speak but was unable.

"Charlie! You're awake." David clasped her to his chest then stood up. "I'll be right back honey."

She groaned softly in reply.

David poked his head out the door and called for the doctor. A moment later a gray-haired man entered accompanied by a young, redheaded nurse.

"She's awake." David cried excitedly.

The doctor bent down and carefully looked her over. "She is." His voice was dumbstruck. He turned to the nurse. "Remove her breathing tube."

The nurse complied without replying. The tube hurt coming out, but Charlie was grateful to be rid of it. After coughing for several minutes Charlie managed to force out a few, faint words. "I'm so glad to see you David."

He nodded. "So am I." Then he took her into his arms.

The two held each other for several minutes before letting go. With David out of the way the doctor stepped forward to examine her. When he was finished he turned to David. "She's out of the woods but she needs her rest."

He nodded. "Give us a few more minutes."

"Okay but don't take too long."

With that he turned and left leaving the nurse behind. David sat with Charlie for another ten minutes before the nurse kicked him out. When he was gone the nurse gave Charlie a pill to take and then left her alone. Charlie sat awake for a few minutes after the nurse was gone just thinking. She was trapped again. Eric would be looking for her as soon as he learned she was still alive and sooner or later he would find her. Everything was back to the way it had been before and yet everything had changed. She was free of the Black Empire for now, but she had not truly escaped that world. In truth she had never left it. She had always been a part of it she had just not known it until now. This world, the earth, was no different than the Black Empire's world. The same people lived there and did the same things. The Black Empire was just more open. She could see that now. The world she had thought she lived in was but a mere facade. A thin glossy veneer beneath which lay an open sewer. She saw that now, but it was not a huge revelation. Deep in her heart she had always known this was how it was.

As she drifted off to sleep Charlie again felt the darkness closing around her and knew that she had never truly escaped it at all. Running had only struck a match against the dark, one that had now burned out letting the shadows close in once more. She knew now. The world was filled with shadow broken by thin panes of light.

ABOUT THE AUTHOR

Brian L. Jackson lives in northeastern Oklahoma with his wife Melanie and two children. In addition to writing fiction Brian practices Domestic and Criminal law, is an avid reader and occasional gamer.

Brian graduated from Lock Haven University with a bachelors in English and went on to earn his Juris Doctor from Oklahoma City University.